ROMANTIC TIMES PRAISES *NEW YORK TIMES* BESTSELLING AUTHOR MADELINE BAKER!

CHASE THE LIGHTNING

"Madeline Baker offers time-travel fans an innovative treat."

UNFORGETTABLE

"Madeline Baker continues to delight fans with her passionate Western adventures that thrill and captivate."

SPIRIT'S SONG

"Madeline Baker consistently delivers winning, heart-wrenching, passionate romances and *Spirit's Song* is no exception."

UNDER A PRAIRIE MOON

"Madeline Baker writes of a ghost, a curse, and a second chance with such power and passion readers cannot help but be mesmerized."

CHASE THE WIND

"This sequel to *Apache Runaway* is pure magic and packed with action, adventure, and passion. Madeline Baker fans, get ready to laugh and cry from beginning to the surprising ending."

MORE *ROMANTIC TIMES* RAVES FOR STORYTELLER OF THE YEAR MADELINE BAKER!

THE ANGEL & THE OUTLAW

"Readers will rave about Madeline Baker's extraordinary storytelling talents."

LAKOTA RENEGADE

"*Lakota Renegade* is as rich, passionate, and delicious as all Madeline Baker's award-winning romances!"

APACHE RUNAWAY

"Madeline Baker has done it again! This romance is poignant, adventurous, and action packed."

CHEYENNE SURRENDER

"This is a funny, witty, poignant, and delightful love story! Ms. Baker's fans will be more than satisfied!"

PASSION'S FURY

He kissed her again, and yet again, kissed her until she thought her bones would melt from the heat of his lips. And then, abruptly, he released her and sat up.

Jesse glared at Dancer as he sat back on his heels, angry with him because he had stopped, and even more angry with herself because she hadn't wanted him to.

"You beast!" she hissed. "You're just like the others. Worse! I hope that posse catches you and kills you. I hope they hang you from the highest tree. I hope they shoot you a thousand times. I hope—"

"That's enough, honey," Dancer drawled, amused by her outburst. "I think I get the drift."

Other books by Madeline Baker:

CHASE THE LIGHTNING
UNFORGETTABLE
SPIRIT'S SONG
UNDER A PRAIRIE MOON
LOVE FOREVERMORE
LOVE IN THE WIND
FEATHER IN THE WIND
CHASE THE WIND
THE ANGEL & THE OUTLAW
RENEGADE HEART
LAKOTA RENEGADE
APACHE RUNAWAY
BENEATH A MIDNIGHT MOON
CHEYENNE SURRENDER
WARRIOR'S LADY
THE SPIRIT PATH
MIDNIGHT FIRE
PRAIRIE HEAT
A WHISPER IN THE WIND
FORBIDDEN FIRES
LACEY'S WAY
FIRST LOVE, WILD LOVE
RECKLESS DESIRE
RECKLESS LOVE
RECKLESS HEART
RECKLESS EMBRACE

Writing as Amanda Ashley:

MIDNIGHT EMBRACE
AFTER TWILIGHT (Anthology)
THE CAPTIVE
SHADES OF GRAY
A DARKER DREAM
SUNLIGHT, MOONLIGHT
DEEPER THAN THE NIGHT
EMBRACE THE NIGHT

MADELINE BAKER

Comanche Flame

LEISURE BOOKS  NEW YORK CITY

To Alicia Condon,
the best editor in the business
who made me do it over...
and over...until I got it right!

A LEISURE BOOK®

April 2009

Published by

Dorchester Publishing Co., Inc.
200 Madison Avenue
New York, NY 10016

ISBN 10: 0-8439-4032-8
ISBN 13: 978-0-8439-4032-9

Printed in the United States of America.

10 9 8 7 6 5 4 3 2 1

Comanche Flame

Prologue

In the press of bodies standing shoulder to shoulder at the polished mahogany bar, one man stood conspicuously alone, one brown-skinned hand draped over the butt of a well-oiled Colt revolver, the other fisted around a glass of the best whiskey the house had to offer.

As new customers entered the hazy, smoke-filled saloon, they invariably headed toward the vacant space beside the solitary man. And after one look into his unfriendly gray eyes, they invariably moved away, seeking more congenial company.

The man smiled wryly as yet another cow-hand edged away from him, wondering idly if it was the wrangler's aversion to gunslingers that sent him skedaddling or merely an aversion to half-breeds. In his younger days, the man would have taken offense to such an obvious slight, but now . . . The man shrugged mentally as he shifted his weight from one foot to the other. Hell, maybe he was just getting too old to give a damn.

He was about to call the bardog for a refill when the boy entered the saloon. The kid was looking for trouble sure as death and hell, the man thought wearily. It was there in the boy's bantam-cock swagger and in the huge old hog-leg holstered at his side.

The young gunsel hesitated just inside the saloon's swinging doors. He was a tall, good-looking kid with corn-colored hair and pale blue eyes. Eyes that darted impatiently from one familiar face to another until, at last, they came to rest on the swarthy countenance of the stranger standing alone at the far end of the bar.

Tall and dark, the stranger was, with long black hair and a sweeping black moustache, high cheekbones, a stubborn jaw, and a hawk-like nose. A .44 Colt with plain walnut grips rode easily in a worn holster tied low on the man's right hip. He was dressed in faded black Levi's and a blue wool shirt, and at first glance looked pretty much like any other drifter save for the fringed, knee-high moccasins that hugged his long, muscular legs.

The boy frowned, experiencing a momentary twinge of gut-wrenching disappointment. He had come looking for a famous gunslick, not some dusty drifter; had expected to find his man attired in rich black broadcloth and white linen, and sporting a pair of matched .44's with creamy ivory or lustrous mother-of-pearl inlays.

The boy was about to turn away in disgust when he noticed the man's eyes—cold and gray, as deadly as the sixgun on his hip, as restless as the wind in the high country. A killer's, the boy mused with a faint smile of satisfaction. Hooking his thumbs in his gun belt, he sauntered over to stand in front of the stranger.

"They say you're fast," the boy drawled. "The fastest around." There was an open challenge in the boy's tone, a subtle shading of the words that implied the boy was faster and eager to prove it.

The man's eyes narrowed to mere slits as he studied the boy, taking note of the well-cared-for gun and fancy hand-tooled holster, the cut of his clothes, and the expensive cream-colored Stetson.

Spoiled rich kid, he mused to himself. Aloud, he said, "Go away, boy. I've no time to play with children."

The implication that he was less than a man brought a quick flush of anger to the boy's cheeks. His right hand came up, hovering dangerously close to the butt of his gun.

"I'm not a child!" he replied hotly. "I'm eighteen and a man growed. I can take you, Dancer, and I aim to prove it, here and now!"

With the mention of the tall man's name, a hush fell over the crowded saloon. Dancer! The man who had outgunned George Buck and cut down all three of the Trenton boys. Hot damn! Men standing nearby hurried to the far side of the room, their faces betraying a mixture of fear and awe as they scrambled out of the line of fire.

Dancer stepped away from the bar, his hands dangling loose at his sides, his manner cool and unruffled. When he spoke, his voice was soft, almost gentle, strangely at odds with the cold fire in his gray eyes.

"Listen to me, boy," he said. "I don't draw on kids. If you need to prove your manhood, go find yourself a woman."

"I didn't know you were a coward," the boy taunted.

"Don't crowd me, kid," the man warned.

"A yellow-bellied, crow-eating coward!" the boy went on in the same impudent tone.

A muscle twitched in the big man's jaw. It was the only visible sign of the tension building within him. How many times, he wondered, how many times had he stood poised to strike? He had lost track. Some said he had killed more than twenty men, and he supposed they could be right. It might easily have been more. Only some men lost their nerve when they gazed into his flat gray eyes. Lost their nerve and backed away, deciding humiliation was better than death.

But not the boy. He was out for blood.

"I'm gonna throw down on you, Dancer," the boy vowed. "And if you don't make your move, I'll gun you down like the yellow, half-breed bastard you are."

The boy's verbal assault sent a shocked gasp rolling through the crowd, and then there was only silence as all eyes in the saloon focused on the life-and-death drama being played out at the end of the bar.

For stretched seconds, the boy and the man faced each other. Then the boy's hand streaked toward his gun, freeing it from the holster, raising it to fire.

But the man was moving, too. Smoother, faster, with the ease that came from years of practice. Afterward, no one remembered seeing him draw. There was only a blur, quicker than the eye could follow, and then the .44 was in the man's hand, a part of him, belching fire and blue smoke, and the boy lay dead on the floor, his lifesblood oozing from a neat hole in his chest.

"Right through the heart," murmured one of the onlookers.

"Just like greased lightning."

"Wait till I tell old Zack I saw Dancer in action!"

The half-breed's narrowed eyes swept the room, choking off the excited babble of voices.

"I gave him his chance," Dancer said evenly. "I let him make the first move."

His hands were moving quick and sure as he spoke, punching the spent cartridge from the loading gate, replacing it with a fresh round before he eased the Colt back into his holster. That done, he crossed the room in long, easy strides, exiting through the batwings without a backward glance.

No one followed him.

"I seen Dancer in Wichita," remarked a grizzled old-timer, addressing no one in particular. "I was there the day he outgunned the Trenton boys. Yessir, he dropped two of them before they cleared leather. He got the third one, too, right between the eyes."

"Somebody better hotfoot it out to the J Bar C and tell old man Clayton what happened," the barkeep suggested. "He ain't gonna like this a'tall."

Several men nodded in agreement, but none of them seemed anxious to leave the saloon's protective walls.

"He's goin'," announced a youthful-looking cowboy, and several men glanced toward the door as the sound of hoofbeats reached their ears.

And now the men in the saloon began to move, clustering around Johnny Clayton's body as they rehashed the shooting, sidling up to the bar to finish their drinks or to order fresh ones.

As the hoofbeats died away, one of the men ventured outside. It was a long ride to the J Bar C, but perhaps J. D. Clayton would be grateful to hear a detailed description of how his boy was gunned down. Grateful enough to offer a monetary token of appreciation. After all, Judge Clayton was the richest man in the whole damn territory.

Chapter 1

Jessica Landry could not help smiling as she gazed at the vast sunlit prairie that stretched endlessly before her. It was a beautiful land, austere and unforgiving, but so beautiful. Excitement fluttered in the pit of her stomach as she contemplated the new life awaiting them in Cherry Valley. She would be practically independent, earning her own living, controlling her own future. It was a heady thought.

"You look like you're going to bust," John Landry remarked, grinning at his sister.

"I am! Oh, John, isn't it exciting?"

"Sure, Jessica," he agreed, but inwardly he was not so sure. Starting a new life was never easy. Jessica thought it was a lark, but John knew it was really up to him to support the two of them. True, Jessica would be receiving a salary for her work as a seamstress, but the amount was a mere pittance, not nearly enough to support her. Still, he knew it gave her a sense of pride to know she would be helping to earn their keep, to know that she would have money of her own and not have to depend on him for everything.

Jesse laid her hand on her brother's arm. He was tall and lean, with hazel eyes, curly brown hair, and a crooked smile. "I just know things are going to be right with us from now on," she said exuberantly.

John nodded. Their parents had died when they were young, and they had spent the last fifteen years living with their maiden aunt, Sally. Now Sally had passed on, too, and they were alone in the world.

"Just think, John, you'll finally be able to teach, just like you've always wanted, and I shall create elegant gowns for wealthy matrons. Between us, I think we shall do quite nicely."

"You're right, little sister," John agreed. "We shall indeed do splendidly."

"I'm always right," Jesse declared, and they both laughed.

A companionable silence fell between them, and Jesse thought how lucky she was to have a brother like John. He was father, mother, adviser, and friend all rolled into one. She had adored him ever since she had been a toddler, and after their parents died, she had looked to John for solace and advice. Though he was only twenty-three, he had always been someone she could rely on.

Humming softly, she turned her gaze to the countryside again. The distant mountains seemed close enough to touch, yet they never seemed to get any closer. The sky was so blue it almost hurt her eyes just to look at it. There was no factory smoke here to dull the vast blue vault, nothing to dim its bright beauty. Occasional stands of timber stood like tall green sentinels in a sea of coarse yellow grass that dipped and swayed to the rhythm of the cool summer breeze.

Jesse smiled as she saw a white-tailed deer dart for cover behind a tangled mass of brush. She was enchanted by the wildlife they saw from time to time: skunks and squirrels, eagles and hawks, even a great black bear.

Jesse let out a long sigh. Perhaps she would find a husband in Cherry Valley. It was said the men far outnumbered the women in the West. It might be fun to be able to pick and choose from a dozen handsome suitors. Maybe two dozen! Not that she hadn't had her share of beaux back East, but somehow none of the young men who had come calling had appealed to her. They had all seemed so shallow and immature, and she wanted a man, not a boy.

She slid a glance at John and smiled. Despite the scarcity of women in the West, she was certain he would attract every female in town, for he was a wonderful man, well-bred, well-mannered, and terribly handsome, with a winning smile that was irresistible.

At sundown, John set up camp while Jesse prepared dinner. She grimaced as she sliced the last of their bacon, heated some red beans, and made a pot of coffee. She was sorely tired of beans and bacon, and she looked forward to arriving in Cherry Valley the following week, her mouth watering as she imagined the thick steak with all the trimmings that John had promised her as soon as they arrived in town.

She was washing their few dishes after dinner when she heard hoofbeats. She threw John a quick look, her expression worried. They had been on the trail for almost three weeks and hadn't seen a soul.

In moments, four men reined in near their wagon. The one in the lead was the biggest man Jessica had ever seen. His eyes were a cold pale blue beneath shaggy brown brows, his nose was broad and flat, as though someone had stomped on it. His brown hair was long and unkempt. He looked, Jesse thought, more like a bear than a man.

The second rider was tall and skinny, with close-set green eyes and a long nose. There was a narrow scar on his left cheek. The last two men were young with regular features, light brown hair, and brown eyes. Jesse wondered absently if they were brothers.

"Smelled your coffee," the bear man said. "Mind if we step down and have a cup?"

John looked apprehensive as he studied the four men. "Help yourself," he said at last. Trying to appear casual, he moved toward the wagon where his rifle rested under the front seat.

The bear man dismounted. Pulling a tin cup from his saddlebag, he poured himself a cup of coffee, his attention apparently focused on what he was doing. The other three men joined him at the fire.

"You pilgrims are travelin' light," the bear man remarked, his eyes drifting over their run-down wagon and meager possessions.

"We'll get by," John said.

The bear man grinned as he drew his gun. "Let's make this short and friendly," he said curtly. "Dig out whatever cash you've got stashed away and me and my pals will be riding on."

John's hand rested on the edge of the wagon near the seat. "We don't have any cash money. We spent it all on supplies."

"Pilgrims always have money," the bear man retorted, his patience gone. "Get it!"

Jesse slid a glance in John's direction and felt her breath catch in her throat as she saw his hand slide under the wagon seat. She screamed as John withdrew the Winchester, screamed again as the bear man fired his sixgun. The slug ripped into John's forearm and the rifle fell from his hands.

"Not very friendly," the bear man remarked as he holstered his weapon and walked toward John. "Not friendly at all."

Jesse choked back a sob as the man's meaty fist hammered into her brother's face and stomach until John went limp and slid to the ground, his nose and mouth a bloody pulp, one eye already swelling.

Jesse turned frightened eyes on the other three men. They had not moved; indeed, they seemed unconcerned by the incident.

The bear man turned away from John and fixed Jesse with a hard stare. "Maybe you've got the money," he mused aloud, and took a step toward her.

Jessica felt her insides grow cold as the big man walked toward her. She bit down on her lip, her eyes frightened, as John made a valiant attempt to reach his rifle.

It was a move the scar-faced man had been expecting. With a cruel grin, he drew his gun and shot John Landry in the shoulder. At the sound of gunfire, the bear man pivoted on his heel, and a second gunshot filled the air. Jesse began to sob as John writhed on the ground. Bright red blood trickled down his shoulder and bubbled from the third wound low in his abdomen. He gazed at Jessica, his eyes filled with pain and remorse, and then he shuddered and lay still.

Jesse swayed on her feet, certain she was going to faint as the scar-faced man callously searched John's pockets, swearing profusely when all he found were a few crumpled greenbacks.

"Let's eat," the bear man said, holstering his gun. "We'll search the girl after we get some grub." He looked at Jessica, his blue eyes hard. "Fix us a little something to eat, missy, then we'll get better acquainted."

Jesse did not answer. Indeed, she did not even hear him. She could not take her eyes from John, or from the bright red blood that stained the ground beneath him. His face was ashen, his breathing shallow and irregular. But at least he was breathing.

"Missy."

His slap spun Jesse half around, nearly knocking her off her feet.

"Fix us some grub," the big man repeated impatiently. "Now!"

In a daze, Jesse did as bidden, quickly frying up the last of the red beans and making a fresh pot of coffee. The four men ate with gusto, smacking their lips.

"About time for dessert, I'd say," the scar-faced man suggested, and four pairs of eyes swung in Jesse's direction.

"Good idea, Matt," the bear man agreed. "Tim, you and Corky grab our filly."

Jessica screamed as the two men advanced toward her, their eyes alight with evil intent. She began to kick and scratch as they grabbed her. Panic lent strength to her limbs, and she fought like a wildcat. A swift kick to the groin sent the man called Tim sprawling, his hands clutching the source of his agony. The scar-faced man hurried to take his place, and then they had her pinned between them. The bear man came to stand in front of her. With a malicious grin, he slapped Jesse across the face.

"I like my women willing," he said curtly.

"Go to hell." She had not meant to speak the words aloud. Retribution was swift and she cried out as the man's hamlike hand slapped her again, the force of the blow splitting her lower lip. She tasted blood in her mouth, felt the cold hand of fear coil around her insides.

"Throw her down," the bear man said, and the two men holding Jesse obligingly wrestled her to the ground. She heard her shirt rip as she tried to twist out of their grasp, and cried out in protest as the scar-faced man tore it from her back so that only her thin cotton camisole covered her upper torso.

Laughing softly, the bear man pushed her skirt up over her thighs, then ripped away her pantalets, exposing long, slim legs and smooth, creamy thighs. There was a sudden silence as the men stared at her, a collective sigh of admiration for the feminine beauty hidden beneath the loose-fitting shirt and full calico skirt.

With a grunt, the bear man began to unfasten his belt. Jesse began to scream wildly. She threw a frantic look in John's direction, but John could not help her now. In fact, she couldn't tell if he were dead or alive.

She lashed out with her foot as the huge man started to lower himself over her, and her heel caught him in the crotch.

He yelped with pain, and then he began to hit her, his fist blacking her eye and bruising her tender flesh. She screamed again, screamed with pain and terror until the world went black....

Dancer rode alone across the grassland, his flat-brimmed black hat pulled low. In the distance, the dying sun was setting in a blaze of glory, leaving a temporary legacy of crimson clouds and a broad sky canvas etched with lavender and scarlet.

It was a beautiful country, he mused. To the east rose towering granite cliffs and lofty pink sandstone spires. To the south lay miles of rolling sand dunes, and in between were miles of grass-covered prairies, endlessly undulating like waves upon the sea.

He had lived most of his life in this part of the country, he reflected, and all he had to show for it was a worn Texas saddle, a well-used Colt, and a reputation as a fast gun. When he was twenty, being the best with a gun had seemed like the most exciting thing in the world. Wherever he went, boys knew his name. Lesser men stepped aside, fearful of incurring his wrath. Saloon girls vied for his attentions. Shopkeepers served him with respect; newspapermen curried his favor, hoping to get the inside scoop on his life story.

Oh, it had been exciting all right, for a while. But now, at thirty-five, the thrill was gone, and there was no going back. He was too old to change his spots, too well known to hang up his gun and take up a new line of work.

Not that he really wanted to change, he admitted ruefully. It was just that gunning down that snot-nosed kid back in Cherry Valley stuck in his craw. After all, it was one thing to gun down a boy of eighteen when you were the same age yourself, quite another when you were old enough to be the kid's father. Dammit, he had not wanted to kill the kid. Why hadn't the boy backed down when he had the chance?

"Shit, I'll be gunning down little old ladies next," he muttered crossly, and wondered how much longer Blue could travel before she dropped in her tracks, and how many more miles he could sit his horse before his backside became permanently attached to the damn thing.

He was thinking of hunting a place to spend the night when he heard it: a long, high-pitched scream filled with pain. Frowning, he reined the big gray Appaloosa to a halt, and swore softly as the anguished cry came again.

Impulsively, he urged the mare into a trot, his hand automatically reaching for the gun holstered low on his right thigh.

Rounding a stand of timber, he saw several people some yards away. He took in the scene at a glance: the woman on the ground, two men holding her down while a third struggled with his pants. A fourth man stood watching, a rifle cradled in the crook of his arm. A fifth man lay sprawled in the dirt near an old wagon.

Muttering an oath, Dancer put the mare into a lope. The sound of a horse approaching quickly attracted the attention of the four men mauling the girl, and they glanced over their shoulders to see a dark figure bearing down on them. Dancer loosed the hair-raising war cry of the Comanche as he rode toward them. The three men nearest the girl scrambled to their feet and ran for their horses. The fourth man lifted his rifle and fired at the approaching rider. The bullet went wide and struck a lantern hanging from the tailgate of the wagon. Hot oil spilled onto the wood, igniting a fire and spooking the two horses grazing nearby.

Dancer grinned as he drew his Colt and cranked off a round, hitting the rifleman in the chest. The other three men hit their saddles running and disappeared into the darkness.

Dancer reined Blue to a halt and vaulted to the ground. Grabbing the man sprawled near the burning wagon, he dragged him out of danger, swearing softly as he realized the man was dead. He carried the girl away from the ruined campsite, then squatted on his heels beside her, his expression grim. She had been badly beaten. Her left eye was already turning black, several ugly bruises marred her face, and her lower lip was swollen and caked with blood.

Dancer glanced at the dead man lying a few feet away. Her husband, no doubt, he mused, and wondered what in the hell a pair of greenhorns were doing alone in this part of the country.

Pity and compassion were emotions Dancer rarely displayed, yet he felt both stirring within him as he gazed at the young woman lying at his feet. There was a look of hurt innocence on her face, and he wondered if she had been raped; wondered, too, if he would have felt the same outrage at what had befallen her if she were old and ugly instead of young and beautiful. For she *was* beautiful. Even the multitude of bruises and the black eye could not conceal the perfection of her finely chiseled features.

For a brief moment he considered hauling her to the nearest town, but that would be foolish, he admitted, especially in view of the posse that was relentlessly dogging his heels, and the Wanted posters that were undoubtedly out by now, making him a prime target for every sheriff and bounty hunter in the territory. Too, riding double would slow him down, and he was a man in a hurry.

With a shrug, he rose easily to his feet. Digging the makings out of his shirt pocket, he fashioned a cigarette, contemplating the girl all the while. She did not look badly hurt. Hopefully, the posse would pick her up before too long. Better she should slow them down than him. And if they didn't find her . . . He let the thought hang, unfinished, then scowled as the girl's eyelids fluttered open.

As her vision cleared, the first thing Jessica saw was a tall form standing over her, and her first conscious thought was that she had died and gone to hell. Surely that dark, forbidding face wreathed in blue-gray smoke belonged to none other than Satan himself!

Thoroughly frightened by his dark mien, Jessica uttered a hoarse cry of terror, then went limp as velvet blackness swirled around her, sweeping her into welcome oblivion.

Dancer rolled a second cigarette as he carefully scanned his backtrail. There was no sign of the posse from Cherry Valley, but he knew they were out there, likely hunkered down around a cozy little campfire, swilling hot black coffee and swapping lies. Well, he'd have a fire, too, once he put a few more miles behind him. And the sooner he got started, the better.

He was about to swing into the saddle when Blue snorted and danced away, her dainty ears laid flat, her nostrils flared. Turning, Dancer glimpsed two dark shapes gliding soundlessly through the underbrush less than a yard away, their hungry yellow eyes glinting fiendishly in the moonlight.

"Oh, hell," the half-breed muttered irritably. "We can't just leave her out here for the wolves and the buzzards."

His mind made up, he quickly stripped the rigging from the big gray Appaloosa, turned the mare loose to forage while he spread his blankets beneath the nearest tree.

The girl whimpered like a wounded cub as he carried her to his blankets. Her long blond hair was silky soft in his hands as he swept it away from her forehead. Playing nursemaid to the sick and infirm did not sit well with the gunman, and he scowled as he splashed water on his kerchief and began washing the blood from her face.

The girl's eyes snapped open as the cold cloth touched her skin and she stared past him, her eyes wide and unseeing. Suddenly she screamed, "John! Help me!" her voice filled with anguish until she began to sob incoherently, like a young child in the throes of a nightmare.

Mouthing a vague obscenity, Dancer doused his kerchief with the last of the water from his canteen, then bathed her battered face again. She was going to have a hell of a black eye, but other than that, she appeared to be fine.

When he'd finished washing her face, he wrapped her in one of his blankets and gathered her trembling body into his lap. The girl snuggled deeper into his embrace, seeking the warmth of his body, and Dancer swore under his breath as her arms crept up around his neck. In less than no time at all, her trembling ceased and she relaxed against him, unconsciously finding comfort in the unyielding wall of his chest and in the strength of the arms that held her close.

Dancer sighed as he became aware of the faint fragrance of wildflowers that lingered in her hair and of the velvet softness of the cheek beneath his calloused palm. He had not had a woman in a long time. Desire stirred in his loins as he vividly recalled the trim beauty of the nubile body enfolded in his arms.

"I must be sinking mighty low to think what I'm thinking," he muttered bleakly. "Mighty damn low."

Chapter 2

Dancer woke with the dawn to find the girl pressed close beside him, her golden head pillowed on his shoulder. She looked incredibly young and vulnerable lying there, he mused, surprised by the protective instincts she aroused in him. She aroused other, less noble instincts as well, he acknowledged with a wry grin. His best bet would be to leave her here for the posse. She would only bring him trouble, slow him down.

Yet even as he tried to convince himself to abandon her, he knew he would not. He wanted her, had wanted her from the moment he first laid eyes on her. And he was a man who always took what he wanted.

Carefully, so as not to disturb her, he eased out of his blankets. Smothering a yawn, he fished a bar of yellow soap, a razor, and a change of clothes out of his saddlebags and ambled off toward the stream he could hear gurgling at the foot of the hill, his mind set on a bath and a shave.

The rising sun coaxed Jessica awake. For a moment she lay still, staring vacantly at the bold blue sky. A weak effort to sit up sent the world spinning out of focus and she fell back, her eyes closed.

There was a dull ache in the back of her head, and for a long moment her mind was mercifully blank. And then, all too clearly, the memory of yesterday's terror returned full force, flooding her mind with grotesque images of John . . . John, wounded and cruelly beaten by that big bear of a man. John, writhing on the ground. John!

She rolled over, her eyes searching for her brother, but there was no sign of him. Where had he gone? Was it possible he hadn't been hurt as badly as she supposed?

She stared blankly at the charred remains of their wagon, too distraught by her brother's disappearance to even care that everything she had owned in the world had been destroyed.

"Feeling better?"

The deep male voice startled her, and she scrambled to her knees, throwing a frightened glance over her right shoulder, the throbbing in her head momentarily forgotten in the surging tide of panic that swept through her.

But the man standing behind her was not one of the four.

"Yes. Yes, I am," Jesse stammered, hypnotized by the cold gray eyes that threatened to devour her in a single glance. Grasping the blanket tighter, Jessica tried to return his gaze with equal force, and failed miserably. It did not occur to her to ask who he was, or how he happened to be there.

He was a big man, broad through the shoulders and narrow in the hips. His hair was thick and black and long, as straight as an Indian's. A drooping moustache added a touch of menace to a face lined by years of living under a harsh sun in a hostile land. He was naked to the waist, and his skin was very dark. Powerful muscles rippled in the sunlight as he slipped a loose-fitting buckskin shirt over his head.

One hand, big and brown, rested easily on the polished butt of the gun holstered at his side as his eyes raked her from head to heel. She blushed scarlet under his bold scrutiny.

"Want to tell me what happened." It was not a question, not the way he said it.

"My brother and I were on our way to Cherry Valley. We had made camp for the night when four men rode up," Jessica explained dully. "They shot my brother." Her eyes searched Dancer's face. "Have you seen him? Have you seen John?"

"I've seen him," Dancer answered, relieved, somehow, to know she had not been married to the dead man.

The tone of his voice told Jessica everything she needed to know, but she refused to believe it. John could not be dead. He was all she had left in the world. "Where is he?"

Dancer jerked his thumb toward a grassy knoll some ten yards away. "I buried him last night."

Jessica stared at him. John was dead. It couldn't be true. She thought of all the hardships they had endured in the East, their hopes for a bright future in Cherry Valley. He was going to teach and they would make a new life for themselves, a good life. . . .

"Can you stand up?" Dancer asked curtly, and the sound of his voice called her back to the present.

"Yes, I think so."

Clutching the blanket in both hands, Jessica rose on wobbly legs, swaying unsteadily. Thinking to help, Dancer reached out to steady her, but she jerked away, clearly remembering other male hands that had grabbed at her, hurting her.

Dancer read the fear in her eyes and took a step backward. "Are you all right?" he asked, not unkindly.

"Yes."

"Here, put this on." He handed her a dark blue shirt, busied himself with saddling his horse while she slipped it on. It was much too large for her but it was soft and warm, faintly redolent of woodsmoke and sage, of sweat and tobacco. She did not find the smell unpleasant.

"Let's go," he said. He secured his bedroll behind his saddle, slid his Winchester into the saddle boot.

"Go?" Jessica repeated, her voice thick with suspicion and distrust. "Go where?"

Dancer stared at her, noticing for the first time that her eyes were blue-green, like the turquoise rocks so prized by the Navajo. Her hair, long and tawny, fell in glorious disarray over her slight shoulders. She looked vastly appealing wearing nothing but his shirt. He felt a peculiar tightness in his belly, a sudden heat in his loins. For a fleeting moment, he thought of taking her there, on the ground, and to hell with the posse! Looking at her, he thought possessing her might be well worth the risk of getting caught.

As if reading his mind, the girl took a step backward.

Dancer answered her question then, his voice strangely thick and uneven. "It doesn't matter where. There's a posse doggin' my backtrail, and it's time to move on."

"I'm not going anywhere with you," Jesse declared resolutely.

"Oh, yes, you are. You might come in handy if that posse gets too close."

"I can't go!" she cried wildly. "Don't you understand?" Her voice rose hysterically. "I can't leave John out here, alone. I can't! I won't!"

Dancer swore impatiently. Taking a quick step forward, he slapped her, hurting her, making her head throb with renewed vigor.

"He's dead and buried," Dancer said brusquely. "There's nothing more you can do for him now."

Wordlessly, Jesse gathered what was left of her clothes. Turning her back on him, she pulled on her skirt and pantalets, her stockings and low-heeled boots, noting as she did so that he had washed her clothes.

She didn't offer any resistance as he lifted her into the saddle. She was numb inside and out. John was dead, and all her girlish dreams of a new and happy life had died with him.

Dancer swung into the saddle behind the girl and took up the reins. "What the hell's your name?" he demanded gruffly.

"Jessica," she answered sullenly. "Jessica Landry."

"Call me Dancer."

She didn't know if it was his first name or his last.

Fatigued physically and emotionally by the events of the past twenty-four hours, troubled by the desire she had seen flare in the stranger's smoky gray gaze, Jesse closed her eyes and retreated into the safe haven of sleep.

Dancer felt Jesse sag against him, and his arm tightened protectively around her slim waist. Why had he brought her along? He had no intention of using her as a hostage no matter how close that posse got. It wasn't in his nature to hide behind a woman, or behind anyone else, for that matter. He'd always faced trouble head-on and alone. Why, then, had he insisted the girl come along?

He knew why, he admitted ruefully.

And so did she.

It was only a matter of time.

Scowling, he urged the mare into an easy

lope in an effort to make up the time he'd lost caring for the girl.

He maintained a hard pace throughout the day, stopping briefly at noon for a quick meal of jerky and cold biscuits, and again several hours later to breathe the mare.

Once, glancing over his shoulder, he saw a faint cloud of dust. The posse? Indians on the prowl? Cowhands, perhaps? There was no telling at such a distance, and he urged the weary mare onward, not wanting to be caught out in the open where there was no cover.

The sun was low in a pale pink sky when he drew the Appaloosa to a halt near a small cave recessed deep in a rocky hillside. He tethered the mare well away from the entrance, lifted the girl from the saddle, then draped his saddlebags over his shoulder and ducked into the cave.

Woodenly, Jessica followed Dancer to the mouth of the cavern and stood there, watching warily, as he spread his bedroll inside the rough shelter, then started a fire in a shallow pit fashioned by some previous occupant.

"You might as well come on in and sit down," he invited, but there was no warmth in his words, and none visible in his eyes.

Jessica covered the distance between them as if treading on hot coals, hesitantly sank down beside him on the hard ground. Hugging her knees to her chest, she stared into the dancing flames.

Dancer rummaged around in his saddlebags

and in minutes served up a meal of bacon, beans, hardtack, and coffee. It wasn't much, Jesse thought bleakly, but at the moment it looked like a feast.

She glanced surreptitiously at Dancer as she ate. Why was he running from the law? Dare she ask? What was he going to do with her? He did not look like the Good Samaritan type, yet he had risked his life in her behalf, had carefully tended her battered face. She lifted a hand to her eye, winced as she felt the swollen flesh beneath her fingertips. She must look a sight, she mused, what with a black eye and a lip the size of a grapefruit.

Still, for all that he had treated her gently thus far, she was afraid of him. Afraid of the ruthlessness she sensed sleeping beneath the surface of his apparent concern; afraid of the lust she had seen reflected in his eyes. Nothing in her twenty years had prepared her to deal with the events of the past two days. Gently reared by a maiden aunt, she had been thoroughly sheltered from life's harsher lessons. She knew nothing of men, especially violent men.

Jesse sighed wistfully. Life had always treated her kindly in the past. Why had it suddenly turned cold and ugly? Even though she had known poverty and hardship, she had never felt abandoned and alone until now. Always, John had been there, giving her moral support, assuring her that things would get better. She had convinced him that moving to

Cherry Valley would be good for them, that the answer to all their dreams lay out West. But now John was dead, and all her courage had died with him.

Dancer stirred beside her, sending a quick shiver of apprehension down Jesse's spine, but he only stood up, stretching his arms over his head.

"Why don't you turn in?" he suggested. "I'm going out to check on my horse."

Jesse nodded. Relieved to be alone, she crawled between his blankets, fully clothed except for her boots. *What happens now?* she thought. What would he expect of her? She supposed he had saved her life. He had undoubtedly saved her from being ravaged. Would he expect her to share his bed in return? Would he take her by force if she refused? After all, he was a wanted man, an outlaw. No telling what crimes he had committed, what violence he was capable of.

Recalling the hunger she'd seen in his cold gray eyes, she drew the blankets up to her chin. Her pulse pounded rapidly in her throat, and she could feel the frightened hammering of her heart. How much longer would he stay outside? And what would she do when he returned?

She risked an apprehensive glance toward the mouth of the cave, blanched when she saw him standing there. He loomed larger than life in the firelight, making her feel small and defenseless, like a rabbit cornered by a lion.

Dancer stood watching Jesse for a long moment, annoyed by her obvious panic, irritated by the strange effect she had on him. His desire to protect her from harm was sorely at odds with his desire to bed her, and these irreconcilable emotions warred within him, stirring his anger.

Scowling, he crawled under the blankets. It was going to be a cold night, and two bodies radiated more heat than one. Still, he was careful not to touch her in any way, afraid any contact between them would cause her to bolt like a spooked mare.

"Relax, honey," he drawled softly. "Get some sleep. Tomorrow's gonna be a long day."

It seemed that only minutes had passed before he was shaking her awake. Wordlessly, he handed her a cup of black coffee, packed his gear while she drank the hot, bitter brew. He slashed a hole in one of his two blankets while she braided her hair into a single thick plait; then he rolled the remaining blanket into a compact cylinder while she pulled on her shoes.

She stared at him askance when he thrust the makeshift poncho into her hands. Offering no explanation, he scooped up his bedroll, saddlebags, and rifle and left the cave.

Jessica followed him outside. Overhead, the sky was a dull leaden gray. A faraway flash of lightning and a rumble of thunder promised rain before the day was out. The big Appaloosa mare shook her head against the rising wind, stamped her foot as Dancer lashed his gear behind the saddle.

Pulling a sheepskin jacket from one of the packs, Dancer gestured at the blanket hanging over Jessica's arm.

"Best put that on," he advised tersely. "I'll see about getting you a poncho and some warm clothes when we come across a town, but for now that will have to do."

"That's very kind of you, I'm sure," Jesse answered politely. "But when we come to a town, I'll be quite able to take care of myself." A faint suspicion worked its way into her mind. "You *are* going to leave me in the next town, aren't you?"

"No." The word came with the finality of a bullet. "That posse is only a day or so behind me at most, and if there's one thing I don't need, it's you waiting in the next town to point out the way I've gone." His eyes bored into hers. "And I might need you to negotiate with if they get too close. I told you that before."

Who are you trying to kid, his conscience taunted, *the girl or yourself?*

"I won't say anything," Jesse said. "I promise."

But he turned a deaf ear to her vow of silence. He picked her up and deposited her firmly in the saddle, then vaulted up behind her with all the grace of a mountain cat. He was very light on his feet for such a big man. She had noticed that before.

They had ridden only a short distance from

the cave when the storm broke, heralded by a deafening crash of thunder. Huge drops of rain pummeled the ground like angry fists while jagged streaks of yellow lightning rent the cloud-darkened sky.

Jessica shivered as the wind howled with all the fury of hell, cutting through her like a knife. She could not remember ever having been so cold and wet and miserable in her whole life, or feeling so helpless and alone. She had no one now that John was dead, buried in an unmarked grave in the middle of the wilderness. Poor John. Killed and buried by strangers. Would that she had died with him! At least then her troubles would be over and she would not be at the mercy of this tall dark man whose only concern for her appeared to be her dubious bargaining power with an unseen posse. And what if they would not grant him his freedom in exchange for her life? Would he kill her then? Or simply abandon her and leave her at the mercy of the animals and the elements? And what were his plans for her in the meantime?

She thrust away the answer that came readily to mind.

She had been so eager to go West, so thrilled with the prospect of venturing into a new land, seeing new sights and meeting new people. She was the one who had persuaded John they should make the move, and now he was dead. John . . . It was too painful to think of him, and she sought another subject to fill her thoughts.

Dancer came quickly to mind. She was physically attracted to him, though she was loath to admit it. Just the thought of him brought a flush to her cheeks and made her stomach flutter queerly. He was disturbingly handsome, and she was ever aware of the viselike grip of his arm around her waist, of his blatant maleness that made her more keenly aware of her own femininity.

The rain continued to fall in icy sheets, soaking both man and beast. The grass went limp, flattened by the relentless downpour. Tall trees bowed before the heavy hand of the wind, while great crashes of thunder shook the earth, and blinding flashes of lightning scorched the clouds.

Dancer felt Jesse shivering against him as he searched the bleak landscape for shelter, and when the squat outline of an old mining shack reared up in the distance, he reined the mare toward it.

The place was a shambles, obviously long unused, but it offered refuge from the wind and rain, and Dancer propelled Jessica up the crumbling stairway and through the sagging front door. Jessica stood in the middle of the room, looking as sleepy-eyed and forlorn as a child suddenly snatched from a warm bed.

"Get out of those wet things," Dancer ordered brusquely, shedding his own jacket and hat. "Shake out the bedroll. And get the coffee pot. It's in the big pack."

Jesse obeyed his curt commands because she

was afraid not to, mentally protesting all the while. Who did he think he was, anyway?

While Jesse grudgingly did his bidding, Dancer broke up the few rickety chairs that were the shack's only furnishings, quietly cursing the last occupant for failing to refill the woodbox before he moved on.

Minutes later, Dancer and Jessica were huddled before a small but cheery fire, a dry blanket draped over their shoulders as they shared a cup of hot coffee.

Jesse glanced furtively at Dancer, relieved to see him staring into the flames, apparently oblivious to her presence. She sighed, wishing the fire's friendly warmth could dispel the ponderous silence between them as easily as it had chased the chill from her bones. She felt terribly ill at ease, sitting in the squalid cabin with a man she did not know and did not trust. A man who was wanted by the law.

She was acutely aware of his presence beside her, of the tension between them. Once, when he shifted his position, his arm brushed her shoulder and she felt the impact of his touch clear down to her toes. She had never been physically attracted to a man before, and the sensations he aroused in her were titillating and scary at the same time.

Gradually, the flames burned low, and when only glowing coals remained, they curled up on the floor in front of the blackened hearth and went to sleep.

Sometime in the night Jesse began to dream;

dark, shadowy dreams peopled with faceless men, men chasing her, catching her, touching her. Horrible men with leering grins and hot, panting breath.

She moaned aloud as the nightmare engulfed her. Dancer woke instantly, hand darting automatically toward his Colt. Beside him, Jesse whimpered in her sleep and he relaxed, recognizing her troubled cry as the sound that had awakened him.

Thinking only to comfort her, Dancer gathered Jesse in his arms and held her close, his hand stroking her hair with a tenderness he had rarely felt or displayed.

Only half awake, Jesse snuggled deeper into the arms that held her. They were such strong arms. Surely they would protect her from the nightmares that haunted her sleep. How wonderful to feel safe and warm. His heartbeat was steady and comforting beneath her ear; his hands were gentle as they caressed her back, then moved up to massage the nape of her neck. He murmured her name as his lips brushed the top of her head.

Jessica's eyelids fluttered open, a startled cry of dismay erupting from her throat as she recognized the man who was holding her. He leaned toward her, his mouth covering hers, stifling her cry with a kiss that threatened to steal the breath from her body.

Jessica twisted her head to the side, trying to evade his touch, but he captured her head in one big, brown-skinned hand, his mouth covering hers in a long, hungry kiss, his tongue slipping between her lips, shocking her sensibilities even as tendrils of pleasure uncurled in her belly. She shuddered as the kiss deepened and waves of heat surged through her veins.

For a moment she ceased struggling, letting herself revel in the unexpected wonder of his kiss; then, with a little cry of triumph, she bit down on his tongue, bit down until she tasted blood.

Dancer swore and jerked away. He stared at her, his expression angry, and then faintly amused. With a low growl, he pressed her to the floor, his body trapping hers, his hands imprisoning her own as his mouth claimed hers once again.

It would be so easy to take her, he mused, so easy to extinguish the flame of his desire in her sweet femininity.

Knowing it was useless, Jesse writhed beneath him in an effort to free herself, to avoid his kisses. But she was powerless against his strength, and as she ceased struggling, a curious warmth crept over her whole body.

He kissed her again, and yet again, kissed her until she thought her bones would melt from the heat of his lips. And then, abruptly, he released her and sat up.

Dancer swore under his breath as he gazed at Jesse. Her eyes were luminous, her cheeks flushed, her lips slightly parted, swollen from his kisses. He was a lot of things, he thought bitterly, and most of them weren't very nice. But he'd never resorted to rape, and he wasn't about to start now.

Jesse glared up at Dancer as he sat back on his heels, angry with him because he had stopped, and even more angry with herself because she hadn't wanted him to.

"You beast!" she hissed. "You're just like the others. Worse! I hope that posse catches you and kills you. I hope they hang you from the highest tree. I hope they shoot you a thousand times. I hope—"

"That's enough, honey," Dancer drawled, amused by her outburst. "I think I get your drift."

"Oh, you're despicable!" Thrashing wildly, Jesse endeavored to climb out of the blanket that was tangled around her feet, desperate to get as far away from him as possible, frightened by the feelings he had aroused in her.

"Just where do you think you're going?" Dancer asked gruffly. "It's raining like hell, and we're in the middle of nowhere."

He spoke to her as if she were a not-too-bright child, infuriating her still more.

"I don't care!" Jessica shrieked. "I'd rather die out in the rain than stay here with you."

"Sorry, honey, but you're not going anywhere. Now settle down and get some rest. And don't think you can sneak away later. I'm a mighty light sleeper."

And so saying, Dancer put his arm around her and held her close while she cried bitter tears, railing at the fate that had left her at the mercy of a stranger.

True to his word, Dancer stopped at the first town they came across and bought Jessica some warm clothes. He bought her a horse, too, a dainty roan mare with a blaze face and three white stockings.

Dancer did not take Jesse shopping with him, however, but left her bound and gagged on the outskirts of town, well hidden from passersby.

It wasn't much of a town, just a few small stores, a hash house, and a saloon. He went to the saloon first, satisfying a deep thirst. Leaning against the rough-hewn bar, he listened to the quiet hum of conversation around him. Most of the talk was about old man Clayton's boy getting himself killed by some fast gun. . . .

Dancer spotted the Wanted poster as he rode out of town. The charge was murder. The reward was five thousand dollars. Alive.

Dancer whistled under his breath. The kid's old man really was rich. But why did Clayton want him taken alive?

Jessica's thoughts went round and round as she waited for Dancer to return. Would he return? Or had he left her out here to die? She could not squeal on him then!

Standing there, fretting over an itch she could not scratch, she tried to hate him, but she could not. Instead, she kept remembering the way his mouth had felt on hers, the touch of his hand in her hair, the husky yearning in his voice when he murmured her name.

"Oh, John," she sighed. "Why did we ever come out here? Nothing has turned out the way we planned."

She was relieved to see Dancer ride up a short time later leading the little roan mare.

Chapter 3

The next two days passed without incident. They left the yellow grassland behind and entered a rolling land dotted with steep rocky mountains and occasional valleys. The earth was a deep rusty red, the sky an unblemished cobalt blue. Wildflowers made bright splashes of color on the hillsides.

Jessica had never seen such vast, beautiful country, or so much wildlife—deer, an occasional elk, birds and squirrels, skunks and foxes, prairie dog towns, and once, in the distance, a tawny mountain lion. Dancer told her there were grizzly bears and black bears, too.

Jessica shuddered. She was afraid of bears, but surely they were in the mountains, not here on the plains.

"Are we still in New Mexico?" she asked as they crossed a dry stream bed.

"Yeah."

"Where are we going?"

Dancer shrugged. His original plan had been to head southeast, toward the Llano, and see if he could find his grandfather. He felt the need to hole up somewhere safe, to take a few months and contemplate his future. He'd been hiring out his gun for over fifteen years and he needed a rest, a change of pace. Killing the kid in Cherry Valley had bothered him more than he cared to admit.

But he couldn't go to Shadow Valley now, not with Jesse.

"Dancer?"

"Bitter Creek," Dancer replied, answering her question. "We're going to Bitter Creek." It was a decision made on the spur of the moment, but it felt right.

"How long will it take us to get there?"

Dancer frowned thoughtfully. "Two weeks; three at the most."

Two weeks, Jesse thought, maybe three. It seemed a lifetime. But at least he was taking her to a town. He couldn't keep her a prisoner in town. People would see her, come to her aid if she cried for help. Somehow, she'd find a way to escape from him before it was too late. . . .

They stopped at noon to water the horses. Jessica sat on a rock beside Dancer, wishing she dared make a grab for his gun. He wouldn't be expecting such a thing. Perhaps she could snatch it from his holster and shoot him in the leg, then make a run for it.

She rubbed her suddenly sweaty palms against her thighs, then curled her hands into fists to still their trembling. She could feel Dancer watching her, and when she chanced a look in his direction, he was grinning at her.

Jessica let out a long sigh of resignation. She probably wouldn't have been able to shoot him anyway.

"See that?" Dancer said. He gestured to a long, thin spiderweb suspended between two tall green shrubs.

"It's a spiderweb," Jessica said sullenly. "So what?"

"The Indians use 'em to forecast the weather. A web like that one, long and skinny, means dry weather. Webs that are short and thick mean rain."

He was full of information like that. He told her that bees would lead her to water, that all the young in an armadillo's litter were always the same sex, that wolves mated for life.

Later that day, walking through some tall grass, he had her study their tracks.

"No two people, and no two animals, leave the same track," he told her. "See that? When you walk through tall grass, you kick the grass away from you, in the direction you're going. Now look at your horse's trail. Cows and horses knock the grass down and back, so their trail shows the direction they're coming from."

Still later they passed the carcass of a deer.

"Wolf tracks," Dancer said, indicating the paw prints circling the deer. "Bigger than a coyote's."

"They look like dog tracks to me," Jesse said with a shrug.

Dancer shook his head. "Dogs walk right up to things, but wolves are suspicious. They circle around, stop to sniff the wind."

Jesse nodded, wondering what possible good all this Western lore would do her. She wasn't planning to become a mountain man, or spend the rest of her life wandering in the desert. She wanted a home and a family, a settled life.

That night he showed her how to build a fire so that the smoke couldn't be seen from a distance.

"Curl-leaf's the best wood for smokeless fires," he remarked, "but if you can't find any, then build a small fire under a tree where the branches will separate the smoke. It's a handy thing to know, especially when you're in Indian country."

"Are we?" Jessica asked, her eyes widening in alarm.

"They're around."

"Here? Now?"

"No. The Apache tend to stay down South, near the Dragoons. The Comanche favor the Staked Plains. Don't worry, I won't let them take your scalp."

His words did little to reassure her. Indians! Good Lord. Wasn't it bad enough she was at the mercy of an outlaw without having to worry about Indians, too?

"Get me some coffee."

"Get it yourself," Jesse retorted, piqued by his high-handed attitude.

"You'd best behave yourself," Dancer warned, "or *Piamermpits* will get you."

"*Piam* . . . who?"

"*Piamermpits.*"

"Is that some kind of Indian?" Jesse asked, glancing anxiously into the darkness.

Dancer chuckled. "No. *Piamermpits* is the Big Cannibal Owl."

"The what?"

"Big Cannibal Owl. Comanche mothers use it to scare their children when they don't do what they're told."

"That's very funny," Jesse muttered as she poured Dancer a cup of coffee.

"If *Piamermpits* doesn't work, there's always *Sehkwitsit-Puhitsit,* the mud men, or the *Nenuhpee.*"

"*Nenuhpee?*"

"They're little manlike creatures about a foot high who shoot arrows that always kill."

Jesse shook her head. Mud men and cannibal owls, indeed! She shot a curious glance in Dancer's direction, wondering where he had heard such outlandish tales, but there was something else she wanted to know even more.

She drew a deep breath, then asked the question that had been troubling her for days. "Why are you running from the law?"

"I killed a man," he answered tersely. "A boy, really. He was out to make a name for himself. He'd heard I was fast and he thought he was faster. I tried to talk him out of it, but he wouldn't back off. Said he was going to throw down on me whether I drew or not. I thought he was bluffing."

A faint note of regret softened the anger in

his voice. "When I saw his hand going for his gun . . ." Dancer shrugged. "A boy can kill you, same as a man. It should have been a clear-cut case of self-defense, only his daddy is a wealthy man, and now the charge is murder."

"Why don't you let me go?" Jesse asked for what was surely the hundredth time. "You could certainly travel faster alone."

"That's true, honey," Dancer drawled, grinning at her. "But then I'd have to get my own coffee."

They were camped in the shelter of a high bluff a couple of nights later. A week had passed since John's death, Jesse thought sadly, and her whole life had turned upside down.

Heavy-hearted, she gazed up at the night sky. A million stars sparkled in the heavens. Away in the distance, a coyote raised a lonely lament to the moon.

Jesse wrapped her arms around her body, discomfited by the unfriendly darkness that hovered outside the fire's warm glow. Western skies were so big they seemed to stretch away into infinity, making her homesick for the East where friendly faces and helping hands waited behind every door.

She slid a glance in Dancer's direction, disliking the heavy silence between them. Abruptly, she asked, "What did you do before you were a gunfighter?"

Dancer gave her a long, quizzical look before he said, "Oh, lots of things. When I was sixteen

I ran off from the Comanches and—"

"Comanches!" Jesse exclaimed. "Whatever were you doing with Indians? Were you kidnapped?"

"Hardly. My ma was a Comanche chief's daughter." Dancer laughed at the look of astonishment on her face.

"I always knew you had a savage streak in you," Jesse muttered dryly, and dissolved into giggles.

"Yeah, well, you bring out the beast in me, honey," he purred, and shot her a wicked grin, like the villain in a stage play.

He was beginning to get that look in his eye, and Jesse asked quickly, "Was your father an Indian, too?"

"No, he was just a farmer down on his luck. He fell in with a couple drifters and they robbed a bank in Tombstone. His partners were killed during the getaway. My old man took a bullet in the back. But he was a tough old bird. My ma found him early one morning slumped in the saddle, unconscious. I guess his horse had wandered into their village. Anyway, she found his pony grazing with the Indian horses. The Comanche planned to fix him up and then torture him, but by the time he had healed up, my ma was in love with him. She went to the chief and begged for his life."

"Were they happy together?"

"Yes." He seemed suddenly restless as he tossed another log on the fire.

"Why did you run away?"

Dancer shrugged. "I don't know. Guess I wanted to see how the white man lived. My old man had filled my head with stories of gunfights and outlaws and fancy saloons. One day I just took off." He pulled the makings from his shirt pocket and rolled a cigarette. "Aren't you bored by all this?"

"No. Please go on."

"Well, I went to the white man's town and lifted some clothes. Cut my hair. Stole a gun from a drunken cowboy I found lying in an alley. I knew the language from my old man, so I didn't have any trouble with that. I got a job bustin' broncs. I soon got tired of that, though, and signed on as a trailhand taking a herd to Texas. It was a long, hard drive, dusty as hell, and I decided then and there that that line of work wasn't for me."

Dancer grinned. "One good thing happened in Texas, though. I discovered white women." He smiled, anticipating the effect his next words would have on Jessica. "I got a job as a bouncer in a fancy whorehouse in Amarillo. The hours were long and the pay wasn't much, but the fringe benefits made up for that."

Predictably, Jesse blushed scarlet as she caught his meaning.

Dancer laughed out loud. "Should I go on?"

"Please," Jesse said in a choked voice. "Don't stop now."

"Well, six months in a whorehouse was all I could take. I left there and went to work for an oilman name of J. J. Jennings. He was a little loco, thought people were trying to kill him, so he hired me as his bodyguard. Easiest money I ever made. But then he up and died peacefully in his sleep and I was out of a job again. I had a big rep as a fast gun by then, and a lot of money. I haven't drawn wages since."

Dancer's voice trailed off and he sat up, reflecting on his past.

Jesse frowned thoughtfully. He had made no mention of anyone in his life, past or present, male or female, who seemed important. Had he spent his whole life alone? Having grown up in the crowded East, surrounded by friends and neighbors, she found the idea incomprehensible.

Wordlessly, she crawled into her blankets. He earned his living by killing people. The thought made her shiver. She had felt safe from harm in his company. Even knowing he was an outlaw, she had felt safe. Until now. And he was a half-breed. She stared at him surreptitiously, afraid to close her eyes for fear he'd pounce on her, and then she grinned into the darkness. She was being silly. He hadn't hurt her so far. Surely she'd be safe for one more night. And with that thought in mind, she closed her eyes and went to sleep.

Dancer was unusually withdrawn the next day, causing Jessica to wonder if talking about his past had stirred unpleasant memories. It puzzled her that he would deliberately choose to live such a lonely life. How could anyone be happy always being alone?

"Dancer?"

"Yeah?"

"Last night, when you were telling me about your past, you never mentioned anyone... anyone special. Don't you have any friends, any family? Anyone you care for?"

"Gunfighters don't make many friends," he replied flatly, "though I guess I do have one, now that you mention it. We rode together for a while down in Texas. I don't see much of him now that he's riding for the law. When you

get right down to it, I guess the only one who means anything to me is my grandfather."

"Haven't you ever wanted to get married?" Jesse asked shyly, and then wondered whatever had prompted her to ask such a question.

"No, can't say as I have. I live the way I want. No strings, no demands. No one to tie me down."

"But aren't you terribly lonely?"

"Lonely? What the hell for?"

"For a home, of course. A family, friends."

"What the hell would I do with a family?" he asked.

"You're going to die a lonely old man!" Jesse snapped, perplexed by her own anger.

Dancer raised a brow in her direction. "A lonely middle-aged man, maybe," he allowed, wondering what he had said to rile her so.

"Most gunmen don't live long enough to make old bones."

Jesse urged her horse ahead. Oh, but he was insufferable! So self-sufficient, so eternally sure of himself, needing neither her friendship nor her sympathy, nor anything else. Still, she could not help feeling sorry for him. How could he go his whole life without wanting or needing anyone at all?

With a toss of her head, she tried to put Dancer out of her mind, together with the niggling thought that she wanted to be more than his friend. Much more. It was a thought she refused to accept. He was an outlaw, a killer, and a half-breed, to boot. Surely he was no fit companion for a decent woman.

That afternoon they stopped atop a shallow rise to rest the horses. Jesse sat on the spongy sod, idly plucking wildflowers as she tried to sort her jumbled feelings. Why should she be so upset because a man like Dancer obviously enjoyed living like a hermit? He was nothing to her. Nothing at all. So why, then, was she so drawn to him? Why did she find his smile so beguiling? Why was it getting harder and harder to repulse his caresses? Why, oh why, did his kisses turn her blood to flame and make her knees go weak with wanting? If only he weren't so damnably handsome, so very, very male. If only he would let her go.

Dancer lay back on the grass, his hands clasped behind his head, watching Jesse through half-closed eyes. And wondering why she intrigued him so. His desire for her was something he could neither understand nor deny. He had known many women, had loved them and left them without a backward glance. No doubt he would tire of Jesse, too, once he possessed her.

"How'd a city girl like you happen to come West?" he asked after a while.

"My brother was offered a job in Cherry Valley. He was going to teach school, and I was going to be a seamstress." Jesse blinked back her tears. It still hurt to think of John, to know she would never see him again. "I wish we'd stayed back East where we belonged. John would still be alive, and I . . ." Her voice trailed off, and she flushed under Dancer's knowing gaze.

"And you wouldn't be here with me," he finished with a wry grin.

"Why won't you let me go?" Jesse wailed. "I won't say anything to anyone, I promise. Oh, why, why, why won't you let me go?"

But he would not answer her.

Chapter 4

The river lay at the foot of a steep incline, partially hidden from view by the tangled mass of dark green foliage that cloaked the hillside, making their descent slow and difficult. The faint hum of winged insects and the cheerful chattering of squirrels and jays filled the late afternoon with music, even as the colorful butterflies flitting lightly from branch to branch filled the air with color. Overhead, a pair of eagles rode the skies with lofty grace, surveying the world through keen yellow eyes.

Dancer and Jesse had ridden halfway down the hill when a sudden break in the dense brush afforded a clear view of the winding river. Jesse experienced a sharp sense of foreboding as she stared at the eerie amber glow emanating from the surface of the shimmering water. Chiding herself for being a foolish ninny, she shrugged her apprehension aside. It was, after all, only a reflection of the setting sun, not a portent of evil.

She was contemplating a long, cold drink of water and a bath when a horse whinnied from somewhere below. As if by magic, Dancer appeared at her horse's head, one big brown hand stroking the roan's velvet nose.

"Stay here," he whispered tersely. "Keep the horses quiet."

Drawing his gun, he made his way toward the foot of the hill, his moccasined feet making no sound as he took cover behind the bole of a fat cottonwood. Several yards away, two men stood talking quietly.

Dancer's eyes narrowed as he recognized the men as two of the four who had attacked Jesse and killed her brother.

"I tell you there's somebody up there," the scar-faced man was saying.

"You're hearing things, Matt," his partner scoffed. "You've been jumpy as hell ever since Corky bought it."

Dancer's gaze drifted from the two men to the three horses grazing near the river. Where was the third man?

"Maybe you're right," the man called Matt allowed without much conviction. "But just in case you're wrong, I think I'll mosey over and have a look-see just the same." And so saying, he walked purposefully toward the hill.

Dancer could have backed off then. There was still time for him to steal away unseen, but his anger held him fast. And as he stared at two of the men who had caused Jesse pain and unhappiness, he was smitten with a burning desire to see them dead. And by damn, he would see them dead before the day was out.

His decision made, he stepped out into the

open, growled, "Hold it, right there!" as the man called Matt reached for his gun.

With a start, Jesse took a few steps forward, and now she had a clear view of the scene below. One hand flew to her mouth to stifle a gasp as she recognized two of the men responsible for her brother's death. There was a dull roaring in her ears as all her senses, her whole being, vibrated with hatred.

Sunlight glinted off the polished barrel of Dancer's .44 as he moved toward the two men. Matt had frozen in mid-stride at Dancer's brusque command, but his hand remained motionless over the ivory butt of his revolver. His eyes, as green as new grass, were focused, unblinking, on Dancer's face.

The other man was unarmed. His eyes darted nervously from the gun in Dancer's hand to the rifle propped against a boulder less than an arm's length away.

A dangerous smile played over Dancer's face as he read the man's thoughts. "Go ahead," he invited. "Make a dive for that rifle. You might even make it."

What followed would be forever etched in Jesse's memory. Dancer and Matt continued to glare at each other, bristling like wolves at bay. The second man began to sweat profusely. He broke suddenly, reaching wildly for the rifle, and the gun in Dancer's hand came alive, spewing smoke and death, and the man fell, was still falling as Matt unleathered his Colt and squeezed the trigger. But Dancer was moving, too, and his .44 flamed a second time and Matt was dead from a bullet in his brain before his partner hit the ground.

It was over in the twinkling of an eye.

Aghast, Jesse stared at the two men lying sprawled in the dirt. Stared, uncomprehending, at the sodden stain spreading across Dancer's shirt front as he turned and started toward her.

Wholly engrossed in the scene at the bottom of the hill, Jesse did not hear the man creeping up behind her, was not aware of his presence until she felt the prick of a knife at her throat. Fear gave strength to her voice, and her terrified cry shattered the deathly pall of silence that had settled over the riverbank.

Dancer knew, then, where the third man was.

Turning, he stared up the hill to see Jesse making her way through the thick brush, the knife at her throat held by a big bear of a man clad in dark twill pants and a dirty red shirt. Jesse's face was stark white beneath her tan, her blue-green eyes wide with unspeakable terror.

"Throw your gun away, easy-like," the bear man growled, and Dancer obeyed without hesitation.

"I should have known it was you, Harry," Dancer remarked caustically, noting that, except for the knife at Jesse's throat, the big man appeared to be unarmed. "You always did run with a dirty crowd."

"Yeah, well, I hear you're running, too," Harry retorted, sounding pleased. "Worth six grand in Cherry Valley. I sure can use the money."

Dancer's face remained impassive. Six grand, he mused. The price had gone up.

Harry's face twisted in an evil grin. "Six grand," he repeated. He glanced briefly at his dead partners. "And no one left to share it with."

Harry's free hand rested carelessly on Jesse's shoulder. Now, smirking at Dancer, he let that hand slide possessively down the length of Jesse's body, fondling every lush curve. Jesse shuddered visibly at his touch, and Dancer tensed, ready to spring, his hands balled into tight fists.

"Don't try anything funny, half-breed," Harry warned. Leering at Jesse, he planted a wet kiss on the side of her neck. "He won't save you this time," the big man murmured huskily, then flung her aside, not caring that she fell to her hands and knees on the rocky ground. "Be a good girl now, while I tie up your friend," he admonished, "and then you and I will take up where we left off."

Harry stepped purposefully toward Dancer, smiling smugly, the knife ready in his hand. And suddenly there was a knife in Dancer's hand, too, hastily drawn from a hidden sheath inside one tall moccasin.

Harry looked momentarily surprised, then

one bushy eyebrow arched upward in amusement.

"Think you can take me?" Harry asked scornfully. "Well, come and try."

The two men circled each other warily, feinting, parrying, taking each other's measure. Harry towered a good six inches over Dancer, was half again as broad, yet for all his vast bulk, he was incredibly light on his feet.

Jesse watched the two antagonists from where she had fallen, mesmerized by the sight of two men locked in mortal combat. A voice in the back of her mind urged her to climb on her horse and ride away just as fast as she could. Dancer was badly wounded. He could not possibly win, and when he was killed, she would be at Harry's mercy. But she could not move, could not tear her eyes from the life-and-death struggle being waged only a few feet away, or from the savage expression on Dancer's face.

Intent only on each other, the two men surged toward each other, knives flashing in the fading sunlight. When they parted, blood was dripping from a deep gash in Harry's left arm. Bellowing with rage and pain, the big man rushed at Dancer, and now they were entwined in a deadly embrace, muscles straining, taut faces sheened with sweat even though the air had grown suddenly cold.

Panting heavily, they parted, only to come together in another frenzied charge, when suddenly Dancer seemed to be falling. Harry grinned with triumph as he leaned forward for the kill, and now Dancer twisted quickly in the big man's grasp and brought his knife up, hard and fast, plunging it to the hilt in the hollow under Harry's ribcage.

Harry screamed his agony, and Jesse screamed with him, then watched, horrified, as the big man spiraled to the ground at her feet, his hands clawing at the knife that was solidly embedded in his flesh.

She felt the nausea rise in her throat as Dancer coolly jerked the knife from Harry's still-quivering flesh and then wiped the blood-stained blade clean on the dead man's shirt-front.

"Jesse? Jesse!"

She looked at Dancer stupidly, her ears still ringing with Harry's last agonized cry.

Taking her arm, Dancer pulled Jesse to her feet.

"No!" she shouted hysterically, pummeling his chest with her puny fists. "No, no, no!"

Swearing softly, Dancer caught her in his arms as she began to cry.

"Let it all out, honey," Dancer murmured, and the sound of his voice slowly dispelled the unspeakable terror that had gripped her. Gradually, she became aware of the strength of his arms around her, of the smell of blood and sweat rising from his body, of the sticky warmth beneath her hand.

"Are you all right now?" he asked quietly, and Jesse nodded, not trusting herself to speak.

"Well, they won't bother you again," he remarked.

"I'm glad they're dead," Jesse declared vehemently. "I'll always be grateful to you for avenging my brother's death."

"I didn't do it for your brother," Dancer replied evenly, and his dark eyes moved over her in a long, possessive glance that told her better than words why he had fought so hard to protect her. And then he heaved a long shuddering sigh, reminding Jesse that he was badly hurt.

Pulling away from him, she cast a fearful look at his side, blanched when she saw the dark red stain that now covered his entire right side.

"Dear Lord," she murmured, and flew up the hill to get their horses and supplies. Returning, she quickly spread Dancer's bedroll on the smoothest stretch of ground she could find. She worried a lock of her hair while he eased out of his blood-soaked shirt, nervously chewed her lower lip as, hand pressed against his side, he stretched out on the blanket and closed his eyes, leaving her to stare in appalled silence at the hideous bullet wound in his side.

Not knowing what else to do, she wadded his shirt into a compact square and pressed it over the gaping hole in an effort to stem the bleeding, sickened, as always, by the sight of blood.

She wished now that she had paid more attention when her aunt had tried to teach her about medicine and healing. "*The day will come when you'll need to know these things,"* Sally had warned.

And that day was here.

Feeling her worried gaze, Dancer opened his eyes. "The bullet's still in there," he rasped. "You'll have to dig it out."

Dismay spread across Jesse's face as his words confirmed her worst fears. She was about to open her mouth to say she could not possibly do such a thing, but he was speaking to her again, his voice low and uneven.

"Go check their packs. Harry never went far without a bottle, and I need a drink."

Jesse hurried to do as bidden, glad for any delay that would postpone the moment when she would have to take a knife to Dancer's flesh.

The first two saddlebags yielded nothing but a ragtag assortment of clothing and cooking utensils, but the third pack contained a bottle of rye whiskey. It was maybe a third full.

Dancer frowned as Jesse handed him the bottle. "Never liked rye," he muttered.

Nevertheless, Jesse noticed he took a good long swallow before surrendering the bottle.

"Take my knife," Dancer instructed. "Pour a little of that rotgut over the blade. When you get the bullet out, pour the rest of the whiskey in the hole, then bandage it up tight."

"I can't do it," Jesse wailed. "I can't! You need a doctor."

"Well, we're not likely to find one out here," Dancer remarked dryly. "It will be all right, Jesse. You can do it."

She looked skeptical. Skeptical and scared.

"It's not as bad as it looks," Dancer lied, hoping to reassure her.

Still, Jesse made no move to take the knife, and Dancer wondered if she would just sit there and let him bleed to death. She had said often enough that she hated him. Perhaps she was thinking about that now, remembering all the times she had said she wished he was dead.

His mouth tightened in a thin line as his anger began to rise. Hell, he wasn't going to beg for her help. If worse came to worst, he'd dig the damn bullet out himself!

He was about to give it a try when Jesse took the knife from his hand, holding the weapon as if it were some kind of repulsive bug.

The wound in Dancer's side was an ugly hole welling with bright red blood. His jaw went rigid as she hesitantly probed his torn flesh with the disinfected blade. She trembled at the torture she knew her unskilled hands were causing him, but he bore the pain without complaint.

I can't! I can't! The words screamed in Jesse's mind even as her hand guided the narrow blade deeper into the wound. Anxiety made her palms run with sweat, and the knife slipped in her grasp, unleashing a fresh river of blood as the blade cut into his side.

A low groan escaped Dancer's lips as the sharp blade sliced into healthy tissue, and Jesse drew back, afraid to go on. What if her poor attempt to help only made things worse? What if he died?

"I'm all right, Jesse," Dancer panted. "Go ahead and get it done."

Encouraged by the sound of his voice, Jesse took a firm grip on the knife, willed her hand to stop shaking as she probed the wound a second time.

The slug was an ugly, misshapen chunk of lead, so tiny to be so deadly. Jesse stared at it for a long moment before she flung it away. Then, remembering Dancer's instructions, she dribbled the remainder of the whiskey over his side. He swore violently as the fiery liquor penetrated the raw wound, searing his flesh like liquid flame.

Searching through Dancer's saddlebags, Jesse found a length of clean white linen, apparently carried for just such an emergency as the one they now faced. As gently as she could, she wrapped the cloth around his middle, stanching the flow of blood. That done, she offered him the last drops of whiskey from the bottle, carefully wiped the perspiration from his brow, and covered him with a blanket. At the river's edge, she scrubbed the blood from his shirt, marveling that a man could lose so much and still be alive.

Darkness had fallen by the time she finished her tasks, and she built a roaring fire to bolster her courage and keep the wolves at bay, afraid they would be attracted by the scent of blood, and by the bodies lying just beyond the fire's friendly glow.

With their horses tethered nearby, and with Dancer's rifle cradled in her lap, she huddled next to the fire, more tired than she had ever been in her life.

Dancer watched Jesse through heavy-lidded eyes. His last thought before sleep claimed him was that she had a lot of grit for a gently reared city girl.

Jesse woke with a start to find the sun high overhead. Jackknifing to a sitting position, she peered anxiously at Dancer. Dear Lord, what would she do if he had died in the night? But no, he still lived, and she breathed a heartfelt sigh of relief, her fear routed by the steady rise and fall of his chest.

Stiff and sore in every muscle, Jesse rose to her feet. It had been a long, hard night, and she had spent most of it wide awake, alarmed by every sound, every drifting shadow.

Pressing a hand to her aching back, she walked toward the river, grimacing as she made a wide detour around the three fly-blown bodies. She could find no cause to mourn their deaths, only grim satisfaction that they would never bother her, or anyone else, again.

All too vividly she could recall the awful panic that had engulfed her when she felt Harry's knife at her throat, the stark terror that had paralyzed her when she thought she was at his mercy with no hope of rescue. Now, as she contemplated the fate that would have been hers had Dancer been less skilled with gun and knife, she felt a deep surge of gratitude sweep away the anger and resentment she had harbored against him since he first carried her off. And with gratitude came a warm rush of affection, and a deep sense of well-being.

The brilliant sun and the cheerful trilling of countless birds made her glad to be young and alive on such a glorious morning, and she laughed aloud as she stepped out of her clothes and slipped into the refreshingly cool water. Eyes closed, she floated on her back beneath the bold blue sky.

Shortly, her eyes flew open. "Why, I'm free!" she mused, flabbergasted by the very idea. "Free as a bird!"

Free to go wherever she pleased, and there was no one to stop her. No one! Dancer was in no fit condition to chase her across the plains. Not now. Not in his present condition. It was a heady thought, and Jesse lingered over it, savoring it like fine wine.

And then reality stepped in, dropping a mantle of discouragement over her shoulders. Ride away to where? She had no idea where she was, could not possibly hope to survive in the wilderness alone. Freedom was only an illusion, a dream with no more substance than a mirage in the desert. She was still Dancer's prisoner, bound to him by shackles of need that were stronger and more binding than iron chains.

Grudgingly, Jesse admitted she did not want to be free of Dancer, not really. She had been drawn to him from the very beginning though she had been loath to admit it.

Dancer. She smiled dreamily, thinking of him. He made her feel vital and alive and terribly feminine.

"Having fun?"

Darn those moccasins, she thought irritably. He moved with all the stealth and grace of a mountain cat on the prowl.

"Yes, I . . . Oh!" Jesse sputtered, flustered by the mental image she had of herself, floating on her back, as naked as a jaybird, and smiling like some insane wood nymph.

She stood up quickly in the waist-high water, her arms crossed over her breasts as hot blood flooded her cheeks.

Dancer laughed aloud at her discomfort. He was bare to the waist, and the linen bandage was very white against the deep bronze of his skin. Jesse thought he looked magnificent standing there against the wild land and the blue sky. The sight of his muscled arms and bare chest did peculiar things in the pit of her stomach and caused her heart to hammer wildly in her breast.

"Too bad I can't join you," Dancer said, chuckling. "I'd let you wash my back . . ." His gray eyes smoldered with subdued passion as his gaze wandered over her bare flesh in a long lazy glance. ". . . Or I'd wash yours."

He seemed to be in very good spirits this

morning, Jesse noted sourly, especially for one so recently wounded.

"Turn around so I can come out," she demanded petulantly.

"Why? There's no one to see you but me."

"Turn around," Jesse repeated, glaring at him.

With a shake of his head, Dancer put his back to her, his imagination running wild as he heard Jesse leave the water.

Jesse kept her eyes on Dancer's back, not trusting him for a minute. Belatedly, she realized she had neglected to bring a towel, and so she stood in the warm sunshine, letting its warmth bake her dry while she admired Dancer's wide shoulders and broad back.

"Need any help?" he inquired solicitously.

"No!" she shouted. "And don't you dare turn around!" The thought of being naked beneath his hot gray gaze made her whole body tremble.

Grabbing her clothes, she tugged them on, even though her skin was still damp. Her pulse was racing wildly, and she wondered if Dancer could hear the fierce pounding of her heart.

"Okay," she murmured breathlessly. "You can turn around now."

"You look like a drowned rat," he observed.

Stung by his uncharitable observation, Jesse frowned at him, but she could not resist the merriment dancing in his eyes, and she began to giggle. No doubt she was a sight, with her hair dripping water and her clothes sticking to her damp skin.

Dancer laughed with her, his teeth gleaming whitely against his black moustache, and Jesse thought anew how handsome he was when he smiled, erasing the hard, forbidding expression he habitually wore. They smiled at each other for a long time.

"We'd best be making tracks," Dancer remarked after a while.

"Do you feel well enough to ride?"

"I reckon," he answered, surprised by the note of concern in her voice. "But you'll have to pack our gear. I'm sore as hell."

"What about them?" Jesse asked, gesturing toward the bodies. She noted with revulsion that buzzards were already gathering in the trees, waiting. "Shouldn't we bury them?"

"I'm in no shape for that," Dancer replied callously. "Anyway, vultures have to eat, same as worms."

Dancer had picked up his Colt on his way to the river and he sat in the shade of a tall cottonwood, carefully cleaning and oiling the .44, while Jesse gathered their gear and stowed it in their saddlebags.

When she had everything packed to Dancer's satisfaction, she handed him Blue's reins and swung aboard her own mount. Dancer stood beside his horse, as if gathering his strength, then climbed slowly into the saddle, wincing as he did so. It grieved Jesse to see him in pain.

"Let's go," he said in a tight voice. "There's

still a posse back there somewhere."

The day passed quietly. Jesse cast several anxious glances in Dancer's direction, disturbed by the tight lines of pain around his mouth, as they made their way through a land broken by deep gullies and sandy swales.

Amused yet pleased by Jesse's concern, Dancer repeatedly assured her that he was fine, just fine. But Jesse noticed they made camp several hours earlier than usual that night.

After dinner, they stretched out under an incredibly blue sky and watched the stars come to life, one by one.

"Harry," Jesse said after a while. "You knew him, didn't you?"

"Yeah," Dancer replied. "We ran into each other a time or two. Once down in Texas, another time over in Dodge."

"Was he your friend?"

"Harry? He was nobody's friend."

"Did you know the others, too?"

"No."

For a while they talked of trivial things, then a gradual silence fell between them, but it was a comfortable silence, not like the ponderous stretches of quiet that had once made Jesse ill at ease.

The direction of Dancer's thoughts became apparent when he muttered, "I've been traveling alone most of my life since I was sixteen. Preferred it that way. But I think I'll miss you when you're gone."

There was the smallest trace of surprise in his voice, as if he had just discovered something new about himself—something he was not sure he liked.

But Jesse was touched by his words. Almost, she leaned over to kiss him. Almost. But then she remembered that he was an outlaw, that he was keeping her with him against her will. And then she reminded herself that he had just killed three men because of her. But by then the moment had passed.

Chapter 5

Things were different after that. Jesse felt it keenly, and she knew Dancer was also aware of the subtle change in their relationship.

She was waiting, she realized with surprise. Waiting for him to make love to her.

She knew it was inevitable.

And so did he.

It was just a matter of time.

The thought made her angry, and she vowed anew that she would never surrender to his touch, never! But she could not ignore the way her heart did crazy flip flops whenever he looked at her, his dark gray eyes warm with longing. Her skin tingled whenever he was near, her heart skipped a beat whenever he touched her. She was attuned to his every look, his every move, all her senses acutely alive, and waiting.

She was aware of his eyes watching her as she washed the dishes that night. She wondered if he knew how devastingly attractive he was, if he was aware of the effect he had on her. His voice was deep, resonant, his eyes were compelling, his arms inviting. Sometimes, to her shame, she wished he would take her by force, thereby taking the decision out of her hands. But she knew intuitively that he would never take her by force, that whatever happened between them would be up to her.

She realized then, as she was drying the dishes, that he had never intended to use her as a hostage. He had brought her with him simply because it pleased him to do so, because he was certain that, in the end, he would have his way with her.

"Of all the arrogant, insufferable . . ." She stamped her foot because she couldn't think of anything bad enough to call him.

She was so engrossed in her inner turmoil that she didn't hear him come up behind her until he whispered her name.

Whirling around, she found herself in his arms.

"Leave me alone," she said curtly.

"No."

He lowered his head, intent on kissing her, but she turned away, so that his lips fell on her hair instead. His hands played over her back as he drew her close.

"Jesse." His voice was soft and deep, like black velvet, gently coaxing. She felt his lips move in her hair, felt the beat of his heart beneath her cheek.

"No, don't!"

She tried to push him away, but her strength was as nothing compared to his. He captured her head in one big hand, forced her face up, and kissed her full upon the mouth.

Oh, the wonder of it, she thought angrily, the warm, sweet wonder of his kiss. His tongue teased her lips, begging for entrance, and she clenched her teeth, refusing to surrender. She was no cheap tart, no woman of easy virtue, to blithely give away that which could not be bought at any price.

But, oh, it was so hard to resist the gentle persuasion of his lips, to deny herself the pleasure he offered. She longed to discover the secrets his hands and lips promised to tell.

He drew her body against his, crushing her breasts against his chest, letting her feel the hard, lean length of him.

She moaned softly, mesmerized by his nearness, aroused by his caresses. His hand stroked the back of her neck, sending shivers down her spine, and she swayed against him, her senses reeling.

Abruptly, she twisted out of his embrace. "No!" She glared up at him, frightened by how easily he had managed to sneak through her defenses. Almost, she had surrendered her virtue. Almost.

Dancer let out a long sigh. She was the most stubborn woman he had ever met. She wanted him. He knew it. *She* knew it!

"Have it your way, for now," he said, and his mouth quirked in a knowing grin that said sooner or later she would be his.

Jesse saw another side of Dancer the following afternoon. They had stopped beside a narrow, winding stream to water the horses and fill their canteens when Jesse spied the deer. It was a young doe, with limpid brown eyes and a dappled chestnut coat. It lay near the water's edge, its slender neck stretched toward the stream, its tongue lolling out of the side of its mouth. A dark, reddish-brown stain covered its right rear leg.

"It's been shot," Dancer remarked as he walked up beside Jesse.

"Poor thing," Jessica murmured. "Look how scared she is."

Dancer nodded. It was a poor hunter who wounded his prey and failed to finish the job, leaving the injured animal to suffer death by thirst or starvation or being mauled by predators.

"Can't you do something?"

Dancer didn't answer, but drew his gun and thumbed back the hammer.

"Not that!"

"She's suffering."

"Please don't."

Dancer let out a long sigh. Unable to resist the silent plea in Jesse's eyes, he holstered his Colt, then knelt beside the deer. The animal began to thrash about, its dark eyes wide with terror.

Dancer swore softly as one of the doe's flailing hooves struck his forearm. Removing his kerchief, he lashed the deer's front feet together.

"Jesse, come here. Hold her head down. Careful now."

Jessica sat at the deer's head, her arm resting across the animal's neck so it couldn't rise.

"The bullet's embedded in her leg," Dancer remarked as he examined the wound. "I'll have to cut it out."

Jessica nodded and looked away as Dancer drew his knife from the sheath inside his moccasin. She felt the doe shudder as Dancer probed the wound.

"Poor girl," Jesse murmured, stroking the doe's muzzle. "Poor little girl, don't worry. We'll fix you up fine."

Dancer worked quickly, removing the bullet from the doe's leg, packing the wound with moss, bandaging it with a strip of cloth pulled from his saddlebag.

"You can let her go now," he said, and when Jesse was in the clear, he released the deer's forelegs.

For a moment, the deer didn't move; then, slowly, she raised her head and looked around, her ears twitching back and forth, her nostrils flaring to test the air.

Dancer shook his head, his expression bemused as he helped the deer to its feet.

"You should be dinner, you know," he muttered as he carried the doe to the water.

Jesse grinned happily as the deer took a long drink of water, occasionally lifting its head to glance at her and then at Dancer.

"Will she be all right?" Jesse asked, her blue-green eyes shining with hope.

Dancer shrugged. "As long as she doesn't run

into another hunter with lousy aim."

Jesse had expected the deer to run away, but apparently it was still too weak to move under its own power and it sank slowly to the ground.

Dancer shook his head; then, with a grimace, he began gathering handfuls of grass which he piled in front of the doe. The animal watched him warily for a moment, then began to nibble at the grass.

"I guess we might as well bed down here for the night," Dancer muttered. "The horses could use some extra rest."

Jesse nodded, her smile widening. He would not admit he was making camp early because of the deer. He wanted to protect the animal from predators, she thought, amused; that was the reason they were making camp so early. And they both knew it.

What a puzzling man he was, Jesse thought as she prepared their supper later that evening. He was a killer, but he was not heartless. He was keeping her against her will, but he had not mistreated her. He desired her, but he would not take her by force.

They ate in companionable silence. Jesse's thoughts drifted toward her brother, to the new start they had hoped to find in Cherry Valley. Poor John. He'd had so much to give, and now he was gone.

She gave a little start when Dancer set his plate aside and stood up. She felt her heart skip a beat as his gaze met hers. Would he take her in his arms? Would this be the night he breached her defenses and won the battle they had been waging since the day they met?

Her mouth went dry as he moved toward her. He was so tall, so strong, so irresistibly handsome. How could she hope to win? She felt his gaze move over her face, felt the heat in his eyes.

Her heart was racing like a runaway train as he drew near. What could she say to stop him? Did she want to stop him?

She could scream, but there was no one to hear her. Her fingers tightened around the knife in her hand and she dropped it to her plate, horrified to even think of using it.

She refused to admit she was disappointed when he walked past her and went to check on the deer.

She hated him then, hated him for making her feel foolish. But she hated herself more for wanting him.

The doe was gone in the morning.

"I hope she'll be all right," Jesse remarked.

Dancer shrugged. "We did all we could."

"I know, but . . ." Jesse smiled sheepishly. "I feel sort of responsible for her."

"How about bein' responsible for me instead?" Dancer suggested with a wry grin. "How about rustlin' us some breakfast?"

With a nod, Jesse began rummaging around in one of the packs.

She caught herself watching Dancer as she fried up a mess of bacon, fascinated by the sight of the deadly-looking straight-edged razor he used to scrape the thick black bristles from his jaw, mesmerized by the width of his shoulders, the broad expanse of sun-bronzed skin that covered his back and chest. She had never seen a man without his shirt until she met Dancer. Her brother had been every bit as modest as she. Now, the sight of Dancer's bare torso and rippling muscles did funny things in the pit of her stomach.

After breakfast, Dancer drew his rifle from the saddle boot.

"Come here, it's time you learned to shoot."

"I don't want to."

"It's necessary."

Jesse shook her head. She did not like guns, could not forget that a man with a gun had killed her brother.

"You need to know how to handle a gun," Dancer explained patiently. "What if something happens to me? You've got to be able to defend yourself."

He was right, Jesse admitted reluctantly, and let him show her how to brace the rifle against her shoulder, how to load it, how to fire it. The recoil almost knocked her off her feet, and she was certain she would never be able to hit anything smaller than a house, but he made her keep at it until she could hit a tree trunk.

"You'll do all right," Dancer remarked, "as long as you don't have to hit anything smaller than a freight train."

He showed her how to fire his Colt, too. It was heavy, somehow even more deadly-looking than the rifle. She had to use both hands to hold it, but her aim wasn't bad.

Unexpectedly, she turned the gun on Dancer.

He stared at her, one black brow lifting in amusement. "Now what?"

"I could shoot you."

Dancer nodded. "I reckon."

"I wouldn't miss at this range."

"Probably not. Of course, it'll make a hell of a hole. You gonna stay around to patch me up?"

"Oh, shut up," Jesse said irritably, and handed him the gun.

He had the good grace not to smirk at her as he holstered the Colt.

Resigned, Jesse began rolling her blankets into a compact cylinder. He couldn't keep her a prisoner forever, she told herself. Sooner or later he would have to let her go.

Chapter 6

There was a town ahead. Indian Wells, Dancer remarked, and Jesse nodded, though the name meant nothing to her. They had bypassed a dozen towns, some fairly large, some no more than a narrow street flanked by a few carelessly built saloons and a store or two.

Jesse's expression turned bleak as she contemplated spending the next hour or so tied up in some secluded spot while Dancer rode into town for supplies and a drink or two at the local watering hole. This was the third town he had considered safe enough to enter. For some reason, he never took her with him. She supposed he was afraid she would try to run away, or maybe make a scene that would attract attention, and possibly the local law.

Head tilted to one side, Jesse watched Dancer toss his saddle blanket over Blue's back, noting that he moved easily now that his wound was nearly healed, leaving a funny, triangular-shaped scar just above his waist. Fingering a lock of hair, Jesse watched the play of muscles in his broad back and shoulders as he swung the heavy forty-pound saddle into place and tightened the cinch.

Raising her eyes to his profile, Jesse felt a thrill of excitement race through her. No matter that he was half Indian and a wanted man, no matter that he had killed many men and would probably kill more, he was by far the handsomest, strongest, most virile man she had ever known.

"Take me with you." The words seemed to come of their own volition, surprising them both.

Dancer threw Jesse a quizzical glance. "Think I could trust you to behave yourself?"

"Yes," Jesse promised. "Please don't leave me tied up out here. It's so hot."

He eyed her for a long moment, as if weighing the sincerity of her request before he shrugged and said, "Okay, honey, saddle up."

They left their horses at the livery stable at the west end of town and walked down the dusty main street. Expecting their first and only stop to be the General Store, Jesse was somewhat surprised when Dancer veered off toward a green-trimmed, two-story building. A large sign in white block letters announced that it was the Empire Hotel and Ale House. Inside, a pasty-faced clerk dressed in a gray pinstripe suit and a black string tie welcomed them with a thin smile.

"I'd like a room with a bath," Dancer stated, signing the register. "And a bed that doesn't sag in the middle."

"Yes sir, Mr. . . . Mr. Smith. Room 16, top of the stairs."

"And send up some hot water right away."

"Yes sir."

Room 16 was reasonably clean, sparsely furnished with an overstuffed chair covered in blue chintz, a dressing table and mirror, and a double bed. Pink flowered wallpaper decorated the walls; dingy white curtains fluttered at the window. The bathtub stood in the far corner.

Jesse sat on the edge of the bed, idly thumbing through an old newspaper, while Dancer relaxed in the chair. His gray eyes moved lazily, suggestively, from Jesse's face to the bed, and Jesse felt a rush of heat suffuse her from head to toe. She rose abruptly, well aware of the thoughts so obviously running through Dancer's mind. But it was her own thoughts that brought a flush to her cheeks. She wanted him. It was as simple as that, yet she was nervous and shy. It was all so new to her, the chaste intimacy they shared, and she didn't know how to behave. Should she be cool and aloof, or eager and willing? What did he expect of her?

After a moment, Dancer pulled off his moccasins and began unbuckling his gunbelt.

"Why don't you wear boots like everyone else?" Jesse asked irritably, then frowned when he replied, with a wry grin, "Because I'm not like everyone else. Haven't you noticed?"

A knock at the door stifled the sharp retort

that sprang to mind, and Jesse glared at Dancer as three young boys burst into the room. They eyed Jesse with bold-faced interest as they filled the tub, then left the room amid ribald giggles and broad winks in Dancer's direction.

Jesse felt a quick anger as she shut the door. No doubt the boys thought she was a woman of easy virtue, some cheap tart Dancer had picked up off the street. And, in truth, she sometimes felt that way.

Turning, she saw Dancer grinning at her and she suddenly wished she weren't a lady so she could punch him in the nose. He looked so smug, sitting there with his long legs stretched out before him and his hands locked behind his head.

"Go ahead," he offered generously. "I'll let you have it while it's hot."

It was obvious he was not going to let her bathe in private. Well, he wasn't going to watch, either!

"Turn your back," she demanded petulantly.

"Don't you think it's time you overcame your maidenly modesty," Dancer asked, "considering all we've been to each other?"

Jesse refused to answer. Instead, she folded her arms over her breasts and stubbornly waited for him to give in and turn around. When, with a scowl, he relented and faced the wall, she hurriedly undressed and stepped into the tub, sighing contentedly as the deliciously warm water closed over her. It was the first hot bath she'd had in months, and she was sure nothing had ever felt so good.

She was drifting in a tranquil sea when Dancer's voice tickled her ear. "Here, let me wash your hair," he volunteered, and rudely dunked her head under the water.

Jesse surfaced spitting and clawing like a scalded cat, infuriated by his amused laughter. Oh, he was incorrigible! Eyes blazing with righteous anger, she squeezed the water from her hair, then washed under his frankly admiring gaze.

When she was finished, Dancer handed her a clean white towel, obligingly turned his back as she stepped from the tub. She could hear him undressing behind her as she hurriedly dried off. There was a loud splash as he lowered his long body into the narrow tub.

"Want to wash my back?" he inquired lightly, and Jesse fumed at the barely suppressed laughter rumbling in his voice.

"No, I don't," she replied coolly, and then stamped her foot in frustrated anger when he laughed out loud.

"You might enjoy it," Dancer coaxed. "I know I would."

"Oh, I hope you drown," Jesse muttered sulkily, but Dancer only laughed at her again, as if she were a spoiled child and therefore not to be taken seriously.

Jesse dressed in sullen silence, aware of Dancer's eyes on her back. She had to get away from him, she thought helplessly, far away before it was too late. Before she fell hopelessly in love with him. Already, she was far too fond of him. Surely he must know how she felt, yet he never spoke of loving her. He was content to drag her across the countryside, certain she would eventually give him what he desired, and then he would no doubt abandon her in some one-horse town, penniless and alone. Yes, she had to get away before it was too late. But how?

She flounced down on the edge of the bed to pull on her boots. That done, she casually surveyed the room, taking particular note of Dancer's gunbelt lying atop the dresser. A quick flutter of excitement started in her belly as an idea began to form in her mind. Surely she could grab Dancer's .44 and be safely out of the room before he could climb out of the tub. After all, he couldn't very well follow her in his present state of undress, and by the time he was decently attired, she would be safe inside the sheriff's office. He wouldn't dare follow her there, dressed or undressed!

Heart pounding, Jesse glanced at Dancer with studied nonchalance, only to find him grinning at her.

"Forget it," he drawled softly. "You'll never make it out the door."

Jesse stared daggers at him. It wasn't fair, she thought hopelessly. Not only was he bigger and stronger than she was, but he read her like an open book.

Dancer lingered in the tub, watching

through half-closed eyes as Jesse fished her hairbrush from one of the packs and began furiously brushing her long golden hair. She was a striking young woman, he mused, modest, well-educated, beautiful beyond description, born to be the mistress of a fine house, surrounded by a loving husband and adoring children. And perhaps she'd have all those things one day, he thought, but not now, not with him.

He did not try to analyze his feelings for Jesse as he lay there, drowsily enjoying his bath. She was here and he wanted her, and that was all that mattered. He could have let her go anytime, in any of a dozen towns, but he was reluctant to part with her. She was a fire in his blood, a thirst he could not quench.

Jesse laid the hairbrush aside and began rummaging through one of the saddlebags. "I'm hungry," she declared, "and there's nothing to eat but this." She held up a withered red apple.

Without warning, she threw the apple in his face and bolted from the room. She heard a splash as Dancer lunged up out of the tub, heard him swear a vile oath as he realized he could not chase after her buck naked.

She was grinning with triumph when she emerged from the hotel. Glancing up and down the street, she wondered which way to go.

Filled with a sense of urgency, she turned left and ran down the boardwalk, her eyes searching for a haven. Spotting a millinery shop, she ducked inside.

The lady standing behind the counter blinked in surprise. "May I help you, dear?"

Jesse shook her head, her cheeks flushing under the woman's curious gaze. She must look a sight, she thought, dressed in men's clothes with her hair streaming down her back.

"Are you all right?" the woman asked.

"Yes . . . no . . . I . . ."

"Here, here," the woman said, coming out from behind the counter to put a motherly arm around Jesse's shoulders. "What's wrong?"

Jesse stared at the woman. She was middle-aged, with graying brown hair and kindly blue eyes.

"Can't you tell me?" the woman asked.

"I need help," Jesse said. "I'm lost, and I don't have any money."

"I see."

"If you could lend me a few dollars, I'd be glad to work for it. I could clean your shop, or . . ."

"There, there, I'll be glad to lend you whatever you need, but first let's get you out of those dreadful clothes."

Jesse nodded, too overcome with gratitude to speak. She'd escaped Dancer and found help.

"I think my daughter's clothes will fit you," the woman said. "They're in a trunk in the back room." The woman smiled at Jesse. "My name's Elsa Linquist."

"Jessica Landry."

"You just wait here a minute, Jessica, while I go see what I can find."

Jesse nodded. She was admiring a feather-bedecked blue bonnet when she heard the shop door open. Glancing over her shoulder, she saw Dancer.

"Let's go," he said curtly.

Jesse shook her head. "No."

He took a step toward her as Elsa Linquist emerged from the back room.

"May I help you?" Elsa asked.

"No, ma'am. I just came to get my wife."

Elsa's gaze darted from Dancer to Jesse.

"I'm not his wife," Jesse declared.

Dancer crossed the room and took hold of Jesse's arm. His dark eyes bored into hers as he dropped his hand to his gun. "Let's go, Jesse," he said, his voice cold and flat.

Jesse stared at him. She saw the warning in his eyes, understood the implication of his hand resting on the Colt.

"Jesse?"

She forced a smile. "I'm ready."

"Are you sure you want to go with him, dear?" Elsa asked, her blue eyes mirroring her concern.

"Yes, thank you."

Elsa Linquist nodded. It wasn't her place to interfere between a man and his wife. But she felt sorry for the girl. "I'll be here if you need me."

"Thank you," Jesse said again, and then Dancer was leading her out of the shop.

"Let's go eat," he said curtly. "There's a decent restaurant down the street."

"No. I refuse to be seen in these clothes. People will think I'm your brother."

"I doubt that," Dancer muttered, staring at Jesse's ample curves. Even clad in dusty trail garb, it was obvious that Jessica Landry was all woman.

"I suppose we could find you a dress somewhere if it will make you happy."

"If you want to make me happy, you can let me go."

"No."

The dress Dancer bought her was lovely, though it was cut daringly low in front. Sea-green in color, it was trimmed with yards and yards of delicate ivory lace. He bought her a pair of new shoes, too, and silk stockings. And because the night was cool, he purchased a white shawl handsomely embroidered with yellow butterflies and pale pink daisies.

He took her to dinner in the town's finest restaurant. Velvet chairs, floor-length draperies, crystal chandeliers, bubbling champagne. Steak two inches thick. Biscuits dripping with butter and rich golden honey. Coffee with thick cream. And hot apple pie for dessert.

Jesse ate two pieces of pie, lingered over a last cup of coffee, and wondered how such a dismal little town managed to support such a wonderful restaurant. And it was wonderful. The food, the atmosphere, the company of other people. And it was heavenly to wear a dress and feel like a lady again.

Her gaze slid in Dancer's direction. He hadn't said anything about her running away. Was he still angry?

He took her arm as they left the restaurant and Jesse looked up at him, a question in her eyes. Was he still playing the gentleman, or was the polite gesture merely his way of making sure she didn't go running off into the night screaming for help? But his expression was closed to her, so she put the thought from her mind, pleased to be in a town again. The noise and the people were exciting after the quiet solitude of the plains.

She was homesick, she thought, for the East, for John, for the companionship of other women, for the security of home and hearth, the feeling of belonging. She did not like wandering from place to place, feeling like a leaf tossed to and fro by the careless hand of the wind.

Dancer paused as he spotted a now-familiar Wanted poster tacked to a bulletin board between a saloon and the newspaper office. His eyes narrowed as he read:

WANTED FOR MURDER
DANCER
$10,000.00 REWARD
IF TAKEN ALIVE
CONTACT JUDGE J. D. CLAYTON
CHERRY VALLEY, NEW MEXICO

He whistled under his breath. Ten grand. That was a pile of money any way you looked at it.

Jesse glanced up at Dancer, puzzled by the grim expression on his face, but before she could determine the cause of his consternation, he was hurrying her toward the hotel.

In their room, Jesse watched suspiciously as Dancer removed a thick roll of bills from one of his saddlebags, then hooked his lariat from the saddlehorn.

"It's not that I don't trust you, honey," he explained, shaking out the rope as he walked toward her, "but I feel like having a drink and playing a few hands of poker, and I'd like to know you'll still be here when I get back."

"Can't I go with you?" she asked, dreading the prospect of being tied up.

"Decent women don't frequent saloons."

"Neither do decent men!"

His grin mocked her.

"I won't go anywhere, I promise," Jesse said, backing away from the determined look in his eyes.

"I know you won't," Dancer said, and his hand reached out to grab her arm.

Jesse scratched and kicked, but to no avail. In a matter of minutes, her hands were securely bound to the bedpost and Dancer's kerchief was tied over her mouth, stifling her protests at being trussed up like a Christmas turkey.

Smiling, he kissed her lightly on the forehead. "Be a good girl now," he admonished, and left the room, locking the door behind him.

Red-faced with anger, Jesse pulled against her tether, but struggling proved futile and only made her wrists ache. Fuming helplessly, she sat in the dark, mentally calling Dancer every bad name she'd ever heard, until self-pity overcame her rage and she cried herself to sleep.

It was after midnight when Dancer returned to the hotel, somewhat richer for his efforts at the gaming tables. Storekeepers, he mused disdainfully; taking their money was too easy.

Jesse was asleep, her cheek pillowed on her bound hands. Silvery moonlight filtered through the open window, bathing her face in a soft, warm glow. He could see from her swollen eyes and tear-stained cheeks that she had been crying, and he felt a sudden wave of remorse for the way he had treated her. She was a good woman, a decent woman, and she deserved better than he was giving her.

With a sigh, he removed the gag, untied her hands, covered her with the quilt that was folded across the foot of the bed.

He swore softly as he brushed a lock of hair from her forehead, but there was no anger in his voice, only a note of soft reproach.

He stood there for a long time, just looking at her.

Chapter 7

Jesse was still angry the following morning, refusing to speak to him, refusing to meet his gaze. They ate breakfast in the same restaurant where they'd eaten the night before. Then Jesse changed back into her trail garb and they were riding eastward again.

Her mood was sullen as they rode. It was hard to remember a time when she'd worn her hair curled attractively atop her head instead of plaited into two long braids, a time when she had worn swirling skirts and starched petticoats instead of coarse denim pants and a cotton shirt. A time when she had worn soft-soled shoes instead of boots, a time when her skin had been creamy white instead of golden brown.

A time when she had been free.

Jesse glared at Dancer, hating him because he would not let her go. What did he intend to do with her? She refused to let him have his way with her, so why did he insist on keeping her with him? She shook her head. Perhaps he was just lonely and wouldn't admit it. Perhaps he really intended to use her as a hostage. Oh, the man was incorrigible!

He continued to teach her how to survive in the wilderness. That day he taught her how to catch a fish using a spear made from a slender willow branch, and that night he showed her how to roast a sage hen underground. He even taught her how to play poker. She was shocked when she discovered the cards were marked, and then she insisted he teach her how to cheat, just to keep things fair. She basked in his praise when she managed to palm an ace without getting caught.

And she admitted, to herself, to her shame, that she was falling in love with him. The hard expression he habitually wore no longer frightened her. There was gentleness in him, though he tried to hide it, a deep underlying sense of right and wrong.

The fact that she was beginning to care for him frightened her, and she renewed her vow to escape before it was too late, before she fell hopelessly, helplessly, in love with a man who was a hired gun, an outlaw. A man who had no future.

The following night they camped in a small wooded valley. After dinner, Jesse crawled into her blankets, her mind plotting and rejecting a half-dozen ways to escape.

She was almost asleep when she felt Dancer's lips in her hair. Her eyes flew open to find him kneeling beside her, his dark eyes alight with desire.

He smiled a slow, lazy smile as he bent his

head and kissed her, his lips warm and coaxing. "Jesse." He murmured her name as he lifted her hand and kissed her fingertips, then let his tongue caress her palm.

"No."

He kissed her again, his hands resting lightly on her shoulders. Her blood grew warm as from heady wine, her breathing became erratic as his kiss deepened. He smelled of leather and sagebrush, of smoke and horse. She grasped his arms and felt the muscles bunch beneath her fingertips.

"Jesse."

There was a world of wanting in the way he murmured her name, and she felt herself drowning, drowning in pleasure, and there was no hope of escape.

She opened her mouth to protest, felt the sweet invasion of his tongue, and knew that she was lost. The passion she had denied for so long would not be thwarted again and she moaned low in her throat, knowing that she had lost the battle.

As from a great distance, she heard Blue whicker nervously.

Quick as a cat, Dancer released her and rolled to his feet, his hand reaching for his gun.

There was a sudden spurt of gunfire and the sharp whine of a rifle as a bullet slammed into the dirt at Dancer's feet.

"Drop it, half-breed!" The harsh command lanced through the darkness.

Dancer whirled around, his thumb easing

back the hammer of his Colt as his eyes searched the shadows, but before he could locate the unseen gunman, there was the unmistakable sound of several guns being cocked.

"Drop it," the voice warned again. "There's more than a dozen of us, and only one of you."

Jesse watched Dancer. Would he surrender? What else could he do? It would be sheer folly to fight.

Slowly, Dancer lowered his arm and dropped his gun. Alone, he might have made a fight of it, but he could not take a chance of Jesse being caught in the crossfire.

"Get those hands up," ordered the same voice. "You, lady, stand up where I can see you."

Jesse scrambled to her feet, her stomach fluttering wildly. She glanced at Dancer, saw his jaw clench as six men materialized out of the darkness, heard him mutter an oath as his hands were tightly bound behind his back.

One of the men came to stand in front of Jesse. "Who are you?"

"Jessica Landry," she replied, certain she was about to be killed. Or worse.

"Are you his woman?"

"No. I'm his prisoner."

The man studied her for a moment, as if weighing the truth of her words, and then nodded. "Sorry if we frightened you, Miss Landry."

"Are you lawmen?"

The man laughed at that. "No, ma'am. A

couple of us were in town the other night. Frank, there, recognized Dancer. We decided to form our own posse and see if we couldn't catch him." The man smiled broadly. "We figure to split that ten grand six ways. Not bad for a night's work."

"I thought there were twelve of you."

"Sounded better that way," he said, grinning. "You'd best turn in now. We'll be wanting to get an early start in the morning."

"Of course." Crawling under her blankets, Jesse turned her head in Dancer's direction. He was sitting cross-legged on the ground, his gray eyes dark with fury.

The men spent the next hour passing a jug and talking about how they were going to spend the reward money. One by one they examined Dancer's gun, their faces grave, almost reverent, as they passed the Colt around. It was an awesome weapon, and if the stories were to be believed, it had sent over a dozen men to their graves.

Gradually the whiskey took its toll and the men turned in for the night, leaving one man to keep watch.

Jesse stared at Dancer. He was still awake, sitting as unmoving as if he were carved from stone. She studied his profile, the high forehead, the straight nose, the strong stubborn jaw, the high cheekbones, the wide sensual mouth, the thick, straight brows and lashes. She felt a queer pain in her heart and she knew she could not let these men take Dancer back to town. They'd hang him, or send him to prison, and she could not abide the thought of seeing him dead or in chains.

Feeling her gaze, Dancer turned to face her. Their eyes met and held for a long moment, and then Jesse stood up.

She smiled at the man on watch as she approached the campfire. "I can't sleep," she said. Squatting down on her heels, she held her palms out, toward the fire. "I thought I'd have a cup of coffee. Would you like some?"

"Yeah, thanks," the man said.

Jesse lifted the coffee pot and shook it. "Almost empty," she remarked. "I'll make a fresh pot."

Rising, she walked toward her saddle and reached for the canteen hanging from the horn with one hand while she quietly put down the coffee pot and picked up a large rock.

The man never knew what hit him.

Dancer grinned as Jesse pulled the knife from the sheath inside his moccasin and cut his hands free.

"Good girl," he murmured; then, lifting a coil of rope from a nearby saddle, he took the knife from her hand and began cutting the rope into three-foot lengths.

Locating his gun, he handed the pieces of rope to Jesse, and then they moved very quietly from man to man, with Dancer rendering them unconscious while Jesse tied their hands behind their backs.

All went well until they reached the last

man. He woke up just as Dancer was about to tap him over the head with the butt of his gun.

The man uttered a startled cry, rolled out of his blankets, and pulled a belly gun. He fired in haste and the bullet meant for Dancer missed its mark and struck Jesse instead. She cried out as the slug plowed into her thigh.

Moving instinctively, Dancer dropped to one knee and cranked off a round, killing the man before he could fire a second time.

Holstering his .44, Dancer knelt at Jesse's side. Her face was pale, her eyes filled with pain as she stared at the dark stain spreading over her thigh.

Pulling his kerchief from his neck, Dancer wrapped it tightly above the wound, then lifted Jesse in his arms and carried her to his horse. Placing her on Blue's back, he grabbed her mount's reins, then swung up behind Jesse and urged the Appaloosa into a lope.

Dancer reined the mare to a walk once they were out of the valley. He had plenty of time to put some distance between himself and the posse. It would be a while before the men regained consciousness. Hopefully, they wouldn't give chase when they discovered the dead man. And even if they decided to come after him, they couldn't track him until morning.

He could feel Jesse trembling in his arms and he swore under his breath. She might have been killed, and it would have been all his fault.

They'd been traveling for almost two hours when he reined Blue to a halt. Jesse was shivering uncontrollably in his arms, her teeth clenched against the pain, her face wan. Dismounting, he lifted her to the ground. Spreading his blankets under a willow tree, he made her as comfortable as possible before tugging down her Levi's to examine the wound.

"Is it bad?" Jesse asked tremulously.

"No." Dancer rinsed the blood from his kerchief, then washed the wound with water from his canteen. The bullet had plowed a shallow furrow the length of her thigh, and while he knew it must hurt like hell, he didn't think it was anything to worry about. His only concern was that he had nothing with which to sterilize the wound, nothing to offer her to numb the pain. He bound the wound with a length of cloth from his saddlebag, tugged her Levi's back over her hips. "Get some sleep."

"But they'll be after us."

"Not for a while."

The strain of the night, combined with the loss of blood and the hard ride, had taken their toll on her strength. In minutes, she was asleep.

Dancer squatted on his heels, an unlit cigarette clamped between his teeth as he stared into the darkness. He had never been responsible for another human being before, never been tied down, never had to alter his way of life to accommodate the wants or needs of anyone other than himself. Until now. He had dragged Jesse with him, never giving much thought to the fact that she didn't want to be there. At first, he had kept her with him simply because he wanted her. It had been in his mind to woo her and win her and then abandon her. But she had stubbornly refused to let him seduce her. And he had stubbornly refused to let her go. It came as something of a surprise to discover that he had grown to care for her. His gaze drifted to the dark stain on Jesse's thigh. She might have been killed, and it would have been his fault. It was a sobering thought, one that kept him awake the rest of the night.

They were on the run again. Jesse didn't complain about the long hours in the saddle, or about the ache in her thigh, fearful that Dancer might slow down and risk being caught again; or, worse, leave her behind.

Each time they stopped to rest the horses, he asked her how she was feeling, and each time she lied and said she was fine, not daring to tell him that her leg was swollen and red, until the night he accidentally jarred her thigh and she choked back a cry of pain.

Face dark with anger, he jerked her Levi's down over her hips, his eyes masking his concern at what he saw. Her thigh was red and swollen. Looking at it, he wondered how she had managed to stay in the saddle.

"You little fool," he hissed. "Why didn't you tell me?"

"I was afraid." Jesse stared at her leg, her

stomach churning at what she saw.

Dancer lifted a hand and placed it on her brow, swore as he felt her fevered flesh. "I ought to whip your little fanny for you," he muttered as he removed her bedroll from her saddle and spread it on the ground. "Sit down."

She did as bidden, her eyes growing wide as Dancer quickly built a fire and placed the blade of his knife over the flames. She felt a sudden nausea as she realized what he intended to do.

She shook her head as he moved toward her. "No."

"Yes. Lie down and close your eyes."

"Don't," Jesse begged, her stomach knotting with fear. "Please don't."

"You want to lose that leg?"

"No."

"Then do as I say. Here." He handed her a twig as thick as his thumb. "Bite on that."

Jesse's heart was hammering wildly as she bit down on the twig. She stared at Dancer's back, her hands clenched into tight fists, her face already damp with sweat, as he pulled the blade from the flames.

The pain was worse than she'd expected, worse than anything she had ever imagined. She bit down on the twig as the long, slender blade pierced her flesh, unleashing a torrent of thick yellow pus and dark red blood. She whimpered as he pressed on the wound, forcing more pus from the abscess, heard him mutter, "Damn!" as a sob escaped her lips.

Dancer let the wound drain until the pus was gone and the blood was a healthy shade of red, then he washed the wound with water, dried it, packed it with moss, and wrapped her thigh in a strip of cloth. Only then did he look at Jesse. Her face was drawn and deathly pale, her eyes tightly closed. Gently he took the twig from her mouth and tossed it aside. Her eyelids flickered open and she gazed up at him, her eyes like blue-green pools of pain.

"It had to be done," he said gruffly.

"I know."

"Try and get some sleep."

"Will you be here when I wake up?"

"I'll be here."

Jesse tossed and turned as the fever burned through her. She was wandering in a dark, shadowy world somewhere between awareness and oblivion; but waking or sleeping, she was ever aware of the man called Dancer. He cared for her with a brisk, efficient manner, insisting she drink what seemed like gallons of water, forcing her to eat when she had no appetite, replacing the blankets she constantly threw aside. Sometimes, late at night, she saw him pacing in the dark, his profile sharply chiseled, clearly etched against the sky. Somewhere deep in the back of her mind she knew they were in danger, knew they should be on the move, but she could not remember why. Her leg pained her constantly, but she could not recall what had caused the pain.

The evening of the third day, her fever broke. She opened her eyes and saw Dancer sitting near a small fire. He was gazing into the distance, his expression brooding, and she burst into tears. She had been hurting for so long. She needed to be held, to know that someone cared, to feel the warmth of another human being.

Dancer turned toward her, his brow furrowed, his expression quizzical. "What is it?" he asked.

Jesse shook her head, irritated that he would have to ask. Did the man have no compassion in his soul, no understanding of human needs and weaknesses? Had he never been in need of comfort, never felt the urge to be held?

Dancer watched Jesse cry for a moment and then, with a deep sigh of resignation, he took her in his arms, his hand lightly patting her back. Jesse's head burrowed into his shoulder as her arms stole around his waist. He was so strong, so solid, and she was so alone.

When her tears subsided, she lifted her face so she could look at him. He had such a strong, handsome face. His eyes were as gray as a winter sky, his lips full, inviting. Slowly she lifted her hand to the back of his neck and drew him down toward her. He gazed into her eyes for a long moment, and then he kissed her, his tongue sliding over her lower lip. Her body responded instantly, straining toward his. He kissed her deeply, intimately, as he molded her body to his, letting her feel his need, letting her know he wanted her.

As she wanted him. It was not in her mind to resist. She had yearned for his touch for so long. She was tired of fighting him, tired of fighting herself.

But Dancer drew back, a wry smile curving his lips. "Get some rest, Jesse."

"Stay with me."

With a nod, he put his arm around her, thinking that denying himself the pleasure of her love was the hardest thing he had ever done.

"What's wrong?" she asked, wondering why he no longer desired her.

"Nothing." He'd hurt her enough, he thought. He wouldn't ruin the rest of her life by taking her virginity.

He smiled down at her, his dark eyes warm and reassuring. "There'll be other nights, when you're better."

Jesse nodded. "Would you tell me something?"

"If I can."

"How'd you get to be a gunfighter?"

Dancer shrugged. "I got tired of backing down when folks called me a dirty half-breed. There's not much you can do to a woman, but I sure as hell didn't have to take it from the men."

"Is that so bad, being called a half-breed?"

"It's not the words, honey, it's the way people look at you when they say it, like you're the lowest thing on God's green earth. I killed a trailhand for bad-mouthin' me when I was seventeen. Then a drifter, then a few others after that. Pretty soon nobody called me a 'breed to my face unless they were willing to back their words with lead. The next thing I knew, I had a reputation as a fast gun. That's why old J. J. Jennings hired me, 'cause he knew I was the best."

Dancer chuckled wryly. "A reputation like that's a hard thing to hang on to. A man figures if he can take you, then he must be the best. That's why Clayton's boy came after me. He wanted to be the best."

"Did you have to kill him?"

"He didn't leave me any choice."

Jesse nodded, feeling she understood him a little at last. Content to be in his arms, she closed her eyes and fell asleep.

Chapter 8

Things had changed between them again, and Jesse didn't like it. She had admitted to herself that she was hopelessly in love with Dancer. With any encouragement, she would have admitted it to him, but he kept her at arm's length.

She often caught him watching her, studying her with a faintly puzzled look in his eye, and it occurred to her that he had probably never been emotionally involved with a woman, had never needed women for anything other than the brief physical relief he found in their arms.

It was strange to think she cared for him. He was so unlike any other man she had ever known. And older than any of the boys who had courted her back home. She had never known a man as self-sufficient as Dancer, or one as hard and self-disciplined. He could be gentle, almost sweet at times, and yet he had a capacity for violence that terrified her. He had killed four men that she knew of, three of them before her very eyes. Still, she was content to be at his side. He had saved her from death and worse. He was all the security she had in the world.

Dancer was keenly aware of Jesse's growing affection, of the tenderness in her eyes when she looked at him, of the covert glances. She had slipped easily into his way of life. She caused no problems, made no demands, no complaints, and as the days went by, he found himself growing accustomed to her company around the campfire at night, caught himself listening for the cheerful songs she hummed as she prepared their meals.

She had stopped asking him to release her, making him wonder if she had accepted their current arrangement as permanent, which it most definitely was not. Jessica Landry was a city girl at heart, and once the novelty of roughing it wore off, she would be pestering him to sink roots in some cozy little town and start thinking about a home and kids.

But he was not ready to be tied down to one place, or one woman, not even a woman as warmly appealing and desirable as Jesse.

But he was not ready to let her go, either, and so he delayed their arrival in Bitter Creek by taking a longer, alternative trail.

They found the cabin on a cool, clear morning. It was nestled in a small emerald valley amidst towering pines and flowering shrubs.

Jesse's eyes lit up when she saw it. "Look!" she cried, pleased by the quiet, pastoral setting. "Do you think anyone lives there?"

Dancer shook his head. "I doubt it. The Comanches swept through here a while back. They drove out most of the settlers in this area." *Or killed them,* he mused.

Comanches. Jesse felt a cold chill slither down her spine at the very thought of Indians.

"Come on," Dancer said, turning his horse away, but Jesse was already riding down the hill toward the weathered cabin.

Muttering an oath, Dancer followed her down the hill.

The cabin was a shambles. The owners had obviously left in a hurry, taking only what they could carry. The Comanches had ransacked what was left. The sofa had been ripped to shreds, the gingham curtains hung in tatters, clothing was scattered over the floor, all the dishes were broken, a charred pile showed where the Indians had burned several wooden chairs. A thick layer of dust covered a three-legged table and the top of the cast-iron stove; cobwebs festooned the corners of the ceiling; there was a rat's nest in the hearth.

"Why would the Indians wreck the place like this?" Jesse asked. "These people probably never did them any harm."

"It's war, Jess," Dancer replied curtly. "I'm surprised the cabin's still standing."

"It must have been a lovely place once," Jesse remarked, glancing around. "It's well-built. The people who lived here probably meant to stay and raise a family."

Dancer grunted softly. The people who had lived here were probably dead.

"Could we stay here a few days?" Jesse asked. "It would be so nice to have a roof over our heads, to stay in a real house instead of a hotel room."

He was about to refuse. He was too old to play house, and Jesse was getting far too serious about their relationship. She was showing all the signs of wanting to settle down, to sink roots deep into the earth, into him. But when he looked into her eyes, so full of hope, he couldn't say no.

They spent the next two hours cleaning up the place. Jesse sang cheerfully as she swept the floor and whisked away the dust. Her voice was lilting and clear as she sang "Onward, Christian Soldiers," wielding her broom as if it were a weapon at war with dirt.

In spite of himself, Dancer was drawn into her merry mood as he hauled the ruined furniture out of the house. He found a hammer and nails in a small shed behind the cabin and repaired the kitchen table and chairs, amazed that he found a certain measure of satisfaction in the work.

He left Jesse puttering in the kitchen while he went out to patch up the small, three-rail corral.

The sun was setting by the time he'd fixed a place for the horses, and as he walked toward the front of the cabin, he was filled with a sense of peace. For a moment he imagined that Jesse was his wife and this was their place and he was coming home after a hard day's work in the fields.

He could hear Jesse inside, still singing, and he knew he was beginning to care for her far more than he should, but for now, for this little while, he was content to pretend.

He was amazed at the change in the cabin. The dust was gone, the floors had been swept clean, the cobwebs were gone, a bouquet of wildflowers brightened the kitchen. And Jesse was there, smiling at him.

She spun tales of a happy future as they ate supper, and then they did the dishes at the dry sink. Dancer felt like a fool as he stood there drying the metal dishes that they used on the trail, and yet it felt right to be there beside her.

When the dishes were done, he built a fire in the hearth and they sat on a blanket in front of the fireplace and gazed at the flames.

Darkness fell and he felt the need growing inside him again, stronger and more demanding than ever. The little cabin enfolded the two of them like loving arms, sheltering them from the outside world, and he was pretending again, pretending she belonged to him, that he had a right to take her in his arms as he was doing now, to kiss her, to caress her.

Jesse returned his kiss passionately, her heart pounding with excitement and dread. It was going to happen, she thought, now, tonight.

It was suddenly hard to breathe and she took a deep breath, her gaze meeting his, then darting away as she saw the hunger in his eyes.

Dancer watched Jesse's cheeks turn scarlet, and the fact that she was young and untouched filled him with longing and regret. He had waited so long to possess her. So damn long. And tonight she was willing. It was there in her eyes, in the becoming flush of her cheeks, in the nervousness that radiated from her.

"Jesse." He stroked her hair, delighting in the soft, silky texture. "Jesse." His voice was low, husky with desire.

She did not pull away when his arms tightened around her, did not resist when he pressed her down on the blanket.

"Tell me to stop," he murmured. "Before it's too late."

Slowly, she shook her head. She knew it was wrong to love him, knew she should tell him to let her go, but she wanted him so desperately, needed him as she needed air to breathe.

He kissed her then, lightly at first, the pressure of his lips increasing, becoming more urgent, more demanding as his hands slid over her arms. She gave a little gasp as he began to unfasten her clothing. It had not occurred to her that he would want to see her undressed, but before she could protest, his hands were touching her, caressing her, and she had lost all desire to make him stop.

He quickly removed his own clothing, and she gazed up at him, shocked and exhilarated by the sight of him. He was beautiful, all rippling muscles and sleek bronze skin. She lifted a curious hand, letting her fingertips trail down his chest, and he let out a little groan and lowered himself over her, his mouth seeking hers, his lips drinking from her own as if he were a man long deprived of sustenance and she his only salvation.

She felt his hands move over her, gently exploring, igniting little fires of desire wherever he touched her, until she seemed to be in danger of bursting into flame.

Dancer made love to her slowly. It pleased him to arouse her, to see the desire blossom in the depths of her sea-green eyes, to know he was the only man who had ever known her so intimately.

Burgeoning passion and curiosity overcame Jesse's initial shyness, and she let her hands roam freely over Dancer's body, thrilling to the hard planes and contours of his chest and arms and thighs. He was all hard-muscled flesh, and she delighted in touching him.

Dancer groaned softly as her hands grew more bold. He had known other women, women more experienced in the ways of men, but he had never known a woman who aroused him as Jesse did, or one who pleased him so well.

He whispered her name, eager to possess her, yet afraid of hurting her. He had no experience with decent women, he thought bleakly, none at all.

Jesse heard him whisper her name, and she murmured, "Yes, oh yes," in answer to his unspoken question, and when he still seemed hesitant, she drew his head down and kissed him, silently urging him to give her that which she longed for.

There was a brief moment of discomfort and then only wave upon wave of pleasure as Dancer's flesh melded into her own. He whispered her name again, telling her that she was beautiful, desirable, and she basked in the sound of his voice and in the touch of his hands, crying his name as his life poured into her, filling her with a sweet warmth and a wondrous sense of peace.

In the morning she was embarrassed to find herself in his arms. She needed time to be alone, time to sort through her feelings, but when she started to rise, he drew her back down beside him.

One big brown hand cupped her chin, forcing her to meet his gaze.

"Are you all right?" he asked.

Jesse shrugged, her expression uncertain. How did one behave after a night of illicit love-making? She felt his leg brush her own, dismayed to realize he was naked beneath the blanket. And so was she.

"Feel like you need a bath?"

Scarlet flames danced in Jesse's cheeks. She *did* need a bath; likely, he did, too.

"It's okay, Jess," he said reassuringly. "There's no reason for you to feel embarrassed."

"Isn't there? We . . . we're not . . ." She glanced away, choking on the words.

"Not married," Dancer said flatly.

Jesse nodded miserably. It had all seemed so right last night, so romantic lying there in front of the fire, alone. It had been easy to pretend that Dancer was her husband, that the little cabin was their home. But now, in the harsh light of day, it all seemed so cheap and tawdry.

Without warning, she burst into tears.

Dancer let out a long sigh. He didn't know much about virgins, but he supposed tears were a normal reaction, especially when the girl was young and unmarried and the man was an outlaw on the run.

He gathered her into his arms and held her close. He had been wrong to steal her virginity. He had known it last night. He knew it now. But, wrong as it was, he didn't regret it.

He murmured her name, his lips brushing hers, and the fire that had been between them since the beginning sparked to life again. There was no denying it now, not when the flames had been fed the night before. He was hungry for her touch, aching for the sweet release he had found in her arms.

Jesse clung to him, her love bursting into full bloom as she returned his kisses. The gentle persuasion of his mouth, the now-familiar warmth of his hands, drove all rational thought from her mind. She forgot that she had been weeping over her lost virtue only moments before, forgot everything but her need to be held in his arms, to hear his voice whisper her name.

His breath was warm in her hair, against the side of her neck. He kissed the lobe of her ear, the curve of her cheek, her eyelids, the tip of her nose, each touch sending shivers of delight down her spine. Her arms drew him closer, closer, and she gave herself to him fully, wanting him to know that she was his, only his, for now and for always.

She was smiling when, much later, she fell asleep in his arms.

She woke to find Dancer gazing down at her, his dark eyes intense with an emotion she could not name, but it quickly disappeared when he saw that she was awake.

"You ready for that bath now?" he asked, grinning.

"Yes," Jesse answered, grinning in reply.

They spent the next hour bathing in the creek behind the cabin, then drying off in the sun. Jesse was excited and modest by turns. Intimacy was all so new. She felt like laughing and crying at the same time. Her gaze was constantly drawn toward Dancer, her eyes filling with admiration for his rugged physique, for the beauty she saw in him. His skin was dark bronze, smooth and sleek as he washed in the shallow water. He seemed amused by her admiration, and when she turned away, red-faced with embarrassment, he caught her in his arms and kissed her soundly.

"It's all right," he assured her. "I like looking at you, too."

She gasped in protest when he took the soap from her hand and began to wash her back and shoulders. She hadn't thought anything could be more intimate than what they had shared in the cabin that morning, but she was wrong. Her cheeks flamed as he washed her neck, her arms, her breasts, her belly, his lips trailing in the wake of the cloth. Each touch was like a brand, making her more fully his. And then he made love to her again, there in the shallow creek, with the sun shining down upon them and the birds singing overhead.

They spent the rest of the day exploring the valley, and when they returned to the cabin at dusk, Jesse felt as though she'd come home at last.

They ate fresh-caught fish and wild cabbage for dinner, then spent the evening talking about what they'd seen that day. The valley was small, but there were fish in the creek. There were quail in the woods, and Dancer had seen deer tracks farther downstream.

Dancer smiled at Jesse as she spun dreams for the future, pretending she was his, would always be his, pushing away the voice that warned him he could never give Jesse the kind of life she deserved.

By morning, he had made up his mind to leave the valley before it was too late. No strings, no ties, no obligations, remember?

But Jesse wanted one more day in the valley, to rest, and then another day to wash their clothes and air the bedrolls. And with each day that passed, it became easier to pretend they could have a life together in the secluded little cabin in the middle of nowhere.

He had never been a man who indulged in make-believe, but it was easy now, with Jesse singing as she puttered in the kitchen. The hunting was good, the water plentiful, there was graze for the horses.

And there was Jesse. How could he leave her? His life had been empty, devoid of purpose, before she came along. His only goal had been to survive one more day. Jesse. She had brought him love and laughter, showed him how good life could be.

They went walking in the forest that afternoon. The ground was carpeted with leaves that whispered and rustled as they made their way along a narrow deer path that ended near a small pool.

For once, Jesse threw her modesty aside with her clothing, and Dancer marveled anew at the sheer feminine perfection of her figure as she waded into the shallow water. She looked like a carefree nymph as she splashed in the pool, and when she called for him to come and join her, he quickly shed his moccasins and clothes and plunged into the water.

Jesse welcomed him with open arms, keenly aware of the changes in him. He smiled more, he talked more, he let her see a little into his heart and soul, and she liked what she saw. If only she could convince him to settle down, to put away his gun, to admit he cared for her. There was warmth in him, and love, and concern. She could feel it now as he smiled down at her, as if he had a secret to share. She could sense his inner struggle as he tried to keep his gentler emotions bottled up, and yet, here, now, she felt she was winning the fight.

She drew him close, her tongue playing in his ear, as she molded her body to his. She saw the fire in his smoky gray eyes as he carried her from the water and lowered her to the ground and she twined her arms around his neck, inviting him to take her. She could not help smiling as she gazed up at him. Nothing could be more beautiful, she thought, than Dancer as he was now, naked and aroused, his eyes glowing with desire. Her whole body was on fire for him, trembling with need. He was Adam, and she was Eve, and they were all alone in Eden.

Later, still folded in each other's arms, he told her about his childhood, about learning to be a warrior, about his grandfather. It was the first time he had ever volunteered anything about his past, and she felt she was beginning to understand him at last.

"We'll be so happy here," Jesse murmured, snuggling closer to Dancer. "We can plant a garden, buy a cow and some chickens. And maybe next year we can add a room to the cabin. Does it snow here? I'll bet the valley is beautiful in the winter."

She bit down on her lower lip as she felt Dancer stiffen beside her. Silently, she cursed her runaway tongue.

"It's no good, Jesse," Dancer said quietly. "I'm no good."

"But . . ."

He sat up, unable to pretend any longer. Jesse wanted a home, roots, security, respectability, things he hadn't had since he left his mother's people, things that were no longer important to him. She wanted a way of life that was no longer possible for him, the kind of life he could never give her.

"Get dressed," he said flatly. "We're leaving."

Some instinct warned Jesse not to argue. It wouldn't be easy for Dancer to change his way of life, to hang up his gun and settle down, but she was confident she would have her way in the end. Dancer loved her, she was sure of it even though he'd never said so. And sooner or later he would realize that he needed her, just as she needed him.

In less than an hour, they were riding southeast.

"Where are we going?" Jesse asked.

"Bitter Creek," Dancer replied resolutely. He might not be the kind of man Jesse deserved, but he knew someone who was perfect, a fine, decent young man who could give Jesse everything she wanted out of life.

Chapter 9

It took a week to reach Bitter Creek. During that time Jesse hovered between ecstasy and despair.

During the day, Dancer kept her at arm's length, rarely speaking to her, avoiding her gaze. She missed his easy banter, his tales of outlaws and Indian lore. But at night, at night all the barriers he'd erected during the day came tumbling down and he made love to her as though he couldn't get enough, as though he must possess her or perish. And she gloried in it, thinking that so long as they shared such passion, everything else would take care of itself.

Once they paused atop a high bluff while hundreds of shaggy buffalo thundered past.

"Oh, they're magnificent!" Jesse exclaimed.

Dancer smiled. "The buffalo mean the difference between life and death to the Indians. The Comanche kill only out of need, using the hair for rope, the skins for lodge covers and clothing, the meat for food. They use the horn for spoons or decorations. The tail makes a handy fly whisk, the paunch can be used as a kettle. Nothing goes to waste."

Jesse listened attentively, pleased by his smile, by the fact that he was sharing his knowledge with her again.

And then, abruptly, Dancer wheeled the big Appaloosa mare around and rode away at a lope.

"Patience," Jesse muttered to herself. "Patience."

Bitter Creek was a large town. The houses were good-sized and well-kept, the main street was wide, flanked by numerous businesses. A dozen well-used dirt roads led to various outlying farms and ranches.

Thus far, Dancer had avoided towns as large and well settled as this one, and Jesse threw him a puzzled glance, wondering at his sudden change of heart.

As they rode down the main street, Jesse saw the usual business establishments: barber shop, mercantile store, telegraph office, bank, smithy, post office, two restaurants, several saloons, a large false-fronted hotel. There were also a red brick schoolhouse, two whitewashed churches, and a jail.

Dancer drew rein at the hotel, and Jesse followed him inside. The clerk treated Dancer to a long appraising glance before handing him a room key, and Jesse had the distinct impression that he wanted to refuse Dancer a room but lacked the nerve to say so.

Their room was lovely, as fine as anything

Jesse had ever seen in the East. Decorated in muted shades of spring green and pale yellow, it reminded her of a quiet park on a cool summer day. Yes, it really was a nice room, she thought, gazing around. There was a large four-poster bed, a comfortable-looking easy chair, a mahogany highboy, a small oak desk, and a commode. And best of all, there was an enameled tub discreetly hidden behind a gaudy Chinese screen.

While Dancer brushed the dust from his pants and hat, Jesse lingered before a full-length mirror, frowning at her reflection. Long hours in the sun had robbed her of the creamy white skin she had once cherished and pampered.

"I'll soon be as dark as an Indian," she muttered, but somehow the thought did not distress her as it should have.

"I have to go out for a while," Dancer said. "Why don't you get cleaned up while I'm gone? I'll have the clerk send up some hot water and clean towels."

Settling his hat on his head, he eased his gun from the holster, carefully checked the loads. Slipping the .44 back into his holster, he reached for Jesse, his arms drawing her close as his mouth sought hers.

At his touch, a quick fire ignited in the pit of Jesse's belly and she returned his kiss hungrily, molding her body to his, marveling anew at the way they fit together, as if they were two halves of a whole. Did he notice how well she fit in his embrace? Was his heart pounding as fiercely as hers?

She was breathless when they parted and she gazed into his eyes, her face shining with love. If only he would say the words she longed to hear! But he only gave her an affectionate pat on the rump and bid her to behave while he was gone.

The El Dorado Saloon was in full swing as Dancer paused at the half-doors, studying the crowd inside. The long mahogany bar was overflowing with cowhands who had come to town for their usual Saturday night fling, and the smoke-filled room seemed to vibrate with boisterous conversation, rowdy laughter, the clink of spurs, and an occasional burst of high-pitched feminine giggles.

His scrutiny over, Dancer stepped inside. As was his wont, he took a place at the far end of the bar facing the door. Ordering a bottle of bourbon, he carried it to one of the tables located in the shadows at the far end of the room. Mindful of the ten-thousand-dollar bounty on his hide, he sat with his back to the wall lest some two-bit cowpoke be tempted to try and collect the reward.

Lost in thought, he was not aware of the girl standing beside his chair until she purred, "Hi, honey, all alone?" in a sultry tone.

She was a pretty thing in a hard, brassy sort of way. Long black hair fell in loose waves over temptingly white shoulders. Brown eyes, deep and worldly-wise, returned his gaze and she leaned toward him, offering a tantalizing glimpse of honeyed flesh. Her lips parted in a knowing grin as his eyes lingered on the swell of her breasts.

"See anything you like?" she asked, one eyebrow arching upward in amusement.

Once he would have taken what she was offering without a second thought, but not now, not with Jesse waiting for him back at the hotel.

"Maybe some other time," Dancer said, and the girl walked away, a pout on her full red lips.

Dancer let out a long sigh as he poured himself a drink. Jesse, he thought. What was he going to do about Jesse? Back at the cabin, he'd thought he could settle down, start a new life, but he knew now it would never work. Jesse had already been wounded by a bullet meant for him. Next time she might be killed. It wasn't a chance he was willing to take.

Discouraged, he stared into his empty glass. His life would be empty without Jesse, he thought bleakly, surprised at how quickly she had taken root in his heart, how deeply he cared for her.

He did not want to need her. He had never needed anyone. No strings, no ties, no obligations...

He sat there for a long time, gazing out the window, watching the day turn to night. Sitting there, staring into the darkness, he had the eerie sensation that he was looking at his future. It stretched ahead of him, dark and empty as the night, and he seemed to hear Jesse's voice whispering in the back of his mind, predicting that he was going to die a lonely old man . . .

"Damn!" he muttered. "How'd I get into this mess?"

Scowling, he pushed away from the table and left the saloon, plagued by an uneasy restlessness and a sense of urgency. He wondered if he was doing the right thing, and cursed under his breath because he'd never doubted his actions before. He'd always been sure of himself, of who and what he was, and he'd been happy with it, until Jesse came along and showed him what he'd been missing. But he was too old to change now, and she deserved better than what he could give her. She deserved a man like Tom.

The thought didn't please him as much as it should have.

The Marshal's Office was a square gray brick building at the far end of Bitter Creek's main street.

Dancer grunted with displeasure as he glanced at the bulletin board outside the jailhouse door and saw the now-familiar poster tacked in the center. Ten thousand dollars, he mused sourly. It wasn't a reward. It was a ransom.

Noiselessly he opened the door to the Marshal's Office and stepped inside.

The marshal, clad in brown trousers, a plaid shirt, and a leather vest, was tilted back in his chair, booted feet propped on a badly scarred desk, black felt hat pulled low over his forehead. He was snoring softly.

Grinning with anticipation, Dancer snarled, "Reach for the sky, lawman!" and slammed the door.

The marshal's hat flew off his head as he bolted upright, his hand reaching for his gun.

"Don't shoot!" Dancer cried in mock terror. "Don't shoot! I surrender."

Tom Brady's sky blue eyes widened in disbelief, then a slow smile spread over his boyish face. "Dancer! You old son of a gun! What the devil are you doing here?" Brady took Dancer's hand and pumped it vigorously. "Don't you know everybody in the territory is after you for that ten grand? Didn't you see the flyer outside?"

"I saw it," Dancer replied curtly. "You got a drink in here?"

"Sure." Tom produced a bottle and two glasses from a drawer in the desk. "I hope you know what you're doing," the marshal muttered dubiously. He poured two drinks, handed one to the half-breed. "Of course, that poster's pretty sketchy, just your name, really. I don't think there's anybody in town who knows you by sight. What happened, anyway?"

Dancer tossed off his drink, then stared into

the empty glass. "You know anything about J. D. Clayton?"

"Sure, who doesn't? He's a judge over in Cherry Valley. Way I hear it, he owns most of the territory thereabouts."

Dancer nodded. "That's him. I was in a saloon there in Cherry Valley a while back when his kid comes in looking for me. Says he heard how I was pretty fast and he wanted to take me on." Dancer snorted in disgust. "He was a smart-mouthed kid. Kept trying to provoke me, and when that failed, he hollered he was gonna draw on me, and damned if he didn't." Dancer let out a long sigh, thinking about it. "He was fast, but not fast enough."

"The charge on that flyer is murder," Tom remarked thoughtfully, "but that sounds like self-defense to me."

"Yeah. Well, Clayton owns more than the territory. He owns the sheriff, too. I guess he can call it anything he damn well pleases."

The marshal nodded. "Have you seen anybody on your trail?"

"Not lately. There was a posse for a while, but they gave up and went home."

"Are you planning to stay in town long?"

"My being here make you nervous?" Dancer asked, grinning.

"You know better than that," Tom chided softly.

"Yeah."

"Are you going to Shadow Valley?"

Dancer nodded. "I thought I'd hole up there

for a while, if they'll have me. Give Clayton a chance to cool off, let things die down a little. How about you, Tom? Still like being on the right side of the law?"

"You bet. It's not as exciting as the old days, but it's a whole lot healthier. You know, we had some mighty close calls."

"*You* did," Dancer said, grinning. "That's for sure. Remember that banker down in Santa Fe?"

"The one with the scatter gun?" Tom mused, nodding ruefully. "I think of that old fart whenever I sit down."

"And the stage drive in Abilene?"

"Don't remind me," Tom begged, rubbing his left hip. "That's one job that was a total disaster from start to finish."

"Yeah. Seems like I was always digging lead out of your hide," Dancer remarked, chuckling.

"And enjoying it," Tom added.

"Yeah. You were the clumiest crook I've ever seen."

Yeah." The grin faded from Tom's face. "Funny, Clayton wanting you alive."

"Better alive than dead," Dancer retorted humorlessly.

"I reckon," the marshal agreed, refilling their glasses. "But why alive? That puzzles me."

"Shit, I don't know. Maybe the old man wants to tie the knot himself and watch me squirm. I heard the boy was his only son. Too bad he didn't teach the little bastard some manners."

Tom frowned. "Sounds to me like this one got to you."

"Maybe," Dancer admitted gruffly. "I don't care much for killing kids."

"He's not the first one."

"Yeah. Listen, I'm beat. Come on by the hotel tomorrow and I'll buy you a drink. I'm at the Banner House."

Jesse spent an hour luxuriating in a hot tub. She washed her hair twice, toweled it dry, then washed Dancer's clothes and her own. Somehow, it made her feel very domestic, washing out Dancer's shirts and socks. For a moment, she imagined herself in her own house, washing out her husband's clothes while she waited for him to come home from work. Thinking of Dancer working at a regular job made her smile. Somehow she could not picture Dancer in a city suit, working for wages like an ordinary man.

Dancer. He had filled her thoughts since that first day.

With the washing done, Jesse sat in the chair by the open window, looking down at the activity in the street below, her thoughts drifting back to John. She spent several minutes remembering the good times they had shared, recalling their hopes for the future, the bright plans they had made that had died with him.

Thinking of her brother filled her with sadness and she thought of Dancer again, instead. His swarthy countenance came readily to mind: his gray eyes dark with desire, his lip curled in a mocking grin. What a mystery he was; such a strange mixture of tenderness and violence, of passion and disdain.

She loved him. She accepted the idea as easily as she accepted the air she breathed. She loved the touch of his hands in her hair, the feel of his body against her own, the way he towered over her, tall and strong and undeniably male.

She wondered if he knew how she felt, and then laughed softly. How could he *not* know?

Closing her eyes, she wished he would hurry back.

Dancer returned to the Banner House well after midnight. He stood on the hotel veranda, an unlit cigar between his teeth as he stared down the darkened street. Tomorrow he would introduce Tom Brady to Jesse. They were much alike in age and temperament, and Jesse would need someone to look after her when he was gone. For a moment, he considered taking Jesse to Shadow Valley, but he doubted she'd enjoy spending the winter with the Comanche, assuming they'd take him in after such a long absence.

Anyway, she'd be better off with Tom. The marshal was the kind of man she deserved. Tom could give her a home, a family, security—things Dancer had never had, or wanted.

Jesse, married. The thought left a bad taste in his mouth, and he scowled blackly as he imagined Jesse kissing Tom, making love to Tom, sharing Tom's bed. Shit!

He tossed the cigar into the street and went into the hotel and up the stairs to his room. Striking a match, he lit the bedside lamp. Soft yellow illumination filled the room and he saw Jesse curled up in the big green chair by the window.

He swore softly, bemused that the mere sight of her should give him such pleasure, such a sense of coming home.

Crossing the room, he bent over and kissed her cheek. "Jesse." He stroked her hair affectionately, sighed as her eyelids flickered open and her arms went around his neck.

"Hi," she murmured sleepily. "I missed you."

"I missed you, too," he admitted gruffly, and drawing her into his arms, he held her close. He knew then that he should never have come back to the hotel. He should have climbed on his horse and ridden out of town just as fast as Blue could carry him. But then, he should have left her long ago, before she started to depend on him . . . before he started to care. It wouldn't be easy, telling her he was going to Shadow Valley, alone.

He carried her to the bed and stretched out beside her. He would tell her tomorrow, he thought, or the next day. But not now. Now he needed to hold her.

Her long golden hair was as soft as cornsilk in his hands; her mouth was warm and sweetly yielding as it parted under his own. He kissed the corners of her mouth, her cheeks, her nose, her eyes, swore softly as he tasted the salt of her tears.

She whispered that she loved him as he began to undress her, and he silenced her words with kisses, not wanting to hear, not wanting to believe.

His breath quickened as he undressed her, his desire rising unchecked as he gazed at the unblemished beauty of her face and figure. Her skin was like fine ivory, her breasts lifting high and proud. Her legs were long and well-shaped, her hips nicely rounded, her waist so tiny he could span it with his hands.

He left her for a moment to shed his own clothes, and Jesse watched him disrobe, her eyes alight with desire, her heart fluttering with excitement as he slipped off his shirt and pants, revealing a broad, black-furred chest, flat brown belly ridged with muscle, and long arms and legs. He was the perfect example of what a man should be, she mused, and clasped him to her as he lowered his body over hers. His hands stroked her thighs slowly, lazily, while his lips covered her face with butterfly kisses, leaving her breathless and eager for more. Her hands moved restlessly over his back and shoulders, delighting in the feel of his heated flesh. He smelled of smoke and tasted of whiskey, but she didn't care. He was here and that was all that mattered. She loved him desperately, loved him with every fiber of her being, and if he did not love her in return, then she would learn to live with it.

She whispered his name as he possessed her, then buried her face in the hollow of his shoulder, surrendering to the wondrous ecstasy that flowed through her, warming her, filling her, making her complete....

Jesse smiled politely at the man Dancer introduced as Tom Brady. The marshal was a handsome young man with an easy smile and warm blue eyes. She was surprised by the fact that the two men were obviously close friends. Somehow a gunfighter on the dodge and a lawman did not seem compatible.

Tom Brady stood with his hat in his hand, staring unabashedly at the vision before him. Jessica Landry was far and away the most beautiful woman he had ever seen.

The three of them spent the next two days together, and it was easy to see that Tom Brady was thoroughly smitten with Jesse. He hung on her every word, complimented her beauty, and gazed at her with rapt adoration. The fact should have pleased Dancer; it was what he had wanted all along. But he was not pleased. He was, in fact, jealous as hell. Every time Tom smiled at Jesse, every time he took her arm or made her laugh, Dancer wanted to smash his face in.

Jesse was confused by the amount of time

they spent with Tom Brady, by the way Dancer seemed to be pushing her at the marshal, encouraging them to get to know each other better. Not that she didn't like Tom, he was a fine man, but it was Dancer she wanted to spend her time with, Dancer she wanted to know better.

It was only at night, when they were alone in their room as they were now, that Dancer seemed to take notice of her. He made love to her, sometimes for hours, as if he couldn't get enough of her. She reveled in the fact that he wanted her, wanted her and needed her, whether he would admit it or not, and she knew she wanted nothing more of life than to spend her days at his side and her nights in his arms.

She smiled as Dancer took the brush from her hand and began to brush her hair, his gaze meeting hers in the mirror, the fire in his eyes hotter than any fire made of wood. Her whole body tingled with anticipation as he drew the brush through her hair. He wanted her. Oh, yes, he definitely wanted her.

Dancer drew a deep breath as he laid the hairbrush aside, then bent to kiss Jesse's cheek, inhaling the warm womanly scent that belonged to Jesse and Jesse alone. He let his lips slide down her cheek to the slender column of her neck, his teeth gently nibbling on her sweet flesh. The quick intake of her breath heightened his desire and he swept her into his arms, hungry for the taste of her, the touch of her hands, the honey of her lips.

And he knew then that he'd kill any man who touched her. She was his, only his. He'd never been in love and now, with his body poised over hers, he realized that he loved Jessica Landry. Perhaps he'd loved her all along and been too stubborn, or too stupid, to admit it.

Jesse gazed up into Dancer's face, thrilled by the passion that burned in his eyes. Someday he would realize he loved her, she was certain of it. And she could wait until someday so long as she could bask in his touch.

She closed her eyes as he began to kiss her, his hands roaming over her body, stroking the soft secret places that only he knew, arousing her quickly, completely, until she was on fire, trembling with a need that only he could quench.

Dancer murmured her name, his voice filled with wonder as they came together, her passion firing his own, his desire satisfying hers, and he knew that his wandering days were over.

An urgent knock at the door roused Dancer from a deep sleep. Carefully disentangling himself from Jesse's arms, he sat up, reaching for his gun. Naked, he padded to the door, thinking wryly that he wasn't dressed quite right for either company or a fast getaway.

"Who's there?" he called softly.

"Tom. Open up."

"I'll meet you downstairs. Give me a few minutes to get dressed." Frowning, Dancer slipped into his shirt and pants, pulled on his moccasins. Something was wrong, very wrong. The warning had been plain in Tom's hushed voice. He was about to wake Jesse when he thought better of it. There was no point in alarming her until he knew what was wrong.

Tom was waiting for him in the lobby, staring out the window at the slumbering town.

"What's up?" Dancer asked.

"This," the marshal replied grimly, and thrust a piece of paper into Dancer's hand.

The poster was smudged but the rough ink sketch of Dancer's face was clear enough, and so was his description. Height, weight, complexion, the color of his hair and eyes, it was all there in black and white. There was even a description of Blue, right down to the jagged scar on her right flank, souvenir of an Apache war arrow.

A muscle twitched in Dancer's jaw. "Where'd you get this?"

"They're posted all over town."

"Damn!"

"I don't know who put them up. I heard someone spotted you in Apache Wells and wired Clayton. As luck would have it, Clayton had a couple of his men in Leadville buying cattle. He wired them to drop everything and hightail it after you."

Dancer's face grew dark, and he swore aloud

as Tom mentioned Clayton. Leadville was less than three days away.

"You'd best be making tracks," Tom remarked soberly. "It's Hardin and his bunch that are after you."

"Cliff Hardin?" Dancer's laugh was grim. "Somehow I can't imagine Cliff *buying* cattle. Stealing's more his style."

"Yeah, but that's beside the point. Anyway, he supposedly gave up that line of work when he went to work for Clayton. Hardin's got orders to stay on your trail until he brings you in, no matter how long it takes."

"Where the hell did you hear all this?" Dancer queried.

"I've got a friend in the telegraph office over in Leadville. He knows I used to ride with you and thought I might be interested."

Tom glanced at the poster, lifted his eyebrow as he mused, "Ten grand. You're lucky I don't need the money."

"You must have improved your fast draw since I saw you last," Dancer drawled with a grin.

"I'm still working on it," the marshal replied, chuckling. "Seriously, Dancer, you'd better get a move on. Hardin can't be more than a day behind you at most."

Dancer nodded absently, thinking of Jesse. He would have to leave her now. Hardin had taken the decision out of his hands.

Chapter 10

Jesse bolted upright, wondering what had awakened her. She reached for Dancer, but his side of the bed was empty. For a minute, she just sat there, her mind a blank. And then, as clearly as if she'd heard the words, she knew he'd packed up and left. Left her without a word.

Grief washed over her. Dancer was gone. She had not felt so utterly alone since her brother died. And yet, even that had been easier to bear than Dancer's unexpected departure.

Dancer, gone. What would she do without him? She had depended on him so, relying on his unfailing ability to protect her, to care for her. Even when she thought she hated him, she had felt safe in his arms. He was strength and security, and she had known that nothing could hurt her so long as he was there.

Like a knight in shining armor, he had saved her life, slain her enemies, and awakened the passion sleeping in her soul. Often his caresses had been rough, and yet he had a capacity for tenderness and understanding that had never failed to surprise her because it seemed so out of character. She remembered his hands, so big and brown and strong, gently stroking her hair, caressing her cheek, exploring her body. She remembered his kisses, soft as a sigh one minute, urgent and demanding the next, evoking feelings and sensations she had never dreamed of.

Last night she had poured out her love for him, responding to his caresses with a passion to match his own. How content she had been then, how sure of his devotion, as she fell asleep in the protective circle of his arms.

And now he was gone, gone without even a word of farewell.

A sudden burst of righteous anger dried her tears. How dare he use her as if she were a woman of easy virtue, to be used and left behind? The cad!

Getting out of bed, she dressed quickly, gathered her belongings, and left the hotel. If he thought he was getting rid of her so easily, he had another think coming, damn him! He could leave her if that was what he wanted, but not until she'd told him exactly what she thought of him. The nerve of the man, riding off and leaving her alone in a strange town without a cent to her name. The least he could have done was left her enough money for a ticket East. . . .

East. She didn't want to go back East, she wanted to stay here, with Dancer.

There was a light burning in the barn. An old man answered her knock and quickly saddled her horse. Yes, he saïd in answer to her question, Dancer had ridden out of town not more than ten minutes ago, headed west.

"You're not thinking of following him?" the old man said. "It ain't safe out there in the dark."

"I'll be fine," Jesse assured him, and climbing into the saddle, she rode out of town.

Tom Brady sat back in his chair, his feet propped on his desk, a pensive expression on his face as he thought about Dancer. They had met years ago, back in the days when Dancer had been riding for Jennings. They had exchanged some heated words over a poker game and gone outside to settle their differences. Tom had always been grateful that Dancer had been arbitrating with his fists that day, and not his iron, because Tom had never seen anybody who could match Dancer's lightning draw. Tom had fancied himself as quite a fighter back in those days, but he'd been no match for the tall half-breed. Dancer had fought exultantly, exuberantly, without caution or mercy, seemingly impervious to the punches Tom meted out. But Tom's best had not been good enough, and Dancer had put him down with a hard right cross. Shaken right down to his socks, Tom had picked himself up, gently massaging his aching jaw.

"Man, you pack more wallop than an Army mule," Tom had remarked good-naturedly, and stuck out his hand.

Later, cleaning up in the horse trough behind the saloon, Dancer had offered to buy the drinks and a lasting friendship had been born over a bottle of Kentucky sour mash.

Tom grinned in retrospect. It had been fun riding with Dancer after J. J. Jennings died. They took to robbing banks. And trains. And stagecoaches. Whatever was handy. They spent their ill-gotten gold as fast as they hauled it in, squandering it on women and whiskey and the turn of a card. But Dancer had grown restless after a while and took off on his own, headed for Abilene.

Following their split, Tom had drifted into Bitter Creek, planning to stay just long enough to rest his horse and maybe earn a little honest money for a change. It had been a nice quiet little town then, as it was now, a perfect place to hide out. And when the old marshal died peacefully in his sleep, Tom had volunteered for the job, wishing Dancer was there to share the irony of the situation. Surprisingly, Tom found he enjoyed being on the right side of the law again, found that he enjoyed the respectability and prestige that went along with the badge.

The courthouse clock chimed eight and he stood up. He didn't relish the thought of telling Jessica Landry that Dancer had left town, but he was definitely looking forward to spending time with her. Dancer had left a sizable sum of money in her saddlebag, enough to tide her over until she decided if she wanted to stay on in Bitter Creek or go back East. Tom smiled. If he had anything to say about it, Jesse would be staying here, with him. He'd known the minute he laid eyes on her that she was exactly what he'd been looking for all his life.

Grinning, Tom grabbed his hat and headed for the hotel, as excited by the prospect of seeing Jesse again as any freckle-faced kid going out on his first date.

Jesse rode as fast as she dared across the gray land, afraid she'd made a terrible mistake.

Back at the hotel, anger had clouded her judgment, so that riding after Dancer to give him a piece of her mind seemed like a perfectly logical thing to do. But now she knew she'd made a dreadful mistake. Dancer had taught her the rudiments of tracking, but she wasn't very good at it. And he had probably taken time to cover his trail, so that the tracks she was following probably weren't even his.

But she kept going. Gradually the sun climbed above the horizon, chasing away the dark, brightening the land, and Jesse's spirits. She'd find him. She refused to believe she wouldn't, or to contemplate what failure meant. Still, she could not completely erase the visions of doom that arose in her mind; visions of herself dying of thirst, being attacked by blood-thirsty Comanches, waylaid by outlaws . . .

Her morbid fantasies scattered as she heard a horse whinny.

Fear took hold of her as she jerked her mare to a halt. Should she ride on, or turn back? Why hadn't she bought a gun? Why hadn't she stayed in Bitter Creek?

A sound from her left spurred her into action and she slammed her heels into her horse's flanks, praying that the game little mare could outrun whoever, or whatever, was chasing her.

She heard hoofbeats coming hard behind her, but she didn't dare look back, too frightened of what she might see. The blood was pounding in her ears, drowning every other sound. Once, she thought she heard a shout and she kicked the mare again, praying that her horse wouldn't fall, that somehow she'd make it to safety.

It seemed as if she'd been running forever when an arm closed about her waist and lifted her from the back of her horse.

She screamed in terror and then, seeing his face, she went limp in his arms. "Dancer."

"Why the hell didn't you stop when I called you?"

"I didn't hear you. I guess I was too scared."

"You should be scared. What the hell are you doing out here alone?"

"Looking for you." She gazed at him for a full thirty seconds, and then she suddenly remembered why she'd come after him in the first place. "Why did you leave me?" she demanded angrily. "What kind of a man are you, to abandon a woman in a strange town with no friends and no money? Even whores get paid, you know."

Her anger had amused him until she compared herself to a whore. Refusing to hear more, he shut her up in the best way he knew how. He kissed her, long and hard.

She was breathless when he drew away.

"You ready to listen now?" he asked.

Jesse nodded, her lips still warm from his kiss, her heart pounding a familiar tattoo.

"I had to leave. Clayton's men are right behind me. There was no time to wake you, no time to explain. I . . . I thought it would be easier on both of us if I just left." He pressed his fingertips to her lips when she started to protest. "And I didn't leave you penniless. There's better than a thousand dollars in your saddlebags."

He took his hand from her mouth and kissed her. "I wouldn't have left you there alone and broke, Jesse. You should have known that."

"Should I? Why?"

"Haven't I taken care of you so far?"

"Yes."

"But?"

"You've never said you cared. I thought . . ."

He knew what she thought, and she had every right. He'd never told her how he felt, but words came hard to him, at least the words she wanted to hear.

"I care, Jesse. You've got to believe that." He swore under his breath. "I couldn't take you with me, and you shouldn't be here now.

The men who are after me are no damn good. They aren't shopkeepers like that posse from Cherry Valley, or law-abiding men hoping to get rich quick like that bunch from Indian Wells. Cliff Hardin is a hired killer, and he's good at what he does. Damn good."

He did care, Jesse thought. He cared, and nothing else mattered.

"Go back to Bitter Creek, Jesse. You'll be safe there. Tom will look after you."

"I don't want Tom. I want you."

"I'm no good for you, Jesse. I've never been worth a damn to myself or anybody else."

"That's not true! I love you. Nothing will ever change that. Nothing." She smiled up at him. "Hadn't we better be moving on? There's a posse back there somewhere, remember?"

Tom Brady shook his head in disbelief. "She went after Dancer, and you let her go? Why the hell didn't you stop her?"

Chet Haskins glared at the marshal. "Just how was I supposed to do that?"

"I don't know. Dammit, Chet..." Tom Brady's voice trailed off. "I'm sorry. It's not your fault."

Frowning, the marshal left the livery barn and made his way back to his office.

She was gone, he thought glumly, and he'd never see her like again.

Dropping into his chair, he put his feet up on the desk and chuckled softly. She was a hell of a woman, that Jessica Landry. Perhaps Dancer had finally met his match.

Jesse stared at Dancer's back, willing herself to stay awake. They'd been riding for hours, stopping only a few minutes at a time to breathe the horses.

It occurred to her that this posse had Dancer scared, and that worried her. He hadn't been afraid before, nor had they ridden so hard or so long. Yes, she thought, he was afraid, not for himself, but for her.

She knew then she should have stayed in Bitter Creek. She was a burden to him now, a hindrance. She should have known he cared for her, even if he had never said so. She should have realized he'd come back for her when he could.

But it was too late to think of that now, just as it was too late for her to turn back.

Finally, at dusk, Dancer drew rein at a stage-coach relay station.

"We'll spend the night here," he said.

"Is it safe?"

"Safe enough."

Dancer swung her to the ground as a man stepped out of the relay station. "Evening, folks," the man said jovially. "Supper's on the table if you're hungry."

"Obliged," Dancer said. He took Jesse by the hand and they followed the man inside.

Jesse could not help staring at the man and his wife as she ate. She was certain the man weighed at least three hundred pounds, his wife almost as much. She smiled politely as the man introduced himself as Gus Maxwell. His wife's name was Zoe.

"You here to catch the stage?" Maxwell asked as he polished off an enormous slice of apple pie.

"Just passin' through," Dancer replied. He hadn't told Gus Maxwell his name, and the man hadn't asked.

Maxwell grunted softly. "We can put you up for the night, if you like. Six bits to sleep in here, or you can bed down in the shed for free."

"We'll take the room," Dancer said. He glanced at Jesse. "When's the next stage come through?"

"Hard to say. The last one's three days late now."

"Indians?"

"More than likely. The Comanch have been on the prowl."

Dancer nodded. The Indians would be raiding hard between now and the first snow.

"More pie?" Zoe asked. She smiled at Dancer.

"No, thank you, ma'am," he said. "It was good, though. Best I've had in a long while."

Zoe Maxwell's face lit up like a Christmas tree. "Breakfast is at six," she called as Dancer and Jesse went to their room. "Don't be late."

"You're thinking about leaving me here, aren't you?" Jesse asked when they were alone.

"I was," Dancer admitted, "until Maxwell

mentioned the Comanches. If you're going to end up in Shadow Valley, you may as well go with me."

"Shadow Valley?"

"It's where I'm headed."

Of course, Jesse thought. He was going home, back to his mother's people. Clayton's men couldn't follow him there.

"How long will it take us to get there?" she asked.

"Two weeks if we keep going in this direction. Hardin will expect me to hole up there, so I've been taking the long way round in hopes of throwing him off the trail."

"Do you think it will work?"

"No."

He put his arm around Jesse's shoulders and stared into the distance, his thoughts drifting toward Cliff Hardin and his gang of ruffians. Wes McDonald was a squat, ugly man, who was rumored to have killed his wife. George Miller was heavy-set. He wore a patch over one eye. He'd killed three men with his bare hands. Baldy Johnson was tall, thin as a porch rail, with a face that was badly scarred. He carried a whip and a knife and could carve a man to bits with either one. Remo Davis was a little man with a face like a weasel and a personality to match.

And Cliff Hardin, leader of the gang, and perhaps the worst of the bunch. The Indians he traded with said he had no soul.

But it was Cliff's sidekick, Man Who Walks,

who worried Dancer the most. He was a renegade Apache, hated and feared by Indians and whites alike. It was said he could track anyone or anything, over rocks and through water, by night or by day.

"Dancer?"

"Yeah?"

"Is anything wrong?"

"No. Come on, let's turn in. I want to be out of here by first light."

Chapter 11

She woke to the sound of Dancer's voice insisting she wake up, now!

"What is it?" Jesse asked groggily. "What's wrong?"

"Hardin's here."

Hardin? Hardin! She sat up, fear for Dancer bringing her wide awake. "You've got to go," she said urgently. "Hurry, before it's too late."

"Jesse . . ." There was a wealth of words that needed to be said, but no time for them now. His hands cupped her face and he kissed her, hoping she knew how he felt, hoping she could hear the words he'd never been able to say.

"Don't wait for me, Jesse," he said quietly. "Go back to Bitter Creek. Marry Tom. Make a life for yourself."

He hesitated a moment, wondering if he should leave her behind when Hardin was here. But he had no choice. She'd be better off here, with Maxwell, than trying to outrun Clayton's men. And if Hardin should catch him, and Jesse was with him . . . no, she was better off here.

He kissed her one last time, hard and quick,

and then he was gone, disappearing out the window like shadows before a storm.

Jesse stared after Dancer, confused by the conflicting emotions in her heart. He had kissed her as if he loved her desperately, as if he could not bear to leave her, and then, in the space of a heartbeat, he had told her not to wait.

The sound of voices in the outer room took her thoughts in another direction. Sliding out of bed, she dressed, put on her shoes, and stepped into the relay stations's main room.

Gus Maxwell, clad in faded long red underwear, stood in the middle of the floor, surrounded by six men. They all swung in Jesse's direction as she entered the room, and she gasped as she saw six guns leveled at her midsection.

"Who's she?" one of the men demanded.

"I don't know her name," Maxwell replied. "She's just waiting for the stage."

"Who are you?" the man asked gruffly.

"Jessica Landry." She kept her head high, refusing to let the man see how afraid she was. They were a mean-looking bunch, and she knew that these were J. D. Clayton's hired guns. Which one was Cliff Hardin? The squat, ugly one? The man wearing the eye patch? The tall, thin one? Or the one standing in front of her, boldly demanding to know who she was and what she was doing here? Yes, she thought, this was Cliff Hardin.

"I'm waiting for the stage to Bitter Creek,"

Jesse lied. "My fiancé, Marshal Tom Brady, is expecting me."

"Brady. I've heard of him. He's supposed to be a hard man, tough as old shoe leather."

"Yes. And who might you be?"

"It doesn't matter. Remo, search the other room. Maxwell, get that fat wife of yours to fix us some grub." Hardin smiled at Jesse. "Join us."

"No, thank you."

"Make her stay, Cliff."

"Leave her alone, Wes. She's a decent woman."

"She could be Dancer's woman, for all you know. Maybe he run out on her."

Cliff Hardin stared at Jesse thoughtfully. "Are you Dancer's woman?" he asked, his voice hard and flat.

"I told you who I am."

"She could be lying," McDonald said. "Give me a minute with her, and I'll find out who she is."

Hardin grunted thoughtfully. She *could* be Dancer's woman, but it was more likely she belonged to the lawman, like she said, in which case he wanted nothing to do with her. Brady had a reputation for being hard and honest and plenty fast with his iron.

"What d'ye say, Cliff?"

Jesse held her breath as she waited for Cliff Hardin's next words, knowing she'd rather die than have any of these men lay a hand on her.

"She could be lying," Hardin mused. "And

she could be telling the truth."

Wes McDonald licked his lips as his eyes roamed over Jesse's breasts. "Let me find out, Cliff. It won't take long."

"No. Dancer's got too much of a head start now."

"If you'll excuse me," Jesse said. Returning to her room, she closed the door, then collapsed on the bed, too weak to stand.

Hurry, Dancer, she thought. *Hurry, please.*

She closed her eyes, trying to erase the sound of Hardin's voice, the feral look in his eyes. He had decided to leave her alone, perhaps because he thought she belonged to a lawman, but he would hunt Dancer until he found him.

And the others . . . They all wore the look of men who killed, men who liked it.

She could hear the men talking in the next room, planning how they'd spend the reward money when they delivered Dancer to J. D. Clayton. Too bad the old man wanted the half-breed alive, she heard McDonald say. It would be so much easier to take the 'breed in tied face down across his saddle.

Jesse drew a deep breath. Alive. J. D. Clayton wanted Dancer alive.

She began to pace the floor, a wild idea forming in the back of her mind. Clayton lived in Cherry Valley. If Dancer were captured, Clayton would be the first to hear of it. And she intended to be the second.

* * *

The sky was dark, overcast, blotting out the moon and the stars. A low rumble of thunder echoed across the vast prairie like the beat of a distant drum as Dancer reined his big gray Appaloosa mare to a halt beside a shallow water hole. He swore softly when he saw the seep was dry.

Dismounting, he loosened the saddle cinch, gave the mare an affectionate pat on the shoulder. Frothy yellow lather dripped from her neck and heaving sides.

Hooking his canteen from the saddlehorn, Dancer swallowed a few drops of the lukewarm liquid. Pouring some of the precious water into his hat, he offered it to the mare.

"No more until you're cooled out," he muttered as he capped the canteen. "Though Lord knows when that'll be."

Dead tired, he rested his back against a scrawny cottonwood, giving the mare a chance to cool off. It had been a long time since they had ridden so hard. Not since his days as an outlaw, he mused, discounting his flight from the posse out of Cherry Valley. He had not had to worry about them. Shopkeepers, mostly, he had dodged them easily, even though Jesse had slowed him down those first few days.

Jesse. Her whispered name was like a sigh on his lips, and when he closed his eyes, her golden-haired image danced before him, kindling a familiar ache in his loins. He wished he'd had time to bring her along. It would have been pleasant, spending the winter with the Comanche, having Jesse there to warm his bed on cold, lonely nights. And yet he wanted more from her than just physical satisfaction. He had enjoyed her company on the trail and by the campfire at night, had welcomed the sound of her laughter. He had been pleased by the wonder in her eyes when she watched an eagle soaring effortlessly overhead, or spied a doe grazing in a meadow.

Jesse. When had he started to love her?

Blue whickered softly, bringing Dancer back to the present, and he swore softly as he tightened the saddle cinch and climbed wearily into the saddle.

Some ten miles later, he made a cold camp in a dry, sandy wash. A couple of cold biscuits and a chunk of cheese, compliments of Zoe Maxwell, eased the hunger gnawing at his belly. He shared the last of his water with Blue; then, with the mare standing guard nearby, he rolled into his blankets and slept.

At first light he was in the saddle again.

Shadow Valley, home of Lame Eagle's Comanche, lay six days away.

Not too many miles behind the fleeing half-breed, J. D. Clayton's hired guns dowsed their fire and broke camp.

They traveled at a steady pace, each man leading an extra mount.

At noon they took time out for a hot meal. There was, after all, no need to run their horses into the ground. They knew where their quarry was headed. And they were right behind him.

Dancer squatted on his heels in the shade cast by the big gray Appaloosa. The mare had cut her right foreleg on a jagged rock the day before, and while it was not a serious injury, it had cost him valuable time; time he could ill afford to lose.

His destination lay a hard day's ride to the west, and as he rolled a cigarette, he wondered if he'd make it. He had detected no sign of Clayton's men, but he knew instinctively that they were closing in on him, could almost feel their malevolent presence drawing ever closer.

He swore softly as he contemplated the glowing end of his cigarette. Like it or not, it seemed his luck was running out.

Frowning, he thought about the men trailing him. Some, like Johnson and Davis, he knew only by reputation. Others, like Miller and McDonald, had been pointed out to him at one time or another. But he knew Cliff Hardin personally, and though he hadn't seen the craggy-faced gunman for several years, he doubted the passage of time had improved Hardin's character any. There had been bad blood between them from the moment they met. It rose without provocation, instinctive, like the enmity between a dog and a cat.

Taking a last drag on his cigarette, Dancer wiped Hardin from his mind and let himself think of Jesse, damning his weakness for her even as he longed for her touch. He was sorry now that he had not been able to possess her slim golden body one last time. His desire for her soft flesh seemed to be unquenchable, and he wondered if it would plague him forever, like the ache from an old wound.

He was tightening the cinch when the mare's sensitive ears flicked forward and she blew softly, warning him that company was coming. He wasted no time looking over his shoulder. Grabbing the reins, he vaulted into the saddle without hitting the stirrup, and the well-trained Appaloosa took off like a shot. Riding low over the mare's neck, Dancer urged her on with the sound of his voice and the touch of his heels. Blue responded valiantly. She ran flat out, belly to the ground, flying hooves sending dirt and gravel skittering in all directions.

Crossing the invisible line that marked the beginning of the Comanche homeland, Dancer felt a swift surge of hope. If he could just reach the foothills beyond, he was home free. Once there, he could disappear into the trees, and then lose his pursuers in the maze of canyons and gullies that crisscrossed the outskirts of Shadow Valley. With hands and heels, he asked the mare for one last burst of speed, felt her willing response.

He was only yards from safety when the mare's injured leg played out and she fell, throwing Dancer into the dirt. Shaken but unhurt, he rolled catlike to his feet, determined not to go down without a fight. But Clayton's gunnies were beating a hasty retreat.

Dancer knew that only one thing would send Clayton's hired guns running for cover, and he felt a quick shiver of apprehension slither down his spine as he turned to face them, careful to keep his hands high and away from his gun. They were indeed an awesome sight as they came down the hill at a brisk trot: twenty Comanche warriors, fully armed and painted for war. Naked save for clouts and moccasins, thick black hair adorned with eagle feathers, heads high and proud, they rode toward him.

Dancer recognized none of them, but that was not surprising. Most of them would have been little more than babies when he had run away.

One warrior broke from the rest and rode forward alone. "Where have your friends gone?" he asked in stilted English.

"They have run away like the rabbit from the lion," Dancer replied in Comanche; his mother's language, unused for a score of years, rolled easily off his tongue.

"Why do you not run away?" the warrior challenged.

"I do not fear the People," Dancer answered arrogantly. "I am Buffalo Dancer, grandson of Lame Eagle."

This announcement caught the interest of the other warriors, and they rode closer in order to get a better look at the white man who claimed to be related to their chief.

"I have been away for many years," Dancer

continued evenly. "Will you take me to my grandfather?"

"Lame Eagle will be pleased to see his lost son return after such a long absence," the warrior replied, his expression skeptical.

They don't believe me, Dancer thought. But it didn't matter. They would let him live until Lame Eagle proved, or disproved, his claim.

The head warrior gestured at Blue. The mare was standing off a ways, her injured leg dripping blood. "What will you do with the mare?" he asked. "She is no good to you now."

"She is not badly hurt," Dancer replied. "In time, she will be as good as new. She is strong in battle and swift as the wind."

The warrior nodded. The Appaloosa was a handsome animal, and he had already decided to claim the mare for his own once the paleface trying to pass as Lame Eagle's grandson was proven a liar and disposed of. The Comanche were the best horsemen on the plains, and the warrior smiled with pleasure as he anticipated the fine foals the mare would throw when mated with his own big black stud. Like the Sioux and the Cheyenne, the Comanche bred their horses for speed and endurance, knowing that a good war pony was as valuable as a good weapon, often meaning the difference between life and death in the heat of battle.

One of the Indians took Blue's reins. A second warrior took Dancer up behind him. Minutes later, the war party was deep in the cover of the trees.

At dusk, the Indians pulled up in the lee of a craggy bluff. While the other warriors set up camp and tended the horses, the warrior known as Yellow Hand informed Dancer that the Comanche were encamped along the banks of Horsetail Creek for the winter.

"Is my grandfather well?"

"You will see for yourself tomorrow," Yellow Hand replied. "Until then, I will take your weapons."

The warrior held out a brown-skinned hand. His deep-set ebony eyes did not change expression as they read the wary hesitation in the half-breed's face.

"Surely you will not need a weapon if you are truly one of us," the Indian challenged slyly.

With a tight smile, Dancer surrendered his Colt, and after a knowing look from the tall Indian, the knife sheathed inside his moccasin as well, knowing he would not see his weapons again until Lame Eagle vouched for him.

After dinner, Dancer sat cross-legged beside Yellow Hand, listening as the warriors exchanged tales of bravery in battle, boasting outrageously as one brave tried to outdo the next. No one seemed to be paying any attention to Dancer, and yet he knew he was being closely watched.

Tomorrow he would see his grandfather for the first time in almost twenty years. He remembered how, as a young boy, he had been completely awed by his grandfather. Lame Eagle had been in his prime then, a powerfully built man, brave in battle, wise in council. Many scalps hung from his lodge pole.

It had been a good life, growing up among the Indians. Dancer had learned to read the signs of the earth and the sky, of man and beast. He had tracked the shaggy buffalo and the grizzly bear and the white-tailed deer. He had learned how to find water where none was visible, how to live off the land. How to track an enemy and cover a trail. Yes, it had been a good life for a boy, even though his father had been a white man, a fact that Elkhorn had never let him forget.

Elkhorn. Dancer had almost forgotten his old enemy. They had been bitter rivals ever since he could remember, but their animosity toward each other had remained passive until the day Elkhorn made a derogatory remark about Buffalo Dancer's mother sharing her blankets with a white man.

Enraged, Dancer had attacked Elkhorn with all the fury of hell, beating the boy without mercy until two warriors stepped in and pulled them apart. The hatred between them had never diminished, though it had never again exploded into physical violence.

The Indians were turning in for the night, save for two who would remain awake, keeping watch.

Feeling naked without his weapons, Dancer rolled into his blankets and gazed up at the bright path of the Milky Way. The Indians called it the Spirit Path, believing that the souls of the dead followed it into the Afterworld. The twinkling stars reminded him of the tears that had glistened in Jesse's eyes that last night in Bitter Creek. She had clung to him, sobbing, crying incoherently that she loved him, would always love him, and he had not had the courage to tell her he was planning to leave Bitter Creek alone; had let her fall asleep in his arms believing that they would leave together.

He had never known a woman like her. She had the courage of a she-wolf, he mused, the tenacity of a mountain lion, to set out after him with no one to help her, no one to guide her. He had made love to her over and over again, certain that once he'd had his fill of her, he would tire of her, as he had tired of others. But that had never happened. The more he held her, the more time he spent with her, the more certain he had become that he could never let her go. But then Cliff Hardin had entered the picture, and the decision had been taken out of his hands.

He closed his eyes, but sleep would not come. Instead, his mind went back in time, back to his fifteenth year, the year he had gone out to seek his vision.

He had never been more aware of his mixed blood than he had been that day. When he had voiced his concern to his grandfather, wondering if the Great Spirit would grant a vision to one who was not wholly of the People, Lame

Eagle had drawn him close and spoken to him face to face, man to man.

"The blood of many brave Comanche warriors also runs deep in your veins," the chief had reminded him gently. *"You have proven that your tongue is straight, your heart is good. The Great Spirit requires nothing more of his children."* Lame Eagle had laid a reassuring hand on his grandson's shoulder. *"Your vision will come, my son. I promise."*

And so he had gone alone to the mountains. Three days and three nights he had huddled in a small pit, wrapped in a special medicine blanket his grandmother had made for him. Three days without food or water. Three days of prayer and fasting.

It was on the evening of the third day that his vision had come to him, and it had been so real, so vivid, he had never been certain if it really happened, or if he had only dreamed it. But it must have been real, else how could he account for the two fallen trees?

He had been on the verge of abandoning his vision quest when a huge white buffalo had appeared before him, its beady red eyes burning into him like twin coals from the bowels of hell. The mammoth head was lowered to charge, and the massive horns, sharp as arrowheads, had gleamed like scarlet scythes in the fading sunlight.

With a mighty roar, the huge beast had pawed the ground, then charged, and the sound of its hooves had been like the echo of thunder off the mountains as it raced toward the boy.

Awestruck, Dancer had cowered in the pit, knowing he was facing certain death, when, at the last possible moment, the great white spike had swerved to the left. Two tall trees had stood side by side in the bull's path, but it had knocked them aside like kindling before disappearing into the sunset.

The *pukahut,* Painted Horse, had been greatly impressed with the vision that had been granted to Lame Eagle's grandson.

"Your puha will be strong," the medicine man had told Dancer. *"Strong like that of the sacred white buffalo. As the earth trembles at the passing of the sacred bull, and the trees fall before him, so will your enemies tremble and fall before you."*

Painted Horse's prophecy had been a true one, Dancer mused. His medicine had always been strong. His enemies had fallen at his feet, and victory had always been his.

With that thought in mind, he fell asleep.

Their arrival in the Comanche camp the following afternoon caused a flurry of excitement. The women left their cook fires to stare at the tall, gray-eyed stranger. Children came to gawk at him, their bright black eyes wide with curiosity. The men regarded him warily, for he was obviously a fighting man.

Some of the older women gathered around

him, their eyes dark with hatred. He was a white man, the enemy.

They think they're in for some fun tonight, Dancer mused, recalling how the women of the tribe tormented captured male prisoners before they were killed. *And they may get their way at that,* he thought abruptly, *if Lame Eagle won't vouch for me.*

It was a sobering thought.

Yellow Hand halted his pony before an empty lodge. "You will wait in here," he directed, "until someone comes for you. Do not try to leave." The warrior smiled expansively. "I will care for your horse as if it were my own, as indeed it will be if your words prove false."

With a nod, Dancer slid from the back of his horse and entered the lodge. It was gloomy inside, empty of personal belongings. Familiar smells filled his nostrils: smoke and sage, grease and rawhide, the aroma of roasting meat from a nearby cookfire. He heard the sounds of children laughing as they ran through the village, the everyday noises of Indian life, and it was as if he had never gone away.

And yet he was not the same man that had left here years before. He was an outsider, a stranger who had turned his back on the People and gone to live with the enemy.

Restless, he prowled the lodge, keenly aware of the two warriors stationed outside, guarding him. He felt a familiar tingle slither down his spine, that peculiar warning chill that presaged impending danger. It brought all his senses into sharp focus.

He did not have to wait long. In less than five minutes a short, hawk-faced warrior summoned Dancer from the lodge and led him to Lame Eagle's dwelling. Three women sat before the chief's lodge, talking and laughing softly as they prepared the afternoon meal.

Stooping slightly, Dancer entered his grandfather's lodge. There were five warriors inside: Lame Eagle, who sat cross-legged on a bright red blanket facing the doorway; Painted Horse, the ancient Comanche medicine man; and two elders of the tribe whom Dancer recognized as Twin Bears and High Hawk. The fifth warrior was Elkhorn.

Lame Eagle spoke first. His voice came strong and clear, and Dancer was glad to see that age had not diminished his grandfather. The chief sat straight and tall, and only the deep creases in his face and the faint streaks of gray in his long black hair betrayed the passage of many years.

"Yellow Hand tells me you were found on our land," the chief began. "He says you speak our tongue, that you claim to be of the People. My grandson. My eyes are gone and I cannot see your face. Therefore, you must convince me with your words that you speak the truth. Our women are anxious to test your courage if you speak with a double tongue."

"My mother was Laughing Deer," Dancer said, weighing his words carefully. "I was her only child. My father was a white man. He came wounded to our village. When he was well again, my mother begged for his life. She died when I was eight. Soon after her death, my father returned to his own people." Dancer paused. Funny, the thought of his father's desertion still rankled after all these years.

"You gave me my first pony," he went on. "A little pinto mare. I called her Nightwind. I ran away when I was sixteen because I wanted to try the path of the white man."

Lame Eagle nodded. If he was moved by any of the memories raised by Dancer's words, it did not show on his face.

"Only my true grandson would know these things," the chief allowed. "Welcome to my lodge, Buffalo Dancer. It has been many years since you left us."

Before Dancer could reply, Elkhorn sprang to his feet. "Buffalo Dancer has no right to be here," he exclaimed. "He turned his back on our people long ago. Why does he come back now, after so many years?" Hate and distrust were thick in his voice; his black eyes glittered with it.

There was some rapid discussion among the assembled leaders, then Painted Horse spoke to Dancer.

"You must answer. It is a fair question."

"I have grown tired of living with the white man," Dancer replied evenly. "It is my wish to return to my mother's people. I have come here seeking peace and friendship. Surely the

People will not turn me away."

The five warriors conferred briefly, then Lame Eagle said, "Elkhorn has challenged your claim to a place among the People, as is his right. He says you are Indian no more, but have grown soft and weak like our enemies, the white eyes. Are you willing to meet him in the old way to prove you are yet one of us?"

Dancer glanced at Elkhorn, saw his own hatred mirrored in the eyes of the man who had always been his enemy. "Yes, Grandfather. More than willing."

A short time later, Dancer and Elkhorn faced each other across six feet of sun-bleached earth, surrounded by every man, woman, and child in the village. Stripped to the waist, each armed with a long knife, they waited in tense anticipation for the signal to begin. The years seemed to melt away as they glared at each other, their mutual hatred from years past still vibrant and alive.

At the medicine man's signal, the two men began to circle slowly, first right, then left. Closely matched in size and strength, their weight balanced on the balls of their feet, their chins tucked in, they made a few sharp passes, searching for weaknesses, testing each other's defenses.

"Are you afraid of me, Buffalo Dancer?" Elkhorn jeered. "Do not run away."

"I do not run from women or children," Dancer replied haughtily. "Come, taste my knife in your flesh."

The watching tribe heard the angry taunts. Many of them remembered another fight, long ago, and they began to murmur among themselves. This would be no ritual fight of honor, the warriors said. There were old scores to be settled here. This would be a fight to the death.

The long, deadly blades seemed to have a life of their own as they flashed in the harsh yellow sunlight. The air rang with the sound of metal striking metal as the two men circled, closed, and parted time and again, their lean bronze bodies sheened with sweat. Bright streaks of blood stained the flesh of both fighters as the battle progressed, crisscrossing their arms and torsos like scarlet ribbons, though neither man had sustained any severe damage. Muscles straining, hearts pounding, eyes narrowed with determination, they closed and parted with savage intent, oblivious to the shouts and cheers of the crowd.

"Come closer, if you dare!" Elkhorn challenged.

"I am coming, old woman." Dancer smiled, but his eyes were as cold as death. "I whipped you once before, remember? I will gladly do it again."

The taunt stung Elkhorn's pride and his black eyes blazed with fury as he hurled himself at the half-breed, a scream of rage on his lips, his blood-stained knife slashing wildly. The finely honed blade opened a wicked gash down the length of Dancer's left arm as tempered steel met yielding flesh, but Dancer was oblivious to the pain as, pivoting swiftly, he powered all his strength into his left wrist and brought it down across the back of Elkhorn's neck.

Stunned by the unexpected blow, Elkhorn dropped to his knees, and then fell flat on his face as Dancer planted his foot squarely in the middle of the Indian's back and pushed down.

With a cry of victory, Dancer straddled the fallen warrior, grasped a handful of hair, and jerked Elkhorn's head up and back. Then, slowly and deliberately, he laid the edge of his blade across Elkhorn's throat.

"Finish me quickly," the warrior rasped, and Dancer felt Elkhorn's body tense beneath him as he waited for the final thrust of the knife.

For a moment, time stood still. The lust for blood burned hot in Dancer's veins, momentarily blinding him to everything but the man beneath him. A single stroke of the ten-inch blade would spill Elkhorn's lifesblood into the dirt, ending their lifelong feud once and for all.

The watching tribe held its breath as endless seconds ticked into eternity.

Abruptly, Dancer released his hold on Elkhorn and stood up in a single fluid motion. He wiped the blade of his knife clean on the side of his pants before slipping the knife into his moccasin, and a collective sigh of relief rippled through the crowd.

"I give you your life, Elkhorn," Dancer said in a hard tone. "Not because I have grown soft like the white man, but because I do not wish to spill the blood of a brother. Not even yours."

Elkhorn rose from the dirt with all the dignity he could muster and stalked away, his face a mask of bitter shame. Never, never, would he forgive Buffalo Dancer for the disgrace he had caused him this day. The half-breed should have killed him, quickly and honorably, for death as a warrior was preferable to humiliation at the hands of a sworn enemy. Somehow, someday, he would get even.

Dancer sat in his grandfather's lodge while the medicine man treated the nasty gash in his arm, then washed the blood from the other minor cuts he had received.

"So, you still fight without mercy, my son," Lame Eagle mused after the medicine man left the lodge.

Dancer frowned as he detected a faint note of disapproval in his grandfather's voice. "Without mercy? I let him live, didn't I?"

"It was a mistake. You should have let him die with honor. He will always be your enemy now."

Dancer scowled at the mild rebuke. "A warrior's death would be wasted on the likes of Elkhorn."

"No matter, it is done now," Lame Eagle stated tersely. "Tell me, did you like living among your father's people?"

"It is very different, Grandfather. There is not much honor among them. I killed a man in a fair fight, but the white man's law is easily bought, and now I am wanted for murder. I lied, Grandfather, when I said I had come to stay. I came because I am being hunted by five whites and a renegade Apache, and this is the only place where they cannot follow me. If this is disagreeable to you, I will leave as soon as my horse can travel. I am sorry I lied to you earlier, but the truth was for your ears alone."

Lame Eagle sighed, deeply disappointed that Laughing Deer's only child had not come home to stay. His sadness was reflected in his voice as he said, "Stay as long as you wish, Buffalo Dancer. I am glad to have you here, if only for a little while. I have missed you."

"I have thought of you often, Grandfather," Dancer replied sincerely.

"And I have thought of you. Tell me, did you seek your father when you ran away?"

"Yes. I found his place but it was deserted. I heard that he died soon after returning to his own people."

"He was better off dead. He had no heart for living after your mother died."

Dancer shook his head, perplexed by the depths of his father's need for Laughing Deer. And then he thought of Jesse.

"Did you find a woman among the whites?" Lame Eagle asked, and Dancer grinned. His grandfather had a knack for knowing what other people were thinking. It was one of the talents that made him a great chief.

"In a way," Dancer admitted, and related how he had found Jesse and all that had happened between them. "She's like a fire in my blood," Dancer muttered, hating to acknowledge it. "I can't seem to put her out of my mind." *Or my heart.*

Lame Eagle smiled knowingly. "Sometimes a second woman can ease your longing for another."

Dancer shook his head. "Not this time," he said ruefully. He had no desire for any other woman. Only for Jesse.

Lame Eagle nodded. Was it possible his grandson had fallen in love? "Storm Woman has offered to take you into her lodge, if you do not object."

"Storm Woman?" Dancer frowned. "Wasn't she captured by the Crow just before I ran away?"

"Yes. But she escaped and returned to us. She was badly mistreated by our enemies and refuses to accept any of our men as her husband. She has no male relatives to look after her."

Dancer nodded. "I will provide for her while I am here."

"Be kind to her, my son. Her face was burned during her escape and she is badly scarred. She is very self-conscious of it."

Again, Dancer nodded.

The two men talked far into the night, and then Dancer left Lame Eagle's lodge, lost in thought.

Elkhorn stood motionless, holding his breath as Buffalo Dancer passed by. So, the half-breed was a hunted man. Perhaps the white men searching for him were still close by, waiting for the half-breed to leave the security of the village.

Perhaps he could shorten their wait.

Chapter 12

The warrior rode out of the village just before daybreak, riding purposefully toward the place where Yellow Hand was known to have spooked the six white men chasing the half-breed. He rode hard, changing horses every few hours, and reached his destination just as the setting sun was turning the prairie to flame. Even in the dim light, the trail he sought was clear and easy to follow.

The Hardin gang had holed up in a grove of cottonwoods less than five miles from where they'd lost Dancer. A small stream gurgled nearby and the disgruntled white men were stretched out near its banks, cleaning their weapons.

"I'm getting tired of sitting around doing nothing," George Miller remarked as he reloaded his rifle and wiped off the stock. "Why don't we mosey over to the Flat and see Lottie?"

Cliff Hardin shrugged. Lottie Deno was a red-haired woman who ran a saloon just over the Texas border. She reigned supreme, and anyone who didn't like her game was quickly disposed of by her hired gunmen.

"I say let's go," agreed Remo Davis. "That 'breed is holed up for the winter."

"We're stayin' put," Hardin said flatly.

"Shit, we could be making a bundle huntin' buffalo," Wes McDonald remarked. "I hear they're payin' $3.75 for hides these days and the pickings are easy. I heard Wylie Poe cut down ninety buffs in one day and never even moved from his spot."

"You damn fool," Hardin sneered. "J. D.'s paying us ten grand to bring Dancer in. Ten grand! You know how many of those smelly hides you'd have to drag into Dodge to make ten grand?"

McDonald shrugged. "A lot, I reckon."

Remo Davis was the first to notice the lone Indian riding toward them. "Heads up," he warned. "We've got company coming."

"I'll take him," Miller said, drawing a bead on the rapidly approaching warrior.

"Wait!" Hardin called gruffly. "Let's see what he's after first." He nodded toward Man Who Walks. "Go out and parley with him, see what he wants. We'll cover you."

Swinging aboard his calico stud, the Apache tracker rode out to meet Elkhorn. The two men talked for several minutes, then Man Who Walks returned to his companions.

"Well?" Hardin asked impatiently. "What's he have to say?"

"Not much," Man Who Walks answered,

shrugging. "Just that there's bad blood between him and Dancer."

"So?"

The renegade Apache grinned wolfishly. "So he says if we still want the 'breed, he'll hand him to us on a silver platter."

"No shit?"

"How do we know this ain't just some kind of redskin trick to sucker us into a trap?" Miller asked suspiciously. "I don't cotton to the idea of my hair decorating some Comanche lodgepole."

"Yeah," McDonald agreed. "How do you know you can trust him?"

"I know," Man Who Walks assured them. "Besides, if Dancer wanted our scalps, he wouldn't have to resort to trickery. He would just send thirty or forty warriors after us."

Miller looked thoughtful. He didn't trust Indians. And that included Cliff Hardin's Apache sidekick. But the decision wasn't his to make.

"What's he got in mind?" Hardin asked.

"He'll go back to the village and keep an eye on the 'breed. Says he'll grab Dancer first chance he gets and hand him over to us."

"That might take weeks," Miller objected.

"You got any better ideas?" Hardin snapped.

"No, but if that redskin wants Dancer out of the way so bad, why doesn't he just stick a knife in him and be done with it?"

"Too risky," Man Who Walks explained. "Seems the 'breed is the chief's long-lost grandson."

Hardin grunted. "And our friend here doesn't want the 'breed's blood on his hands, right?"

"Right. What do you think?"

"I think if he wants to hand Dancer to us on a silver platter, we'll take him. There's just one more thing. We're sitting ducks out here. Ask our friend if he knows of some place where we can hole up till he snatches the 'breed."

Elkhorn knew a grim sense of satisfaction as he rode back to the village. He had left the white men upriver, hidden in an ancient burial ground where they would be safe. They had complained at being left so near the village, but he had assured them that no one would find them there. The Comanche feared the dead and avoided the ancient burial ground.

The warrior urged his horse downriver. Soon Buffalo Dancer would be in the hands of the *tabeboh*, the white men. No longer would he, Elkhorn, burn with shame each time he saw his defeat mirrored in the half-breed's mocking gray eyes.

Chapter 13

Jesse felt a sudden surge of excitement as the Concord pulled into Cherry Valley. At last, after two weeks of jolting over rough trails, of eating dust and sleeping on lumpy mattresses in dilapidated relay stations, her destination was in sight.

It hadn't been easy, traveling alone, mostly because she'd never been on her own in her whole life. She'd always had someone to look after her. First her parents and John, then Aunt Sally, and then Dancer.

Dancer. She inquired about him at each town and relay station, but no one knew of his whereabouts. They'd heard of Dancer, though, and she'd listened to countless stories of his legendary skill with a Colt .44. She wondered if all the stories could possibly be true. Certainly he couldn't have survived as many gunfights or killed as many men as people said.

Three stories were repeated time and again. One involved a shoot-out in Wichita between Dancer and the Trenton brothers. There had been three of them: Joe, Hiram, and Rufus. No one was certain what had started the fight, but

Dancer had ended it with three well-placed shots, killing all three Trenton brothers in less than a minute.

Another concerned the killing of a man named George Buck. The way Jesse heard the tale, George Buck had challenged Dancer in the middle of a crowded El Paso street. Buck was well-known in his home town, with a reputation almost as big as Texas. He had swaggered back and forth, bragging about how fast he was, daring Dancer to face him. Dancer had obliged him, and George Buck had died of a bullet through his heart.

The third story involved Johnny Clayton.

Jesse leaned out the window, eager to see the town that was to have been her home. It was here, in Cherry Valley, that she and John had planned to start a new life.

It was a large town, well-kept, laid out in an orderly fashion. The buildings were in good repair, the outlying houses neatly painted. There were several shops along the main street, as well as a doctor's office, a dentist, and a lawyer. She also saw a newspaper office, a barber shop, a dry goods store, and a Chinese laundry. She noticed the name Clayton on several of the establishments.

She saw a red schoolhouse at the far end of town, and quick tears burned her eyes as she thought of her brother again, of the life they had dreamed of. John would have loved it here, she thought sadly. He had wanted so badly to teach, to encourage young minds to learn, to grow. He'd had such wonderful plans. . . .

Blinking back tears, Jesse stepped from the coach, collected her meager baggage, and made her way to the hotel.

At the desk, Jesse stared at the clerk in disbelief. "What do you mean, I can't stay here?"

"I'm sorry, ma'am, but no single women are allowed," the clerk replied patiently. "Mrs. Holden's Boardinghouse is just down the street. I'm sure you'll be comfortable there. Her rates are cheaper, and she's a mighty good cook."

Annoyed, Jesse swept out of the hotel and made her way down the boardwalk until she came to a large, neatly painted sign which read:

MARTHA FAYE'S BOARDINGHOUSE
LADIES ONLY
RATES BY THE DAY, WEEK, OR MONTH

Martha Faye Holden proved to be a tall, angular woman with short white hair, sharp brown eyes, and a friendly smile. She welcomed Jesse warmly, showed her to her room, and informed her she was just in time for the noonday meal if she was of a mind to eat.

Jesse followed Martha Faye into a large, wood-paneled dining room and smiled as Mrs. Holden introduced her to the other tenants.

Lydia Bascomb was the schoolmarm, Ramona Dawson was a seamstress, Margaret Nelson was a retired nurse who had come West for her health, and Frieda Merriweather ran a small bakery across from the Cherry Valley *Gazette*. It being a Sunday, all the ladies had just returned from church and were still attired in their Sunday best.

Taking a seat across from Margaret Nelson, Jesse ate quietly, listening politely to the conversation of the other women. They were all middle-aged, and seemed to have strong opinions about everything.

The main topic of conversation was the scandalous behavior of the blacksmith's new wife. She was fifteen years his junior and inclined to wear more makeup than Mrs. Holden's boarders thought proper.

There was a lull in the conversation. From outside came the hollers of several children running up and down the street.

Lydia Bascomb pursed her lips in disapproval. "That child!" she said in a voice heavy with disapproval. "Out there running around with the Parker boys again. I declare, if her grandfather doesn't do something to discipline that child soon, she'll be nothing but trouble in a few years, if you know what I mean."

"Now, Lydia," Frieda Merriweather said calmly, "she's just a little girl. You can't blame J. D. for being a little bit lenient with the child; after all, she's had a rough time of it these past two years."

Jesse gazed out the window, eager to see the subject of the conversation. She saw three boys and a small girl chasing each other in the dusty street. The girl's dress was mud-stained, the hem torn. A smear of something that looked like chocolate covered her lower lip.

Martha Faye smiled indulgently. "Lizzie is a sweet child. I'm sure Judge Clayton will take her in hand when the time comes."

Clayton! Jesse's ears perked up.

Lydia Bascomb shook her head. "The child doesn't even attend school, Martha Faye. She's going to grow up wild and uneducated if Judge Clayton doesn't do something mighty darn quick!"

The conversation turned to other things, but Jesse's mind was on Lizzie Clayton. Perhaps this was the answer to her problem of how to meet J. D. Clayton.

Early the following morning, dressed in a subdued skirt and shirtwaist, Jesse hired a carriage and drove out to the Clayton ranch. She was awed by the vastness of it, but she forced herself to stay calm as she knocked on the front door.

It was opened by the girl she had seen playing in the street the day before.

"Good morning," Jesse said, smiling at the girl. "Is your grandfather home?"

The girl nodded. "He's in the kitchen."

"Could I speak to him, please?"

Lizzie Clayton shrugged. "I guess so. Grandpa! There's a lady here to see you."

Jesse heard his footsteps, and then she saw him, Judge J. D. Clayton, the man who had put out a reward for Dancer's capture. He wore an expensively tailored suit of black broadcloth. A large diamond stickpin sparkled in his cravat.

"Something I can do for you, miss?" he asked gruffly.

"Yes, I . . ." His presence flustered her. It was hard to think rationally, knowing this man wanted Dancer dead. "I'm new in town and I'm looking for work."

"What kind of work?"

"I've been trained as a governess," Jesse lied. She smiled at Lizzie. "I'd be willing to hire on as a maid or cook, though. I really need the work."

Clayton studied Jesse intently for a moment. She looked a mite young to be a governess, but he could forgive her for that. She was a pretty thing, and it had been a long time since there was a pretty woman in the house. Not since Lizzie's mother died. He glanced at his granddaughter, standing at his elbow. She needed a woman's influence.

"Come in," Clayton said. He gestured down the hallway toward the parlor. "Make yourself comfortable."

Jesse entered the parlor, awed by the size of the room, the expensive furnishings, the opulent crystal lamps, the carpets and drapes. A huge stone fireplace took up one entire wall.

"Sit down, please," Clayton said, entering the room. He sat down in the chair beside Jesse, his gaze moving over her face. He was captivated by her beauty, charmed by her smile. Looking at her, he was aware of a sharp stab of desire, something he had not experienced in years.

Jesse drew her gaze from his, embarrassed by his frank admiration. Everywhere she looked, she saw signs of wealth, from the ornate vases and clocks to the paintings on the walls. She had never seen such riches, never imagined that such splendor existed in the untamed West.

"Lizzie is my granddaughter," Clayton said, smiling at the girl who had followed him into the parlor. "She's in need of a governess, someone to teach her to read and write, someone to teach her some manners, remind her that she's a girl."

"I don't want to be a girl," Lizzie said, wrinkling her nose. "Girls never get to have any fun. I want to hunt and fish and ride astride."

Clayton looked at Jesse and shook his head ruefully. "You see what I mean," he lamented. "We haven't had a woman in the house since her mother . . . since her mother. Except for the cook, and she's no help at all in persuading Lizzie to act like a young lady."

"Ladies never have any fun," Lizzie retorted.

"Of course they do," Jesse said. "Ladies can hunt and fish if they like. And they can ride."

Lizzie looked dubious. "Can I ride astride, like Grandpa?"

"If you like, but riding side-saddle is much more difficult. Perhaps you can't manage it and that's why you don't want to try."

"I can do anything," Lizzie said firmly.

"I'm sure you can," Jesse agreed.

Clayton grinned. "You're hired, Miss . . ."

"Landry," Jesse said, offering him her hand. "Jessica Landry."

"It's done, then. We'll discuss wages and responsibilities later." He squeezed her hand. "Welcome to the family."

Jesse moved into the Clayton household the following day, unable to believe her good luck. She'd been afraid that meeting J. D. Clayton might take weeks, months even, and yet here she was, living in his house, eating at his table. It was almost as if Fate had taken pity on her and paved the way.

In the days that followed, Jesse learned a great deal about Lizzie and J. D. Clayton. Lizzie was a remarkable little girl, quick to learn and quick to laugh. She had a soft heart, and was moved to tears by the sight of anyone or anything that was hurt or in trouble. She was forever bringing in stray cats, and the back porch harbored a constant stream of lost or injured birds, squirrels, rabbits, and baby possums.

Lizzie Clayton was also spoiled rotten, and could be quite stubborn when it suited her. But, for all that, Jesse quickly found herself growing very fond of the child.

J. D. Clayton was another matter entirely. He was rich, proud, stubborn, and accustomed to having his own way. He was also accustomed to being obeyed without question. He ran his ranch with an iron hand and he was judge and jury when trouble or disputes arose. Though he was old enough to be Jesse's father, it was obvious that he found her attractive, and just as obvious that he was willing to be more than her employer if she but said the word.

She'd been at the Clayton ranch a little over two weeks when she heard Clayton's side of what had happened to his son, Johnny. They had been discussing Lizzie's mother, who had died in childbirth when Lizzie was four. Clayton had been fond of his daughter and had grieved for her when she died, but it was clear to Jesse that J. D. Clayton had thought the sun rose and fell for his son.

"He was killed," Clayton said gruffly. "Gunned down by a dirty half-breed."

"Yes," Jesse said. "I heard about it in Bitter Creek. I heard it was a fair fight."

J. D. Clayton glared at her as if she'd just profaned the Deity.

"He killed my boy," Clayton said, and his eyes blazed with a cold and bitter hatred the likes of which Jesse had never seen. "Killed him in cold blood. But he won't get away with it. Sooner or later, he'll be mine, and then I'll have my revenge."

"I'm sure the law will catch up with him before long," Jesse mused.

"To hell with the law!" Clayton said. "Out here I'm the law, and I intend to hang that half-breed bastard myself. I don't want to *hear* about Dancer being dead. I want to *see* Dancer dead." A malicious smiled curved his lips. "I intend to tie the knot and spring the trap."

Jesse nodded, repelled by the hatred in Clayton's eyes and voice. Repelled and afraid. Surely it would be up to a court of law to decide if the shooting had been murder or self-defense. Surely a man like Clayton, a man who was himself a judge, would not take the law into his own hands.

And yet, looking into J. D. Clayton's cold blue eyes, she knew he would not rest until Dancer was dead.

Chapter 14

Dancer found himself falling easily into the Comanche life-style as the old ways came back to him. Village life had not changed since he left. The women still did all the work, the children laughed and played, and the warriors hunted and protected the village.

The Comanche were a ferocious people. They called themselves Nermernuh, meaning People. The Cheyenne called them *Shishin-ohts-hit-ahn-ay-oh*, meaning Snake People. The Utes called them *Koh-mats*, or Those Against Us. They had no written record, only stories and legends passed from generation to generation by word of mouth. They believed they had sprung from a magical mating of animals—the wolf, perhaps, for, like the wolf, the Nermernuh were wild creatures with a strong sense of family. To their own they were loving and loyal, to their enemies they were ruthless. They respected the wolf's cousin, the coyote, and they did not eat the coyote's relative, the dog. Children were cherished, and orphans were cheerfully adopted into the tribe. The People were wary of spirits, but they were not afraid of death itself; it was only a doorway to a better life.

Dancer spent the first few days idle, stretched out lazily in the late summer sun, or swimming with long, powerful strokes in the river that ran behind his lodge. Little by little, he began to relax. Here in the land of his birth he was no longer Dancer, the wanted gunman, but Buffalo Dancer, the warrior. It was no longer necessary to be constantly alert and on guard; no longer a matter of survival to watch his back, or to sleep with one eye open lest some bounty hunter take him unawares. He began to leave his gun in the lodge, content to go unarmed save for the knife sheathed inside his moccasin.

Storm Woman took good care of him. She was a quiet, soft-spoken woman in her early thirties. The left side of her face was badly scarred, the skin fish-belly white, puckered and lifeless. She spoke little, but she had a kind heart and a good soul. She kept the lodge clean, made certain he had enough to eat, tobacco for his pipe.

They got on well together, the silent woman and the gunfighter. Dancer hoped one of the warriors would win Storm Woman's heart, for he knew she would make a fine wife for any man, a loving mother. But it would not be him.

He sighed heavily as his thoughts turned to Jesse, always Jesse. Come winter, he intended to return to Bitter Creek for her. Hopefully, Clayton's hired guns would have called off the hunt by then and gone home. If not . . . he let out a heavy sigh. If not, he could always form a war party and get rid of Cliff Hardin and his bunch of curly wolves once and for all.

But he would worry about that when the time came. For now, he was tired of running, tired of fighting.

And so the days passed, and it was as if he had never gone away. He renewed old acquaintances, made new friends, and when Yellow Hand and some of the other warriors organized a raid against the Apache, he just naturally went along. And had a hell of a good time.

They returned victorious, brandishing several Apache scalps, a dozen stolen rifles, and a wealth of Apache ponies. One of the captured mustangs was a fine young mare the color of new-fallen snow. White horses were prized by the Comanche, and Dancer had claimed the mare as part of his share of the spoils, thinking the horse would make a good mount for Storm Woman. It pleased him to think of giving her a gift; she had given him much, and he wanted to give her something in return.

The women and children clamored around the returning war party as they rode into the village, singing praises to their bravery and cunning, and to Yellow Hand's flawless leadership. Not one Comanche warrior had been lost in the raid; only two men had been injured, neither seriously. Later, there would be a feast in Yellow Hand's honor.

Storm Woman came out to meet Dancer, her smile expressing her happiness at his safe return. Looking into her face, Dancer saw the love shining in her luminous black eyes before she quickly turned away. He sat there for a long moment, wondering how he could have been so blind for so long. Storm Woman loved him.

Dismounting, he tethered his horse outside the lodge, then followed Storm Woman inside.

"Welcome home, Buffalo Dancer," she murmured. "Are you hungry?"

"No. Storm Woman, look at me."

She met his eyes reluctantly, her cheeks flushing under his probing gaze. She had never meant for him to know how much she cared for him. She had not meant to fall in love with him, had been certain she would never love a man after the dreadful indignities she had suffered at the hands of the Crow warriors. She had never meant to fall in love. And it was just as well, for no man could ever love her. They felt only pity or revulsion when they looked at her.

"Storm Woman, I . . ." Dancer let out a long breath, at a loss to express what he was feeling.

"You need not speak," Storm Woman said. "I know your heart lies elsewhere."

"I'm sorry," Dancer murmured with a slight shake of his head. "I would love you if I could."

"You have given me enough already."

"I've given you nothing."

She smiled at him, her dark eyes warm and

sad. "You have made my lodge a home. You have brought meat to my table." She lowered her eyes. "You have given me a reason to live."

She knelt quickly and pulled a pair of moccasins from beneath her sleeping robe. "These are for you."

Dancer stared at the moccasins Storm Woman handed him. They were exquisitely wrought. The upper portion was of tanned doeskin, soft and pliable, reaching to mid-calf; the soles were made of thick buffalo hide.

Dancer lifted his eyes to Storm Woman's face and knew he had never received a gift of such value in his entire life. "My thanks," he said, pulling off his worn moccasins and replacing them with the new ones. "Come," he said, taking her by the hand. "I have a gift for you."

Storm Woman's eyes grew round when she saw the white mare. She looked at Dancer, certain he must be making a joke, for the mare was beautiful and of a color prized by Comanche men. Surely he did not mean to give the horse away.

"Do you like her?" Dancer asked, stroking the mare's neck.

"She is lovely," Storm Woman replied. "So very lovely. My gift pales in comparison."

"Not true," Dancer argued. "I did little to capture the mare, but your gift took many hours of time and effort."

Storm Woman smiled at him, and Dancer felt a warm rush of affection for her. Impulsively, he pulled her into his arms and kissed her.

Storm Woman's body went rigid as his lips touched hers, and Dancer released her immediately. Gazing into her eyes, he read the stark fear in her expression and cursed under his breath. Caught up in the moment, he had forgotten that she had been abused by the Crow, that many men had used her body.

"Forgive me," Dancer said. "I did not mean to frighten you."

"Thank you for the mare," Storm Woman whispered hoarsely, and turning on her heel, she ran back to the lodge. For weeks she had yearned to have Dancer make love to her, certain that with him she would not be afraid. But it was no use. She could not bear the touch of a man's arms around her, could not forget how awful it had been in the Crow camp. No matter how she had fought, the warriors had come to her, forcing her to accept their rough caresses, ignoring her cries of protest as they vented their lust on her unwilling body.

She looked up, startled, as Dancer entered the lodge. He paused inside the doorway, his gray eyes filled with understanding.

"Do not be afraid of me," he said quietly. "I will not hurt you."

"I know."

"Then why did you run away from me?"

"I could not help it. Please do not be angry."

"I could never be angry with you." He crossed the lodge and knelt before her. "Do not be afraid of me." Gently, he reached out to stroke her cheek. "Do not be afraid," he murmured again, and leaning toward her, he placed a kiss on her lips.

Storm Woman sighed with pleasure as his mouth moved over hers. She had never known tenderness from a man, never known gentleness. She gazed up at him in wonder as the kiss ended. "How can you bear to touch me?" she asked as she lifted a hand to her scarred cheek. "Do I not repulse you?"

"I do not see your scars," Dancer replied. "I see only a woman with eyes as black as night and a heart filled with kindness."

His words drove all the bitterness from her heart even as his kiss had eased her fears.

Storm Woman underwent a remarkable change in the days that followed. She laughed more, she smiled often, she began to take part in the tribe's social activities.

Dancer was pleased to see her getting out more, to know he had helped her overcome some of her fears. Perhaps she would eventually find a man to marry. If he were still here, he would shower her with horses and robes, so that she would be a wealthy woman in her own right. If only she might find a man . . . it grieved him to know that Storm Woman loved him and he could not love her in return, but his heart belonged to Jesse.

Jesse. He longed to hold her in his arms, to feel her soft curves pressed against his body, to taste the sweet honey of her lips and see her eyes grow cloudy with passion.

Jesse. She had satisfied more than his physical needs. Like Storm Woman, she had accepted him without question, trusting him, depending on him. He had been captivated by her smile, by the sound of her laughter. She knew him for what he was, a man who lived by his gun, but she had never reviled him for it, never accused him of being a killer, though that was what he was.

Jesse. When had he started to love her? He felt a deep need to hold her in his arms again, to feel her love.

He let out a long sigh as Storm Woman entered the lodge and began to prepare for bed. He felt her eyes on his back, felt her need to be loved.

His pulse quickened when she came to stand before him. She had removed her doeskin tunic and stood naked beside the fire, the flickering flames caressing her copper-hued skin, dancing in the long black hair that fell to her waist.

"Storm Woman." His voice was low and husky.

"Love me, Buffalo Dancer," she pleaded softly. "Love me just this once."

Slowly, he shook his head. "Storm . . ."

"Please." She knelt beside him and placed her hand on his chest. "I have never willingly bedded a man before, never known tenderness. Show me what it is like between a man and a woman when the woman is willing and the man cares, even a little."

He could not refuse her. Gently, he took her in his arms and kissed her, his body responding to the touch of warm feminine flesh. Yet even as he made love to Storm Woman, he was thinking of Jesse, yearning for a girl with flaxen hair and eyes the color of the sea. . . .

Chapter 15

The days were growing shorter, the nights longer and colder as autumn gave way to winter, but in the Clayton household it was always warm and cheerful. Fires blazed in the hearths night and day; candles and lamps turned away the early evening darkness.

Jesse was almost a part of the family now. She took her meals in the big paneled dining room with Lizzie and J. D., sat with them in the parlor after supper. She tucked Lizzie into bed at night, read her a story and heard her prayers. She often spent long hours playing chess with J. D. after Lizzie was asleep. J. D. made no secret of the fact that he found her attractive and desirable. In the back of her mind, Jesse knew that sooner or later J. D. Clayton was going to propose marriage. But she refused to think about it, or how her negative answer would affect her job as Lizzie's governess.

She attended the lavish parties he hosted, standing at his side as he received his guests. If people thought it strange that Lizzie's governess was included in J. D.'s social gatherings, no one ever said anything, at least not to his face. Or hers.

Jesse had never known such luxury, such wealth. J. D. had bought her a dozen ball gowns, and when she protested that such a thing was improper, he merely shrugged and said it was necessary. She was a part of his household, not a servant, and she had to dress accordingly.

It was impossible to refuse his kindness. The dresses were costly and beautiful, accompanied by white ruffled petticoats, pantalets trimmed in pink ribbon, chemises edged in white lace. She had never owned such lovely undergarments, or such elegant gowns. Sometimes, looking in her mirror, she felt like a princess waiting for the prince.

Dancer. As busy as Jesse's days were, Dancer was ever in her thoughts. He had planned to winter with his mother's people, and she wondered if he was still there. Did he think of her often? Or had he found someone else? Her jealous heart quickly conjured up a beautiful Indian maiden with ebony hair and dark eyes and soft copper-hued skin. There were bound to be single women in the Comanche village, women who would be attracted to a man as tall and handsome as Dancer.

The thought of Dancer in another woman's arms filled her with such intense jealousy it was like a physical pain, and she put the thought from her, refusing to believe he would be unfaithful to her. And yet, hadn't he told her to find someone else? *"Don't wait for me, Jesse,"* he'd told her that last night at the relay station. *"Go back to Bitter Creek. Marry Tom. Make a life for yourself."*

Had he meant it? She thought of Clayton. She could be happy here, surrounded by comfort and luxury, happy with Lizzie. But could she be happy with Clayton? The thought of being in J. D.'s arms, of being his wife, filled her with despair. As much as she had come to love Lizzie, she could not marry J. D.

Clayton often went into town to see if there was any news of Dancer's whereabouts. He haunted the telegraph office and the jail, waiting for some word from Hardin, but to no avail. He would return home in a foul mood, often locking himself up for hours on end, and Jesse would sigh with relief. Dancer was still alive, still free. And as long as he lived, she had hope. Hope that she would see him again, feel his arms around her, hear his voice.

His image paraded through her dreams at night, and she often woke, breathless and in tears, after dreaming that they had made love and then he had left her again. Some of her dreams were so vivid, so real, that she woke in a warm sweat, surprised to find herself alone in bed. Was he dreaming of her, too? Did his body ache with the same need hers did? Or had he found someone else?

Chapter 16

The days ran by on winged feet, and Dancer felt as though he had truly returned home. He was a warrior again, accepted as such, and he spent his days with the men, smoking and talking, listening to the young men complain about the encroachment of the whites. Settlers were moving into their hunting grounds, hunters were coming from across the water to hunt the buffalo, taking the head and the tongue and leaving thousands of pounds of meat to rot in the sun.

Dancer listened to their complaints and felt a quick sympathy for his people. He knew, better than they, that the days of the warrior were numbered.

Many tribes had been confined to reservations where they sickened and died, having no resistance to the white man's diseases, having no desire to live as the white man thought they should live. Many Indians left the reservations in the summer, raiding and dodging soldiers when the grass was new, then returning to the reservation in the winter.

He had no doubt that one day all Indians

would be penned on reservations. The whites were determined to kill them or cage them. General Sherman had decreed that the more Indians he killed in one year, the fewer he would have to kill the next. An editorial in an Austin newspaper had stated that "the idea of making treaties with the Comanche is supremely absurd; just as well make treaties with rattlesnakes and Mexican tigers. Property will be stolen, men murdered, women ravished and children carried into captivity on our frontier until the Indians are all killed off, or until they are all caught and caged."

But Dancer did not dwell on that now. Lame Eagle's people were at peace, far from the grasping hand of the whites, at least for the time being.

For Dancer, living with the Comanche was like being set free. He felt young, vital, alive, and if the women did all the work while the warriors played, well, that was the way life was, the way it had always been.

Soon, inclement weather would force Clayton's men to go home if they hadn't already, and he would ride back to Bitter Creek. Hopefully, he would find Jesse there, waiting for him even though he'd told her not to. And if she'd taken him at his word and left town, Tom would know where she'd gone, and he would go after her. If she was willing, he would bring her back to Shadow Valley. They could have a life together here. It was the only place he'd ever felt safe, the only place he'd ever be safe from bounty hunters and would-be fast guns like Johnny Clayton.

He grinned ruefully as he imagined Jesse living with the Comanche, making her home in a hide lodge, cooking over an open fire. Would she be willing to give up the comforts and conveniences of town living to have a life with him? Could he ask her to leave everything she knew behind?

Beautiful, flaxen-haired Jesse. She was ever in his thoughts, even now, as he left Storm Woman's lodge and made his way to the river. It was his favorite time of day, that peaceful time just before full dark. Tonight the weather was cold as a whore's heart; soon the river would be as cold as ice and he would have to give up his moonlight swims until spring. Usually Storm Woman accompanied him, but tonight she was caring for an elderly woman who was seriously ill.

From a distance, Elkhorn watched as Buffalo Dancer made his way down to the river. A smug smile tugged at his lips when he saw that the half-breed was alone. At last the night he had been waiting for had come. The white man, Hardin, possessed the patience of a hunting cat, Elkhorn thought with grudging admiration, to wait so long for his prey. The other white men would have left long ago but for him.

Silent as a snake, Elkhorn glided through the trees toward the wide ribbon of water shining in the distance.

At the river's edge, Dancer drew in a deep breath as he slipped out of his buckskin shirt and tossed it over a flat-topped rock.

He was bending over to pull off his moccasins when he felt the jab of cold steel against his spine.

"Do not make any sudden moves," warned a whispered voice.

"What do you want?" Dancer asked, feeling every muscle in his body tense.

"Walk upriver, slowly. There are horses waiting around the bend."

"Horses?"

"We are going for a short ride."

Dancer felt the short hairs stand up along the back of his neck as he recognized Elkhorn's voice.

"Go."

Moving cautiously, Dancer did as he was told, acutely aware of the gun barrel resting against his spine. They had reached the bend of the river when Storm Woman came running up behind them, softly calling Dancer's name.

He halted in mid-stride, mouth open to warn her away, when the world exploded in a blinding flash of light. . . .

He swam back to consciousness through shimmering red waves of pain. Cracking his eyes open, he glanced around, frowning when he realized he was in the ancient burial ground, his hands bound behind his back, and that Storm Woman was sitting beside him, her hands lashed behind her back, a dirty kerchief tied over her mouth. Her eyes were wide with fright.

Why was she afraid? he wondered groggily. And why was he trussed up like a Christmas turkey? Damn, but it was hard to think.

Turning his head, he saw two men conversing a short distance away. Man Who Walks and Elkhorn, he thought dully.

Man Who Walks! His mind screamed the name as he squinted into the darkness. If Man Who Walks was here, then Cliff Hardin would not be far behind.

Hardin and Elkhorn. Between them, they would see him safely delivered into J. D. Clayton's hands.

Muttering a vile oath, he closed his eyes against the pain pounding in his head, felt himself falling into nothingness. . . .

Someone was shaking him. Whispered voices buzzed around his head like angry hornets. It was an effort to open his eyes, and when he did, it was to find Elkhorn staring down at him.

A sinister smile played over the warrior's face as he grabbed the half-breed by the arm and hauled him to his feet. It took the combined efforts of Elkhorn and Baldy Johnson to boost Dancer onto the back of a dun gelding. Mounted, he swayed in the saddle, only dimly aware of what was going on around him. There was the clank of spurs and bit chains, the sound of cloth scraping leather, a muffled oath as one of Hardin's men dropped a cigarette. As from far away he heard Hardin utter a crude remark about Storm Woman's anatomy as he lifted her onto the back of his big chestnut stud.

"Everybody ready?" Cliff asked gruffly. "Then let's ride. We haven't got all night."

Elkhorn took the lead while Hardin and his men fell in behind, neatly boxing Dancer between them.

Dancer rode slumped in the saddle, quietly cussing the man who had betrayed him. It was obvious that Elkhorn had gone out looking for Hardin, and between them they had devised a near-foolproof plan to whisk him out of Shadow Valley and turn him over to Clayton. No one would come looking for him right away, not as long as Blue was still at camp. Everyone knew he would not leave without the mare. Likely, people would think that he and Storm Woman had gone off together. In time, people would wonder about their prolonged absence, but by then it would be too late.

The trail veered left and Dancer scowled. Elkhorn had planned well. The trail they were following was an old game trail. Seldom used, it was heavily carpeted with leaves and pine needles, muffling the sound of their passage so that they moved down the narrow twisting path like so many mounted shadows.

They rode steadily, silently, over narrow switchbacks and through passes barely wide enough for horse and rider. Cresting a humpbacked ridge, they dropped down into a shallow gorge, threading their way between high granite cliffs until they reached what appeared to be a dead end. There was some angry muttering from Miller about a trap, but Hardin followed Elkhorn confidently into a rocky defile and then along a narrow winding ribbon of ground that ended abruptly at the base of a waterfall. Without a break in stride, Elkhorn urged his calico pony behind the towering curtain of water. Hardin and his men followed apprehensively, and found themselves in a grassy moonlit meadow.

A collective sigh of relief rose in the throats of the white men as they recognized the surrounding countryside. The trail to Cherry Valley lay only a few miles to the south.

Dancer sat motionless astride the dun, concentrating all his energy on remaining upright in the saddle. With the cessation of movement, the ache in his head receded, clearing the cobwebs from his mind.

Elkhorn rode over to him, a satisfied smirk on his swarthy face. "I hope they kill you slowly, by inches," the Indian hissed. "Remember, each time you cry out, that it was Elkhorn who betrayed you."

A voice echoed in the back of Dancer's mind: *"You should have killed him honorably,"* the voice said. *"He will always be your enemy now."*

Well, Lame Eagle had certainly called that one right, Dancer mused, meeting the warrior's hate-filled gaze with one of his own. Imperceptibly, he shifted his weight in the stirrups as he eased back in the saddle. Then, bracing himself against the high Mexican cantle, he powered his left leg up and out, catching Elkhorn flush in the side and toppling him off his horse to the ground.

Elkhorn sprang to his feet with murder in his heart, his lips curled back in a hideous grin as he clawed his knife from the beaded sheath on his belt. A pale shaft of moonlight glinted on the blade as he hurled himself at Dancer.

A gunshot rang out across the meadow, the echo reverberating through the stillness like the sound of distant thunder.

Dancer's horse reared, pawing the air in panic as Elkhorn's lifeless body fell at its feet, and only Man Who Walks' quick thinking kept the dun from bolting down the meadow toward home. Vaulting from his pony's back, the Apache grabbed the dun's reins.

Looking immensely pleased with his marksmanship, Cliff Hardin dropped his rifle back into the saddle boot and turned to the man beside him.

"Johnson, get the redskin's horse for the girl and let's make tracks. I want some miles between us and the Comanche before dawn."

It was mid-morning before Hardin called a halt. A quick meal, a few hours' rest, and they were on the move again.

Dancer shifted his weight in the saddle. His head throbbed like a Comanche war drum, making coherent thought difficult, but one thing remained clear. He had to get Storm

Woman away from Hardin and his pack of curly wolves before it was too late, but how? With his feet secured beneath the dun's belly and his hands tied to the saddle horn, he was virtually helpless.

Storm Woman, mounted on Elkhorn's big calico gelding, was similarly bound.

He drew a ragged breath. Behind him, he could hear Miller and McDonald bragging about their sexual prowess, and he knew it was only a matter of time before they began cutting the cards to see who would get her first.

Glancing at Storm Woman, Dancer saw that she, too, was aware of the danger she was in. She didn't have to understand English to comprehend the lusty ribald tone of George Miller's laughter. And the lewd gesture Wes McDonald made in her direction was understood the world over.

Dancer swore under his breath, knowing that Storm Woman was in for a much worse time than he was. Hardin needed him alive, and that gave Dancer a certain advantage, up to a point. J. D. Clayton wouldn't buy a corpse. But Storm Woman was completely at the mercy of the Hardin bunch, and of no value whatsoever once they tired of her. And when that time came, he knew they would dispose of her with no more thought than they would give to swatting a fly.

Darkness had overtaken them when they stopped at a deserted squatter's cabin for the night. A chill wind blew through the cottonwoods, howling mournfully as it rattled the windows, whistling shrilly as it found its way through the numerous cracks in the old building. Gray-black clouds scudded across the sky, gathering ominously overhead, shutting out both moon and stars. A sharp crack of thunder rocked the cabin, then another, and it began to rain. A heavy silence fell over the shack as Hardin's men stared at Storm Woman, their unspoken desire louder than the raging storm.

Hardin tossed one of the packs at her. "Dancer, tell the woman to fix us some grub. And see you make it short. Long conversations make me nervous." He dropped into a rickety old chair. "Miller, untie the squaw."

"Storm Woman," Dancer said quietly. "Fix them something to eat."

"You do not look well," she remarked, moving toward him.

"I'm fine," he assured her. "Do as I say. You must not make these men angry. And try not to worry. I'll get you out of this somehow."

"What are you telling her?" Hardin asked suspiciously.

"He told her not to worry," Man Who Walks said, grinning.

Laughing mirthlessly, Hardin sauntered over to Storm Woman and ran his hand down her arm. "She's got a right to worry, half-breed. We've been sitting on your tail a hell of a long time, and we're all a little lonesome for some female company, even if she is as ugly as a warthog." Hardin pinched Storm Woman's cheek. "Tell me, squawman, how is she under the buffalo robes?"

Dancer's face clouded with anger. "Leave her alone, Cliff," he rasped.

"What's the matter, half-breed?" Hardin sneered. "You want her all for yourself? Well, be a good boy and maybe we'll cut you in for a piece."

"You slimy bastard. Keep your hands off of her!"

"Shut up, squawman," Hardin said mildly, and sent a vicious blow into Dancer's midsection.

Fighting the urge to vomit, Dancer doubled over. It was then, as he fought down the hot bitter bile that rose in his throat, that his dislike for Cliff Hardin blossomed into full-fledged hatred.

Dinner was a quiet meal, and when it was over, Davis and Miller donned their slickers and went out into the driving rain to check on the horses. Minutes later, Man Who Walks gathered his blankets and headed outside, preferring the wind and the rain to the cabin's musty interior.

With a frown, Hardin glanced at Dancer. The half-breed was naked save for leggings and moccasins. Pulling a buckskin jacket from one of his saddlebags, he tossed it at McDonald.

"Wes, cut the 'breed loose so he can slip that on. He ain't worth shit if he freezes to death."

Smothering a yawn, Wes McDonald crossed

the room to where Dancer was sitting with his back against the wall.

"You heard him," McDonald growled. Cutting Dancer's hands free, he dropped the jacket in his lap.

Dancer rubbed his chafed wrists, stalling for time as he remembered the knife sheathed in his moccasin. Perhaps there was a way out of this mess after all. Hardin always tied his hands behind his back, but if he could manage to get the knife out of his moccasin and hidden behind him, he could cut himself free later, when everyone was asleep, take Storm Woman, and get the hell out of there.

"Move it, Dancer." McDonald's voice prodded him to action and he eased slowly into the jacket, one eye on Wes, who was yawning again.

Across the room, Hardin and Johnson were exchanging lewd remarks about Storm Woman as she moved about the shack, cleaning up the dinner debris. With a grin, Hardin reached out and grabbed her breast as she walked by.

Uttering a hoarse cry, Storm Woman jerked away, dropping the pot she had been wiping dry. It landed on the raw plank floor with a loud clatter, momentarily drawing McDonald's attention from Dancer.

It was now or never, Dancer thought, and eased the knife from its sheath. He was sliding the blade behind his back when McDonald glanced down at him.

"What the hell!" Wes exclaimed, then grunted as Dancer rose to his knees and drove the eight-inch blade into his belly.

Quick as a cat, Dancer clawed the dead man's gun from its holster and leveled it at Hardin.

But he was too late. Cliff stood behind Storm Woman. One hand was tangled in her long black hair; the other held his gun, ready-cocked, against her right temple.

"Drop it," Hardin ordered quietly. "Drop it or I'll scatter her brains all over the floor."

Dancer believed him. Without hesitation, he let McDonald's Colt fall to the floor.

"Johnson! I thought you said you searched him good!"

"I did. He didn't have that knife on him when we left the canyon."

"Then where the hell did he get it?"

"I don't know," Johnson said defensively. "Maybe—"

"Maybe, hell! Get over there and tie him up tight!"

Scowling, Hardin pushed Storm Woman aside as Remo Davis entered the cabin.

"What the hell happened?" Davis demanded, glancing from McDonald's body to Hardin's taut face.

"Stupid mistake, that's what happened," Cliff growled. "The 'breed had a knife hid on him. Get over there and make sure he ain't hiding any more surprises."

"Sure." Remo Davis shook the water from

his hat, shrugged out of his slicker. "You ain't gonna let him get away with carvin' up old Wes?"

"For now," Hardin replied indifferently. "Anyway, ten grand is easier to split five ways."

Davis considered that for a moment, and then shrugged. He'd never liked McDonald all that much anyway. And ten grand was easier to split five ways.

Chapter 17

They were camped in a small green valley that was watered by a crystal river and sheltered by timbered hills. Alone, they were, just the two of them, and happy to be that way.

We'll build our house here, he said, and Jesse smiled with heart-felt joy as he took her in his arms and kissed her deeply, tenderly.

I love you he said, and she wept softly because he had finally spoken the words she had so longed to hear.

It was hard work, building a cabin in the wilderness with no one to help them, but she never complained because he was there beside her. She was never afraid when he was near, never lonely, never discouraged. He was there, working beside her during the day. And each night she found comfort in the circle of his arms, in the sound of his voice as he whispered again that he loved her, would always love her.

They worked all summer, and when winter came, the cabin was finished and she had never seen anything more beautiful.

Home, she said. *Home at last.*

They spent the winter in cozy seclusion, and

when spring came, her belly was round with new life, and her world was peaceful and complete.

He threw away his gun and turned his hand to farming, and they were happy, so happy.

And then the men came. They came with rifles and all her pleas for mercy fell on deaf ears. The gunshots echoed in her ears like thunder in the mountains....

"J. D., don't!"

Jesse sat up in bed, her cheeks damp with tears, the sound of her own anguished cry still ringing in her ears, and then she heard it again, the sound of thunder rumbling across the sky.

It had only been a dream, after all.

She slid out of bed and went to the window to stare out at the storm. A great jagged streak of lightning brightened the sky. Thunder echoed in the distance, and then there was only the heavy sound of the rain on the roof.

As she gazed into the darkness, her thoughts went back in time, back to the days when she had ridden at Dancer's side. How she missed those days, and the nights she had spent in his arms. She refused to believe that she would never see him again, refused to believe that the love they had shared had been lost forever. For he had loved her. She refused to think otherwise. Someday she would find him again and he would say the words she longed to hear, the words she knew were in his heart.

She thought of the peaceful days they had

spent in the cabin in the valley. She had never known such happiness. He had not been Dancer the gunman then, simply Dancer the man. If she could only see him again, make him believe that they could have a life like that, together.

Jesse folded her arms over her breasts and closed her eyes, remembering how wonderful it had been to fall asleep in his arms, to wake up with her head pillowed on his shoulder, to watch his eyes turn smoky with desire as his hands caressed her. A quick warmth enflamed her as she relived the hours she had spent in his arms, the joy of discovery, the ecstasy they had found in one another.

With a sigh, she opened her eyes and watched the trees as they swayed back and forth, blown by the heavy hand of the wind. She told herself that Dancer had survived this long, that not even a man like Cliff Hardin would be able to catch him.

Hardin. She had heard his name often since she had come here. His reputation was well-known, and he was feared and hated by the people in town.

But Dancer was safe, Jesse thought, safe with his mother's people. Surely not even a man as fearless as Cliff Hardin was reported to be would have guts enough to ride into a Comanche village and try to take Dancer out at gunpoint.

Returning to bed, Jesse let out a deep sigh

and closed her eyes. He was safe. He had to be safe. And if she didn't lose hope, she would see him again.

She fell asleep holding fast to that thought.

Chapter 18

The Hardin gang was on the road again shortly after dawn the following day. There was no sun to warm them, only thick gray clouds and a chill wind that blew out of the northeast.

The gloomy weather suited Dancer's mood perfectly. Captivity was a worm in his belly, twisting, turning, gnawing at him continually. If only his hands were free! If only he had killed Elkhorn that first day when he'd had the chance. If only he hadn't let himself get taken like a green kid!

If, if, if. Dammit, this whole mess was his fault, but it was Storm Woman who would suffer the most. It was only a matter of time.

The rain came in blinding flashes of lightning and drum rolls of thunder. The horses plodded sluggishly through the ankle-deep mud, their heads hanging, their hooves making ugly sucking noises in the thick slush. Miller and Davis pulled bright yellow slickers from their bedrolls. The others huddled deeper into their jackets, collars turned up, hats pulled low.

Dancer endured the cold with stoic acceptance. What could not be changed must be endured. He had traveled in worse weather in days gone by. And if he didn't have a hat to keep the rain out of his face, at least he had Hardin's buckskin jacket to block the wind. But Storm Woman had only a doeskin dress to ward off the wind and the rain. She was shivering violently.

It was going on noon when Hardin reined his big chestnut stud to a halt before a mountainous pile of rocks. Several large boulders formed a cave of sorts, offering a degree of protection from the elements.

"We'll stop here," he called, shouting to be heard above the deluge.

Cold and soaked to the skin, the travelers crowded under the rough shelter. A rat's nest provided fuel for a small fire. It was a pitiful blaze at best, but it was better than nothing. Outside, the horses stood with their backs to the wind, their heads low.

"Doesn't look like it's gonna clear up today," Man Who Walks opined.

Time proved him right. The thunder and lightning tapered off, but the rain continued to fall in icy sheets.

Storm Woman sat close to Dancer, her head pillowed on his shoulder. Hardin and his men huddled under their blankets, impatient with the delay. One by one, Hardin's men stretched out and went to sleep, leaving the boss to guard the prisoners.

Dancer glanced at Cliff Hardin. "How about a blanket for her?" he asked stonily, though it galled him to ask the gunman for anything.

With a grunt, Hardin pulled a blanket from his bedroll and tossed it over Storm Woman.

Dancer stared into the gathering darkness, his mind bleak, like the landscape. Storm Woman moaned in her sleep and he gazed at her fondly, then shifted his gaze to Hardin. Cliff's swarthy face was expressionless, his brown eyes as cold as yesterday's ashes. His right hand, as big as a bear's paw, absently caressed the stock of the rifle lying across his lap.

Their eyes met briefly, and though no word was spoken, both men knew that there would be no quarter given on the trail that lay ahead.

It was still dark the next morning when they climbed dispiritedly into the saddle. There was no dry wood, and that meant no fire and no coffee and nothing but beef jerky for breakfast. There was considerable grumbling among Hardin's men as they rode through the wet brown slush. It was going on noon when the sun fought its way through the clouds, transforming the pallid wilderness into a sparkling wonderland of unblemished beauty, lifting their sagging spirits with its delicious warmth.

A cowtown loomed ahead and Hardin decided to ride in, ostensibly to wire Clayton with the good news that they had Dancer and were on their way home. He took Johnson with him. It was going on dark when Hardin and Johnson returned, carrying several bottles of rotgut.

"Bought you fellas a little something to take the chill outta your bones," Hardin said. His words were slurred, his grin crooked.

"Took you long enough," Miller muttered caustically.

"Shut up!" Hardin snapped. "I had some things to do."

"Blond or brunette?" Davis asked sulkily.

Hardin scowled, then shrugged. It was none of their business how he spent his time and he offered no explanations. If they didn't like the way he ramrodded the gang, they could get the hell out.

Opening a bottle of rye, Hardin sat cross-legged before the fire. One by one, the others drifted over and squatted down beside him. Cliff passed the bottle, and the whiskey warmed them, dispersing some of the gloom that had settled over the gang while they cooled their heels waiting for his return.

"Isn't it time we tried out that squaw?" Davis asked, his voice thick with drink.

"Sure, Remo," Hardin said magnanimously. Sated from an afternoon with one of the local whores, he could afford to be generous with the scar-faced Indian woman. "Just keep the noise down. I've got a hell of a headache."

"No!" The word exploded from Dancer's lips.

"What do you mean, no?" Hardin asked contemptuously. "Since when have you got anything to say about it?"

Dancer stood up, his hands clenched as he

tried to control his anger. "Leave her alone," he said quietly. "She's got no part in this."

"She's whatever I say she is," Hardin retorted. "Of course, if you was to ask me real nice, I might let you have a turn when my men are through."

"Go to hell."

"All in good time," Hardin replied smoothly. And then he laughed. "Perhaps I'll let my men rough you up a little first. Kinda whet their appetite for something more pleasant."

Dancer swore under his breath. Perhaps if he could make Hardin and his men angry enough, they would be content to torment him and leave Storm Woman alone. It was a slim chance at best, but it was all he had.

"Do what you want with me, Cliff, but leave her alone. Or maybe defenseless women are all you and your mangy cutthroats can handle."

"I can handle you!" Hardin snarled. "I could have you crawling in the dirt like a whipped cur!"

"You're all mouth," Dancer said with a sneer. "But then, you always were."

"Shut up."

"Sure," Dancer said, and spit in Cliff Hardin's face.

Hardin went stiff-legged with rage. As from far away, he heard his men urging him on, shouting for him to bring the half-breed to heel, to show the redskin who was boss. And show them he would! Only the sight of Dancer groveling in the dirt at his feet would satisfy him now.

Dancer saw the fury building in Hardin's eyes and steeled himself for the beating that was sure to come, but Cliff had something else in mind.

"Remo, get the woman," Hardin barked. "I want her to see this." He smiled with diabolical cunning. "I know you've got too much arrogance to ask for mercy for yourself; too much heathen pride. But how about for that squaw, half-breed? How far will you go to save her?"

Lazily, Hardin reached out and grabbed Storm Woman's arm as Davis dragged her into view. Storm Woman choked back a sob of pain, her eyes sending a look of mute appeal in Dancer's direction, but the half-breed's eyes were riveted on Cliff Hardin's face. Indeed, the two men might have been alone on the prairie, for Dancer took no notice of the woman at Cliff's side, or of the four grim-faced men clustered around them, waiting to see what would happen next.

"How far?" Hardin repeated, and the question seemed to hang in the air, like smoke.

Hardin was a sly bastard, Dancer thought bitterly. He had not counted on anything like this, had assumed Cliff would threaten him with some kind of fiendish torture. He could have tolerated that. But begging . . . his pride rebelled at the very idea.

"Well?" Cliff prompted in a bored tone. "Do I let my men have her or not?" Hardin tightened his hold on Storm Woman's arm and gave it a cruel twist. She whimpered with pain as Cliff's fingers dug into her arm, and Dancer looked at her for the first time.

He no longer noticed the grotesque scar on her cheek. He saw only a lovely woman who had been kind to him, who loved him without question. He could not let her suffer because of him, and if that meant he had to lick the dust from Cliff Hardin's boots, then, by damn, he'd do it.

"If I do what you want, will you call your men off? For good?"

"Sure." Hardin's voice was silky soft. "All you gotta do is ask me nice."

Storm Woman's gaze was fixed on Dancer's face. She could not understand the words of the white men, but she knew they had something to do with her and she was afraid again, as afraid as she had been in the Crow camp.

"Buffalo Dancer." She called his name, her voice begging for reassurance.

"Don't be afraid," Dancer told her in Comanche. "Everything will be all right."

"What you'd tell her?" Hardin demanded angrily.

"I told her not to be afraid," Dancer replied.

"She should be," Hardin said, his eyes cold. "It's your move, half-breed."

Dancer forced the word through clenched teeth, knowing it would not be enough. "Please."

Hardin snickered. "Please what?" He was

thoroughly enjoying himself, and it showed.

"Please leave her alone."

"Down on your knees, pig," Hardin ordered brusquely.

For a moment, Hardin and Dancer glared at each other. Then, with a sigh of resignation, Dancer dropped to one knee, cursing himself for being a fool. Worse than a fool. The odds were a million to one that Hardin would play square.

"Both knees," Hardin drawled.

Storm Woman shook her head in despair. The white men were trying to humiliate Buffalo Dancer, and she knew that somehow she was the cause of his shame.

"Now, crawl on over here and beg me to save her," Hardin drawled, grinning expectantly.

"Dammit!" Dancer exploded. "That's going too far!"

"Make him do it, Cliff," Davis coaxed, enjoying the game.

"I'm running out of patience," Hardin warned. "Either do as I say, or I'll let Remo stake her out here and now."

Despising himself, Dancer crawled awkwardly toward Hardin. Rocking back on his heels, he rasped, "Please save Storm Woman from your friends."

Man Who Walks chuckled. "Now that he has learned to beg, perhaps you can teach him to roll over."

"Or fetch a stick," Davis chortled.

Their taunts were childish, yet humiliation

and rage washed over Dancer as he sat there, listening.

"We could teach him to play dead," Miller suggested scornfully. "I'll bet he'd be real good at that."

"Forget him," Johnson said impatiently. "Let's get the woman."

Hardin grinned. His headache was gone and he was ready for some action. His eyes filled with contempt as he stared at Dancer. "Hold her down, boys," he called cheerfully. "We'll cut the cards to see who goes first."

A cold fury engulfed Dancer as he looked up and met Cliff's gaze. "I should have known," he said quietly.

"Yeah," Hardin agreed. "You should have known."

The atmosphere was suddenly charged with tension as the men turned toward the Indian woman.

Storm Woman saw the lust in their eyes and her heart went cold with fear. For days the white men had gawked at her, letting their hands slide suggestively over her body. She had known it was only a matter of time before they forced themselves on her. And that time had come.

She glanced at Buffalo Dancer, a mute plea for help in her eyes, but he could not help her now.

Heart pounding with dread, she backed away as two of the men started toward her, their eyes hot as they lunged forward and grabbed her by the arms.

With a cry, she twisted out of their grasp and ran into the dark, fear adding wings to her feet.

"Get her!" Johnson hollered, and all the men turned and gave chase.

Dancer quickly scrambled to his feet. It wouldn't take them long to catch Storm Woman. Walking swiftly toward the fire, he dropped to his knees and seized the knife Storm Woman had used to prepare dinner. The blade was razor sharp, and he nicked his arms several times as he sliced through the rope that bound his wrists. And even as the rope slipped to the ground, he could hear the men returning, could hear Storm Woman's frantic cries as she begged for her freedom, for mercy.

There was no time to search for a gun. Instead, he backed away from the fire and dropped to his knees, his arms behind his back, the knife clutched in his right hand.

Cliff Hardin frowned thoughtfully when he saw Dancer still kneeling in the dirt. He had expected the half-breed to make a run for it; indeed, he had been looking forward to the chase.

Davis and Man Who Walks wrestled the woman to the ground while Miller and Johnson argued over who would go first.

"Get the cards and cut for her," Davis snapped impatiently. "I ain't gonna hold her down all night."

Miller nodded and pulled a worn deck of

cards from one of his saddlebags. Walking back toward Johnson, he made the mistake of passing too close to Dancer, who immediately sprang to his feet and buried the knife in Miller's back.

Miller grunted softly and fell forward. He was still falling as Dancer lifted the gun from his holster and lined the sights on Remo Davis.

All the color drained out of Remo's face when he saw the murderous rage blazing in the half-breed's eyes. With a wordless cry, he lurched to his feet and drew his gun.

Seeing a chance for freedom, Storm Woman jerked free from the Apache's grasp. Scrambling to her knees, she started toward Dancer.

She gained her feet as Remo Davis pulled the trigger.

The shot echoed and re-echoed in the sudden stillness.

For a moment, Storm Woman stood still, and then she staggered forward, one arm extended toward Dancer.

"My God, no," Dancer cried hoarsely, and forgetting everything else, he dropped the gun and caught Storm Woman as she collapsed in his arms. A thin trickle of blood oozed from the corner of her mouth.

Hardin swore under his breath as he picked up the gun Dancer had dropped and tossed it at Man Who Walks. Jerking the knife from Miller's corpse, he stuck it in his belt.

Hardin's gaze swept the camp. Davis, Johnson, and Man Who Walks were standing together. The half-breed was sitting on the ground, his face like something carved from stone as he cradled the squaw in his arms, his right hand splayed across the slight swell of her abdomen. The woman was whispering, her voice faint, faltering. Hardin wasn't fluent in the Comanche tongue, but he caught a few words and he frowned when the woman mentioned a child.

He stepped forward, ears straining to hear the half-breed's reply.

"I promise," Dancer murmured. He placed his right hand on Storm Woman's blood-stained chest, then lifted his hand to his right cheek. "Blood for blood," he said hoarsely. "A life for a life."

He uttered a strangled cry as Storm Woman shuddered convulsively, then lay still.

For a moment, it was as if they had all been frozen in time. Then Dancer eased Storm Woman's body to the ground and stood up, his dark eyes glittering with fury.

There was no mistaking the hostility of that countenance, and Hardin drew his gun and leveled it at the half-breed's chest. "Don't try anything else, Dancer, or I'll blow your guts out."

Hardin and Dancer glowered at each other while Davis and Johnson dragged Miller's body into the woods.

"I need a shovel," Dancer said, his voice flat, concealing the pain splintering through him.

"You can bury her in the morning," Hardin replied crossly.

"I'll do it now." The words came quietly, harmless in and of themselves, but the tone of Dancer's voice and the look in his eye spoke volumes.

Cliff Hardin scowled blackly as he sent Man Who Walks after a shovel, convinced that if he pushed the half-breed another inch, he'd have to kill him. And kiss the reward goodbye.

Hardin and his men squatted on their heels, guns drawn, while Dancer dug her grave. Remo Davis smoked one cigarette after another, while Baldy Johnson and Man Who Walks passed a bottle back and forth. Cliff Hardin never took his eyes off Dancer's back.

When the hole was deep enough, Dancer knelt beside Storm Woman's body. With gentle hands, be brushed the dirt from her dress, tenderly wiped the blood from her face. And all the time he was remembering—remembering the good times they had shared in Shadow Valley, the way she had always come running to meet him whether he'd been gone an hour or a week, the night he had made love to her. He had been happy with Storm Woman, at peace for the first time in his life. She had been a good companion, cheerful, tolerant of his moods, eager to please him in every way. And now she was dead, and he was to blame.

Wrapping her body in a blanket, he held her close one last time, plagued by a terrible sense of loss. A burning pain tore at his throat as he placed her in the shallow grave, carefully shoveled the soft brown earth over her still form, painstakingly smoothed the dirt. That done, he collected several large rocks and placed them over the grave to protect it from predators. If only he could have protected her from Hardin, he mused bitterly, burdened by grief such as he had never known.

Brushing the dirt from his hands, he picked up the shovel, only to stand staring down at her final resting place, unable to believe she was really dead.

"Drop the shovel, Dancer."

Hardin's deep bass voice pierced the night, and when there was no response to his command, he stood up, jacking a shell into the breech of his rifle. The rasp of the Winchester's mechanism was very loud in the quiet of the night.

Dancer turned stiffly toward the sound, his knuckles white around the handle of the shovel.

"I said drop it!" Cliff snarled. It was time to re-establish his authority, time to remind the prisoner, and his own men, who was the boss.

"You gonna kill me, Cliff, and lose all that money?" Dancer asked disdainfully. "I doubt it."

"You willing to bet your life on it, Dancer man?" Hardin countered. "Besides, you might not die from a gut wound, but you'd sure wish you had!"

Hardin's expression changed from anger to

smug satisfaction as he added, "I don't think the judge'll care what shape you're in, so long as you're still breathin'."

Dancer's eyes narrowed thoughtfully as he considered Hardin's words. Cliff was an adversary to be reckoned with, especially with Johnson and Davis standing there watching his every move. Hardin could not afford to make idle threats, not if he wanted to maintain his position as head honcho. The first time he displayed the slightest trace of weakness or indecision, he was finished as their leader.

The cool hand of caution tempered Dancer's anger. The chance of escape, slim as it was, would disappear entirely if he took a bullet in the belly. With a sigh of resignation, he dropped the shovel.

"Johnson, find some rope and tie him up," Hardin growled. "Davis, put the coffee on. You." He nodded in Dancer's direction. "Turn around and put your hands behind your back."

Perversely, Dancer held his ground, thoroughly fed up with Cliff Hardin's orders and his insufferable arrogance.

"I said turn around, squaw lover."

It was the wrong thing to say. Dancer's gray eyes blazed like twin coals in hell, radiating a white-hot hatred, and the force of his gaze was like touching a match to gunpowder. Hardin's volatile temper exploded. With an oath, he reversed the rifle in his hands, swinging it like a club. The heavy walnut stock caught Dancer low in the belly.

Grunting with pain, Dancer doubled in half, his arms folded across his stomach as he waited for the worst of the pain to pass. Then, moving quickly, he jerked upright, lunged forward, and powered his clenched right fist into Hardin's jaw.

Hardin grunted with pain and surprise, the rifle flying from his hand as he staggered back, shaking his head to clear it. A second blow followed the first, and then a third as Dancer unleashed the pent-up fury and sorrow that churned deep inside, demanding release.

Seeing that Hardin was losing the fight, Johnson and Davis sprang into action, drawing Dancer's anger, giving Cliff Hardin a chance to crawl away and catch his breath.

Johnson tried to pin Dancer's arms to his sides, but it was like trying to harness a whirlwind until Davis picked up the shovel and struck the half-breed across the back, hard. The blow drove the breath from Dancer's body and he went to his knees, gasping for air.

Hardin staggered to his feet, massaging his battered jaw. "Hold the 'breed right there," he said hoarsely. He cocked his fist, and Davis and Johnson quickly moved to either side of Dancer, grinning expectantly.

"Shit, I've got a better way to take the sand outta his craw," Hardin rasped. "Tie him to that tree yonder. I'll be right back."

Dancer shuddered imperceptibly as a warning chill snaked down his spine. Davis drew his sixgun and pressed the barrel against Dancer's left ear.

"Hug the tree, half-breed," Remo purred, and Dancer did as he was told, resting his head against the cool bark while Johnson secured his hands around the broad trunk.

"You're in for real trouble now," Man Who Walks promised. "Hear that? It's the boss, shaking out his cat."

In spite of himself, Dancer shivered, his fingers digging into the bark of the tree as his body tensed with dreadful anticipation. Behind him, he could hear Cliff snapping the whip, getting the feel of it.

Too soon, the wait was over. There was a sharp whistling sound as the lash slithered through the air to land with sickening force on his back, biting through cloth and flesh, driving the breath from his body.

Again and again the whip fell across his back, bringing white-hot agony. He felt his skin split under the crushing blows, felt the warm rivers of blood course down his back. Clenching his teeth against the excruciating pain, he summoned every ounce of self-control he possessed to keep his tongue silent and his mouth shut.

His body jerked convulsively as the whip played its song endlessly over his back and shoulders until it seemed he had always stood thus, helpless, mindless, unable to escape the burning flame that danced relentlessly over his shrinking flesh. And then, when he thought he must scream or die, merciful velvet blackness swirled between his cringing flesh and the pain and he drifted into oblivion on an ebony sea that carried him away from all thought, from all feeling.

Hardin coiled the whip as the unconscious Dancer slid slowly to his knees. With a satisfied nod of his head, he handed the whip to Man Who Walks.

"He won't be giving us any more trouble," Hardin said confidently. "Let's get some sleep."

Morning. Dancer came slowly, achingly, awake. Hugging a tree was not the best way to spend a night, he mused sourly. His arms and legs were stiff, cramped, his throat dry as the Arizona desert. The slightest movement unleashed incredible agony across his back and shoulders, and he cursed himself for defying Hardin. What had he hoped to gain?

He groaned softly, searching his mind for something to focus on besides the terrible fire that engulfed his back, and Jesse came unbidden to mind. Jesse, with her lush golden body and hair like smooth silk. Jesse, laughing softly, her sparkling sea-green eyes half-closed in passion, yielding sweetly as she whispered that she loved him....

Man Who Walks squatted on his heels beside Hardin, prodding the sleeping man in the ribs with his finger. "Cliff?"

Hardin woke instantly, scowling his annoyance at being disturbed. "What do you want?"

"You did a hell of a job on the 'breed's back," the Indian remarked. "Such a hell of a good joh, I'm not sure he'll be able to fork a bronc today. And maybe not tomorrow."

"He'll ride," Hardin said succinctly. "You do what you can for him while I get Davis to plant Miller." He glanced up at the sky. "It's early yet. If we ride hard, we can be home late tonight."

Man Who Walks whistled a mournful tune as he went to cut the half-breed loose. Dancer cringed as the Indian smeared a handful of bear grease over his back and shoulders, then bandaged his back with strips of cloth torn from one of Miller's extra shirts. Waves of nausea assailed him each time the Indian touched him.

With a shrug, Man Who Walks bound Dancer's hands together, then stood up. He'd done all he could.

An hour later, Hardin nudged his prisoner in the ribs. "Get up, you," he growled. "We've wasted enough time here."

Dancer stood cautiously, swaying unsteadily on his feet as the world spun out of focus. Davis led the dun forward and Dancer grabbed hold of the saddle horn and climbed slowly, painfully, into the saddle, each movement bringing added torment.

Sitting there, his back a solid sheet of flame, he silently upbraided himself for riling Cliff

Hardin, vehemently cursed J. D. Clayton for having fathered a pig-headed son, damned Elkhorn for a black-hearted traitor. Elkhorn! He should have killed the sneaky bastard when he had the chance. Damn! What a mess.

His thoughts turned to J. D. Clayton. Just what did the old man have in store for him?

Man Who Walks was the last man in the saddle. Swinging aboard his big calico mustang, he caught up the dun's reins and fell in behind Hardin's chestnut stud.

It was going to be a long, long day, Dancer thought bitterly, but it was one he never clearly remembered. It was lost in the bright haze of pain that clouded his mind, blinding him to everything but the memory of a freshly turned grave hastily dug in the midst of a lonely trail.

Twelve hours later, they rode under the elaborately carved double arch of the J Bar C Ranch.

Chapter 19

Judge J. D. Clayton sat up in his big four-poster bed, sleepily brushed the hair from his eyes with the back of his hand. Had he dreamed it, or was someone knocking at the front door? Listening, he heard it again, louder and more insistent.

Striking a match with his thumbnail, he regarded the clock on his bedside table. It was near eleven. Grumbling, he lit the lamp and climbed out of bed, swore aloud as he stubbed his toe against a chair. Still muttering crossly, he reached for his robe, shrugged it on as he stomped downstairs, threw open the massive oak door.

Pete Akins, foreman of the J Bar C, stood on the porch wiping sleep from his eyes.

"Well, what is it, Pete?" Clayton rumbled. "It's nigh on to eleven o'clock."

"You said you wanted to know the minute Hardin got back. Well, he's here, and he's got that gunfighter with him."

The old man's jaw dropped, then a slow smile spread over his leathery face. Dancer, here at last. Hot damn!

* * *

Hardin sent the others to unsaddle the horses and shake out the bedrolls while he waited for the judge. Lighting a cigarette, he felt the tension of the past weeks drain out of him like water through a sieve. It was good to be back on the home place, and he grinned as he contemplated the fat reward coming his way. He'd earned his money this time, he mused ruefully. Bringing the half-breed in had cost him two good men and a lot of aggravation.

Still mounted on the dun gelding, Dancer surveyed Clayton's domain through eyes dulled with pain and fatigue. A brilliant yellow moon hung low in the sky, highlighting a massive two-story house situated atop a small rise some two hundred yards away.

The whole place reeked of great wealth and the power it could buy. Power to control land and water and votes. Power to influence congressmen and lawmen. Power to buy anything the world had to offer. Including people, Dancer mused bleakly. He, himself, was proof of that.

Hardin ground out his cigarette with his boot heel. "Wonder what the old man has in store for you," he remarked casually. "Bound to be something special, I reckon, considering the trouble and expense he's gone to."

"I don't suppose I'll get a trial?"

"Already had one. The judge found you guilty as hell."

Dancer grunted. "Guess there's no point in saying I shot the kid in self-defense."

Hardin chuckled as he rolled another smoke. "You know, we heard it was self-defense, but J. D. didn't see it that way. He figures it was murder, nothing less, on account of you're a famous shootist and Johnny was just a green kid."

Dancer made a sound of disgust low in his throat. "For a kid, he was packing a hell of a weapon. And he sure as hell knew how to use it."

"Yeah, he was good," Hardin agreed. "I taught him everything he knew."

Dancer nodded, grimacing as a sharp pain cut across his back, followed by a creeping numbness that started between his shoulder blades and slowly worked its way down toward his waist. He smiled grimly. Clayton would be executing a corpse if he waited too long.

Hardin snuffed out his cigarette, stood away from the corral. "Here comes the old man now," he murmured, and Dancer detected a grudging note of respect in Cliff's tone.

J. D. Clayton strode briskly into view, exuding wealth and power. He cut a commanding figure as he stood in the moonlight, his vast bulk swathed in a red silk robe, his feet encased in black leather slippers. A mane of shaggy white hair framed a face the color and texture of old saddle leather. Crystal blue eyes, like chips of cut glass, scrutinized Dancer from head to foot.

"So this is the jasper that gunned Johnny down, eh?" he boomed. "What the hell's the matter with him? He looks half dead."

"He gave us a little trouble on the trail," Hardin explained with a shrug. "I had to work him over some."

"Some!" Clayton repeated harshly. His frigid blue eyes bored into Cliff Hardin, and there was no mistaking the menace in that cold stare, or the barely controlled anger in his voice. "I will hold you personally responsible if this man dies before I am ready to see him dead. Is that clear?"

"He ain't gonna die, boss," Hardin assured the judge. "He's tougher than a nickel steak."

"He'd better be," Clayton retorted. "Because if he dies, you die. Is *that* clear?"

Hardin nodded, his expression sullen.

Clayton stared at Dancer, a small smile of satisfaction playing over his lips. He had never doubted that, sooner or later, Dancer would be his. He had built a special cage to hold his son's murderer, had planned his revenge very carefully. And now, at last, he was about to put those plans in motion.

"Pete will show you where to put the 'breed. Have Willow Woman look after his wounds. You and I will settle up in the morning."

So saying, Clayton turned on his heel and walked swiftly up the hill to the big white house. Inside, he filled a water glass with double-bonded bourbon, sighed with pleasure as the smooth amber liquid mingled with his satisfaction at having his son's killer in custody at last.

Pouring himself another drink, he raised the glass in a silent toast to the smiling photograph of the son he had idolized.

"I'll make him pay, Johnny boy," he vowed. "He'll rue the day he tangled with the Clayton family."

The cage stood atop a small grassy knoll. A stand of timber rose to the west, a square wooden building was at the foot of the rise.

"That's where the chain gang sleeps," Hardin said as he pulled Dancer from the back of his horse. "You'll be one of 'em as soon as your back heals up." He removed a large brass key from his pocket and unlocked the cage door. "Get in."

Dancer stared at the cage with loathing. He had never liked small rooms, small houses.

Hardin gave the half-breed a shove. "Get in."

Dancer entered the cage with great reluctance. It was small, rectangular in shape, made of thick iron bars, and reminiscent of a jail cell except that the top, bottom, and all four sides were covered with wood, limiting his vision to what he could see through the narrow, iron-barred door.

He turned to face Hardin, and it was then he saw the hanging rope swinging from a tall tree.

A wry grin twisted Dancer's lips. *Subtle*, he mused, *very subtle*.

"Lay down and make yourself comfortable," Hardin ordered brusquely. "Willow Woman's coming to take a look at your back." Cliff snorted derisively. "The Old Man thinks she can work miracles."

With great care, Dancer stretched out on the wooden floor, his gaze drawn toward the rope. He'd never figured to hang, he mused bleakly. It was a bad way to die.

Moments later, he heard the sound of a wagon, and then an old woman stepped into the cage. She wore a shapeless red dress and moccasins. Two long gray braids fell over her shoulders.

Ignoring Hardin, Willow Woman put her flowered carpet bag on the floor, then knelt beside Dancer.

Reaching into her bag, she withdrew a pair of scissors and cut Dancer's hands free. Lifting his shirt, she began cutting away the dirty strips of cloth swathed around his midsection.

Her eyes widened and she made a soft clucking sound when she saw the results of Hardin's handiwork.

Dancer's back was a mass of ugly red welts and scabbed-over lacerations. One area near his waist was yellow with infection.

Working efficiently, she poured water into the bowl and began to sponge the dried blood and dead skin from the prisoner's back, paying particular attention to the area around the festering cut.

Dancer grunted softly, his hands curling around the iron bars, his knuckles turning white, as the woman meticulously cleaned his back. He shuddered each time she touched him.

When his back was thoroughly clean, Willow Woman withdrew a long-bladed knife from her bag and Dancer sucked in a deep breath, knowing she intended to lance the festering wound in his back, and that it was going to hurt like hell.

He groaned softly as the keen-edged blade pierced his flesh, releasing a stream of thick, foul-smelling pus and dark red blood. Sweat ran down his face, oozed from every pore.

Reaching into her bag yet again, the old woman withdrew a tiny bottle of ointment prepared by her own hand. Dancer grasped the iron bars tighter as she began to smear the pungent salve over his back and shoulders. His back began to tingle, then burn, as she spread the thick concoction across his mutilated flesh, and he began to tremble uncontrollably. And then, when he thought he must scream or die, the pain subsided, magically extinguished by an ancient Indian remedy.

She did work miracles, Dancer thought as he watched the old woman gather her belongings and stuff them back in the bag.

"No shirt," the woman said, rising to her

feet. She sent a warning glance at Hardin. "No work."

She left the cage without a backward glance.

"Old crone," Hardin muttered as he locked the door, and then he, too, rode away, leaving Dancer alone with his thoughts.

Chapter 20

Six days passed and he saw no one except the frightened-looking man who brought him his meals morning and evening.

Six days. They were the longest six days of his life. He prowled the cage restlessly. All his life he'd been free, free to come and go as he pleased. He had been born to sunlit skies and endless horizons, had grown up free in a way white men were never free.

Time dragged. Anger festered deep in his soul, bitterness as black as the bowels of hell took hold of him, pushing him to the brink of despair.

Hour after hour, day after day, he paced, restless as a caged tiger. Three long strides carried him from one end of his prison to the other.

He spent his days yearning for his freedom, hungry for the sight of cool forest streams and vast sunlit prairies, haunted by the memory of snow-capped mountains and tall timber.

And always the noose drew his eyes, reminding him that his days were numbered. Sometimes he stared at the rope in grim fascination, trying to imagine what it would be like to feel the rough hemp around his neck as he waited for the awful moment when the horse would be whipped out from under him. If he was lucky, the fall would break his neck; if not . . . he shuddered as he imagined himself gagging and choking as he slowly strangled to death.

But as bad as the days were, the nights were worse. His dreams were troubled, filled with old ghosts, haunted by the skeletal images of the men he had killed. Sometimes he dreamed of Jesse, beautiful, golden-haired Jesse. He would see her smile, and then he would hear her prophetic words whispering in the back of his mind as she predicted that he would die a lonely old man. Well, he was lonely, sure enough.

Sometimes, as now, his dreams were filled with images of Storm Woman. He would see her dark eyes filled with pain and fear, her chest covered with blood, one hand outstretched in silent entreaty as her lifesblood flowed from the killing wound in her back.

"I promise," Dancer murmured, tossing restlessly on the hard wooden floor. "Blood for blood, a life for a life."

He woke with a strangled cry to find a girl of perhaps seven or eight staring at him through wide, sapphire blue eyes.

"What are you doing here, girl?" Dancer asked.

"Everyone on the ranch is talking about

you," she answered candidly. "I wanted to come see you for myself."

"Well, you've seen me, now get lost."

The girl cocked her head to one side. "Why did you murder my Uncle Johnny?"

"I didn't murder him," Dancer protested wearily.

"My grandpa says you did."

"Who the hell are you, anyway?" Dancer asked, hoping to change the subject.

"Lizzie Clayton," she answered proudly.

The old man's granddaughter. Fancy that.

"Grandpa's awful mad at you because you killed Uncle Johnny." She stared at him for a minute, as if considering the wisdom of her next question before asking, in a small voice, "Does it hurt to die?"

"Sometimes," Dancer replied honestly. He glanced at the bars that surrounded him, thinking sometimes it was more painful to live.

"Did it hurt when my Uncle Johnny died?"

"No, kid, it didn't hurt."

"Are you afraid to die?"

"No." He grinned under her solemn appraisal. "Shouldn't you be home in bed?"

Lizzie shrugged. "I wasn't sleepy. Are you?"

"No."

"Good! Shall I tell you a story?"

"Why not?"

Pleased, she folded her hands in her lap and told him, in spritely fashion, a story about a fairy princess and a frog who dreamed of being a king.

"And," she finished, "they lived happily ever after."

Dancer grinned. "I'm glad you came to see me, kid. You're like a wildflower in a patch of weeds, but you'd better vamoose before someone misses you."

"Okay," Lizzie said agreeably. "Good night."

"Good night."

He stared after her for a long time, and when he closed his eyes, he heard a small voice asking, *Does it hurt to die,* and then he heard Jesse's voice predicting that he'd die a lonely old man, and he wished suddenly that Clayton would hang him and get it over with.

The old Indian woman came with a fresh dressing for his back the following morning. Hardin stood watch, lounging against a tree a few yards away, a rifle cradled in the crook of his arm.

Dancer stretched out on the hard wooden floor while the old woman peeled away the soiled bandages, then lightly ran her gnarled fingers over his back and shoulders, judging by look and feel and smell how well he was healing.

"Will I live, old woman?" Dancer asked, speaking Comanche.

"For now," she answered, her voice pitched for his ears, and his alone.

"Now's all I've got," Dancer replied fatalistically.

"Your Comanche is very good," Willow Woman remarked. "Are you of the People?"

"Yes. Lame Eagle is my grandfather. I am called Buffalo Dancer."

"Lame Eagle was yet a young man when I was captured by the whites," she said softly. She sighed as she began to coat his back and shoulders with her magical salve.

"You will have many scars," she informed him, "but you are strong and will soon heal. I should not be talking to you," she confided with a shrug. "Clayton has forbidden it. He is filled with rage because you killed his son. He will destroy you when he feels you have suffered enough."

Dancer nodded. "I don't suppose you could bring me a weapon?"

"I will not be allowed to come here again," she said with regret, and then she grinned. "If I could get a weapon, don't you think I would have killed him by now?" Dancer sat up and she touched his cheek, her expression suddenly sad. "I had a young son when I was captured by Clayton's men. They killed him, and my husband, too. I like to think my son would have grown straight and tall, as you are."

She looked away quickly, lest he see the tears rising in her eyes. "It is good to see a Comanche face again and speak the language of the People."

Impulsively, Dancer kissed her withered cheek, his arm curling around her frail shoulders. She looked up at him in surprise, a smile lighting her wrinkled face, a trace of deviltry in her eyes.

"Too bad I am not forty years younger," she teased boldly.

Dancer laughed, genuinely amused. "Thank you for your strong medicine, *kaku*," he said, using the Comanche term for grandmother.

Willow Woman smiled. "I will pray to the Great Spirit for you," she murmured.

Touched by her concern, Dancer took her tiny, clawlike hand in his and gave it a squeeze. "If I find a way out of this, I'll come back one day and take you home," he promised.

"Come on, you old hag," Hardin called from the doorway. "I've got better things to do than hang around here all day."

Ignoring Hardin, Willow Woman caressed Dancer's cheek. "May the Great Spirit watch over you," she said softly, then, rising to her feet, she walked slowly to the door.

Cliff Hardin did not like being ignored, especially by someone he considered inferior. With an oath, he reached out and grabbed the old woman by the arm and yanked her through the doorway, laughing as she stumbled over a rock and fell to her knees.

Quick as a cat, Dancer lunged toward Hardin, outraged by his rough handling of the old woman, only to come to an abrupt halt when he found himself staring into the business end of Hardin's Winchester.

"Come on, squaw man," Hardin growled. "I'd love an excuse to cut you in two." Sneering, he took a step back, slammed the door to the cage, and locked it with a flourish.

"Chain gang tomorrow, half-breed," Hardin called over his shoulder. "Vacation's over." The sound of his mocking laughter trailed behind him like smoke.

Chapter 21

Jesse sat across the table from Clayton, listening attentively as he told her of the property he had just purchased on the outskirts of Cherry Valley. As he went on, she found herself wondering what drove him to try and own the whole town. He had so much land now, so much money, what could he possibly need with more?

She glanced around the candlelit dining room. Never in her life had she been surrounded by such luxury. The whole house was beautifully and tastefully decorated. Expensive paintings and costly sculptures filled every room. Plush carpets covered the hardwood floors. The furniture was richly carved, heavy, upholstered in fine fabrics. Clayton smoked the most expensive cigars, drank the finest wine and bourbon, wore tailor-made suits and shirts. His boots were the best that money could buy.

He spared no expense where Lizzie was concerned, either. The child had more clothes than she could ever wear, enough shoes and boots and slippers for a dozen children. She had a pony of her own, a shelf full of books, her own paints and an easel, music lessons, and every kind of toy imaginable. No wonder the child was spoiled!

Clayton was equally generous with Jesse. He paid her a lavish salary, enabling her to buy any number of lovely frocks and gowns. She was quite likely to become spoiled herself, she mused. It was so easy to get used to being waited on, to have enough money to buy whatever trinket caught her eye, to have people defer to her simply because she worked for J. D. Clayton, the richest man in the territory.

Clayton had finished speaking and he was looking at Jesse, waiting for her answer.

"I'm sorry, J. D.," she said, grinning sheepishly. "I was daydreaming."

"No matter," Clayton said. His eyes were filled with admiration when he looked at her. "It wasn't important." Rising, he walked around the table and held her chair. "I'm going outside for a smoke."

"Very well. I'll take Lizzie upstairs and help her with her homework."

"Do we have to?" Lizzie complained.

"We have to," Jesse said firmly.

"You do as Jesse tells you, Elizabeth," Clayton said. "I'm paying her good money to turn you into a young lady."

"I know," Lizzie said. With an air of exaggerated resignation, she left the table and went to her room.

Jesse laughed. "I don't know how much of a

lady we'll make of her, but I'm certain she'll make a fine actress."

Jesse lingered in the dining room after Clayton went outside. She had been here for several months now, and she was no closer to finding out what had happened to Dancer than she had ever been. She had tried, as furtively as possible, to question the men who worked on the ranch, but either they knew nothing about Dancer or they weren't talking.

Once, in Cherry Valley, she had overheard two men talking. They had been sitting in the shade near the mercantile store and Jesse had overheard Dancer's name. Ashamed of herself for eavesdropping, she had moved closer, straining to hear what they were saying.

"Heard he'd been gunned down by some bounty hunter," one of the men had said.

"Bound to happen sometime," the other had remarked. "Even a fast gun like Dancer can't live forever."

Jesse had reeled back, unable to believe her ears. Dancer, dead? It was impossible.

Knowing she was asking for trouble if Clayton found out, she approached the two men and asked if they were talking about the half-breed gunman known as Dancer. Yes, they'd assured her, none other.

"He's dead, then?" Jesse had asked.

"Yes, ma'am," one of the men had replied.

But when she pressed them for details, they didn't know anything else. Not where he had died. Not who had killed him. Only that the sheriff had been notified that he had been killed.

She refused to believe it. He could not be dead. Surely she'd know, deep inside, if something had happened to him.

She had sent a wire to Tom, asking him for information, and received a letter in reply. A long letter. In it, Tom informed her that he had indeed received word that Dancer had been killed by a bounty hunter somewhere in the Texas Panhandle. The reward had been paid, but the name of the bounty hunter remained unknown.

Tom went on to say he was sorry for the way things had turned out, and then he had urged her to return to Bitter Creek. He had mentioned his love for her, his hope that she would be his wife.

She had sent him a short reply, saying that she had not yet decided whether she would return to Bitter Creek or not, telling him, briefly, of her life at the Clayton ranch, of her deep affection for Lizzie.

She had read Tom's letter several times in the past few months, still refusing to believe that Dancer was dead.

She frowned as she recalled Clayton's reaction to the news. She had expected him to be angry, outraged because he had been robbed of his revenge, but he had only shrugged and said he was glad the "damned 'breed was dead at last."

J.D.'s words had lacked conviction, and it

was his easy acceptance of Dancer's death that had convinced her Dancer was still alive.

Now, standing in Clayton's lavish dining room, she pondered her future. Clayton was growing more fond of her with each passing day. His affection for her was a complication she had not counted on when she agreed to work for him. In truth, she liked him well enough, as a friend and an employer, nothing more. But she was beginning to think he wanted more than her friendship. He had made no overt passes at her, but he often caressed her with his eyes, and sometimes he held her hand or touched her shoulder in a way that told her more clearly than words that he found her desirable.

With a sigh, she wondered what she'd do if Clayton tried to seduce her. She had grown terribly fond of Lizzie, and, if she was going to be honest, she had grown fond of living in luxury, too. It was so nice to be waited on, to know that she had only to ask for something and it would be provided.

But she could not marry Clayton. She didn't love him. Nor could she marry Tom. She wanted Dancer, only Dancer, and he was the one thing all Clayton's money could not buy her.

But she would not give up hope, not yet. Telling herself that everything would be all right, she went upstairs to help Lizzie with her homework.

But later, when she was lying alone in her

big canopy bed with the covers drawn up to her chin, Jesse's thought again turned to Dancer. Where was he? Did he ever think of her? Had he gone back to Bitter Creek to look for her? What if he were truly dead?

She shook the thought away. Closing her eyes, she summoned his image to mind: hair as black as Satan's heart, eyes as gray as a stormy sky, skin the color of freshly turned earth. Even now, after so many months had passed, she could recall the fire in his eyes when he looked at her, the taste of his lips on hers, the way her body had instantly responded to his touch.

He could not be dead.

She could not bear to think she would never see him again. She remembered his easy strength, the wariness that had been as much a part of him as the color of his eyes. She could not make herself believe that he had been bushwhacked. No, he was alive and well, hiding out someplace. Sooner or later, someone would see him and notify Clayton. And she would be here when news of his whereabouts came.

Until then, she would continue to host Clayton's parties and teach Lizzie how to be a proper lady.

She felt sleep closing in on her and, as always, her last thoughts were for Dancer. Where was he now? Did he think of her at all?

Chapter 22

The chain gang. Dancer viewed them with a mixture of fear and pity. Ten men, if they could still be called men. Mostly Mexicans. Clayton hired them from the territorial prison. It was an arrangement that benefited both the warden and the judge, padding the warden's pockets with a little extra cash while providing Clayton with a steady stream of cheap labor.

The prisoners were overworked and underfed, and if one died, or was killed, no one cared. Heavy leg irons hugged their ankles, and when the day's work was done, the men were shackled leg to leg, discouraging individual attempts to escape during the night.

The lucky ones died.

The men looked up only briefly as Dancer was added to their number. If they wondered why his hands were shackled as well as his feet, they gave no evidence of it. Curiosity had gone the way of pride and self-respect, annihilated by hunger and brutality, and the swift punishment of the lash.

One of the guards thrust an axe into Dancer's hands as he barked out the rules of the gang:

no talking, ten minutes rest every two hours, no trips for water, or anything else, without permission.

Any hope Dancer had of escape shriveled and died as he studied the three guards who would rule his life in the days to come. They were all big men, each well over six feet tall, each packing over two hundred pounds of solid muscle.

The guard known as Dirty Tom was a Negro, with kinky jet-black hair and hostile brown eyes. A jagged scar, souvenir of a riverboat knife fight, ran the length of one ebony arm.

A. J. was built like a bull buffalo, with massive shoulders, a shock of shaggy blond hair, pale blue eyes, and a nose that proudly advertised it had been broken more than once.

Smith had a face that could have been carved from granite, all lines and angles, with no trace of softness or humor.

They were all men in their prime, hard as nails and good at their work. Each man packed a Colt .45 in a tied-down holster, and a six-foot rawhide whip that could gently brush a fly from a horse's ear, or flay a man's flesh to the bone.

It didn't take long for Dancer to realize that Clayton had warned the guards of dire consequences if he escaped. Each day one guard watched Dancer, and only Dancer. And that guard was always armed with a sawed-off Greener, to remind Dancer they meant business.

* * *

Spring was in the air and Dancer took a deep breath, filling his lungs with the sweet fragrance of earth. Wildflowers, pink and yellow and white, grew in colorful abundance on the outskirts of the heavily wooded forest away off in the distance. Lord, it was good to see trees again! Good to see bright blue sky and billowy white clouds. Good to feel the sun on his back. And yet, in some ways, being out in the open was harder to bear than confinement in the cage for it only increased his desire to be free.

"Get to work, Comanche!" Smith barked sourly, and with practiced ease laid the lash across the half-breed's back, smirking at the look of defiance that blazed in the prisoner's eyes.

"We'll soon take the fight out of you," the guard promised with smug assurance. He jerked a callused thumb toward one of the convicts working alongside Dancer. "A month, maybe two, three at the most, and you'll be nothing but a cowering animal, just like the others."

A chill ran down Dancer's spine as he took a good look at the convicts. Their expressions were blank, dead, as if they had lost the power to hope for anything but death, to feel anything but pain. *How long,* he wondered, *how long had it taken to reduce them to the pitiful creatures he saw now? How many months of captivity, how many beatings, to strip them of their manhood?*

Fear's clammy hand twisted around Dancer's insides. How long would it take until he became one of them?

He swung the heavy axe rhythmically, his thoughts turned inward as he reflected on the events that had brought him to this place. He had been seventeen when he killed his first white man. Seventeen and he had discovered he had an uncanny feel for guns, a natural ability that came as easy as breathing. Practice had perfected his draw, steadied his aim. Sure of his ability, he had faced every challenge eagerly, knowing somehow that he could not be beat, not while he was in his prime. He had liked being a gunfighter, liked the risk that made each day sweeter because it might be his last. You never knew, not when you were a gunfighter.

There were disadvantages to the life he had chosen, of course, one of them being that you could never really trust anyone, never knowing when a supposed friend might decide the price on your hide was worth more than your friendship. But he had been a loner by nature, and friends and family only tied a man down. He had gone through life like a bat out of hell, uncaring and untouched by those around him, content to come and go as he pleased and to hell with the rest of the world.

Until Jesse. Stopping to care for her that day had been his undoing, though he hadn't realized it at the time. She had been the first crack in his armor.

But it had been Storm Woman's needless

death that had wrought the final change, resurrecting emotions and passions he had thought long dead. Anger, guilt, remorse, grief, all had been reborn as he held her, dying, in his arms.

Jesse and Storm Woman. They had burrowed into his heart, making him care for someone other than himself.

He stared at his shackled hands, at the leg irons that shortened his stride and tarnished his soul. Bitterness churned inside him and his eyes grew dark, cold as a wintry night, reflecting the depths of his inner turmoil.

Recognizing the dangerous glint in the half-breed's eyes, Smith tilted the shotgun upward until it was leveled at Dancer's midriff.

"You're not thinking of causing any trouble, are you?" the guard asked dubiously.

Dancer stared at Smith for a long time, and then shook his head. He had trouble enough.

Slowly the months slipped by. Clayton's visits to the chain gang, once as regular as clockwork, tapered off until Dancer began to hope the old man had lost interest in him, in which case the guards might relax their constant vigil and he might yet escape.

But no opportunity presented itself, and after a couple of months he found himself drowning in despair.

Tonight he felt the cage closing in on him. From the guard shack, he heard one of the prisoner's cry out in his sleep. It was a haunting cry, filled with anguish, and Dancer shuddered.

Death held no terror for him; he had faced it too often in the past to be afraid of it now, but the thought of becoming like the other prisoners chilled him to the depths of his soul. They were all dead inside, stripped of everything that made a man a man, leaving only a pathetic craven shell in human form.

How long did it take to reduce a man to an animal?

How long had he been here?

A tide of anger washed over him. Dammit! If Clayton was going to kill him, why in hell didn't he do it and get it over with? Surely death would be infinitely preferable to sleeping in a cage, shackled hand and foot, whipped daily like a damned dog!

Death. He had pondered it often in the last few months. He thought of the white man's belief in heaven and hell and knew that, according to that philosophy, he would surely be damned. The Comanche view of the afterlife was more to his liking. The People believed that everyone went to heaven. It was not a reward for having lived a good life on earth, although it was believed that a warrior who died defending the People, or women who had died in childbirth, might receive special consideration in heaven. The only thing that could keep a man out of heaven was having his hair cut off after he was dead. Comanche males were very vain about their hair, and it was never cut, except perhaps to express a deep grief. Scalping annihilated the human spirit; death by night made it doubtful if the soul could find its way to heaven. Mutilation of the dead was an act of vengeance because it was believed that the dead would be so deformed in the next life.

Death. No matter how it came to him, he thought he would welcome it. Better to spend eternity hunting spirit buffalo than live in a cage with no hope of escape.

"Pst, Dancer?" The muffled voice came from his left and he twisted around, peering into the darkness.

A small, slim shape separated itself from the shadows. It was Lizzie Clayton.

He'd never been so glad to see anyone in his life. "Hi, kid."

Her smile was brighter than the sun. "Hi." She moved closer to the cage door, her smile fading when she saw the raw red welt on his cheek. "They treat you mean, don't they? A. J. and Smith and the dark man?"

"Sometimes."

A single tear glistened in the corner of her eye.

"Hey," Dancer admonished lightly. "No one's ever cried for me before. Don't you be the first." Awkwardly, he reached between the bars and wiped the tear away. "Come on, kid, give me a smile."

Lizzie obligingly rewarded him with a crooked grin. Head tilted to one side, she asked, "Are you really an Indian, like Willow Woman?"

"Yeah, a Comanche," Dancer acknowledged, and then, because she asked, he told her about the People, and how they lived. How the women and dogs had carried the lodges on their backs before the Indians had horses. He told her of war dances and friendship dances, of sacred rites and ancient traditions, of long winter nights and sweet summer days, and as he talked, he was overcome with a terrible longing to see Shadow Valley once more before he died. To see the sun climb in all its golden splendor over the dark purple mountains, to swim in the placid stretch of river behind his lodge, to speak with his grandfather, to hunt the buffalo with Yellow Hand and the other warriors, to make love to Jesse . . . Oh, Lord, how he ached for Jesse.

"I'd like to see the Comanche," Lizzie said, her eyes aglow with excitement. "Could you teach me to talk like an Indian? I asked Willow Woman to teach me, but she said Grandpa wouldn't like it."

"Sure, kid, if you want to learn."

"How do you say grandpa in Comanche?"

"*Tawp*."

"*Tawp*." Lizzie repeated the word.

"You'd better get back to your *tawp*'s house before they miss you."

"Okay," Lizzie said. "Bye."

She came to see him often after that, whenever she could sneak out of the house. She brought him friendship and laughter, and after he mentioned one night that he was hungry, she brought him food. Cake and pie, cold chicken, thick slices of roast beef a loaf of bread, an apple, whatever she could safely smuggle out of the kitchen.

Surrounded by ugliness and cruelty and scowling faces, Lizzie's radiant countenance was like a breath of spring on a wintry day, reminding him that there was still beauty in the world.

He didn't know why she liked him, or why she had decided to befriend him, but he looked forward to her midnight visits, grateful for her cheerful company, for her ability to make him laugh and forget, if only for a little while, the utter misery in which he lived.

Jesse stared at the ceiling, unable to sleep. Four months had passed and she had heard nothing of Dancer. Where was he? Dancer, Dancer, he haunted her dreams and filled her waking moments, as well.

Rising, she drew on a long yellow wrapper and went to stand at the window. She guessed the time to be close to midnight. The ranch was peaceful, quiet. Gazing out into the moon-dappled yard, she realized how much she had come to love this place, and Lizzie. She spent most of her waking hours with the child, and the two of them had become good friends. Lizzie was a winsome child, eager to learn, eager to please. Clayton was amazed by the girl's progress, and he showered Jesse with gifts and praise. Often, she caught him watching her, his blue eyes alight, his expression thoughtful. She told herself she was being foolish, that the man was old enough to be her father, but she could not ignore the flare of desire she sometimes saw in his eyes, nor dismiss the fact that he found any number of excuses to touch her arm, her shoulder, her cheek.

Troubled by thoughts of Dancer, and by a growing fear that Clayton was becoming overly fond of her, she left her room and went downstairs to the kitchen, hoping a cup of hot tea would relax her so she could sleep.

Nearing the kitchen, she frowned when she saw a light burning. On tiptoe, she approached the open door and peered inside.

"Lizzie! What on earth are you doing up at this hour?"

Lizzie whirled around, her cheeks flushed with guilt as she tried to hide a small burlap bag behind her back.

"What are you hiding?" Jesse asked, stepping into the room.

"Nothing," Lizzie answered quickly.

"Lizzie."

"If I tell you, will you promise not to tell Grandpa?"

"Lizzie, I can't keep secrets from your grandfather. I work for him."

"Please, Jesse."

"Very well, I promise. Now what are you hiding in that sack?"

"It's just some ham left over from dinner," Lizzie said, handing the sack to Jesse.

"Just some ham," Jesse exclaimed, looking inside the bag. "Lizzie, you've got six slices of ham, half a loaf of bread, two apples, and a piece of chocolate cake."

Lizzie shrugged. "I know."

Jesse sighed with exasperation. "What are you going to do with all this food?"

"There's a man in a cage," Lizzie said, the words coming in a rush. "He's lonely and unhappy. And hungry. He needs me, Jesse. I take him food almost every night."

A man in a cage. Good Lord. "Lizzie, who is this mysterious man?"

"He works on the chain gang."

"Chain gang!" Jesse exclaimed in horror. "What chain gang?"

Lizzie stared at Jesse. "Don't you know anything? They're prisoners who work for Grandpa, cutting trees and doing stuff the cowboys won't do."

"How did you meet this man? Not out on the range, certainly."

Lizzie looked down at the floor, her hands twisting together nervously. "I heard the cowboys talking about him and I . . ." She sent an anxious glance in Jesse's direction. "I wanted to see what he looked like. He lives in a cage." Lizzie smiled shyly. "He told me I was like a breath of spring."

Jesse's hand went to her heart. Merciful

heavens, was the man trying to seduce the child!

"Lizzie, darling, if your grandfather finds out what you've been doing, he'll send you East for sure."

Lizzie's eyes grew wide. Before Jesse's arrival at the ranch, her grandfather had often threatened to send her to school in the East if ever she displeased him.

Lizzie didn't really believe he would send her away, but she wasn't willing to find out.

In the end, it was the threat of being sent away to school that finally persuaded Lizzie to do as she was told. Reluctantly, she promised never to visit the man again. With one stipulation. Jesse must go to him that very night and explain why Lizzie couldn't come.

"Very well," Jesse agreed.

"Don't forget this," Lizzie said, scooping up the bag Jesse had dropped on the table. "He'll be hungry."

A short time later, Jesse was riding through the darkness, wondering what on earth had ever possessed her to make such a ludicrous bargain with Lizzie. What could she possibly say if someone should find her riding around in the middle of the night?

The cage was situated on a small rise a goodly distance from the house. Dismounting, she left her horse tethered to a tree and crossed the last few yards on foot.

As she drew near the cage, she could see a dark figure sitting cross-legged inside. His clothes were ragged, crusted with dirt and dried sweat and dark brown stains that could only be blood. One pant leg was ripped, exposing a long, muscular flank. His hair was long and shaggy; the lower half of his face was concealed by a moustache and a coarse black beard. His shoulders were broad, and she had the impression he was a tall man.

She stopped just out of reach of the man in the cage, wondering what there was about this filthy, bearded man that Lizzie found so fascinating.

Jesse cleared her throat. "Lizzie won't be coming out here anymore," she said bluntly, not looking at him, but at the ground at her feet instead.

Dancer stared at the vision before him, unable to believe his eyes. Had he finally gone completely mad? That could not be Jesse standing there in the moonlight, her cheeks flushed, her hair falling like a honey-colored cloud about her shoulders.

"Jesse." He breathed her name, his voice husky with disbelief.

Jesse lifted her head, her eyes baffled, her heart racing as the man murmured her name again. Dancer! It couldn't be. But it was.

Sobbing his name, she crossed the short distance separating them, her eyes searching his face. It was him. It was really him.

He was reaching between the bars, his hands closing over her shoulders, traveling up her neck to cup her face.

"Jesse, my God, Jesse, what are you doing here?"

"I work for Clayton. I'm Lizzie's governess." She leaned forward, her heart thundering with happiness as he kissed her, and kissed her again.

The burlap bag dropped from her hand as she reached for him, her arms slipping past the bars to wrap around his neck. He was here. He was alive. Thank God.

After a long time, they parted. Breathless, Jesse gazed into his face. "How long have you been here?"

Dancer shook his head ruefully. "I don't know. I've lost track of the time." His eyes filled with the sight of her. He had forgotten how beautiful she was. She looked like an angel, he thought, a golden-haired angel newly fallen from heaven. Her eyes were bluer than he remembered, her skin felt like smooth velvet beneath his callused hands.

"Kiss me again," Jesse murmured, and he willingly obliged. Her hair was like silk, her skin warm, inviting. He took a deep breath and his nostrils filled with the delicate fragrance of lavender soap, and the provocative scent of woman.

After a long while, Dancer took his mouth from hers. "Tell me how you came to be here," he said, his hands sliding up and down her arms.

It was hard to think clearly when he was so close, when she wanted him so desperately.

Taking a deep breath, she told him how she had taken the stage to Cherry Valley, and how she had met Lizzie and Clayton.

"I heard you were dead, but I refused to believe it."

"Clayton put that word out so the bounty hunters would stop looking for me," Dancer said, his voice bitter.

"What right does he have to keep you here? I know you killed his son, but aren't you entitled to a trial?"

Dancer shrugged. "He's a wealthy man, Jesse. He owns the town and just about everybody in it. I don't imagine anyone would argue with Clayton's right to take the law into his own hands."

"I'll go to the sheriff," Jesse said fervently. "Surely he can do something."

"He's Clayton's man. He won't do anything except maybe string me up."

"There has to be something I can do."

"There is," Dancer said. He drew her close and kissed her again, his mouth hard upon hers, his body on fire at her nearness.

Jesse reached through the bars, her arms twining around his waist, slipping under his shirt to caress his back. His tongue was teasing hers, his hands sliding up and down her ribcage, sending shivers of pure delight coursing through her, making her knees weak and her heart sing. He was here. He was alive. Somehow, she would find a way to get him out of that dreadful cage.

A sound from below drew Jesse's attention and she peered around the side of the cage. She could see a shack at the bottom of the incline, and a long line of men who appeared to be sleeping.

"I'm surprised Lizzie was never caught up here," Jesse remarked.

"The guards rarely come up here after dark," Dancer said with a wry grin. "They know I'm not going anywhere."

Jesse nodded, her heart aching as she thought of the long nights he had been forced to spend in such a dismal place.

"I'm sorry I can't let Lizzie come to visit you anymore," she said. "You understand why, don't you?"

"Yeah. I could never figure out why she came out here in the first place."

"She said you needed her, but I suspect the opposite is closer to the truth. Lizzie's father was killed in a snow storm two years ago. She misses him terribly. Her mother died when she was only four. And then Johnny . . ." Jesse's voice trailed off. "I think she needs a father figure."

"Well, she sure picked a strange one," Dancer muttered.

Jesse pressed her head against the bars, her hand on Dancer's thigh, unable to believe he was really here.

There was a clank of chains from below, the sound of voices. She felt Dancer's body tense.

"You'd better go," he said thickly.

"No." She could not bear to leave him.

"Go on, Jesse. It won't do either one of us any good if you get caught here."

She blinked back her tears. He was right, of course, but how could she leave him in such misery?

"I'll come back tomorrow night," she promised.

"No!"

"You don't want me to?"

He groaned low in his throat. "There's nothing I want more, but it's too dangerous for you to be coming here. What if you're caught?"

"You didn't tell Lizzie to stay away."

"She's Clayton's granddaughter, and she's just a kid. If she got caught here, they'd just chalk it up to a childish prank of some kind. But you're a grown woman. What possible excuse could you have for being out here in the middle of the night?"

Jesse nodded. His reasoning made perfect sense. She hated it.

"Go on, Jesse," Dancer urged. He swore as he heard the door to the shack swing open, its hinges squeaking loudly. "Hurry."

She nodded, too choked up to speak. As she turned to leave, her foot hit the burlap bag, dropped and forgotten in the surprise of seeing him. "Here." She shoved the sack through the bars, then hurried into the shadows where she had left her horse.

Dancer stared after her. Jesse was here. Incredible as it seemed, she was here.

* * *

Jesse spent a sleepless night. Every time she closed her eyes, she saw Dancer locked inside that awful cage. His eyes had been haunted and filled with bitterness. And he was thin, so thin. Despite the food Lizzie had been taking him, she could see he had lost a lot of weight. She thought of the hard wooden floor he slept on and felt guilty for sleeping on a soft feather bed between clean sheets. She thought of the filthy clothes he wore, of the unwashed smell that clung to him, and thought of the clean clothes and hot water she took for granted each day. She recalled the sumptuous dinner she had eaten that night, thought of the food that was wasted at every meal, and remembered Lizzie telling her he would be hungry; he was always hungry.

She rose early the next morning. Immediately after breakfast, she instructed Lizzie to do her lessons, and then she left the house. Minutes later she was riding toward that part of Clayton's ranch where Lizzie said the chain gang worked.

She found the prisoners toiling on a stretch of high country grassland, removing decaying timber and stringing wire. Dancer was easy to spot, even from a distance. The other men might shuffle along like so many beasts of burden, but not Dancer. He carried himself erect, head high, eyes looking up and out. He had talked one of the guards into letting him remove his shirt, and sweat ran down his broad chest and heavily muscled arms in muddy rivulets.

Jesse felt a slow heat ignite within her. In spite of his unkempt appearance, he was magnificent. Months of arduous physical labor and scant feed had trimmed away every ounce of excess fat, leaving only taut bronze flesh and corded muscle. Like a well-oiled machine, he swung an axe against the bole of a gnarled pine, the muscles in his back and arms flexing as he swung the heavy blade. She felt a flurry of excitement in the pit of her stomach, stirred by the raw untamed power that emanated from him.

She gasped when he turned away from her, revealing his broad back and shoulders, and the scars that marred his flesh.

While she watched, the guard Smith swaggered over to Dancer and there was a brief exchange between the two men. An order Dancer refused to obey, or just some taunting words, she could not tell, but Dancer's terse reply incurred Smith's wrath. With a vile oath, the guard jerked his whip to life. The rawhide whistled through the air, landing with a sharp crack across Dancer's back where it raised a long red welt.

Dancer flinched, but he held his ground and Jesse silently applauded his quiet defiance, his stubborn refusal to bend.

Smith made an obscene gesture and then stalked away, and Jesse saw Dancer smile bitterly before resuming his work.

And still she remained, studying him, noting that, in spite of the chains that hampered his movements, he carried himself with a kind of stubborn pride, his whole attitude one of unspoken defiance. Whether cutting down a tree or stringing wire, his movements were quick and sure, graceful as a cat's.

She longed to go to him, to wipe the sweat from his brow, to offer him a drink of cold water. She longed to remove the shackles from his hands and feet and wash the dirt from his body, to lie with him in the shade of a tall tree and feel his arms around her, his lips trailing fire as they kissed her hungrily, passionately.

Feeling her persual, Dancer glanced up, the axe suspended in midair as his dark eyes raked her from head to heel. The longing in his eyes brought a flush to Jesse's cheeks, and she wondered if he had somehow divined her thoughts.

So near, he thought, and felt his whole body burn with the need to hold her, to be held by her. She was constantly in his thoughts now; the fact that she was so near was the cruelest kind of torture, like being hungry and unable to eat, or being thirsty and denied water when it was near at hand. He yearned for her by day and dreamed of her at night, dark, sensual dreams that caused him to wake in a sweat, his body weak and aching inside.

The distance between them seemed to shrink as their eyes met and held, his filled with longing, hers filled with determination to free him from captivity.

* * *

Jesse went to the cage that night. Knowing he was there, so near, she could not stay away.

She had expected to find him asleep, but he was sitting up, staring into the darkness.

"Jesse." He breathed her name like a prayer as she pressed against the bars, and then he was kissing her, his mouth hard, his hand closing around her neck to hold her close as though he feared she might slip from his grasp.

"You're hurt," Jesse murmured as they drew apart. Her voice was soft and sympathetic, her eyes filled with compassion.

"I'm fine."

"You're hurt," she insisted.

"Why did you come here tonight?" he asked, his voice harsh with anger. "Do you think I like having you see me like this?" His gaze moved to the iron bars that imprisoned him, to the chains that hampered his every move.

Pain tore at Jesse's heart. She had never realized how humiliating it must be for him to be locked up, how degraded he must feel.

"I'm sorry," she murmured. She had forgotten how proud he was. In her eagerness to see him, to touch him, she had forgotten he had enough pride for ten men. "I won't come here again."

She turned away from the cage, heartsick at the thought of leaving him alone. How could she stay away now that she knew he was here? Now that she'd seen him, touched him? But if her presence caused him distress, she would do as he asked. Difficult as it would be, she would stay away from him.

It was then she saw the noose. It was swaying ever so slowly in the slight breeze. She knew immediately why Clayton had put it there, and she was outraged at the cruelty of it. How many times a day did Dancer stare at that noose and wonder what it would feel like around his neck?

Dancer watched Jesse walk away and it was like saying goodbye to his last reason for living. "Jesse," he called softly. "Don't go!"

Relief washed through her as she hurried back to him. "Don't ever send me away again," she whispered brokenly.

He reached for her, swearing under his breath as the chains on his wrists rattled against the bars. "I'm sorry, Jess."

She leaned against the cage door, content to be held in his arms, to know he needed her.

"Do they beat you very often?" she asked after a while.

"Often enough," he replied bitterly.

"Let me see your back."

"No."

"Please."

Muttering an oath, he turned around, flinching as Jesse lifted his tattered shirt to examine his back.

Even in the moonlight, she could see the old scars, and the fresh red welts that marred his flesh. How many times had he been whipped? How much more could he stand?

"Oh, Dancer," she wailed softly. "How do you bear it?"

"Dammit, Jesse, I . . . hey," he said, turning to face her once more. "Don't cry. For God's sake, don't cry."

"I'll bring something for that tomorrow night," she promised, blinking back her tears.

Dancer grinned wryly. "Yeah, you do that," he said, chuckling softly. "I'm sure A. J. will understand."

She felt a rush of anger. He was hurting and she could do nothing to help him. She couldn't even spread ointment on his back to ease his pain.

Dancer's hands curled over Jesse's shoulders, quietly cursing the bars that kept them apart. He had been long without a woman and it was torture to touch her, to kiss her, to inhale the warm womanly scent of her, and not be able to satisfy the need that plagued him.

Jesse strained toward him, unmindful of the hard iron bars that flattened her breasts as she wrapped her arms around Dancer. He was here, close enough to touch, and yet not close enough. She felt his lips move in her hair, heard his voice whisper her name, and she wished fervently that she could crawl into the cage and comfort him. She longed to kiss away his pain, to erase the bitter discouragement in his eyes, to satisfy the yearning she heard in his voice.

There had to be a way to help him escape from this place, she thought, but she couldn't do it alone and she had no one to turn to for help.

She thought briefly of sending for Tom, but he had no authority in Cherry Valley, and she feared that Clayton might execute Dancer immediately if he suspected that an outsider knew Dancer was still alive. And yet, there had to be a way.

She moaned softly as Dancer claimed a kiss. It was heaven to be in his arms, to feel his lips on hers after so long, and yet it was exquisite agony to have him so near and not be able to love him as she so longed to do.

Such sweet pain, she thought as his hands caressed her. *I wish it could last forever....*

She stayed with him as long as she dared, hating to leave him in the cage, hurt and alone.

She felt his gaze following her until she was out of sight.

Chapter 23

It was a sultry Sunday, the kind of day that made you long for the coolness of winter. J.D. and Lizzie had gone on a picnic, just the two of them, leaving Jesse alone in the house. Bored, she wandered from room to room, looking for something to occupy her hands, but nothing appealed to her. She wished she could ride out to the cage to see Dancer, but she dared not do so in broad daylight.

Exasperated, she grabbed a book of poetry from the shelf, slipped off her shoes and stockings, and padded barefoot down the carpeted stairway, bent on spending a pleasant hour reading down by the lake. As she stepped out the back door, she felt as though she had stepped into a furnace. A blazing sun beat down upon the earth, wilting the flowers and bringing an immediate sheen of perspiration to her face.

She was about to go back into the house when she happened to glance down the road and saw Dancer and Smith standing beside the huge old oak that towered menacingly over the smokehouse. Snarling orders, Smith thrust an axe into Dancer's manacled hands, then moved off to sit in the shade, his shotgun within easy reach.

After a moment, Dancer got down to work, his lean face void of expression as he swung the heavy axe. It was hard, back-breaking work, and within minutes he was sweating profusely.

Jesse sat on the porch rail, her book forgotten. How cruel, she thought angrily, to make him work now, during the hottest part of the day.

A few minutes later, A. J. ambled into the backyard and dropped down beside Smith.

"Thought you were going into town," Smith remarked.

"Later," A. J. said. "It's too damn hot to make that ride now." He jerked his chin in Dancer's direction. "You think he was as fast as they say?"

"Who cares?"

"They say he killed better than twenty men. I've heard some say closer to thirty."

"Well, then," Smith retorted sarcastically, "he sure as hell can't be slow."

"Wish I could have seen him in action just once," A. J. murmured wistfully. "I'll bet he was something to see." He drummed his fingers thoughtfully on the ground as he said, "Hardin's the fastest gun around here. Say, that would be a match. Hardin and the 'breed."

"Maybe you could arrange it," Smith suggested, annoyed by A. J.'s chatter and his endless fascination with guns and gunfighters.

"Maybe I could at that," A. J. mused, mopping the sweat from his brow with a dingy kerchief. "Think Hardin would go for it?"

Smith stared at A. J. as if he'd gone crazy.

"Well, I'm gonna ask him anyway," A. J. decided, rising to his feet. "All he can do is say no."

"That's not all he can do," Smith muttered caustically, but A. J. was already gone.

Twenty minutes later, A. J. was back, with Hardin in tow. Jesse leaned forward, wishing she knew what was going on.

Smith shook his head as he lumbered to his feet and went over to hear what Cliff had to say.

"C'mon, Cliff, it won't take long," A. J. was saying.

"I told you to forget it," Hardin growled. "I just came up here for a cold beer."

"Afraid the 'breed's too fast for ya?" A. J. queried slyly, and Smith shook his head, amazed by his partner's nerve. Hardin was not a man to run afoul of.

But the taunt worked. "Arrange it," Cliff snapped, and stalked off to wait in the shade.

Looking hugely pleased with himself, A. J. approached Dancer.

"Take a break, Comanche," he suggested, and offered the half-breed a thin black cheroot.

Dancer's dark eyes regarded A. J. warily as

he accepted the cigar. Something was up. He could smell it in the air.

The guard smiled affably. "We"—he included Smith and Hardin with a jerk of his head—"been talking about ya, about your rep as a gunslinger. Are you as fast with a .44 as folks say?"

Dancer grinned coldly. "Faster."

Surprised by the half-breed's answer, A. J. blurted, "Did you really cut down George Buck? And the Trenton brothers? I heard you nailed Joe and Hiram before they cleared leather, and then drilled Rufus right between the eyes."

Dancer shrugged. "That was a long time ago."

"But you did it? You really did it?"

"Yeah, I took the Trentons and Buck and a few others. So what?"

"Do you think you could take Hardin?"

"Maybe," Dancer replied softly. His dark eyes glinted with a curious light as his gaze slid in Cliff's direction. "Why?"

"I've got two hundred bucks that says you can take him."

Dancer's black brows rushed together in a frown as he mulled that over. Slowly he blew out a thin column of smoke, his eyes intent upon A. J.'s face. "Just what exactly are you leading up to?"

"A match between you and Hardin," A. J. said, his voice choked with enthusiasm. "It's all arranged. Just like a real shoot-out, except your guns will be empty."

"Naturally," Dancer replied dryly, amused by the genuine note of regret in the guard's voice. It was obvious A. J. would have preferred to see the real thing. "Well, you can take your little shooting match and shove it."

"What? You mean you won't do it?"

"That's exactly what I mean."

"But I gotta chance to win two hundred bucks."

"Yeah? You gonna split it with me?"

A. J. snorted in disgust. "What use have you got for money?"

"About as much use as I've got for you," Dancer retorted curtly.

"Dammit, what would you do it for?"

"A woman, perhaps," Dancer answered, and his gaze slid down the road to where Jesse sat on the porch rail.

"A woman!" A. J. exclaimed. "Dammit, Dancer, how the hell am I gonna get you a woman?"

Dancer shrugged. "That's your problem."

"What else would you do it for?" A. J. asked doggedly. "There must be something else you want? How about a bottle of whiskey, or maybe a box of cigars?"

"No."

"What, then?" He was practically shouting now.

"A bath," Dancer said, returning his gaze to A. J.'s face. "And a shave."

"A bath!" A. J. repeated incredulously. "Are you serious?"

"And a shave. Is it a deal?"

"Hell, yes," A. J. said, stunned by the half-breed's terms. A bath!

"When's this little shooting match supposed to take place?"

"Right now, before the judge gets back. Come on."

Minutes later, Hardin and Dancer faced each other across six feet of sun-washed ground. The animosity between the two men rose like an evil presence in the yard, permeating the atmosphere like smoke, until the day seemed dark and ominous.

Smith and A. J., armed with a shotgun and a .45, stood on either side of Dancer, guns leveled at his chest.

Temporarily freed of his shackles, Dancer buckled A. J.'s gunbelt around his hips, slipped the empty Colt from the holster. The big weapon nestled snugly in his hand, and a flicker of a smile played over his face. Now, for the first time in months, he felt whole again.

From her position on the back porch, Jesse watched in wide-eyed fascination as Dancer hefted the heavy pistol, getting the feel of it, she supposed.

Wanting a better view, she moved from the rail to the top step of the porch and now had a clear view of Dancer's face. Frowning pensively, she recalled the first time she had seen him. He had looked dangerous then, and he looked dangerous now.

Giving the Colt a last spin, Dancer dropped it smoothly into the holster. And now he stood easily, his feet spread ever so slightly, his hands hanging loose at his sides. Completely self-assured, his gray eyes glittered with cynical amusement as he waited for Hardin to make the first move.

Cliff Hardin's countenance was grim, his jaw rigid. Ill-disguised loathing burned in his blue eyes as he glared at the tall half-breed.

Smith and A. J. waited in tense anticipation, bets temporarily forgotten in the excitement of the moment, and Jesse had the distinct impression that all four men were wishing this showdown was the real thing.

Tension stretched like fine wire between the two men standing in the center of the yard, and then, when Jesse thought she would scream with the agony of waiting, Hardin made his move. Swiftly, smoothly, with little wasted motion, his hand streaked for his holster.

Dancer's draw was a blur. The Colt appeared in his hand as if conjured there by magic and he held it, aimed and cocked, before Hardin's gun cleared leather.

With defeat staring him in the face, Hardin let his .45 drop back into his holster. Scowling, he glared at the half-breed.

There was a cold smile on Dancer's face as he gently squeezed the trigger, a hollow click as the hammer fell on an empty chamber. Hardin flinched involuntarily and a red flush climbed up the back of his neck.

"Bang, you're dead," Dancer muttered under his breath, and dropped the Colt into the holster. Unbuckling the gunbelt, he returned it to a jubilant A. J.

"Hot damn!" the guard chortled. "You're slicker than shit. Fastest thing I ever saw."

Grinning from ear to ear, he replaced the shackles on Dancer's wrists. Then, still grinning with delight, he swaggered over to Smith and Hardin.

"Pay me!" he demanded, and slapped his thigh, laughing gleefully. "Hot damn! Easiest money I ever made in my life," he crowed, following Hardin down the hill. "Man, if I ain't gonna have myself one hell of a time at the Golden Goose tonight!"

Grumbling, Smith returned to his place in the shade. Damned Indian! Betting against the 'breed had cost him a hundred bucks. Well, he'd take it out of the half-breed's hide one way or another, that was sure. Glowering at the source of his irritation, he pulled a kerchief from his back pocket and wiped the sweat from his face and neck while he watched the prisoner toil in the hot sun.

Jesse sat on the porch steps, fanning herself. Dancer's face was dark, impenetrable, his eyes as cold as death. What was he thinking, she wondered. Was he remembering other gunfights, other men he had faced across a stretch of barren ground? And just what was there between Dancer and Hardin?

Perhaps twenty minutes had gone by when Dancer paused to rest, wiping the sweat from his face with the back of his hand. Damn, it was hot enough to melt iron!

In a remarkably agile movement for one so big, Smith rose to his feet. Without warning, he grabbed the whip he'd been carrying in his back pocket and laid it across the half-breed's back. Three times the heavy lash cracked in the sweltering stillness.

"Get back to work, Injun," Smith drawled softly. "It ain't time for a break until I say so."

Pivoting on his heel, Dancer shot the guard a look laced with venom. The whip fell again, harder this time, and Dancer winced as the rawhide opened a long thin gash from his ear to his collar bone. A muscle worked in Dancer's jaw and his knuckles went white as he tightened his grip on the axe handle.

Unaware that she'd done so, Jesse stood up, one hand at her throat, as it occurred to her that the tool in Dancer's clenched fist would make a formidable weapon if he chose to use it as such.

Apparently Smith was entertaining the same thoughts, for he suddenly snatched up the ten-gauge and eared back both hammers, then reddened as he realized he had telegraphed his apprehension to the half-breed.

For several taut seconds the two men glared at each other, and Jesse wondered if Dancer would hurl the axe at the guard, risking a double dose of buckshot for the satisfaction of injuring his tormentor. But then the tension drained out of Dancer and he relaxed his grip on the axe. With a bitter smile, he turned to face the huge old oak again, and as he did so, Jesse caught his eye.

He looks tired, she thought compassionately. *Tired and hot and thirsty.*

She was debating the wisdom of offering him a drink of water when J. D. and Lizzie rode into the yard.

Clayton drew rein near Smith, and the guard respectfully removed his hat. Lizzie guided her pony closer to Dancer. Her friend. He looked so hot. And so uncomfortable, all sweaty and bound in heavy chains. Childlike, she did not question the way things were, only wondered at the strange behavior of grown-ups.

"Let's go, Lizzie," Clayton called. "There's a new horse I want you to see."

"Wait, Grandpa. Can't we give him a drink?" She pointed at Dancer. "He looks so thirsty, and it's so hot." She gave Clayton her sweetest, most angelic smile. "Please."

Clayton frowned, his love for his granddaughter battling with his raging hatred for the half-breed. Lizzie won.

"Very well," Clayton said, not wanting to appear cruel in front of the child. "Jesse, fetch the prisoner a drink. Come along, Lizzie."

Lizzie threw a brilliant smile in Dancer's direction before she urged her pony after Clayton's horse.

Drawing the bucket from the well, Jesse carried it to Dancer, held it for him while he dipped into it once, twice, three times, quenching a powerful thirst. Their eyes met as he dropped the ladle into the bucket and the unveiled desire in his flinty stare smote Jesse like a flaming brand, scorching her flesh.

"Thanks, honey," he murmured huskily, and the sound of his voice sent a shiver down her spine.

"Wait." She pulled a handkerchief from her skirt pocket and gently wiped the darkening blood from his face and neck. His breath was warm against her cheek, his nearness made her tremble. She longed to touch him, to kiss him, but she didn't dare, not with Smith looking on. She made one last swipe at the blood on his neck, then stepped away.

"Thanks," he said again, and in a single fluid motion he scooped up the heavy axe, swinging it with renewed vigor against the drooping oak, handling the heavy tool as if it were a toy.

With a sigh, Jesse walked back to the house and went inside. Somehow she could not bring herself to seek out a shady glen or go for a swim while he was out there laboring in the hot sun. Instead, she sat watching him through the kitchen window, admiring the rhythmic play of muscles in his scarred back and broad shoulders, wondering if, in the end, Clayton would break his rebellious spirit as he had broken the spirits of the other prisoners.

A sudden warmth surged through her as she recalled the hungry look in his eyes, and the husky yearning in his voice. Closing her eyes, she imagined herself in his arms, her breasts flattened against the hard wall of his chest, his mouth crushing her own.

If only she could find a way to get him out of that cage, she mused. If only . . .

Chapter 24

Dancer swung the heavy axe one more time and the stricken tree crashed heavily to the earth, raising a thick cloud of red dust. At Smith's command, three convicts shuffled forward to haul it away while Dancer moved to the next tree, a live oak that was twisted and blackened where it had recently been struck by lightning.

Two days had passed since his mock shootout with Cliff Hardin. And two nights. Long, lonely nights spent in bitter isolation. Lying on the floor of the cage, his body weary and hurting after a hard day's work, he could think of nothing but Jesse, the ache in his loins stronger than the pain in his back. He recalled each look, each touch that had passed between them. His desire for her was like a living, breathing thing. The knowledge that he would never again hold her in his arms was the worst torture he had ever known.

He swung the axe automatically, his thoughts dismal. The present was bleak, the future grim, the past painful and unpleasant.

With a sigh, he let the axe fall still, his gaze

moving to the distant mountains visible beyond the trees. Far beyond the jagged mountain peaks lay the land of the Comanche. If only he were free to . . .

The crack of a whip shattered his reverie and he swore aloud as the weighted tip bit into his back, drawing blood.

"What'd you say, you whoreson Comanche half-breed?" Smith demanded, swinging the lash again.

But the blow fell on empty air as Dancer dropped the axe, reached out and caught the end of the whip in midair, wrenching it from the guard's fist.

With an oath, Smith raised his shotgun and eared back both hammers.

"Clayton won't like it if you kill me," Dancer warned sardonically. "That's a job he wants to do himself."

There was truth in the half-breed's words and Smith lowered the Greener, his hand reaching for the gun holstered at his side. If he couldn't splatter the 'breed's guts in the dirt, he could sure as hell cripple him.

He was raising the .45 when Dancer struck the weapon from his hand with a flick of the whip. Instinctively, Smith covered his face with his hands to ward off the blow he saw coming.

Dancer swung the whip with all his might, his smoldering fury building with each stroke of the lash as all the pent-up hate and anger he carried for his tormentors, and for this guard in particular, burst into flame.

The whip hissed through the air like an angry snake, exacting vengeance for hours of toil in the hot sun, for jeering taunts, for endless hours in a steel-barred cage.

Smith bellowed for help as the lash cut into his hands and forearms. Despite the pain, he stood solid as a rock, keeping his bulk between his weapons and Dancer, knowing Clayton would kill him an inch at a time if the half-breed got hold of a gun and managed to escape.

In minutes, Dirty Tom and A. J. came running up behind Dancer, their guns drawn. Blinded by his rage, Dancer was unaware of their presence until Dirty Tom jabbed the business end of his .45 into his back.

"Drop it, Comanche!" the big Negro snarled.

Dancer froze as the muzzle of the Colt dug into his spine. Reluctantly, he lowered his arm, his gray eyes blazing as he turned to face the two guards. His dark eyes were still bright with the satisfaction of drawing the blood of an enemy, and for a moment A. J. feared the half-breed might take them all on with his bare hands.

But then Dancer shrugged and dropped the whip.

"I'll get you for this, you bastard," Smith promised. "I'm gonna wear my arm out on you."

"No, you won't, Smitty," A. J. said, casting a sidelong glance at Dancer. "The boss said to go easy on the 'breed from now on. He wants

Dancer to be in good shape for his birthday next week."

Smith's face split in a spiteful grin, the expression made grotesque by the blood dripping down his right cheek.

"Sure, A. J.," Smith said. "Whatever you say. I guess I can wait till the old man's birthday." He glared at Dancer. "That's one shindig I wouldn't miss for all the money in the world."

Dancer remained impassive, his eyes focused on A. J.'s face. What he read in the guard's expression sent a warning tingle down his spine.

Jesse sat in her room, patiently waiting for the hours to pass so she could go to Dancer. She hadn't seen him for two days and she couldn't wait any longer. Something was up, but she couldn't find out what. All she knew was that it had something to do with Dancer, and with Clayton's birthday, which was the following Saturday.

At last she heard the downstairs clock strike midnight and she tiptoed out of her room and down the stairs. Her horse, corraled near the house, whickered softly as she led it from the corral. And then she was riding toward the cage.

Dancer sat up at the sound of footsteps, his heartbeat quickening in anticipation of seeing her again. But it wasn't Jesse who materialized out of the shadows. It was A. J.

"I thought you'd be awake," the guard remarked.

Dancer grunted, his eyes wary. The guards rarely came to check on him after dark, never at midnight.

"Pretty night," A. J. said.

"What are you doing here, A. J.?" Dancer asked.

"I come to tell you what to expect on the old man's birthday. We've been warned to keep our mouths shut, but I think you've got a right to know what he's got in mind."

"Prepare myself, you mean?"

"Yeah, something like that."

"Well?"

"You want a cigarette?"

"Yeah."

There was a brief silence while the guard rolled and lit two cigarettes, then passed one to Dancer.

"Come on, A. J., spill it."

"He's gonna torture you. At least, he's gonna let Man Who Walks do it. I don't know if the judge will take a hand in it or not."

"Smith will," Dancer muttered. He stared at the noose, thinking of all the hours he'd spent worrying about a hanging. Hell, that would be a cakewalk compared to what A. J. had just told him.

"Yeah. Anyway, the judge promised Man Who Walks five thousand dollars if he could keep you alive for at least three days."

Three days. Dancer shuddered involuntarily. Three days. And it could be done, he thought bleakly. Three days of torture. Three days of excruciating pain while Clayton and Hardin looked on, laughing and making jokes, betting on how long it would take to make him scream, to make him beg, to die.

"I just thought you'd wanna know." A. J. took a deep drag on his cigarette, exhaled slowly. "I . . . uh, I want you to know I ain't gonna take any part in it."

Dancer nodded. Of all the guards, A. J. was the only one who had treated him decently.

"Well, I gotta go," A. J. said, snuffing out his cigarette.

"Thanks for the smoke."

A. J. waved and went down the hill.

A moment later, Jesse stepped from her hiding place in the timber and hurried up to the cage.

"Oh, Dancer," she whispered brokenly. "It can't be true."

"Jesse!"

"I heard everything. I can't believe Clayton means to do it. I just can't believe it." Tears flooded her eyes and cascaded down her cheeks.

"It's probably just talk," Dancer said.

"Dancer, I can't bear it. What if he means it?"

He swore under his breath. "Dammit, Jesse, don't go soft on me now. Damn, I wish I had a drink. Do you think they'll ask me if I have any last requests?"

He was smiling at her, urging her to smile

back. His dark eyes held a tacit plea, asking her to save her tears, to cry later, if she must.

Jesse wiped her eyes and managed a weak smile. "Is that what your last request would be?" she teased halfheartedly. "A drink?"

"You know better than that," he answered, and suddenly neither of them were smiling.

Jesse moved against the bars and he reached for her, his hands caressing her arms, moving up to touch her neck, her cheek, to stroke her hair. His eyes were dark, intense, as he bent to kiss her. He did not close his eyes and neither did she.

Jesse sighed as his hand slid down her arm, then moved to cup her breast. The heat of his touch seared her skin, spreading outward like the petals of a rose, engulfing every part of her until it settled in the warm womanly depths of her being. She groaned with a sudden need that would never again be satisfied.

She stood quiescent as his hands moved over her, as though to memorize each curve. How could she live without him?

She reached an eager hand through the bars to stroke his cheek, her eyes intent upon his face as her hand moved over him, refamiliarizing herself with the hard planes of his chest, the width of his shoulders, the rough silk of his hair.

She smiled suddenly. "You've had a bath!" she exclaimed softly. "And a shave."

"Pretty slow to notice, aren't you?"

"When? How?"

"It was my reward for that stupid showdown."

Jesse nodded. "What's between you and Hardin? Why do you hate each other so much?"

"I don't want to talk about that now. Come here."

She pressed herself against the bars again, eager for his kisses, knowing she could never have enough to last for the rest of her life. She felt the tears start again, and forced them back. He did not like her tears.

"Jesse, what are you going to do with the rest of your life?"

"What do you mean?"

"You ought to get married, have kids."

"Dancer, please . . ."

"You should give Tom a chance. He's a good man, the kind of man you deserve."

"Do we have to talk about that now?"

"I just want to know that you'll be all right after . . . that you'll be all right."

"I'm fine."

"What'd you do with the money I left you?"

"It's in the bank in Cherry Valley. Dammit, Dancer, why are we talking about me?"

It was the first time he had ever heard her swear and he chuckled softly, amused.

"Dancer." She drew his head down and kissed him, her hands kneading his back and shoulders.

His tongue plunged into her mouth, sending a bright shaft of flame to her loins, and she moaned softly, her need for him a sweet torture. His hands cupped her breasts, and she remembered the last night they had spent together. If only they could share one more night like that, before it was too late . . .

She stayed as long as she dared, and then lingered a few minutes more, hating to leave him, not caring who saw her with him. She loved him desperately, and she didn't care who knew it.

But Dancer cared. "Don't come back here, Jess," he said quietly. "Clayton's bound to have the guards keep a close eye on me now. And there's nothing you can do."

"I want to come."

He shook his head. "No, Jesse. Please. I . . ." He bit off the next word. What good would it do to tell her he loved her now, when he had less than a week to live? Why burden her with that? She didn't need his ghost haunting her the rest of her life.

"Dancer, please don't send me away."

"It's better this way."

She didn't understand, and he couldn't explain it to her, couldn't tell her he needed time to be alone with his thoughts, time to meditate, to draw on whatever inner strength he had left to face what was coming.

"Please, Jesse," he said quietly. "For me."

How could she deny him? Standing on tiptoe, she kissed him one last time and was gone.

Dancer stared after her. So, Clayton intended to have him tortured to death? Deep down, hadn't he known it all along?

There were a multitude of favorite Indian tortures. He had seen the Comanche skin prisoners alive, inch by inch; seen men roasted over a slow fire; heard men scream when they were staked out over an anthill, their faces smeared with honey. He had seen an Apache who had lasted almost a week. The women had tormented him with hot knives and sticks, and when that failed to bring a scream to his lips, they had lit a fire between his legs. Finally, they wrapped him in a green hide and left him out in the hot sun where he was slowly crushed to death by the shrinking hide. But he never screamed.

Man Who Walks would know all these tricks and more. Few men died well when confronted with slow, agonizing death.

Dancer swore as a shiver of apprehension crawled down his spine. Would he die well? Or would Clayton break him at last?

He drew a deep breath, felt a cold knot of dread form in the pit of his stomach as he wondered just how skilled Man Who Walks was in the fine art of torture. The Sioux were known for their cunning, the Cheyenne were thought to be the most handsome Indians on the plains, the Comanche were renowned for their riding ability, but the Apache had always been feared for their expertise in the art of inflicting pain and slow, agonizing death.

Sitting there, staring into the darkness, he grinned ruefully. "I'm thirty-five years old," he mused aloud, "and what have I got to show for it? Not a damn thing." And yet he'd had a hell of a good time. He had seen most of the country west of the Missouri, won and lost a dozen fortunes on the turn of a card, ridden the owlhoot trail with Tom.

Now, as he faced certain death, he regretted only two things: that he could not keep his promise to Storm Woman, and that he could not make love to Jesse one last time.

He stared through the bars, gazing up at the night sky, and suddenly it was not a woman he longed for, but the cool green mountains and valleys of home.

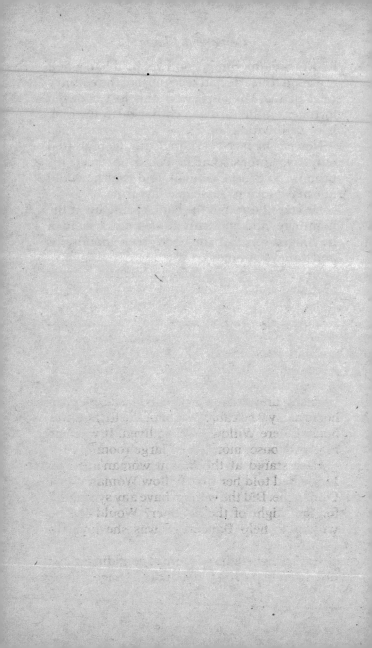

Chapter 25

Jesse rode back to the house, her thoughts churning wildly. She dashed the tears from her eyes, angry with herself because she could not stop crying. There was no time for tears now. Later, if Clayton did indeed kill Dancer, would be time enough for tears. For now, she needed a plan.

If only she had someone to help her, but there was no one on the ranch to turn to. Clayton wanted Dancer dead. Lizzie was too young to be of help. The hired hands would not help her.

As she drew rein at the corral and put her horse away, she caught sight of the little white house where Willow Woman lived. It was not really a house, more like a large room.

Jesse stared at the Indian woman's home. Lizzie had told her that Willow Woman was a Comanche. Did the woman have any sympathy for the plight of the prisoner? Would she be willing to help Dancer, or was she loyal to Clayton?

Jesse weighed the wisdom of confiding in the old woman against the judge's anger if he found out she'd tried to help Dancer escape, and decided the risk was worth it. She was not a prisoner, after all. If Clayton found out, she would leave the ranch.

Squaring her shoulders, Jesse went to the Indian woman's house and knocked on the door.

Chapter 26

Dancer swore as he tried to get comfortable. The cage seemed to grow smaller each day, and he cursed Clayton for having built the damned thing.

Scowling, he gazed into the darkness, wishing he had not told Jesse to stay away. She was the only bright spot in his life. But for her, he thought he would have gone mad during the last few weeks of his captivity.

A faint sound drew his attention and he glanced over his shoulder to see Jesse gliding toward him. She was dressed in black, her face ghostly white in the faint glow of the moon.

"Jesse." He breathed her name, pleased beyond words that she was there.

Jesse lifted her face for his kiss, the touch of his mouth on hers making her forget, for the moment, why she had come.

Dancer's hands closed on her shoulders, holding her tight, wishing he could take her in his arms and make love to her as he so longed to do. Why had he realized, too late, that he loved her?

Jesse was breathless when he released her.

For a moment, she blinked at him, her heart hammering with desire, and then she recalled her reason for being there.

"Dancer, listen, I have a plan."

"Jesse . . ."

"Listen to me. You're going to get sick tomorrow. Willow Woman will be called to look at you. She's going to tell J. D. that you've contracted some highly contagious virus and must be quarantined in her care. J. D.'s bound to listen to her. Lizzie said he thinks she's some kind of miracle worker. Anyway, he won't want you dying of some illness when he wants to kill you himself."

Dancer looked skeptical. "What's going to cause this sudden malady?"

Jesse reached into the pocket of her skirt. "This." She handed him a small brown bottle. "Drink that tomorrow morning when you wake up."

Dancer looked at the bottle for a moment and then grinned. Hell, he'd try anything if it would get him out of this cage.

"Jesse, I—"

"Shhh! Someone's coming!"

Before he could say anything else, she was gone.

The liquid in the bottle had a strange bittersweet smell and a strong sour taste. An hour after he drank it, he began to vomit, his body wracked by violent chills. Within minutes, he was unconscious. A. J. hurriedly sent for Clayton, and Clayton summoned Willow Woman. Everything went according to plan.

Dancer regained consciousness slowly, a layer at a time, hearing the song of a bird, feeling the warmth of the sun on his face, tasting the bitter dregs of bile in his mouth. Opening his eyes, he found himself alone in a small room only a little larger than the cage. The whitewashed walls were bare. Curtains of red and white gingham fluttered at the window over his head. A chair and a small table were the only furnishings in the room other than the bed he occupied and the tall cupboard against the far wall.

It was when he tried to turn over that he discovered his left foot was shackled to the heavy metal bed frame. His hands were still manacled as before: wrist to wrist with a length of chain between. He also discovered he was stark naked beneath the sheet.

Minutes later the door opened and the old Indian woman entered the room.

"How are you feeling, Buffalo Dancer?" she asked solicitously.

"Like I fell off a mountain. What the hell was in that bottle? Poison?"

Willow Woman nodded matter-of-factly. "Only a mild one. Rarely fatal in so small a dose."

Dancer grinned at her emphasis on the word *rarely*, then smiled ruefully. Whatever Jesse hoped to gain from this bit of deception was beyond him, but he was more than happy to be out of the cage and off the chain gang.

"Who stole my clothes?" he asked.

Willow Woman wrinkled her nose in disgust. "I burned them."

"My moccasins, too?"

"No. They are under the bed. There are still a few miles left in them." Willow Woman smiled sagely. "I have never seen moccasins made so well. Whoever made them put much love into her work."

An image of Storm Woman flashed into Dancer's mind, and he shook it away. "What happens now?"

"Would you object to a bath and a shave?"

Dancer glanced at her quizzically. "From you? I don't know. I've never been shaved by a woman before."

"Are you afraid I might cut your throat?" she asked, grinning, and Dancer laughed.

"Better you than Clayton!"

He was on the brink of sleep when the door opened and Jesse stepped into the room, a dark silhouette in the open doorway.

Willow Woman rose to her feet, smiled knowingly at Dancer, and left the room.

Dancer gazed at Jesse, unable to take his eyes from her face. Her hair fell over her shoulders in glorious disarray. He could not make out her expression in the dim light, but he could hear the sudden change in her breathing as she slipped the robe from her shoulders and let it fall to the floor. She stood beautifully naked before him.

The chains on his hands rattled as he held out his arms and Jesse went to him eagerly. Sliding beneath the sheet, she felt the heat of his body as he drew her length against his. His mouth quickly covered hers as his hands caressed her back and buttocks, sending shivers of delight racing through her.

He murmured her name as he rose over her, and she shivered as the cold chain fell across her breasts.

"Jesse." Her name was a groan on his lips as he thrust into her, taking her with quick savage strokes. He had not had a woman in months and now that she was here, he could not hold back. He buried his face in her shoulder, his body convulsing as his life flowed into her.

It was over in moments. Jesse could not contain her disappointment. She had expected to be cherished and loved, had dreamed of having him pleasure her the whole night long, and now it was over before it had even begun.

Dancer loosed a long sigh of contentment. And then he smiled at her. "Sorry, Jess," he apologized, somewhat sheepishly.

"It's all right," she said, not meeting his eyes.

He didn't argue. Instead, he began to kiss her, his touch gentle, his expression tender. The chains on his hands hampered him only a little as he caressed her, his hands and mouth moving over her lazily, deliciously, arousing her to fever pitch, until she trembled in his arms. And still he held back. His kisses were long and hot, his tongue a flame of fire as it tasted her own, then slid down the side of her neck to lave her breast.

Jesse gasped with pleasure, needing him, wanting him, as never before. And still he held back, until she was riding a wave of passion and pleasure that swept her out of the realms of reality and into a turbulent sea of ecstasy such as she had never dreamed of. Her arms drew him close, reveling in the powerful muscles that rippled beneath her fingertips. He was a strong man, so strong, and she gloried in his strength and power. He could easily break her in two, yet he was infinitely gentle with her as he swept her higher, higher, until she whimpered for him to possess her.

And still he held back, his hands turning her flesh to flame, her blood to fire. She moaned low in her throat, certain she would die of wanting him. And then, at long last, he entered her, his manhood filling her, completing her, until the waves crested and broke, leaving her weak and utterly content.

Dancer smiled down at her, his eyes drinking in the beauty of her. "If I die tomorrow, I'll die a happy man," he whispered, his finger toying with a lock of her hair.

"We're getting out of here tomorrow," Jesse said. "Willow Woman is going to try and steal the key to those shackles from A. J."

"Are you serious?"

"Yes. I'm only sorry I waited so long to ask for her help."

Dancer sat up, his dark eyes bright. To be free again! It was a heady thought.

Jesse sat up, too, hugging her knees to her chest. "Just think, tomorrow night we'll leave all this behind."

"No, Jesse."

She looked at him incredulously. "Don't you want to go?"

"Of course. But I'm going alone."

"No, I'm going with you. Please, Dancer." She could not bear to let him out of her sight, not now, when she'd just found him again.

"Don't argue with me about this, Jesse," he said quietly. "My mind's made up."

When she started to protest, he placed his hand over her mouth. "Clayton's bound to send his men after me when he discovers I'm gone. I can travel faster alone."

She could not argue with the logic of that, and so she nodded slowly, agreeably.

"I'll meet you in Bitter Creek."

"I'll be there."

Dancer put his arm around Jesse and drew her down on the bed beside him. Content, she rested her head on his shoulder, her arm draped across his waist, and that was how she fell asleep.

Jesse woke slowly, aware of a great heaviness across her legs. Glancing down, she saw that Dancer's leg was across hers. Lifting her gaze to his face, she studied him while he lay sleeping, her heart swelling with tenderness.

She glanced at the door as Willow Woman slipped into the room.

"Hurry," the Indian woman said, her face wrinkled in a worried frown. "It is almost dawn."

Dancer woke as soon as Jesse slid out of bed. His eyes grew warm as he saw her bend over to pick up the yellow wrapper she had dropped on the floor the night before.

"I've got to go," she said. "I'll be waiting for you in Bitter Creek. Come as fast as you can."

"I'll probably get there before you," he said. Reaching up, he curled his hand around the back of her neck and drew her toward him, his lips slanting over hers in a long, lingering kiss.

"Be careful," Jesse said. Quickly she placed a kiss on his cheek and hurried out of the room, knowing that if she stayed another minute she would wind up back in bed.

Dancer stretched luxuriously, thoroughly rested after the first good night's sleep he'd had since Elkhorn had betrayed him.

The day passed slowly, and he chafed at the inactivity. He did not enjoy sweating on the chain gang, but at least working made the hours pass quickly.

And then, at last, it was dusk. Willow Woman entered the room, a smile on her face as she held up the keys to his shackles, a dark shirt and a pair of denim pants.

In moments, his hands and feet were free. He accepted the clothes Willow Woman gave him, dressed quickly. Freed of the heavy iron manacles, he left as light as a feather. It was a heady feeling, and he picked up Willow Woman and swung her around the room.

She was breathless when he released her. "Are you going to stay here and play with an old woman all day," she teased, "or are you going to go while you can?"

"I'm going," Dancer assured her. "But what about you?"

"I am going home," she said.

"I promised to take you."

"You will have enough to do, just getting away from here. Do not worry about me. I will make it."

"Perhaps we'll meet again one day."

"I hope so." She touched his cheek, her eyes suddenly bright. "Take care, Buffalo Dancer."

"You, too." With a last look at the aged woman, he left the room. There was a horse waiting for him outside, saddled and ready to go. He swung effortlessly into the saddle and urged the gelding into a lope.

He turned the horse toward the trees, pausing once to look back. In the distance, he could see the main house and he wondered if Jesse had already left the ranch, and then he put her from his thoughts.

He was certain Clayton would send Hardin after him as soon as it was reported that he was missing, and he wanted to leave a trail Hardin couldn't miss. . . .

Chapter 27

J. D. Clayton was furious when Hardin told him that Dancer had escaped.

"How?" the judge shouted, his face livid, his blue eyes bulging. "How'd he get loose?"

Hardin shrugged. "Someone lifted the keys and turned him loose."

Clayton glared at Hardin, his mind racing. "Willow Woman," he muttered at last. "It had to be that damned squaw. Where is she?"

Hardin cleared his throat. "She's, uh . . . she's gone, too."

Clayton swore a vile oath. Moving to the liquor cabinet, he poured himself a drink, downed it in one swallow, and threw the glass into the fireplace.

"I want Dancer back," he said vehemently. "Dead or alive, I don't care which, but I want him back. Take every man on the ranch, if necessary. But bring him back!"

"I'll leave at first light."

"First light, hell. You'll leave now."

The morning after Dancer's escape, Jesse tendered her resignation. That afternoon, she was on a stagecoach bound for Bitter Creek.

It had been hard, saying goodbye to Lizzie. Clayton had been too wrapped up in his anger to give more than a passing thought to her sudden departure, but Lizzie sobbed as though heartbroken.

Now, staring out the window of the coach, Jesse felt her eyes burn with unshed tears as she recalled the forlorn expression on the child's face as they said their final goodbyes. Jesse had grown to love the little girl in the time they had been together, loved her as dearly as if the child had been her own. But she couldn't stay on at the ranch now that Dancer was free. She had waited too long to be with him again.

With a sigh, she settled back against the seat and closed her eyes. Soon, she thought happily, soon she would be with Dancer. He would tell her that he loved her, couldn't live without her, and they would be married. They'd find a town where no one had ever heard of him and settle down and raise a family.

She was smiling as she drifted to sleep.

Chapter 28

He rode most of the night and all the next day, stopping briefly at the first waterhole he came across to breathe the gelding and fill the canteen hanging over the saddle horn. He had left a trail a blind man could follow, certain that Clayton would send Hardin after him. He was eager for Hardin to catch up with him, but not until he was ready.

He rode most of the second day as well, pausing only to rest his weary mount, wanting it to look as though he were running for his life. It would never do for Hardin to suspect that his quarry wanted to be caught.

On the morning of the fourth day, he drew rein beside a wide river. Dismounting, he stripped the rigging from the gelding, then hobbled the animal in the lush grass that grew nearby so it could graze.

The gurgling water was an invitation he couldn't refuse, and he threw off his clothes and moccasins and plunged into the river. Damn, but it felt good, and he floated there, soaking away three days of trail dust as he bitterly contemplated the scars on his wrists and ankles. He would carry them always, a constant reminder of the months he had spent on the chain gang. They would fade in time, as would the tracks the whip had left on his back, but they would never completely disappear.

He owed Hardin for that, too.

A long time later, he stepped briskly from the water, stood naked on the bank while the warm, late-summer sun baked him dry. He dressed quickly, then sat on a flat rock and pulled on his moccasins, the ones Storm Woman had made for him a lifetime ago. They were badly worn now, torn and scarred like the man who wore them, and he knew he would not rest until the men responsible for her death were dead.

He was reaching for his saddle when a sudden uneasiness prickled the short hairs along the back of his neck.

Hardin was here.

He felt a sudden excitement build within him as he thought of facing the man.

A twig snapped, loud in the eerie stillness of the day. In a smooth, flowing motion, Dancer pulled the Winchester from the saddle scabbard, dropped into a crouch, and fired at the man stepping from the brush less than ten yards away.

There was a deafening explosion as both men fired at virtually the same time, and then Cliff Hardin pitched forward, gun in hand. He crashed heavily to the ground and lay still.

Knowing Hardin wasn't dead, Dancer walked cautiously toward him, his rifle aimed at Hardin's inert form. He would have killed anyone else instantly, but he didn't want Hardin dead. Not yet.

Feigning death, Cliff Hardin lay perfectly still, ignoring the blood seeping from a bullet hole low in his left side. His right arm, flung out in front of him, still grasped his pistol.

He timed his next move perfectly. Just when he figured Dancer was within easy range, he rolled over, jerked his arm up, and squeezed the trigger. The bullet, meant for the half-breed's heart, went high and wide and caught him in the left shoulder.

Dancer rocked backward, momentarily thrown off balance, but he recovered quickly, and before Cliff could pull the trigger again, he fired the Winchester, and Hardin's gun flew from torn and bloody fingers.

Cradling his shattered hand, Hardin struggled to his feet, mentally cursing himself for tracking the half-breed alone.

"I knew Clayton would send you," Dancer remarked quietly. "How much is he paying you this time?"

"Twenty grand," Hardin replied sullenly.

Dancer gave a low whistle. "And you came all alone so you wouldn't have to split it. But then, you always were a greedy bastard. Too bad you won't live long enough to spend it."

"How do you know I came alone?"

"Because I'm still alive."

"What are you gonna do?" Hardin asked gruffly.

"I think you know," Dancer replied, and his voice was silky smooth and soft, sharply at odds with the angry glitter in his deep gray eyes.

Hardin shuddered imperceptibly, not liking the predatory gleam in the half-breed's stare.

"You're gonna kill me out here, in cold blood," Cliff mused glumly, and flinched as Dancer's lips curled back in a mirthless grin.

"Remember the night Storm Woman died?" Dancer asked. "I made her a promise that night. I promised her that you'd die at my feet, begging for mercy."

Hardin had always fancied himself as a brave man, but the look in the half-breed's eyes turned his legs to jelly and his blood to ice. Still, he held to a sliver of hope, praying desperately that the half-breed was toying with him in an effort to make him crawl. And crawl he would, if it would help.

But Dancer's next words extinguished whatever mercy Cliff Hardin had hoped to find, and he knew with terrible certainty that he was a dead man.

"You never should have laid hands on my woman," Dancer said flatly. "She was carrying my child."

"Hell, we didn't know she was your squaw!" Hardin shouted, but the lie fell flat and he took a step backward, as if to flee the wrath in the half-breed's eyes.

"You know now," Dancer retorted, and as he spoke, he lowered his rifle until the barrel was leveled at Hardin's groin, like an accusing finger.

Hardin's eyes bulged with fear as he threw his good hand out in front of him in a futile effort to ward off the threatening menace of the rifle.

"We never touched her!"

"You would have if you hadn't killed her first."

Dancer's finger curled around the trigger and Hardin shrieked, "Wait!" as he dropped to his knees. "I've got money," he babbled, "plenty of money. You can have it. All of it."

"I don't want your blood money, Cliff, I want your life. Your life for the life of my child. That's what I promised Storm Woman and that's what I'm going to give her. Stand up."

"No." Hardin shook his head and scrambled backward.

"Stand up!"

Hardin levered himself to his feet, his shattered hand cradled against his chest. "Go ahead, you dirty 'breed," he snarled. "Do your worst."

A cruel smile twisted Dancer's lips as he squeezed the trigger. The sound of a single gunshot shattered the peaceful stillness, mingling with Hardin's animal-like scream of pain as he fell to the ground clutching his ruined manhood.

A second shot followed hard on the heels of

the first, and then there was only quiet.

Face impassive, Dancer watched the gunsmoke drift away, and then he went in search of Hardin's horse.

There were two of them, a rangy bay mare and a tall black gelding with a crooked blaze. He took the mare because he preferred mares, swung into the saddle, and rode back toward the river.

Ripping a strip of material from the bottom of his shirt, he jammed it against his wounded shoulder. And then, with a last look at Hardin's body, he headed for Bitter Creek.

Morning found him dozing in the saddle. With no hand to guide her, the bay came to a weary halt at the river's edge and plunged her nose into the placid water.

Satisfying her thirst, the bay began to graze on the sparse yellow grass that grew in scattered clumps along the shore. She stretched her neck to reach an especially tempting thistle, and the movement jerked the reins from Dancer's hand.

He woke with a start, instantly aware of his injured shoulder. What had started as a dull throb the night before had progressed into a steady, monotonous pain. A warm stickiness told him he was bleeding again.

Hardin's canteen was empty, and the river called invitingly, but Dancer remained in the saddle, knowing that if he dismounted he would never find the strength to remount.

He stared at the slow-moving river. It was deep and inviting, blue-green, like Jesse's eyes. Jesse. She was waiting for him in Bitter Creek. Jesse. He longed to lay his head against her breast, close his eyes, and sleep.

He felt himself growing weaker as he studied the terrain, looking for familiar landmarks, then swore softly as he realized he'd missed the shortcut to Bitter Creek while he dozed in the saddle.

But Shadow Valley was not far, and he felt a sudden yearning for home, a longing to see the land of his birth once more before he died.

Overhead, a huge white cloud caught his eye and he stared at it, unblinking. Slowly the cloud began to move, changing shape, coming to life, until it was not a cloud at all, but the horned image of his medicine dream.

With a strangled cry, he reached out to grasp the shaggy white mane.

Chapter 29

He was lost in a fever born of exhaustion and infection. Shadowy figures peopled his dreams and he was defenseless against them.

Storm Woman came to him, shrouded in blood, a dead child cradled in her arms;

Lizzie floated toward him, her laughter like the tinkling of tiny silver bells;

Jesse danced before him, radiant in a sea-green gown, a seductive smile lighting her lovely face;

Willow Woman hobbled toward him, a bent figure with long gray braids and Comanche moccasins, chanting his death song.

Suddenly he was hurled into the dark confines of the cage. And then he was working on the chain gang, his back raw, his ears filled with the sound of the lash. And then he was crawling in the dust at Hardin's feet while Cliff's laughter rang in his ears.

And then Jesse came to him, offering him a small brown bottle, and they were side by side on Willow Woman's narrow cot and for a brief, fleeting moment he was content. He opened his mouth to tell her he loved her but before he could form the words, Hardin's last anguished cry echoed in his mind, chasing all the phantoms away....

He woke to pain and darkness. It required too great an effort to keep his eyes open and he closed them again, frowning as he tried to recall what he had wanted to tell Jesse. It seemed terribly important that he remember, but the moment was gone and he slept again, unaware of the woman seated in the rocking chair beside the bed.

Jesse sat quietly, listening to Dancer's breathing grow slow and even as sleep claimed him once more. Leaning forward, she sponged the sweat from his brow, replaced the covers he had thrown aside. She let her hand linger on his shoulder, reassuring herself that he was really there.

Rocking quietly in the dark room, Jesse felt sleep creeping up on her. Tom thought she was foolish to wear herself out staying at Dancer's bedside when there was a nurse available, but she refused to leave Dancer's room, afraid he might disappear on her again.

She filled her eyes with the sight of him. His face was drawn and haggard, bearded, his hair long. His back was badly scarred, and months of wearing heavy shackles had left telltale scars on his wrists and ankles.

She brushed the hair away from his face. She had been afraid when he hadn't shown up at the expected time; afraid he'd changed his mind about returning to Bitter Creek, afraid he'd been killed leaving Clayton's ranch, afraid he'd decided to go back to Shadow Valley alone.

He tossed restlessly, mumbling in his sleep, and she caught the name of Storm Woman again. He had called out for the mysterious Storm Woman several times, and Jesse felt a sharp twinge of jealousy as she wondered who the woman was, and what she had meant to Dancer that he called for her again and again, his voice filled with anguish and bitter regret.

Dancer moaned and his hands clutched the bedclothes in a viselike grip, twisting the covers furiously, as if he would rend them into shreds. It grieved her to see him in pain, to see his indomitable strength humbled by fevered nightmares.

She stared at the hands restlessly worrying the covers, remembering how deadly they had looked when fisted around a gun, and yet how gently they had stroked her willing flesh. . . .

In a tortured voice, Dancer cried out for Storm Woman again, and his right hand moved along the edge of the bed, as if he were searching for the woman whose name he called again and again.

Impulsively, Jesse laid her hand over his and he grasped it tightly, mumbling incoherently in a guttural language she assumed was Comanche.

The minutes ticked by. Jesse's hand, firmly clasped in Dancer's, began to grow numb but she made no effort to draw it away.

In his sleep, Dancer whispered her name and she began to weep.

The sun rose lazily in all its brilliant glory, painting the eastern sky with subtle shades of yellow and bright bands of vermillion as it blessed the new day.

Dancer stirred restlessly as the golden sunlight flooded the room, coaxing him awake. He looked around, wondering where the hell he was.

The room was pale blue. White lace curtains fluttered at the open window. A carved oak dresser stood against one wall. There was an oak table on one side of the bed, a rocking chair on the other. A multicolored rag rug covered most of the floor. His moccasins were beside the bed. Someone had brushed away the layers of dust and grime.

A sharp pain rocked him when he tried to sit up, and he fell back against the pillows, noticing for the first time that his left shoulder was heavily bandaged.

He let his mind go back in time as he tried to recall how he'd gotten from the river to this quiet blue room, but his mind was blank after Hardin.

There were footsteps in the hall, then the door across from the bed swung open and Jesse entered the room. The mere sight of her stirred a warm tingle in the pit of his stomach. So, she had not been a dream after all.

Jesse's smile was radiant when she saw that

Dancer was conscious. She moved quickly to his bedside and placed her hand on his forehead.

"How are you feeling?"

"Kind of groggy." His gaze settled on her face, his eyes dark with longing. "Come here."

She went into his arms eagerly. She had been so worried about him, hardly leaving his side since he arrived, refusing to think he might die.

"Jesse." He murmured her name as his hand found its way to her neck, curling in her hair as he inhaled the sweet scent of woman. He thought of the months he'd spent caged like an animal, of the nights he had dreamed of her, yearned for her, ached with the need to hold her. And now she was here, in his arms, his for the taking.

He closed his eyes as he kissed her, felt her willing response, heard her muffled laughter as his desire sprang to life.

"Love me, Dancer," Jesse murmured, snuggling closer. "Love me now."

The words, so like those once uttered by Storm Woman, smothered the fire in his blood. Wordlessly, he put Jesse away from him, refusing to meet her puzzled frown.

"What's wrong?" she asked. "Is your shoulder bothering you?"

He nodded, though it was a lie. It wasn't his shoulder, but his conscience, that was hurting.

He drew a deep breath, let it out in a long sigh before asking, "How'd I get here?"

"A prospector found you passed out near the Dirty River and brought you into town. You were at death's door. Dr. Peters removed a bullet from your shoulder. He said you were suffering from exhaustion and loss of blood and a bad infection."

"Anything else?" Dancer asked wryly.

"That about covers it, I guess."

Dancer grunted as he glanced around the room. "Where am I?"

"The hotel. My room is next door." Her face flushed a pretty shade of pink. "I've been looking after you."

"Thanks. Where's Tom?"

"Over at the jail." Jesse stood up, smoothing her skirt as she crossed the room and poured Dancer a glass of water. Tom had been extremely pleased to see her again. He had insisted on taking her out to dinner and keeping her company while they waited for Dancer to arrive. Once, Tom had even kissed her.

"I'm crazy about you, Jesse," Tom had murmured fervently. "You can't imagine how worried I've been, wondering how you were, afraid I'd never see you again." He had gazed deep into her eyes. "Is there any chance for me?" he had asked. "Any chance at all?"

"I love Dancer," she had replied.

"And he loves you?"

"I don't know. I'd like to think he does, but he's never said so."

"I don't think he knows how to love," Tom had remarked, and Jesse had steered the conversation into safer waters. She liked Tom. Perhaps, if she'd never met Dancer, she would have loved him.

"Here," Jesse said, handing the glass to Dancer. "Dr. Peters said you were to drink lots of water."

Obligingly, he drained the glass, then placed it on the bedside table. "Did you have any trouble getting away from the Clayton place?"

Jesse shook her head. She did not miss the bitterness in his voice when he mentioned the judge's name.

"No," she replied, "no trouble." She grinned. "He was too upset over your escape to worry about me, or wonder why I was in such a hurry to go." The smile faded from her face. "It was hard to leave Lizzie, though."

"She was a sweet kid," Dancer remarked. "How's Tom?"

"Fine."

He nodded. "How long have I been here?"

"Nearly a week. You were out of your head most of the time." She moved to the rocking chair beside the bed and sat down. The chair was like an old friend. She had spent hours sitting here, just watching Dancer, her heart aching because he was in pain.

She studied his profile, puzzled by the change in him, wondering why he had pushed her away. It wasn't his shoulder that was bothering him, it was something else. But what? He was free now. Flyers had gone out months ago saying he was dead, and surely even Clayton had extracted vengeance enough. Surely now she and Dancer could have a life together. He cared for her; she knew it. He had been glad to see her when he first woke up, eager to hold her in his arms.

Dancer frowned, perplexed by her scrutiny. "What is it?" he asked. "What's bothering you?"

"Who's Storm Woman?" Jesse blurted. As soon as the words were out of her mouth, she was sorry she had mentioned the woman's name. Sadness dragged at Dancer's features, pain flickered in the depths of his eyes.

"I'm sorry," Jesse apologized quickly. "I had no right . . . it's none of my business."

"It's all right, Jess," Dancer said quietly. "She was a Comanche woman. I shared her lodge while I was in Shadow Valley. She was captured with me."

Pain and jealousy warred in Jesse's heart, but she had to ask the question anyway. "Did you care for her?"

He was staring out the window and it was a long time before he said, "Yeah, I cared."

Jesse went suddenly still, as if she were dying inside. "Where is she now?"

"Dead," he rasped. "She caught a bullet that was meant for me. She was pregnant with my child. Damn!" he whispered in a voice thick with pain and anguish. "I didn't even know she was pregnant until the night she died."

Jesse stared at Dancer, her emotions in turmoil. He had made love to another woman.

She felt hurt, betrayed. Dancer had shared a lodge with a Comanche woman and gotten her with child, and now he was feeling guilty because Storm Woman was dead and he was still alive.

"I'm sorry," Jesse murmured, ashamed because she was jealous of a dead woman. "So sorry."

Dancer seemed not to hear her. Still staring out the window, he might have been alone in the room. When he spoke again, his voice was low and edged with remorse, and Jesse had the distinct impression that he was not speaking to her, but to the distant mountains.

"She loved me," he murmured, "and it cost her her life." His right hand balled into a tight fist and he banged it against the bedside table. Storm Woman had loved him, and now she was dead, and his child with her. Would he ever be free of the guilt that twisted through him when he thought of her?

He looked at Jesse and remembered how he had thought of her while making love to Storm Woman. A muscle worked in his jaw. Storm Woman had asked for one night and he had obliged, physically, but he had closed his eyes and pretended it was Jesse he held in his arms. He had refused to think of Storm Woman while he was in chains. He had buried her memory deep in the recesses of his mind, spending all his energy on the task of surviving. Now he could think of little else. She was dead, and it was his fault. If she had not loved him, she would not have come running after him the night he had been captured.

As if reading his mind, Jesse said compassionately, "Dancer, it's not your fault."

He looked suddenly old and tired as he drew his gaze from Jesse's face and stared out the window again. "Isn't it?" he asked bitterly. "I should have done something. Anything."

"What could you have done?"

"I don't know," he admitted. He knew only that he had allowed himself to care for Storm Woman and now she was dead, and he didn't intend for anything like that to happen again. No strings, no ties, no obligations.

Try as she might, Jesse could find no words to comfort him. She had never seen him like this, with his guard completely down and his cynical good humor gone. The hard mask he habitually wore had slipped away, too, leaving his grief and his guilt clearly etched in the lines of his face, in the depths of his slate-gray eyes. She had always thought him invulnerable to sorrow, immune to remorse, would have sworn that no one in all the world could penetrate the hard shell of his indifference and reach the man inside. But she had been wrong, for he was hurting now, and hurting deeply.

"Do you think Hardin will come after you again?" she asked, hoping to take his mind off the Indian woman.

"No."

"You seem very certain."

"I am," he said curtly, and Jesse wisely asked no more questions that day.

The next few days passed peacefully. Dancer recovered quickly, though he was still confined to bed. Jesse spent a good deal of time with him, yearning to reach past the invisible wall he had erected between them. He was friendly, talkative, but he kept her at arm's length, and she didn't like it.

Tom came to visit Dancer twice a day, and Jesse found it awkward to be in the same room with the marshal, knowing how he felt about her. She had the feeling Tom was waiting, waiting for Dancer to recover, waiting for Jesse to admit that Dancer wasn't good enough for her, waiting for her to realize that what she thought was love was nothing more than infatuation.

Four days after Dancer regained consciousness, Tom burst into the room, a worried expression on his face.

"What's wrong?" Jesse asked, alarmed.

"Clayton's in town."

Jesse stared at Tom in disbelief, and then she looked at Dancer. She felt a peculiar catch in her heart when she saw the expression on his face, saw the hatred that burned in his eyes.

"Where is hé?" Dancer asked.

"Over at the saloon. He's not alone, Dancer. Davis and Johnson are with him. My deputy heard the Judge asking about you."

Dancer swung his legs over the side of the bed, his face hard.

"Forget it," Tom said.

"Get out of my way."

"I said forget it," Tom repeated. He took a step back, his hand resting on the butt of his gun. "As far as Clayton knows, you rode through here eight days ago on your way to Shadow Valley. I won't have any killing in my town."

"Dammit, Tom—"

"You're a wanted man, Dancer. I've got a flyer in my office with your picture on it."

"It's no good. Haven't you heard? I'm dead."

"I know differently, and I'm sticking my neck out by harboring a fugitive. I don't mind, because we're friends and because I believe you killed Johnny Clayton in self-defense. But if you gun down Clayton, I'll throw your ass in jail. Do I make myself clear?"

"Crystal clear," Dancer replied flatly.

"Good. I'm going down to make sure Clayton and his men are out of town by nightfall."

A noise in the next room caught Jesse's attention and she frowned as she heard Dancer moving around in the room adjoining her own. Goodness, was something wrong? He wasn't supposed to be on his feet for another three days.

Slipping out of bed, she drew on her wrapper and hurried to his room where she knocked lightly on the door.

"Who is it?"

"Jesse. May I come in?"

"Sure."

Turning the knob, she opened the door and stepped into the room, which was dimly lit by a lamp with the wick turned low.

"Something wrong?" Dancer asked.

Jesse shook her head. He was standing at the window, stark naked. She couldn't help staring at him at the sheer masculine beauty of sun-bronzed flesh highlighted by the soft yellow glow of the lamp. Desire washed through her, instantaneous, undeniable

"I'm glad you're here," he said, apparently unconcerned that he wasn't wearing a stitch.

She felt her cheeks grow hot as she lifted her gaze to his face.

Dancer grinned at her. "I need some clothes."

"Yes," Jesse said dryly. "I can see that."

"Now."

"Now?" Her surprise at finding him naked was forgotten as worry took its place. "You're not supposed to be out of bed yet," she reminded him.

"I know, I know. Will you get me something to wear or not?

"And if I refuse?"

Dancer shrugged. "I guess I'll have to do my own shopping. He glanced at his nude form in the mirror and grinned. "Should cause quite a stir."

"All right, you win," Jesse muttered.

She had her hand on the door knob when he realized he probably wouldn't be back this way after he killed Clayton. Tom would never forgive him for what he was about to do, and Jesse . . . He loved her, he thought bleakly, loved her too much to ask her to share his life. For one fleeting moment he thought of forgetting about Clayton, of taking Jesse and heading for California. But Storm Woman's ghost rose up before him and he knew he couldn't let Clayton go. Even now, the need for vengeance was clawing at him. And yet, he had to hold Jesse one more time, bury himself in her softness, taste her sweetness. Just once more.

"Jesse."

She turned away from the door, the need in his voice unmistakable. Her heart fluttered in her breast as he crossed the floor and took her in his arms. At last, she thought, at last the walls are tumbling down.

He was kissing her, his lips moving slowly over her eyes, her nose, her mouth, his hands kneading her back, stroking her shoulders, drifting down to caress the curve of her thigh. She wrapped her arms around his neck as he lifted her into his arms and carried her to the bed.

He undressed her slowly, his dark eyes admiring her, his hands moving lightly over her flesh in slow exploration, as if he meant to memorize every inch of her body.

A small warning bell went off in the back of her mind, but then he was kissing her again, pressing her down on the mattress, his long, lean body covering hers, the look in his eyes heating her blood even as his caresses scorched her flesh. And there was no time to think, no time to worry about the future. There was only now and the never-ending wonder of his touch as they came together, closer, closer, until their bodies blended into one, his heart beating in time to hers, his flesh her flesh, his need her need.

Head thrown back, she moved in rhythm with Dancer, felt herself spinning out of control, racing toward the light, until it burst, raining down on her in all the colors of the rainbow as his life poured into her, filling her with warmth and peace and a delicious sense of well-being.

She released a long sigh as the flood of passion receded, leaving her drifting on a golden cloud of contentment. Dancer's face was buried in her shoulder and she stroked his hair, his weight a welcome burden. His skin was damp, and her nostrils filled with his musky scent. When he started to move, she put her hands on his back and held him close.

"Don't go," she murmured. "Not yet."

He shifted his weight so she didn't bear the brunt of it, hating himself for what he was going to do. How could he leave her?

"I love you."

He closed his eyes, as though to shut out her words, and Storm Woman's image flashed across his mind, her face contorted with pain, her mouth stained with blood. Storm Woman had loved him, too. All she'd wanted was his love in return, and now she was dead.

Love. It was what Jesse wanted, too. And he did love her. God help him, he loved her more than his life. And that was why he was going to leave her. She deserved a better life than he could give her. Clayton wouldn't rest until one of them was dead. And even if Clayton was out of the way, there'd always be some bounty hunter out to make a few bucks, or another kid like Johnny Clayton who thought he had lightning in his hands.

He rolled away from Jesse and stood up, a muscle working in his jaw, his hands clenched at his sides.

Jesse stared up at him. "What's wrong?"

"Nothing." He reached for her hand and helped her to her feet. "I still need some clothes," he said.

"Not for me, you don't," Jesse remarked, trying to keep her voice light.

He forced a smile as he playfully slapped her rump. "Move it, woman."

Knowing it was useless to argue, Jesse washed quickly, dressed under his hooded gaze, and left the room.

With a sigh, Dancer began to pace the room, stretching his arms and legs. It was time to go, time to find Clayton before the man left town.

Jesse returned a short time later bearing a large package wrapped in brown paper. A black hat rested on top of the package.

"Mr. Phelps wasn't very happy about having to open the store at this time of night," Jesse said, dropping the package on the bed. "I told him it was an emergency."

Dancer nodded as he unwrapped the parcel, removing a pair of black whipcord britches, a black shirt, and a suit of underwear. He grimaced as he tossed the long handles aside, then turned to face Jesse, an amused grin on his face.

"You always made me turn my back when you were dressing," he teased, "but I don't mind if you want to watch."

Jesse stared at him, speechless, as the hot color washed into her face and neck. Oh, but he was incorrigible!

She whirled around, crossing her arms over her breasts, listening to the sound of material sliding over skin, wishing she knew why he was suddenly so cheerful.

"Thanks, Jess," he said, and she turned around to find him fully dressed, the familiar moccasins on his feet, the hat on his head.

"You're not leaving?"

Dancer nodded. "I appreciate you looking after me."

"But I thought that we . . . that you would . . ." Comprehension dawned in Jesse's eyes. "You're going after Clayton, aren't you?"

"Yeah."

"But Tom said—"

"I don't give a damn what Tom said. This is

something I've got to do, and nothing is going to stop me."

He couldn't go, Jesse thought, her mind racing. Clayton wanted to kill him, Tom had threatened to put him in jail if he tried to kill Clayton.

From the corner of her eye, she saw Dancer's rifle standing in the corner. Without quite realizing what she was doing, she darted across the room, grabbed the Winchester, and aimed it at Dancer's chest.

"You can't go," she said, her voice unsteady. "You're not supposed to be out of bed."

"Put that rifle down, Jesse."

"Why are you so determined to go after Clayton? Surely you must realize he'll shoot you on sight! And what about Tom? He jeopardized his career by not arresting you. Doesn't that mean anything?"

"I don't want to discuss it," Dancer said curtly. He took a step toward her, his dark eyes wary.

Jesse lowered the barrel until it was leveled at his right thigh. "I don't want to hurt you," Jesse said, "but I'll shoot if I have to. I know how."

"I know," Dancer acknowledged quietly. "I taught you. Now put that rifle down."

Jesse shook her head. "I'm not letting you leave this room until you come to your senses."

Dancer took another step forward, his eyes riveted on her face, ready to hit the floor rolling if she found the courage to pull the trigger. But it was one thing to shoot at targets, and quite another to shoot a man. And he didn't think she had the nerve.

Jesse paled considerably as Dancer took another step toward her.

"You'd better make your first shot count," he warned. "You won't get another."

With a deep sigh of defeat, Jesse lowered the Winchester.

Dancer's face was grave as he reached forward and took the rifle from her hands. Bending, he kissed her on the cheek, his hand caressing her hair.

"So long, Jesse," he murmured, and then he was gone.

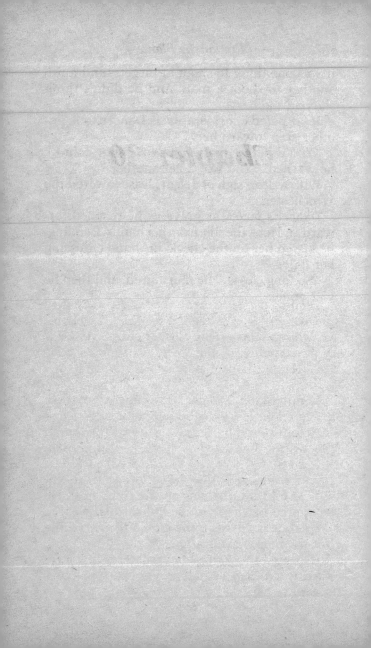

Chapter 30

Dancer moved noiselessly down the stairs and left the hotel. Pulling his hat low over his eyes, he made his way to the saloon. He paused at the doorway, his narrowed eyes raking the bar and tables. There was no sign of Clayton or his men.

Turning on his heel, he walked swiftly toward the livery barn. Yes, the stablehand said, a man answering J. D. Clayton's description had ridden out of town less than an hour ago. No, he hadn't noticed which way they went.

Minutes later, Dancer was riding out of town mounted on Hardin's big bay mare.

He quartered back and forth until he found the tracks of four shod horses heading east toward Shadow Valley. They were the freshest tracks leading in that direction, and his instincts told him he was on the right trail. He wondered briefly who the fourth man was.

He rode hard, his mind closed to everything but the men he was after.

He found them three hours later. They were making camp in a small grove of cottonwoods.

Clayton was squatting near the fire, smoking a cigar, while Davis and Johnson took care of the horses. Man Who Walks stood in the shadows, his rifle resting on his knee.

Silent as the clouds moving across the sky, Dancer made his way toward the camp until he reached a large tree. Using the trunk for cover, he jacked a round into the breech of the Winchester.

Man Who Walks whirled around. Throwing his rifle to his shoulder, he fired in Dancer's direction. The bullet slammed into the tree near Dancer's head, and he fired the Winchester, his first shot drilling a neat hole in the Indian's chest. Remo Davis jerked his gun from his holster and fired at the rifle's muzzle flash, but his shot went wide. He gasped as Dancer's second shot found its mark.

Clayton scrambled to his feet, his hand reaching for his gun as he hollered, "Johnson, kill that sonofabitch!"

Johnson swore under his breath as he dived out of the firelight. Rolling nimbly to his feet, he raced toward his horse, tethered in the shadows nearby, but he could not outrace the bullet that buried itself in his back, just left of center.

Clayton's face was pale as he stood up, his hands over his head. "Who are you?" he called. "What do you want?"

"Drop your gun," Dancer ordered quietly.

Clayton's eyes narrowed as he tried to recall where he had heard that voice before.

"I said drop it, old man."

J. D. Clayton's face turned pasty white. "Dancer," he murmured. "What's the matter, half-breed? Afraid to face me like a man?"

Soundlessly, Dancer moved into the open, the rifle at his side. "I'm here."

Hatred burned in Clayton's blue eyes as he quickly lowered his hands and fired his Colt. But he was too slow. He uttered a hoarse cry of pain as the slug from Dancer's Winchester slammed into his forearm, knocking the gun from his hand.

"Go ahead," Clayton challenged. "Kill me."

"All in good time," Dancer replied. Taking the knife from the sheath on Man Who Walks' belt, he cut a length of rope from the riata coiled around Clayton's saddle, deftly tied the old man's hands behind his back. Removing the kerchief from the judge's neck, he tied it around the wound in Clayton's forearm, then saddled the old man's horse.

"Mount up," Dancer said curtly.

"I can't," Clayton retorted.

Dancer swore under his breath. "Put your foot in the stirrup and I'll give you a leg up."

Clayton nodded. Lifting his foot, he started to place it in the stirrup, then whirled around and kicked Dancer in the groin.

Dancer muttered an oath as pain exploded through him. He doubled over, grunting as Clayton's knee smashed into his nose. Clayton was preparing to kick him again when Dancer drove his fist into the old man's face. The blow, filled with furious anger, sent Clayton sprawling to the ground, unconscious.

Fighting the urge to vomit, Dancer doubled over. Gradually the pain lessened and he wiped the blood from his nose. Cursing softly, he dumped Clayton over the back of his horse, lashed the man's hands and feet together under the animal's belly, then swung aboard the bay mare.

It was a long ride to Shadow Valley.

Tom stared at Jesse, his eyes dark with anger. "I should have known," he muttered between clenched teeth. "Dammit, I should have known he'd do something like this. How long ago did he leave?"

"Not more than an hour at the most."

"Why didn't you tell me sooner?"

"He was determined to go, and I knew you were just as determined that he stay." Jesse spread her hands out, palms up, in a gesture of hopelessness. "I didn't want to see either one of you get hurt."

Tom nodded. For a moment he stood staring out the window. Then he drew his gun and checked the cylinder. Replacing the gun in his holster, he jammed his hat on his head and stalked out the jailhouse door.

"Where are you going?" Jesse called.

"After Dancer. I've got to stop him before he kills Clayton."

"Wait for me. I'm going, too."

"No."

Jesse didn't argue. And she didn't follow him, at least not right away. Instead, she waited until he was headed out of town before she hurried to the livery barn for her horse. Once they were well on their way, Tom would have to take her along. It would cause too big a delay for him to take her back to town. And she was certain he wouldn't let her ride all the way back to Bitter Creek alone.

It was late afternoon almost two weeks later when Dancer reached the Comanche village. Dismounting, he pulled Clayton from the back of his horse. The trip had been hard on the old man. His face was haggard, he had lost weight, and there was a look of resignation in his eyes. But Dancer felt neither pity nor compassion for Clayton. The man was responsible for Storm Woman's death, and Dancer would not rest until Clayton had paid the ultimate price for his treachery.

Dancer's arrival caused quite a stir, but he ignored the crowd gathering around him as he took Clayton by the arm and hustled him toward a stout post near the edge of the camp. Clayton shuddered as Dancer lashed his hands and feet to the post. The half-breed's eyes burned with a need for vengeance, and J. D. Clayton knew, with a cold and bitter certainty, that he was going to receive the kind of death he had once planned for Dancer.

Turning away from Clayton, Dancer saw Lame Eagle standing a short distance away.

"Grandfather," Dancer said as he approached the aged warrior. "It is good to see you again."

"Welcome home, my son," Lame Eagle replied. "Do you want to eat?"

"No."

Lame Eagle's sightless eyes gazed into Dancer's soul. "Do you want to talk?"

"No."

"I wish it," Lame Eagle said, and turning, he made his way toward his lodge, certain his grandson would follow him.

"What do you wish to talk about, Grandfather?" Dancer asked as he entered the chief's lodge.

"I would know what has happened to you since you left us. I am told you have brought a white captive to our village, and that Storm Woman is not with you."

Dancer let out a long sigh. "It is a long story, Grandfather."

"Then it will be a long night. Begin."

Knowing it was useless to argue, Dancer sat down across from the old chief. Staring into the dead embers of the previous night's fire, he began to talk, telling Lame Eagle of how Elkhorn had betrayed him. His voice grew cold and bitter as he told of how Storm Woman had been captured with him, of the child that had died with her, how Hardin had whipped him the night of her death, of the long months he had spent laboring on Clayton's ranch.

Dancer paused for a moment, then went on,

telling how Willow Woman had helped him escape, how he had killed Hardin and the rest of Clayton's men, and how he planned to kill Clayton, an inch at a time.

"You did not mention the white woman, Jesse."

"What do you know of her?"

"Only what Willow Woman has told me."

"I do not wish to speak of her."

"She loves you, this white woman?"

"Yes."

Lame Eagle sat quietly for a long time, his head cocked to one side, his expression thoughtful.

"Revenge is like a sickness that eats at a man's insides," he said slowly. "Nothing you can do will bring back that which has been lost. Sometimes it is better to forget old hurts, old wounds, old enemies. Sometimes, in hurting others, we hurt only ourselves."

"I cannot forget, Grandfather. I cannot forget Storm Woman and the child that died with her. I cannot forget the months I spent locked in a cage, being whipped like an animal. I cannot!"

Lame Eagle nodded. There were some things a man had to learn for himself, the hard way.

"I hear the hot blood of vengeance in your voice, Buffalo Dancer," the chief said with regret. "I know you will not rest until you have dipped your hands into the blood of this white man. I hope his death will bring you the peace you seek."

A short time later, Dancer left Lame Eagle's lodge. Restless, he went to stand before Clayton, his eyes hooded as he contemplated the satisfaction he would derive from the old man's death.

Clayton stared into the half-breed's face and saw his own death lurking in the cold gray eyes. He had rarely known fear, but the taste of it was strong in his mouth as he felt the full force of Dancer's hatred. His mind filled with a bright recollection of the pain and humiliation he had inflicted on the man standing before him, and he knew there was no chance for mercy or forgiveness.

"Listen, Dancer," Clayton said, his voice sounding weak in his ears. "Can't we talk this over? I'll pay you—"

"No!" The word cracked through the air like a rifle shot. "You can't buy your way out of this the way you bought me, old man. An innocent woman is dead because of you. But you're going to pay all right, in blood!"

Pivoting on his heel, Dancer stalked away from Clayton. He was heading for his lodge when he heard an excited shout and saw a dozen braves ride into the center of camp brandishing their rifles and lances overhead. The warrior bringing up the rear was leading two horses, and Dancer felt a quick surge of dismay when he saw the faces of the prisoners.

Tom Brady struggled violently as two warriors yanked him from the back of his horse. He muttered an oath as a third warrior dropped a noose around his neck, then the three Indians dragged him toward a stout tree. Throwing the loose end of the rope over a limb, one of the warriors tied it off, leaving Tom no choice but to remain standing.

Jesse screamed as several of the warriors grabbed at her, dragging her from the back of her horse. She heard laughter as the women encouraged the warriors, cried out in fear and shame as the bodice of her dress ripped, exposing a lacy white camisole and the curve of her breasts.

A tall warrior with a hideously scarred face drew Jesse into his arms, his hand locked in her hair as he forced her head back.

"No!" Jesse screamed. "Oh, God, no!" It was like a nightmare, the copper-hued face leering down at her, the shouts and laughter of the crowd, the awful sense of unreality as the man's mouth covered hers.

"Cuchillo, let her go."

Dancer's voice silenced the boisterous crowd, and Jesse felt a ray of hope as the warrior drew away from her, though he kept a tight hold on her arm.

"Do not interfere, Buffalo Dancer," the Indian warned. "She is my captive, and I claim her as such."

"She is my woman," Dancer replied calmly.

Cuchillo shook his head. "That cannot be. She was traveling alone with another man."

"The man is my friend. He was bringing my woman here, to be with me."

Cuchillo glanced at Jesse. She was beautiful and he wanted her. Slowly he turned and met Dancer's eyes; what he saw there convinced him to let the white woman go.

"Jesse, come here," Dancer said, holding out his hand.

He did not have to ask her twice. Clutching her torn bodice in one hand, she placed her other hand in his.

"This is my woman," Dancer said so all could hear. "Any man who touches her will have to answer to me."

Still holding Jesse's hand, he led her to the lodge he had shared with Storm Woman, knowing that the only reason it was still standing was because Lame Eagle had never given up hope that his grandson would return.

"Go inside," Dancer told Jesse. "I'll be back as soon as I can."

"Where are you going?" she asked, frightened at the prospect of being left alone.

"To see if I can persuade my grandfather to release Tom."

"What if you can't?"

Dancer shook his head. "Let's not worry about that now."

"I saw Clayton," Jesse said, not meeting Dancer's eyes. "Why did you bring him here?"

Dancer grinned. It was not a pleasant expression. "Why do you think? Go inside."

He was gone before she could argue, and Jesse entered the hide tipi with a mixture of apprehension and curiosity.

As her eyes grew accustomed to the dusky interior, she noticed that the lodge was quite spacious and not as empty as it first appeared. There was a wide, comfortable-looking bed made of buffalo robes to one side. Several cooking pots were stacked beside the entrance. A feathered lance hung from one of the lodge poles. A tawny-colored skin covered a low backrest made of willow branches.

Skirting the firepit hollowed out in the center of the floor, Jesse sank down on the buffalo robes, frowned as her hand encountered something hard beneath the soft robes. Lifting the top hide, she discovered a .44 Colt snuggled in a worn holster. It was Dancer's gun, she was certain of that. All those days on the trail, it had been the last thing he touched at night, the first thing he reached for in the morning.

She felt a sharp stab of jealousy as she stared at her surroundings. So this had been the lodge he had shared with the Indian woman, and this had been their bed.

Grimacing, Jesse stood up, trying not to think of Dancer lying naked in the furry bed, his body poised over that of a dusky-skinned woman.

She began to pace the lodge, unable to quell the jealousy that clawed at her heart. Had the other woman been beautiful? Young? Voluptuous? Had she heard the words that Jesse so longed to hear? She knew it was foolish to be envious of a woman who was dead, but she couldn't help it.

It seemed as though an eternity had passed before Dancer returned. One look at his face told her that Lame Eagle had refused to release Tom.

"What happened?" she asked. "What did your grandfather say?"

"Cuchillo refused to surrender his claim to Tom. He said I had taken you from him, but he would not give up the white man, and my grandfather agreed with him."

"Why? Didn't you tell them Tom was your friend?"

"I told him. But Lame Eagle hates white men."

"What do we do now?"

"Nothing."

"Nothing!" Jesse exclaimed. "I thought Tom was your best friend. Are you just going to stand by and let these savages kill him?"

"Trust me, Jesse. They won't do anything right away. They'll give Tom a couple of days to think about what's coming, and then they'll have a big shindig to celebrate his capture. Until then, we'll just sit tight."

"And what about Clayton?"

"He's mine." Dancer's eyes were hard as flint as he looked at her. "Stay away from Clayton. And stay away from Tom. There's nothing you can do for them, and if you try to interfere, it will only make things worse."

Jesse nodded, chilled by the look in his eyes and by the tone of his voice.

Chapter 31

Jesse sat outside Dancer's lodge, her thoughts glum. Never had she felt so helpless, or so discouraged. In the distance she could see Tom, still tied to the tree. How tired he must be, she mused sympathetically. He had been standing there since yesterday afternoon, unable to sit down because of the rope around his neck. Even as she watched, she saw his eyes close, saw his shoulders slump, his legs sag as weariness overtook him. His body began to slide down the tree, and then he jerked upright as the noose cut into his throat, choking him. She could not see Clayton, but she knew that the old man must be equally uncomfortable, equally frightened.

As she, herself, was frightened. She fought down the panic that surged within her whenever she thought about how uncertain her future was. Dancer had left the lodge early this morning, left without a word to say where he was going or when he would be back. She knew he would come back sooner or later, if not for her, then for Clayton, but she could not help wondering what would become of her if he didn't return. Would the Indians tie her to a post and torture her as they meant to torture Tom? Or would she become a plaything, to be passed from man to man until she was driven out of the village and left to die in the wilderness?

Hugging herself, she watched the hum of activity around her. The women seemed to be constantly at work, mending worn moccasins or fashioning new ones, fetching water from the river, tanning hides, which was a disgusting process that involved the use of buffalo brains and animal fat. They sewed new clothing for their husbands, nursed their children, cooked huge pots of food. Unlike the whites, the Comanche did not eat three meals a day, but whenever they were hungry, so food was always available.

In the distance, she could see two women erecting a new lodge. The frame consisted of twenty-two slender cedar poles and over this they were fitting tanned skins and sewing them together.

Some of the women smiled at Jesse shyly, admiring her golden hair and pale skin, while others glared at her, their eyes filled with loathing.

The warriors did not seem to be busy at all. To Jesse they seemed terribly spoiled and lazy as they strutted about the camp, talking and laughing, or sitting in the shade repairing their weapons.

She knew, of course, that they did more than

that. Dancer had told her that the men were responsible for feeding the village and protecting it from harm. They kept watch at night, and were often away from home for long periods of time to search for game.

That afternoon, several warriors rode into the center of camp, their horses laden with gaily colored Mexican blankets and clothing, rifles and tequila, *pulque,* and hard candy. Women and children clustered around the triumphant raiding party, talking and gesturing excitedly as the warriors boasted of their success and divided the spoils.

And still Dancer did not return.

Toward evening the Indians began to gather in the center of the village. Jesse was wondering what was going on when Willow Woman came to sit beside her.

Jesse smiled fondly at the old woman, thinking she had never been so glad to see a familiar face in her life.

"So," Willow Woman said, grinning. "Our paths cross again."

"Yes," Jesse agreed. "What's going on?"

"They are celebrating the return of the raiding party." Willow Woman nodded at the warrior who was striding into the center of the circle. "That is Red Shield. He was the leader of the raid. His dance tells of his courage, of how he guided his men against our enemies and stole their horses and blankets, and how he counted coup on two men and killed a third."

Jesse nodded, fascinated by the intricate steps of the warrior's dance. Drumming filled the air, and another man joined the first.

"That is Night Sky. He was Red Shield's second in command. He is boasting of Red Shield's cunning, and also his own. None of our men were lost on the raid, and that, too, is cause for celebration."

So lost was Jesse in the scene before her that she did not see Dancer come up beside her was not aware of his presence until Willow Woman said,

"Buffalo Dancer, come sit with us."

Jesse stared at him as he dropped down between them. His long hair hung loose at his shoulders, his torso was bare. Fringed buckskin leggings hugged his long, muscular legs like a second skin. The familiar moccasins that were as much a part of him as his arms and legs covered his feet.

She gazed into his eyes, hoping for a sign of affection, but she saw only the deep burning anger that had held him since they'd arrived at the village.

There was a pause in the dancing and one of the young girls called Willow Woman's name. Dancer helped her to her feet and the old woman moved into the center of the circle.

"Is she going to dance?" Jesse asked.

No," Dancer replied. "Winter Blossom has asked for a story."

"A story? Really?"

"The Comanche love stories. Adults as well as children."

"What is she saying?" Jesse asked as Willow Woman began to speak.

"She is telling the story of Buffalo Woman," Dancer said, and Jesse listened with interest as he interpreted the story for her.

"Once there was a handsome young Comanche boy of well-to-do parents who went out to look for buffalo. The boy selected an attractive young calf for his prey. He struck the calf with two arrows, but the animal did not fall.

"It was very unusual for an animal shot in such a way to stay alive, but the young buffalo had fallen in love with the boy and had used magic powers to sustain her life. The young buffalo cow rejoined the herd and in time gave birth to a calf, which had been fathered by the two arrows of the Comanche boy. In time, the bull calf saw all the other calves standing around with both their mothers and their fathers and he asked his mother where his father was. His mother explained that his father was 'one of those who eats us.' The bull calf then insisted on seeing his father.

"So the two set off on a long journey toward the Comanche village. When they came in sight of the circle of lodges, the mother buffalo began to roll around on the ground and told her calf to do the same. When she stood up, she had become a woman dressed in a buffalo robe. Her son became a handsome boy, wrapped in a beautiful yellow calf robe.

"Following his mother's instructions, the boy went into the village, found his father, and told him his story. The Comanche boy, now grown to manhood, remembered the day he had shot a buffalo calf who refused to die. He took his son and the buffalo woman to live in his lodge. The woman had saved the young man's arrows and she returned them to him, telling him that she could help him and his people, but he must promise never to drink water out of any stream unless she had given him permission.

"During the time she lived with the Comanche, Buffalo Woman helped the tribe many times. Once when they were all starving, she gave just a small piece of dried meat and fat to the man with whom she lived. He ate his fill and passed it on to the next family, who also satisfied their appetites and passed the remainder to others. The little piece of meat went from family to family without ever being entirely consumed. Another time, when the tribe was out of food, Buffalo Woman instructed each family to pack a parfleche as if it were full of jerky. In the morning, every parfleche was full of dried meat.

"One day the father of the buffalo calf was riding across a dusty prairie and became very thirsty. He remembered being warned not to drink from any stream, but thought he would just rinse out his mouth. As soon as he touched the water, the woman and the boy were instantly transformed back to their old forms, and as a buffalo cow and calf they ran from the village. Everyone was very sad, for they had grown to love the beautiful buffalo woman and the handsome boy."

The Indians clapped and cheered as Willow Woman finished her story and sat down.

"Did you like my story?" the old woman asked Jesse.

"Yes, it was very entertaining."

"What did you learn from it?"

"Learn from it?" Jesse frowned. "I don't know. Perhaps that things are not always what they seem. Or perhaps the wisdom of obedience."

Willow Woman nodded, then, with a mysterious smile, glanced from Jesse to Buffalo Dancer.

"Perhaps," the old woman mused, "the story is about the power of love." And with that, she rose to her feet and walked away.

Jesse thought about the old woman's words as she followed Dancer to his lodge later that evening. *The power of love.* Had Willow Woman been trying to tell her something?

She watched Dancer as he drew off his moccasins and stepped out of his leggings, then crawled into bed. Last night she had tried once again to convince Dancer to free Clayton, to do something about Tom.

"Revenge is a terrible thing," she had said fervently. "No matter what you do to Clayton, how much you hurt him, you'll be hurting yourself more."

His dark eyes had narrowed ominously, his fury building because she continued to defy him. "I remember you were quite pleased when I tangled with the men who abused you," he had remarked cuttingly. "And quite happy to see them dead, as I recall. Revenge didn't seem so bad to you then, did it?"

Jesse had faced him squarely, her chin high. "I *was* glad to see them dead," she had admitted. "But that was different. If you hadn't killed Harry and the others, they would have killed you."

"How is that any different from this?" Dancer had demanded. "Dammit, Jesse, don't you think Clayton would kill me now if he could? If I let him go, I'll be looking over my shoulder as long as he lives."

"But this is so cold-blooded," she had argued, "You can't just—"

"Let it be, Jesse," he had snapped angrily, and left the lodge.

Now, watching him, she was filled with sympathy. Could she really blame him for hating Clayton? The judge had hounded him and mistreated him. Had hurt and humbled him. In her mind's eye, she saw the horrible scars that disfigured Dancer's broad back and shoulders, the other, fainter scars on his wrists and ankles. Bad as those were, she knew intuitively that they were not the demons that drove him.

His pride had been hurt, she thought. That fierce pride that was so much a part of him. And Storm Woman had been killed, and his child with her. No wonder he was bitter. No wonder he hated Clayton. But killing the old man wouldn't solve anything. She thought of the Indian woman. Dancer had confessed he had cared for her. Perhaps he had loved her. The thought of his loving another woman was painful. She wanted to be the first woman he had ever loved. The only woman.

Quietly she slipped out of her clothes and went to him. Timidly, afraid she might be rebuffed, she placed her hand on his shoulder.

Dancer opened his eyes to find Jesse kneeling beside him. How often in the past months had he dreamed of her, ached for her? Their brief interlude in Bitter Creek had only whetted his appetite for more. He would have taken her in his arms last night, but he had not been able to reach past the pity and disapproval he had seen in her eyes.

Taking her hand in his, Dancer gently pulled Jesse down beside him. She did not resist, but joined him beneath the buffalo robes, her body pressing eagerly against his. She let her hands wander over his chest, along his arms, over the hard plane of his stomach. She heard his breath quicken as her fingers stroked his thigh, felt the slight tremor in his limbs as she washed his ear with her tongue.

With a low growl, Dancer tucked Jesse beneath him, his mouth covering hers, his hands cupping her face. She wound her arms around him, her hands sliding up and down his back, feeling the scars that crisscrossed his flesh like a fine spiderweb.

She touched him tenderly, willing him to know by her kisses and her sweetly whispered words that she loved him, that nothing else mattered but the feelings they shared.

She felt his hunger build, felt the heat of his body against hers, heard him murmur her name as he lifted her hips to receive him. He took her masterfully, and she gloried in it, reveling in his hard masculine strength, in the sweet seduction of skin sliding over skin. His tongue singed her lips as it darted into her mouth, filling her with an urgent sense of need as the rough velvet of his tongue tasted hers.

She whispered her love for him as her pleasure crested, clutched him to her as she felt his warmth spill within her, pleasuring her again.

Dancer shuddered, then sighed as he let his weight sag briefly against her and then he rolled over onto his side, carrying Jesse with him. Jesse buried her face in the hollow of his neck, her heart gradually slowing from its wild hammering.

The power of love, she thought drowsily, and fell asleep in his arms.

But Dancer could not sleep. Rising, he drew on his leggings and moccasins and left the lodge.

Outside, a pale yellow moon hovered over the mountains, while a million stars glittered against the black velvet sky.

He moved quietly through the village to

where Tom was leaning against the tree, his eyes closed, his face drawn with the strain of the last two days.

"Tom?"

The marshal's eyes opened at the sound of Dancer's voice.

"How are you doing, lawman?" Dancer asked.

"Not good," Tom admitted ruefully. "I'm about dead on my feet, and I'm dying for a drink. I haven't had anything to eat or drink since day before yesterday."

Dancer nodded sympathetically. "The Comanche don't usually waste food or water on the enemy."

Tom grunted. His legs were weary, his arms ached, and his neck was raw where the rope had rubbed against his flesh each time he started to dose off.

"I'll be back," Dancer said, and going toward Lame Eagle's lodge, which was the closest, he found a water gourd and carried it back to Tom. "Here, drink this."

Tom gulped the cold water gratefully, certain that nothing in life had ever tasted quite as good or been so welcome.

"Thanks," he said when he'd emptied the gourd. "You may have saved my life."

"Yeah."

"Where's Jesse? Is she all right?"

"She's fine. She's asleep."

"I asked her to marry me," Tom said quietly.

"But she turned me down. I thought you should know."

"If I can get you out of this mess, you can ask her again."

Tom blinked at Dancer. "I thought . . ."

Dancer shook his head. "I've got no right to love her. Jesse wants a home, security, respectability. I can't give her those things. I can't live summer and winter in the same place, cooped up in a little house. I'll always have the itch to move on, see new places. I've got to be able to just get up and take off when the mood hits me. Jesse couldn't live like that and be happy, and I don't think I could live any other way."

"But it's you she loves," Tom said bitterly. "She told me so back in Bitter Creek."

"Maybe. But it's you she'd be happy with."

"I can't argue with that." Tom looked around at the Indian lodges. "I guess I'll never know if she'll have me or not." Tom's face paled in the moonlight. "How soon, Dancer? How much longer have I got?"

"Till tomorrow night."

"Cut me loose."

"I can't."

"Do you want me to beg?"

Dancer shook his head. "There are guards posted all around the village. You'd never get out of here alive."

"I'm willing to take my chances. Just get me a horse and a gun."

"No. If you killed any of the men trying to make your escape, I'd catch hell. I'm not willing to take that chance, or do anything that might jeopardize Jesse's safety."

"Yeah. I guess I understand."

"I doubt it, but you will." Dancer glanced up at the sky. "Try to get some rest."

"Yeah. Thanks again for the water."

"Keep smiling," Dancer muttered with a wry grin.

Padding silently through the village, he went to where Clayton was being held prisoner. The old man was awake, hunkered down on the ground at the foot of the post.

Clayton struggled to his feet, unable to mask the fear that swamped him when he saw the half-breed striding toward him.

"How's it going, old man?" Dancer asked.

"Why don't you just kill me and be done with it?" the judge snapped.

"All in good time." Dancer's eyes glowed with a sinister fire. "Mark my words, old man," he said, his voice harsh. "You'll pray for death a thousand times before I let you die."

Clayton shuddered as he recognized the words he had once said to the half-breed. It was in his mind to plead for mercy, but Dancer was already gone.

Too restless to sleep, Dancer walked down to the river where he sat cross-legged on the sand, staring into the dark swirling water.

Hours passed. And still he sat there, staring into nothingness.

The sky was still dark when he went to the corral and whistled for Blue.

The big gray Appaloosa came at his call, blowing softly as she nuzzled his arm. Slipping a bridle over her head, he led her out of the corral, swung easily onto her bare back.

Given her head, the mare broke into a lope and ran down the valley, effortlessly covering the miles until the village lay far behind. They passed two sentries and Dancer signaled that everything was all right.

They were high in the hills when Dancer reined the mare to a halt and slid to the ground. Sitting beneath a rocky ledge, he gazed into the distance, feeling a closeness to the land where he'd been born.

He sat there a long time, his thoughts wandering back in time. He'd been a man apart all his life. As a boy on the Llano, his white blood had made him different from the Comanche. In the white world, his Indian blood had been like a gulf between himself and everyone else. And when he became a fast gun, his reputation had erected a barrier of its own. And he'd been content to live that way. Until Jesse. Beautiful, flaxen-haired Jesse.

He closed his eyes and the night closed around him like a living, breathing thing. Not awake, not asleep, he hovered in a world filled with peace, and then, abruptly, he knew he was no longer alone.

He opened his eyes to find Storm Woman standing before him. Her dark eyes were calm and serene. Her skin was smooth and unblemished, her face no longer disfigured by the ugly scar.

He murmured her name, his voice tinged with wonder, and she smiled down at him, a gentle smile filled with love and understanding and forgiveness.

Hate is not the answer.

Did she speak the words aloud, or were they only an echo in his mind?

Only love lasts forever.

He heard the words whisper in his mind, and it was as if someone had pulled a thorn from his heart.

He closed his eyes again, feeling the guilt and the hatred drain out of him, cleansing him, healing all the old wounds, the old hurts.

A faint breeze stirred the wind, its touch on his cheek like a gentle caress. He knew she was gone even before he opened his eyes.

Dancer let out a long sigh, filled with a sense of peace such as he had never known.

And then he thought of Clayton. Clayton who had offered a king's ransom for his capture, who had been responsible for Storm Woman's death, for the months of misery he had endured on the chain gang and in that damnable cage. Clayton, whose need for vengeance outweighed his own.

Clayton. If not for Clayton, he would never have met Jesse on the trail to Cherry Valley. If not for Clayton, he would not have returned to his mother's people, or known Storm Woman. If not for Clayton, he would not have met Lizzie. . . . Lizzie. Her ready smile and happy laughter had brightened many a dreary night. How could he repay her by killing the only family she had left?

Blue came at his call and he vaulted effortlessly onto the mare's back and headed for home.

J. D. Clayton's mouth went dry when Dancer drew rein beside him and slid to the ground. The half-breed's eyes were as dark as the night, burning with an intensity that made Clayton's blood run cold. *So,* he mused, *the time had come.* As of this moment, he was a dead man.

He clenched his fists as Dancer moved to stand directly in front of him.

Dancer smiled faintly, feeling a twinge of genuine admiration for Judge John David Clayton as he drew his knife from its sheath. Clayton was a tough old bird, tough and brave even now, when he thought he was facing certain death.

Clayton drew a deep breath as the half-breed ran his thumb over the edge of the blade. "What happened to Hardin?" he asked gruffly. His eyes focused on the knife as he waited for the half-breed's reply.

"He's dead," Dancer said curtly.

Clayton licked his lips as he lifted his gaze to meet Dancer's. He was afraid, more afraid than he'd ever been in his life. He longed to ask for mercy, but he knew it would be a waste of breath. He hadn't shown the half-breed any mercy and in his heart he knew he'd do it all again. The man had killed Johnny. He had deserved every bit of misery he'd received.

"Go ahead, kill me and be done with it," Clayton said boldly.

His heart began to pound as the half-breed raised his knife. But the blade did not strike his flesh. Instead, Dancer cut his hands free.

"What is this?" Clayton asked suspiciously. "Some kind of trick?"

Dancer whistled softly and Yellow Hand emerged from the shadows leading Cliff Hardin's big bay mare.

"Mount up," Dancer told Clayton. "Yellow Hand will see you safely out of camp."

Clayton made a sound of disbelief low in his throat.

"What's the matter, old man, don't you trust me?"

"Not by a damn sight."

"No reason why you should. Now mount up before I change my mind."

Clayton needed no further urging. Scrambling onto the bay's back, he took up the reins and then paused to look back at the half-breed. "Why?"

"Don't come after me again," Dancer warned, ignoring the old man's question. "I'm tired of being hunted and you might not get off so easy the next time. And another thing, I killed your son in self-defense. Now go on, get the hell out of here."

Clayton had never been one to push his luck, and he saw no reason to start now. Without a backward glance, he put the horse into a trot and followed Yellow Hand out of the village.

Dancer sighed heavily as he watched Clayton out of sight. No one would object to his setting the old man free. J. D. had been his prisoner, his to do with as he pleased. Freeing Tom would not be so easy.

It was just past dawn when Dancer returned to his lodge. And Jesse.

She was asleep beneath the buffalo robes, her cheek pillowed on her hand, her eyelashes making dark crescents against her smooth skin. Never had he seen anything more beautiful, known anyone more desirable.

Stripping off his leggings, clout, and moccasins, he slid under the blankets and drew her close, his lips moving in her hair, his heart hammering wildly as he drank in the sight and the scent of her. She was naked beneath the robes and his hands traveled leisurely over her hips and thighs, the curve of her buttocks, before he drew her length against his own.

Slowly Jesse's eyelids fluttered open. "Dancer . . ."

He smiled at her, his dark eyes aflame, his voice husky with yearning as he whispered, "Let me love you, Jesse. Don't ask questions. Just let me love you."

He had never asked her permission before and she wondered what it meant.

"Jesse."

His voice was soft, husky, filled with a deep yearning. The arm that held her was rock hard, quivering slightly, as if he were keeping all his emotions in check until she said the word that would unleash the passion that blazed in the smoky depths of his eyes.

Slowly she nodded, unable to speak for the wild pounding of her heart, for the sudden need that pulsed through her.

She slipped her arms around his neck as his mouth closed over hers, his tongue tickling her lower lip. She felt her breath catch in her throat as his hands caressed her, his touch lazy and bold by turns. Pleasure suffused her as he rained kisses, feather-light and wonderfully sweet, over her face, her neck, her breasts and belly.

She knew he wanted her, wanted her desperately, She could feel the passion that was barely contained within him as he made love to her with all the tenderness and gentleness a woman could ask for. She writhed beneath him, wanting him, needing him, certain she would burst into flame if he didn't quench the fire his hands and kisses had ignited.

She cried his name, her voice thick with desire. Slowly he rose above her, his dark gray eyes smoky with desire, the muscles in his arms taut as he held himself over her for just a moment before he possessed her, his flesh now a part of her own. Jesse gloried in his touch, in his strength. In his gentleness.

She wrapped her arms and legs around him, wanting to be closer, and closer still, shuddering with ecstasy as his life flowed into her, the pulsing warmth bringing her own desire to full flower.

Now, Jesse thought exultantly. *Now and forever we are one.*

Slowly, reluctantly, they returned to earth.

With a sigh, Dancer rolled onto his side, carrying Jesse with him, so that they lay locked together, facing one another.

"Dancer . . ."

"No questions now," he murmured as he stroked her cheek. "Later, but not now."

He was still holding her close when he fell asleep.

Something had happened, Jesse thought with certainty. But what?

She felt a sudden fear as she realized that the restless anger no longer haunted his eyes. Had he killed Clayton? Was that why he seemed to be at peace? Had he finally taken the vengeance he had so yearned for?

The thought filled her with regret, and she knew she would never feel quite the same about Dancer if he had taken the old man's life.

And then she thought about Tom. He had been on his feet for the last three days, forced to remain awake lest the noose tighten around his neck and choke the life from his body. How much longer could he stand there? How much longer until the Indians killed him?

And what of herself? What did Dancer intend to do with her? Would he keep her here, to be his squaw? She would stay if he asked her to, if only he would say he cared, admit that he loved her. And if he should send her away, what then?

So many questions, she mused wearily, and no easy answers to any of them.

She pushed her worrisome thoughts aside and nestled closer to Dancer, certain that he could make everything come out right.

Chapter 32

Jesse awoke to find Dancer smiling at her, a beguiling smile that tugged at her heart and brought all her senses to life.

Her stomach fluttered with anticipation as he took her face in his hands and kissed her, the pressure of his lips gentle at first and then building in force and intensity until they were straining toward each other, arms and legs entwined in a graceful dance of desire.

He made love to her slowly, leisurely, as if he had nothing else on his mind, nothing but time. His hands whispered over her flesh, tantalizing, possessive, even as his lips bathed her in sweetness. All her questions of the night before seemed suddenly unimportant as she returned his kisses, basking in the fire of his need, warmed by the love that burned in her heart for this man, and this man alone.

She studied his hand as it moved over her breast, his skin as dark as the earth, hers as pale as the moon.

Dancer drew back, his expression troubled as he followed Jesse's gaze. "What is it?"

"We're so different," she murmured, "yet

our bodies fit together so perfectly."

Dancer nodded, bewildered by the turn of her thoughts.

"Do you think our souls are also touching?"

"I'm sure of it."

Jesse smiled, her eyes cloudy with passion as she drew him to her. "Heart to heart," she whispered fervently, "and soul to soul. . . ."

A long time later Dancer stood up and pulled Jesse to her feet.

"I need a bath," he remarked, drawing on his leggings. He waited while she dressed, then took her hand and led the way to a secluded place at the river.

They bathed leisurely, kissing and caressing as the water swirled around them. She thought he looked like a pagan warrior as he stood waist deep in the water, his long black hair flowing over his shoulders, his skin like sleek bronze, his gray eyes untroubled for the first time since she had known him.

She uttered a soft moan of pleasure as he drew her near, tucking her buttocks against his thighs while his hands took the soap and began to wash her breasts. The water, the soapy bubbles, and the touch of his hands sent shivers of pleasure coursing through her and she rested her head against his chest, giving herself up to the wonder of his touch, the heavenly sense of well-being that filled her.

They spent the day at the river, swimming and loving, not talking of the future, but living each moment as it came. Dancer left her side only once to get them something to eat, and then they made love in the shelter of a shady glen, surrendering to the desire they could not seem to quench.

It was only later, as they stood on the bank getting dressed, that Jesse's thoughts turned to Tom.

"What's going to happen to him?" she asked.

Dancer shook his head. "Nothing good, you can bet on that, but whatever it is, it will happen tonight."

Jesse glanced at the darkening sky. She could hear the sound of drums coming from the village, the low, steady throbbing sounding like a death knell to her ears.

"Aren't you going to do anything to help him?"

"If I can. Come on, let's go."

He had kept her at the river all day in hopes of keeping her mind off Tom, but now it was time to face reality again, time to put his own life on the line and hope they'd both survive the night.

Jesse trailed after Dancer, agitated by his apparent lack of concern for the man who was supposed to be his best friend.

Inside their lodge, Dancer removed his buckskin leggings and loincloth and pulled on a black wolfskin clout. He left his hair loose, held away from his face by a narrow strip of red cloth. Dipping his forefinger into a pot of war paint, he drew a single black slash across his left cheek.

Dancer gazed at Jesse for a long moment. "I think it would be best if you stayed here."

Jesse shook her head vigorously. "No. I want to go with you."

He fixed her with a hard stare. "You must do exactly what I say," he warned. "Whatever happens, you must not interfere. Do you understand? No tears, no hysterics."

Jesse nodded, wondering what terrible things he was expecting to happen.

"Let's go."

Jesse followed Dancer out of the lodge and had the feeling she had stepped into a nightmare. A huge fire burned in the center of the village. Curling orange and yellow flames danced against the dark sky, casting eerie shadows on the lodgeskins, bathing the faces of the Indians with a fiendish glow, reminding her of creatures from hell. A cold wind moaned through the trees, dark gray clouds scudded across the sky. She could not help noticing that the clouds were the color of Dancer's eyes.

The Comanches fanned out in a wide circle around the fire, their voices lifting in shouts of derision and contempt as two burly warriors dragged the prisoner into the circle.

Tom Brady's gaze swept over the crowd and the hatred he read in their eyes chilled him to the bone. He stood there, his arms tightly bound behind his back, while the Indians danced and sang and feasted on roast buffalo hump and venison. He'd had little to eat or drink in four days, had gotten very little sleep, but hunger and rest were far from his mind now. He was aware of nothing but the fear that pounded in his brain and left a brassy taste in his mouth.

He was going to die. Hard.

Gradually the singing and the dancing came to an end and the tribe's attention focused on the white man standing in their midst.

The warrior who had captured Tom strutted into the center of the circle. He wore elkskin leggings and a fringed war shirt. Yellow paint streaked his face, and there was a single white eagle feather braided into his long black hair. But it was the long-bladed knife in the warrior's hand that held Tom Brady's attention.

The warrior circled Tom, the knife snaking out to jab at Tom's flesh, opening a half-dozen shallow cuts on Tom's arms and chest. Tom clenched his teeth, choking off the urge to groan as the blade sliced into his skin.

The watching Indians laughed and joked among themselves as blood dripped from the white man's flesh.

Tom drew a deep breath as he caught sight of Dancer standing on the edge of the crowd, Jesse at his side. Jesse's face was the color of chalk, her sea-green eyes wide with horror. Dancer stood straight and tall beside her, a speculative expression on his face as he met Tom's gaze.

And Tom felt a sudden chill in the pit of his

stomach. He had known Dancer for years, known that his friend was an Indian, but the fact had never hit him with such force before. There was no hint of civilization in the half-breed's appearance, nothing to indicate he was anything but Comanche.

Tom swore under his breath as Dancer made his way toward the center of the circle, wondering, morbidly, if his best friend intended to finish him off.

Jesse stared at Dancer as he entered the circle, seeing him as if for the first time. His face was calm, devoid of expression, darkly handsome, yet she sensed the tension lurking beneath his impassive facade. He exuded a raw, animal-like power and she was chilled by the hint of violence that lay behind his frosty gray eyes. But, more than that, she was hit by the startling realization that here, for this moment, he was wholly Indian. His hair was as long and black as any warrior's, his skin as dark, his features those of the Comanche. But it was the single streak of black paint that made him seem like a stranger, a single streak of black paint that seemed to sum up the vast difference between them. And made him all the more fascinating, all the more desirable.

She pressed her hand to her heart as Dancer plucked the knife from Cuchillo's hand.

Cuchillo whirled around, his face dark with anger as he grabbed for his knife.

"No," Dancer said. "This man is my friend. I will not see him killed."

"He belongs to me," Cuchillo countered angrily. "It is my right to dispose of him as I see fit."

A low murmur rippled through the crowd as the two warriors glared at each other. Jesse threw an anxious glance at Tom, but Tom's gaze was fixed on Dancer's face, his brow furrowed as he sought to understand what was going on.

"He is mine," Cuchillo said again.

"If you want his life, you will have to fight me for it," Dancer said flatly.

Jesse watched, aghast, as Dancer tossed the knife in his hand to Cuchillo, then withdrew his own knife from inside his right moccasin. The two men moved apart, both slightly crouched as they circled each other.

Jesse sent a quick glance in Tom's direction, then turned her gaze toward Lame Eagle, who was engaged in conversation with a tall, barrel-chested warrior.

There was a gasp from the crowd and she swung her gaze back toward Dancer, felt her stomach coil in horror as she saw the long gash across his chest. The two men came together in a rush, and when they parted there was blood dripping from Cuchillo's left arm, just above his elbow.

Before they could close in on each other again, Lame Eagle's voice pierced the air.

"Enough!" He walked into the center of the circle, guided by the barrel-chested warrior. "I will not have Comanche blood spilt over the life of a white man. If Buffalo Dancer is willing to risk his life to save that of his friend, then the white man must be a man of courage, a man with a good heart, a good soul. Is this not true, Buffalo Dancer?"

"The white man is my friend. He is a brave man. I will not let him be killed."

"What say you, Cuchillo?"

The warrior grinned. "I will not free a white man, but"—he gazed at Dancer—"if this paleface is as Buffalo Dancer says, then I say he should be one of the People."

Dancer chuckled. "It shall be as you say."

"Buffalo Dancer?"

"Yes, Grandfather?"

"I was told that the man Clayton has been set free by your hand."

"Yes, Grandfather."

Lame Eagle nodded, a slight smile playing over his wrinkled features. It had taken time, but Buffalo Dancer had finally realized the futility of revenge.

Tom Brady breathed a sigh of relief as Dancer cut his hands free. "What's going on?"

"We're going to become blood brothers," Dancer explained. "It's a solemn rite. Look properly grave and respectful," he admonished, wiping the grin from his own face and replacing it with a sober expression.

"Blood brothers," Tom said, frowning. "Why?"

"To save your ass. Now, hold out your hand,

palm up," Dancer told him, extending his own hand.

Tom winced as the tall warrior standing beside Lame Eagle made a shallow slash in the palm of his hand, then made a similar cut in Dancer's palm. Gravely the warrior pressed their two hands together.

The *puhakut*, Painted Horse, stepped forward. "Now your blood is one and you are brothers," he proclaimed in a loud voice. "From this day forward, the white man shall be known in the lodges of the People as Pale Warrior."

When the medicine man finished speaking, Lame Eagle began to talk.

"My grandfather says you are now one of us," Dancer said, translating the chief's words for Tom's benefit. "He says you are welcome here anytime, and that anyone who hurts you will be punished."

Tom nodded. "Am I expected to say anything in return?"

"Of course. The Indians love speeches, the longer the better, but I'll just tell Lame Eagle that you're honored to be a part of the great Comanche nation, and that you'll bring him some tobacco the next time you come to visit."

Dancer rattled off some rapid-fire Comanche and Lame Eagle nodded, obviously pleased.

"That should about do it," Dancer said. "Come on, let's go get those cuts cleaned up."

"You look like you could use a little patching up yourself," Tom replied, yawning.

Dancer glanced at the blood dripping down his chest and shrugged. "It's just a scratch."

Jesse had been watching from a distance; now, as the crowd broke up, she hurried forward, her eyes reflecting her concern as she glanced from one man to the other.

"Do the two of you plan to stand here and bleed to death, or are you going to let me look after those cuts?" she exclaimed, arms akimbo.

The two men grinned at each other. "After you," Tom said, and followed Dancer and Jesse into Dancer's lodge.

Inside, Jesse quickly took charge. Finding a length of clean cloth, she began to wash the blood from Dancer's chest, some of her anxiety draining away when she realized the knife wound was not as deep as she had feared.

When she had the cut cleaned and dressed to her satisfaction, she turned toward Tom, only to find that he had fallen asleep. He did not awaken when she began to wash his cuts, nor did he stir as she bound up the worst ones.

"He must be exhausted," she murmured sympathetically.

Dancer nodded. The last four days hadn't been easy on Tom. He probably hadn't managed to get more than a few minutes' sleep at a time. But he'd be all right. Dancer had managed to sneak him enough food and water to keep his strength up; a good long sleep would have him feeling as good as new.

"I'm beat," Jesse said, dragging a hand across her forehead.

Dancer nodded. "I guess it's been a rough night for everybody."

"Yes, but it's over now. What would you have done if Lame Eagle hadn't stopped the fight?"

"I don't know. If I'd killed Cuchillo, Lame Eagle could have demanded my life in payment." Dancer shrugged. "I was betting my grandfather wouldn't let that happen."

"He loves you."

"Yes," Dancer said at last. "He does."

"Dancer, I . . ."

"Not now, Jesse." He saw the hurt flicker in her eyes, knew she had been about to tell him she loved him. But he was not ready to face that now. He was too uncertain of his own feelings, his own future. He knew he loved her. But was that enough?

He waited until she was asleep, and then he left the lodge and went down by the river, a lonely, brooding figure of a man caught between two worlds.

It was quiet, there by the water. A bright yellow moon hung low in the sky, surrounded by a million stars that twinkled on a bed of black velvet like dewdrops spread by a careless hand. A deer came down to drink, never knowing Dancer was there.

His thoughts turned to Jesse, always to Jesse. Since the day he met her, she had never been far from his thoughts. He loved her, and it frightened him. He had never been in love before, had never realized its power, or thought himself capable of loving another person. It was hard to accept the fact that he loved her even now.

He loved her, he thought bleakly, and that was why he had to let her go.

He spent the rest of the night beside the river, remembering all they had shared, and when he returned to the lodge, his mind was made up, his heart heavy.

Tom slept all the next day, and Jesse hovered over him, checking often to make certain he didn't have a fever. She examined Dancer's wound as well, shuddering to think that he might have been killed.

She tried several times to engage him in conversation, but he didn't seem inclined to talk, merely sat on a pile of robes, smoking a long-stemmed pipe and watching her.

It was late evening when Tom awoke. Jesse offered him a bowl of soup, and he ate it quickly and asked for more. He glanced at Dancer several times, and when he'd finished eating, he cleared his throat, then took a deep breath.

"Dancer, I'd like to . . . I mean, do you mind if I talk to Jesse alone for a few minutes?"

Dancer shook his head. He knew how Tom felt about Jesse. His eyes met hers for a moment, and then he left the lodge.

When they were alone, Tom knelt before Jesse and took her hands in his. "I love you, Jesse," he said simply, fervently. "Is there any chance for me? Any chance at all?"

"No. I'm sorry, Tom. Truly I am. But I love Dancer."

Tom nodded. "I guess I knew you'd say that, but I had to try." He rose smoothly to his feet, his gaze lingering on her face. "If things don't work out between you and Dancer..." He shrugged. "What I mean is, you can always count on me to be your friend, or whatever else you need."

"Thank you, Tom."

"Well, I guess I'll be going. I've been away from my job long enough."

"Not tonight," Jesse protested. "It's too late."

"Tonight," Tom said firmly. He kissed her once, briefly, and then he was gone.

Jesse sat in the lodge for a long time, waiting for Dancer to return. A sudden fear that he might have left the village without her drove her outside, and she walked through the camp, her eyes searching for him but to no avail.

Truly alarmed, she made her way to the river, her emotions close to panic, when she saw him standing beside the water. She hurried toward him, and then paused, wondering if she should intrude. Perhaps he wanted to be alone.

"What is it, Jesse?" he asked. He did not turn around and she wondered how he knew who it was.

"Tom left."

"Did he?"

"Yes, he said he had to get back to Bitter

Creek. I...I was wondering what happens now?"

He still did not face her. "We'll spend the night here and then I'll take you home."

"I have no home," Jesse remarked quietly.

"But you want one?"

"Yes. I want a home and a family. I can't just..."

Dancer swung around to face her as her voice trailed off. "Can't just keep following me from place to place," Dancer concluded.

Jesse nodded. "Tom asked me to marry him again."

A muscle worked in Dancer's jaw as he pondered that for a moment. "Do you love him?"

"I could learn to."

"Is that what you want?"

"You know what I want."

He did know, but he was afraid he was not the man who could give it to her. Perhaps she would be better off with Tom. Brady had a career, a solid reputation, roots. He would be good for her. But the mere thought of another man touching her, holding her, filled him with rage. He admitted then what he had known all along. He couldn't let her go. Selfish as it might be, he could not let her go.

He let out a long sigh of resignation as he took her in his arms. He kissed her then, one hand tangled in the golden mass of her hair, the other pressed against her back to hold her close. It was a long, lingering kiss, full of passion and promise, and in that kiss was his unspoken question and her heartfelt reply.

Reluctantly, he took his mouth from hers. "You're sure, Jesse?"

"Yes, Dancer."

"It won't be easy. My reputation will likely follow us wherever we go."

"Yes, Dancer."

"And you know I'll probably never settle down?"

"Yes, Dancer."

He fell silent then and Jesse waited patiently, her sea-green eyes focused on his face, a ghost of a smile playing over her lips.

"Do you have to have the words?" he asked gruffly.

"Yes," Jesse replied with a hint of regret in her voice. "This once I do."

Scowling fiercely, Dancer said, "Dammit, Jesse, I love you! I love you," he said again, and this time his voice was as soft as a caress, as warm as the winds that blew across the prairie.

And then he was kissing her again, and as Jesse's arms went around his neck and her lips met his, Dancer knew he had come home at last.

Dear Reader:

COMANCHE FLAME is the first book I ever wrote. It's taken over ten years and numerous rewrites to get it published, but it does prove that persistence pays off.

I appreciate all the letters I've received this past year. They've come from as far away as Canada, Stockholm, England, New Zealand and the Republic of South Africa. I've read them all, and I'm still trying to answer them, so if you haven't yet received a reply, please be patient. Unfortunately, I received a few letters where the return address was illegible or missing. My regrets in being unable to answer these.

I love to hear from my readers. Please write me at P.O. Box 1703, Whittier, CA 90609–1703. Please include a self-addressed stamped envelope if you wish a reply.

Cordially,

Madeline